LEVI'S LEGEND
STONE'S SURRENDER
MERK'S MISTAKE

Dale Mayer

Books in This Series:

Levi's Legend: Heroes for Hire, Book 1
Stone's Surrender: Heroes for Hire, Book 2
Merk's Mistake: Heroes for Hire, Book 3
Rhodes's Reward: Heroes for Hire, Book 4
Flynn's Firecracker: Heroes for Hire, Book 5
Logan's Light: Heroes for Hire, Book 6
Harrison's Heart: Heroes for Hire, Book 7
Saul's Sweetheart: Heroes for Hire, Book 8
Dakota's Delight: Heroes for Hire, Book 9
Michael's Mercy: Heroes for Hire, Book 10
Jarrod's Jewel: Heroes for Hire, Book 11
Heroes for Hire, Books 1–3
Heroes for Hire, Books 4–6
Heroes for Hire, Books 7–9

Books in the SEALs of Honor Series:

HEROES FOR HIRE, BOOKS 1–3
Dale Mayer
Valley Publishing

Copyright © 2017

ISBN-13: 978-1-773360-49-2
Print Edition

Back Cover

Levi's Legend

Welcome to Levi's Legend, book 1 in Heroes for Hire reconnecting readers with the unforgettable men from SEALs of Honor in a new series of action packed, page turning romantic suspense that fans have come to expect from USA TODAY Bestselling author Dale Mayer.

Nothing stays the same...

Since his accident Levi has been driven to find the men who betrayed him. Everything else is secondary. Now he's recovered, started his own company, and he's caught the scent of the last man on his list. Only to find the same man intends to finish the job he originally started – and kill Levi once and for all.

Ice has been at Levi's side every step of his new journey – well almost. It's the places where she hasn't been that are the hardest. Her relationship with Levi is at a critical point. One wrong word and her hopes and dreams will be gone. They almost are now.

But she can't resolve her love life until the man who forced change into their world is taken care of. Only he's on the attack, and his target is right at the heart of everything that's important to her, and to Levi.

They'll have to move fast to stop the man who wants them both dead or they won't have a future at all...

Stone's Surrender

Welcome to *Stone's Surrender*, book 2 in Heroes for Hire reconnecting readers with the unforgettable men from SEALs of Honor in a new series of action packed, page turning romantic suspense that fans have come to expect from USA TODAY Bestselling author Dale Mayer.

Life is on the move again...

After a long slow-ass recovery, Stone finds himself triumphantly back at work at Levi's new company. The action comes fast and furious on his first run out as they rescue a senator's daughter who's been kidnapped in the Middle East.

Lissa will do almost anything to thwart her father's plans for her. Getting kidnapped wasn't on her list. And once she meets Stone no other man matters. She falls, and she falls hard. But even on home soil, there's no respite as she finds the nightmare has followed her home...and she's caught in the middle of it.

It's a battle that requires both of them to not only clear her name but to keep her safe...especially when a twist is thrown at them that they didn't see coming...

Merk's Mistake

Welcome to *Merk's Mistake*, book 3 in Heroes for Hire reconnecting readers with the unforgettable men from SEALs of Honor in a new series of action packed, page turning romantic suspense that fans have come to expect from USA TODAY Bestselling author Dale Mayer.

Time never fades...

After months of recovery, Merk is moving from mission to mission, happily back in his active life again. But when his ex-wife sends out a panicked call for help, he rushes to meet her – only to see her snatched away in front of him.

Katina has only one person in mind when she finds herself in trouble. Merk. They haven't spoken for ten years, but time hasn't changed some things. The attraction between she and Merk is as deep and strong as it was back then. Even more so. But with her life on the line, she can't focus on him… and can't get her mind of him.

She has something others want, and they will do anything to get it back. No matter how nefarious. No matter how evil. No matter who they kill.

Sign up to be notified of all Dale's releases here!
http://dalemayer.com/category/blog/

COMPLIMENTARY DOWNLOAD

DOWNLOAD a **_complimentary_** copy of TUESDAY'S CHILD? Just tell me where to send it!
http://dalemayer.com/starterlibrarytc/

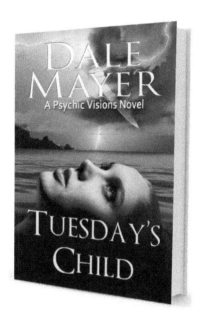

LEVI'S LEGEND

Heroes for Hire, Book 1

Dale Mayer

Chapter 1

G *ET UP, LEVI. Damn you, get up.*
Two more shots slammed into the tree, splintering bark in every direction. A hard *boom* exploded and then ... silence. Leaves drifted toward him from above.

Levi rolled to his back, his eyes open to the hot sun bearing down on them. Dear God, he hurt.

Damn it, Levi.

Ice's voice raged through his head. Only she wasn't at his side. She hadn't been for a while.

Yet her words urged him on.

To keep you alive.

He waited for the pain to stop thundering through his body.

Who knew being in the blast radius of a grenade could still hurt so much? That damn thing had blown seconds ago, sending him tumbling under the tree.

He shifted in place and groaned. Please let him have all his body parts. Again ... And why the hell did Mexico always mean a FUBAR mission? This place was cursed. Or he was. Either way it was a deadly combo. And one he couldn't seem to turn away from.

Of course you can't. You've got a death wish. Why the hell do you think I didn't want you to come on this one? You shouldn't be out there. You need to let this go.

Ice's voice still echoed in his head.

"Nice. Sometimes death is preferable to listening to the living." Not that he had a death wish, but he'd certainly been through the wringer. And sometimes it just seemed much easier to do what he was good at than to stay behind, working on the stuff he wasn't.

And some things were meant to stay a certain way. He knew Ice would never bring it up, and he'd never bring it up. But, if he had one regret in his life, it was letting her step away from what they had. He'd been trying to get her back ever since. And, although she still stuck close, she wouldn't take that final step. Not the one he wanted. Needed. But he understood. They'd had a whopper of a fight over having a family. She wanted one, and he didn't. She'd been devastated. But she was also the bravest woman he'd ever met. She had more courage than most men. Considering his training and skills as a former SEAL, that said a lot. He should have fixed things immediately, but he hadn't. And then, well ... life had changed ... and he'd been badly injured.

Each no longer in the navy, Levi now ran his own private security company, saving people as before, along with her. Where he should be right now. Only this tip had come through. The info he'd been waiting on since forever, it seemed. The location of one of the last two men who'd betrayed him and his unit almost one year ago, which had gotten his ass kicked and his friends blown to shit, ending their careers and lives as they, and others, knew it. Yet the assholes had gone free. Levi had slowly taken care of most of them, except for these remaining two.

So he'd dropped everything and came running here as soon as he got this intel.

One of those two, Herrara, was downhill. There was

always a chance the other man Levi was chasing was here too. Levi couldn't *not* come.

Ice had wanted him to walk away from this mission. But, in order to move forward with his future, he had to put his past to rest first. He'd hoped she'd understand. He'd left her home, in charge of the company, but she'd been cold. Angry.

Hence he found himself now lying flat on his back in the middle of Mexico with bullets flying overhead. "Dear God," he said, "I've got to stop this."

"Damn right you do."

Merk's hard voice rolled over Levi, making him realize he'd spoken out loud.

"Get your ass up off the ground. Let's move it. Still four tangos down with Rhodes."

Levi gathered his strength and, in a smooth but painful movement, rose to his feet and slipped behind the trees. From the new vantage point he could survey the shacks below. His team had checked first to make sure there were no more women and children. But it was always a gamble. Lately these drug warehouse factories were working underground. So, when it appeared the building above was empty, it didn't mean all was *empty*. And these guys wouldn't give a damn. He'd watched them single-handedly shoot a dozen women and a couple kids. That was before Levi himself and his unit got blown apart. "Where did you see the four?"

"Two on the left, one on the right, and another hiding inside the vehicle." Merk took up his position on the ground beside Levi. "I can take out the two on the left."

Levi's comm unit buzzed quietly in his ear as Rhodes said, "Don't bother. I've got them." They watched Rhodes creep up behind the men and put a bullet in both their heads.

Levi smiled. Such a great sense of justice. These men had been responsible for not only the deaths of women and kids who had worked for them but for all his SEAL unit had suffered. An informant in the States had betrayed Levi, setting up a sequence of events that had caused the injuries sustained in this hellhole and then had cost all of them their careers.

Only two of his team had come with him. The third, Stone, was still in therapy and pissed at being left behind—wanting at least to run communications—but Levi had put his foot down. He could only hope that when he returned, Stone would be over his anger and ready to get on with it. Levi's new company had several potential jobs coming in, so he needed to take care of this asshole now and forever.

Another bullet passed overhead. He swore and dropped flat to the ground. "You sure there are only two left?"

Beside him, Merk laughed. "Yeah. But, as we well know, for every one of *these* men, several more are ready to step up to take their place. And they have a ton of firepower."

Levi nodded. He watched as the shooter slipped from the vehicle to the side of the building and around the back. Levi just wished he could find the leader, Rodriguez, and finish this once and for all. Levi'd hoped the head asshole would be here, but the intel hadn't confirmed his presence, just Herrara's.

Levi pulled out his gun and waited for his chance. Whispering to Merk, Levi said, "I'm going after him." He quickly retreated down the back of the hillside and came up behind the structure. Before they burned this place to the ground, he wanted to make doubly sure there weren't any innocents like last time.

He crouched down, peered around the corner, and came up behind one gunman.

The gunman pivoted and fired, the shot going wild. Before the guy could aim again, Levi took him out. "Number three's down."

Rapid gunfire spat to the left from the other side of the building. Levi turned, raced back the way he had come and scoped out the front of the structure, only to see Rhodes down and the final gunman holding an assault rifle to his buddy's chest.

"Hey, asshole, remember me?" Levi called out.

The man turned, a grin on his face. "Oh, I do. This bullet's got your name on it."

For the first time since arriving in Mexico, Levi could see Herrara's face clearly, matching the sneer to the name of one of the two assholes in Mexico who had used the US contact to take out Levi and his SEAL unit.

The man squeezed the trigger with the sound of return gunfire coming immediately afterward. The idiot's body danced midair, riddled with bullets from Levi and Merk's weapons. And the last of the four tangos went down. Levi waited in place for a moment and called out to Rhodes, "You badly hit?"

"No, just my shoulder."

The two team members did a swift recon and then hustled back toward Rhodes, who was now sitting up. Levi took a quick look at the injury. The bullet was still inside. That might be nasty, but they could only do so much here. Hurriedly, Levi bandaged Rhodes up. "Stay here while we check out the buildings."

Levi and Merk went through the two shacks. In the second they uncovered a trapdoor and stairs. Guns up and ready for more fighting, they went down and found a large group of crying women huddled in a corner. With a sense of déjà vu, Levi motioned for them to escape up the stairs. His Spanish sucked, but Rhodes was pretty good. He could explain what was going on.

Scanning the dark basement, Levi saw the money and drugs. Levi hated to touch the tainted money but if it could help the women escape ... he snagged up a pile from in front of him and stuffed it in his pockets.

In seconds, he and Merk were certain that the place was truly empty of people. Outside again, with everybody clear of the area, they lit the shack on fire.

While the broken-down structure burned, Rhodes explained everything to the women who were hugging each other in fear. "*Tranquila*, senoras."

Levi approached and pulled the money from his pocket. With Rhodes explaining it was to help them escape, Levi handed it over. Heads slowly nodded, eyes wide as if in disbelief; shoulders straightened, and the women scattered, running back to wherever they had come from.

Levi turned to Merk. "Let's go."

Slipping his arm around his buddy's waist, Levi helped Rhodes up the hill.

Behind them, Merk noted, "Helicopter is four minutes out."

Levi nodded. Only four minutes meant they were out of time to see if Rodriguez had run for the nearby hills when all the gunfire first erupted. Damn.

The helicopter blades whirred in the distance. Levi liked to think his heart knew who was in the cockpit, yet he'd hired another pilot for this mission. Since Ice had always been the one to pull Levi's ass out of the fire, he'd been counting—deep down—on her not giving up on him this time either. It was a slim chance considering how pissed she was, but hope was a hard thing to kill ...

As the helo came in for a landing, he did a final sweep, ensuring all was clear with no more targets left alive. The old Blackhawk, fully refurbished and outfitted, that now belonged to his company settled on the hilltop beside him. He helped Rhodes up first and then turned to see Merk getting in and—a flash came from the left.

Strong hands grabbed at his camo vest, dragging him inside as gunfire erupted around them.

From the corner of his eye, he spotted the pilot's pro-file—one he knew well and loved.

Ice. She'd come after all. His heart warmed. She was the best pilot he knew. And, so far, she'd never let someone else pick him up. She'd never be able to forgive herself if some-thing had gone wrong. He knew that. Because when they'd been in the military together, that's how he'd felt watching her head off on a flight without him.

He'd hated it. And waiting until she returned safe once again, time after time, had damn-near killed him. But he'd never let her know. Her work was every bit as important as his had been. And he'd kick the ass of anyone who didn't get it.

Being separated for missions was one thing he did not miss once they'd both walked away from the navy. Now they were together all the time. Just not in every way. The helicopter rose, tilted, and pulled out as he struggled to see what was happening. That was the thing about Ice. She never wasted any time. He shuffled to his seat and turned to find out who had grabbed him.

"Son of a ... Goddammit, Stone, you were supposed to

stay home."

Stone gave him a hard look. "Yeah, by whose orders? The day you guys go into battle without me watching your back is the day after I'm dead."

Levi rolled his eyes. No longer being in the military had given them all some moments of adjustment. But, as the boss, Levi expected to have his unit follow his orders. Even now. They'd always been tight, and he knew he'd have done the same.

Levi had a few more specialists working for him now—one who had always been a phone call away but was a resource most would have laughed their fool heads off, had they known. Merk's brother. Merk was a hell of a military man, but his brother was something else—in a whole different way. Merk's instincts were solid. Levi's were spookily good, but Merk's brother, Terkel ... he had something otherworldly going on. Their Creole grandmother was a well-known fortune-telling figure in her town. Terkel had called Levi and Merk on several occasions to warn them about missions going bad. They'd learned to listen.

Terkel had also warned them not to go on the Mexico job last year—that it was a bad deal.

Merk had tried to make Levi listen to Terkel that time too, but Levi had refused. He'd been so sure he was right. So sure how the play would go down.

Instead Terkel had been right. The mission had blown up. With Levi's men taking the worst of the hit. Levi would forever feel guilty for not having listened back then.

None of which helped right now.

Stone's artificial leg didn't work worth shit, a prototype Merk and Rhodes were working on but hadn't finished. Stone's stump had swelled with irritation, and all involved had to be careful there was no permanent damage. So Stone shouldn't be out here in the Mexican field.

Levi opened his mouth to say so when Rhodes nudged him and shook his head. With a glare Levi's anger subsided quietly. So not his usual form. Pissed at Stone, even more at himself for not finding his ultimate target, Levi settled back and closed his eyes.

The thing was, what made his men so great was also what pissed him off. Men he could trust. Men who would always have his back. Men who would do what was right, regardless of orders. And they'd do it well.

That was worth any amount of frustration.

"Take us home, Ice," he called to the front.

As usual he got no response.

Chapter 2

One month later ...

ICE WALKED INTO the office, stopped, and stared. Four desks for four men but only one was seated here. Stone. He flipped through papers with a frantic movement, as if searching for something he had absolutely no hope of ever finding but desperately needed. Stone, on desk duty. She quietly snickered, but he heard the sound. He looked up and glared at her, and her chuckles turned to full-blown howls.

"Oh, my God, you're actually on desk duty." She bent over, barely able to stay on her feet. "This is your worst nightmare."

"And that means it's funny?" Stone growled. "You think living my worst nightmare is a piece of cake?" His glare deepened. "Mary quit. That's the fourth secretary in as many months. And Alfred is not here to deal with the mess."

She held back her laughter as she headed to the spare chair and sat down on the other side of the desk from him. "I never imagined you as a secretary after being such a fine military specimen. But you know? It could grow on me," she said with a huge grin. "Hope you got payroll all arranged. The men need to be paid today." She leaned forward in a conspiratorial manner and whispered, "As you're such a pro, Alfred might even want to keep you here."

Stone raised his face and his glare turned to horror as he

understood. "No way. Oh, my God, payroll? That's not for me to do. I don't know the first thing about it. Hell, I don't even know what to do with this paperwork." He waved his arms. "This shit here is all invoices and receipts."

With an imploring look, he added, "Tell me Alfred is back today. Please ..."

She shook her head. "Nope. So *not* your lucky day."

Alfred had arrived at the compound's doorstep sometime during the first week and had immediately taken over the administration of it. They'd known him in the military though not well. They did now. Well ... partly. The man ran a tight ship. He was the engine of the office.

Levi was the heart.

"This is not my deal," Stone protested. "I need to be out there, building and hammering away, at least blowing shit up. That's what I'm good at."

"And apparently you're also very good at overdoing it." She nodded to his injured leg, then shot him a pointed look. "I'm pretty sure you were told to take it easy and not irritate that stump again."

He glared at her and opened his mouth.

She tilted her nose in the air, looked down over the tip of it, in one of those moves that she'd perfected over the years, and said in a hard and cold tone, "Or have I got it wrong?"

He deflated.

She chuckled and got to her feet. "I see Levi has found the perfect way to rein you in. Paperwork. Any time you don't follow orders, instead of cleaning the latrine, you get working in the office." She turned toward the doorway.

"Alfred better be hiring secretary number five and damn fast." He glared at Ice. "I am not staying here a moment longer than I have to."

"Alfred returns tomorrow," she reassured him. "I doubt finding our next secretary will be at the top of his list once he finds out why you're here, since that leg of yours needs another week to heal." She walked out, letting the door close behind her, leaving Stone alone to ponder his fate.

Rhodes waited in the hallway for her, a big grin on his face. "You've got a mean streak, you know that?"

She laughed. "I do. Hanging around you guys, that's how I developed it."

"Ha. You can't blame me for Levi," Rhodes said. "That's all between you and him."

"Exactly," she said smoothly. "That's between him and me."

With her flat tone, he backtracked for the moment to the proper side of the Levi-and-Ice boundary, a topic never to be discussed. But she also knew the men she worked with were not wusses, and they'd cross the line when needed to make things happen.

"You could go to bed again. It's not like you guys didn't have a hot relationship for a long time." With that parting shot, Rhodes took off down the hallway.

She watched him go. Sometimes the compound wasn't big enough for all of them. And at 25,000 square feet of furnished living space, and even more in development, it was damn big.

Levi's uncle had died a year ago and had left the property to Levi. The timing had been perfect as Levi had just set up his private security company and needed a base. He and Ice had become business partners, with the men in his old unit all now looking for a new career and joining in. Together they worked on the modifications they wanted. There weren't many, as his uncle had been all kinds of crazy. And paranoid was at the top of that list.

Every kind of protective measure was available, including panic rooms, secret entrances and exits, and even hidden hallways leading to the rooftop garrets. The place suited their purposes perfectly.

One of the first things they'd done was expand the parking lot and put in helipads. One on the roof and, in case needed, a second near their new medical facility. Just because …

They all had medical training, but Ice's was more extensive. Still it wouldn't hurt if they had a fully trained medic on the team, like Bullard, another former-active SEAL who'd gone private. They'd all been friends for over a decade, but Bullard was in Africa with his own security company; however, his focused on the hardware and software elements instead of safeguarding people, like Levi and his team did.

Another SEAL they knew and loved, Cooper, had a partner, Sasha, who was a doctor. Maybe if they could convince him to join them, she'd be happy to come too. And Ice's own father. As it was just the two of them, she knew one day he'd like to settle close to her. But that didn't necessarily mean at the same compound …

After she and Levi had had a serious discussion of what they needed security wise, they'd spent a week in Africa to talk to Bullard and his team, figuring out what parts of their system would work for Levi's new company. Besides, it was the only way to get Stone over there to spend some time with Dave.

Dave lost his leg a good ten years ago and was quite well-adjusted to it at this point in time. Stone, while he *said* he was, was no way in hell even close.

They needed Stone back physically and mentally. And that meant he must adjust. And fast. He'd come a long way and was anxious to get back to work in every aspect, but he wasn't healing fast enough. And he kept pushing it, which slowed his healing …

One sure way to make Stone behave himself so he could heal and become strong again was to give him a shit duty—like paperwork.

Still laughing, Ice headed to the kitchen. Today was her turn at cooking. Alfred, the office guru, was also their chef and majordomo, by his choosing. He'd adopted them, not the other way around, and had taken over and organized them in a big way. He'd been a godsend, and no one crossed him. He cooked like a dream and managed all the day-to-day stuff that kept their world functioning.

He'd been gone three days. Three long days. And was due back anytime, likely tomorrow, given the hour now. He was as mysterious as any of them. He'd asked for a lift to town, saying his brother had passed away, and he'd be back soon. They'd watched him go in silence.

She knew she wasn't the only one afraid he wasn't coming back. And, if Stone hated being in the office, Ice wasn't particularly fond of being in the kitchen. But they all had to do what they had to do.

Just as she threw the pot roast and vegetables into the oven, the phone rang. Was it the call they'd been waiting for? The kitchen didn't have a phone, but somebody elsewhere in the house picked it up. That was good. She hated answering the damn things. She was no secretary.

The thought of Stone answering the phone all day made her smile all over again.

Her cell phone buzzed within minutes. The text was

clear and blunt.

**Ice, the drop is confirmed for today. We need to
be in the air in two hours.**

She looked at the oven. No way in hell was she getting a
chance to eat any of this pot roast.

Another meal she would miss. Damn. She raced to the
helipad. Two hours was nothing. She checked the gas; she'd
already done the maintenance this morning, knowing this
call was a possibility. With everything looking good, she ran
back to her room, grabbed her bag, and headed to the
kitchen, snagging a bunch of apples and muffins, plus a big
thermos of coffee.

The skies were clear, and, as this was their third trip giving a routine feel to it, she felt confident about the
conditions they faced.

Being a private organization had another advantage. She
could rig out her helicopter the way she wanted, not the way
the military demanded. Sure, the company didn't have the
money for some of the latest and greatest, but they would
soon. In the meantime her helo was primed with the best in
weapons and navigation systems they could manage. She
patted the dashboard. She loved these machines.

This was the same helicopter she'd completed her training on. The military had sold off several dozen machines
when they'd upgraded theirs. She and Levi had scraped
enough funds together to buy two. Private investors, friends
of hers, had backed them.

She'd take one of these tried-and-true helicopters over
the new ones any day. Not everyone would appreciate the
constant dependability of these older ones. But *she* did. If she
got herself into some deep shit, these babies had always

brought her back home again.

Levi opened the door and hopped up beside her. She glanced at him. When only he and Rhodes jumped into the back, she silently raised one eyebrow.

Levi shrugged. "It's a small job."

A two-man job. Just doing another delivery. They'd been running supplies to a wilderness camp in Mexico for several weeks now. She swiveled to see Rhodes checking off the boxes they'd loaded earlier. She watched as he signed the clipboard and gave a nod. Then he hopped off and signaled they were good to go.

Rhodes closed the door, smacked the side of the helicopter, and backed up to where she could see he was free of her blades. His shoulder was healing nicely but not enough that he could return to active duty yet, even for this simple run.

As jobs went, it wasn't much, but it paid the bills. The good news was, it wouldn't take that long. Four hours round-trip if all went well—not that anything ever went smoothly anymore.

She and Levi buckled up, the weapons were safely stowed, and she slowly lifted the bird into the air. This trip would be easy. Just a quick hop over and back. What the hell? Maybe she'd be lucky enough to get to eat dinner after all.

LEVI KEPT A close watch on the land far below. They'd done this trip several times, and so far each had been uneventful. But he was always prepared, just for the one time that didn't go the right way. Cockiness made for accidents. And that was not in the cards. He'd worked hard to pull together his private security venture. He knew it was only a matter of time, and then they'd be swamped with jobs.

Alfred had set up this job, and it was a good one. Less danger than their usual assignments. Nice for a change.

Stone could have come on a run like this. Except he'd pushed being actively involved by overdoing it. Now he was stuck in the office.

Levi grinned. Stone had no freaking idea how to handle that. Too bad. He'd have to learn. But, until then, this milk run entailed just Levi and Ice. And he was handling that. At this point, the two of them were friends, but still not lovers, and it was killing him.

He relaxed into the seat, loving the way Ice handled the helicopter. She was not only a gifted pilot, but one of those special people who seemed to blend with the machine itself. She took pride in her work and was one of the most capable beings he had ever met. That she was also the woman of his heart didn't hurt. He wanted her back in his bed, and he wanted, no needed, her back in his arms. But he knew they were a long way away from that. He could hope. Still they couldn't go on this way. He wanted so much more.

"Ten minutes," Ice said quietly.

He didn't bother to answer. He just kept a close watch on the ground below. It was a beautiful afternoon. As they approached to land at the same clearing as last time, he recognized several from the group of men meeting the helicopter from before. It was a simple maneuver to unload, get the paperwork signed, all while Ice prepped the helo for the return journey. Fast and efficient and a repeat of the last time—until the number of men on the ground doubled. Levi took one look and yelled at Ice, "Go, go," racing to the helicopter.

Ice had the rotors spinning and happened to raise her

head from her pre-flight check. He waved his arms urgently at her.

She turned to see the circle of men rushing toward them.

He caught sight of her face as she lifted the helicopter to hover just above ground. He threw himself in, grabbed his assault rifle, rolled, and raised it.

As he spun to line up with the action below, he realized the men he'd done the delivery run for were now on their knees, hands behind their head. Two men holding semiautomatic weapons kept them in place.

Another seven lifted their weapons to the helicopter. And those were just the guys they could see. Gunfire filled the air. But Levi and Ice were already airborne. Ice tilted the helicopter and slipped to the side as she peeled away from the danger below.

Levi returned fire. The first man hit was flung back with the force of the bullet. The second Levi missed, but he took out the third as Ice flew them out of range and low enough to be under the cover of trees in case the crazies had rocket launchers.

Another few seconds and they were clear.

He grinned. Yep. He'd take Ice over all other pilots any day.

Staying in position for a few minutes longer to make sure all was well, he hopped up and made his way back to his seat. As soon as he was buckled in, he sent out a distress call for the camp. He highly doubted any were still alive, but he could hope.

As far as he'd seen, they were all good men. He hadn't had an issue until now. And even then, it wasn't their fault. But who were those gunmen? Rebels?

Ice spoke as soon as she got off the call. "Is someone on

the way to help them or are we going back?"

"We'll be outnumbered," he said.

She gave him *that* look. And he realized they'd been circling and were almost back to the camp. Ice had already made the decision for them.

Grinning, he chuckled, and as they came up on the rear of the camp, he was already in position. Damn, she was good.

He watched the line of men still kneeling and the other men yelling at someone standing out of sight. A strident voice snapped out a stream of Spanish. Rifles were raised.

Shit. *Here we go again.*

Levi quickly fired on the men threatening to shoot the research team. The place erupted in chaos. Return fire slammed into the side of the helicopter, and Ice swore like the sailor she was. She hated when her machines were hit. If it had been through an act of carelessness, she'd go on a rampage. But *deliberate* meant she'd be on the warpath. And that's what she was doing now.

She dropped the helicopter fast, pivoted so he was on the far side, the machine between him and the shooters, and lined him up for two of the assholes trying to escape. He took them out in seconds, and she spun the helo around again. He could see the exploration team was no longer lined up on the ground.

Good. Hopefully they'd made it to safety.

One more asshole … Another shot and one more man was down. Like shooting ducks at an arcade. Fast math and he figured he had them all but… He searched the treeline as Ice lowered the helicopter to the ground.

Two loud shots rang out behind him. Twisting, he could see two dead on the far side. Ice had brought out her own weapons. Damn, he loved that woman and there were never enough.

His attention swiveled back to movement near the woods; his gaze landed on a face twisted with anger—Rodriguez. His arm wrapped around the neck of Jimmy, one of the young men Levi had dealt with before.

Goddammit.

Levi lined up his sights, and then the young man was propelled forward so hard he stumbled and fell. The space where Rodriguez stood one second before was empty.

The bastard had escaped again.

Chapter 3

ICE LANDED ONCE more, and they'd ensured the exploration team was okay. Several were injured but nothing so bad to demand a helicopter ride out of here. She'd helped patch up everyone who'd needed it.

Finally everything returned to normal with authorities promising to be here within hours to collect the bodies and to investigate. With that reassurance, the exploration team sent Ice and Levi home.

They weren't sad to leave.

Tired but happy with the outcome, and with promises of a continuing working partnership—not to mention the men's gratitude—Ice set out to double-check the damage to her helicopter.

At least she considered the aircraft hers. She was a full partner in the company after all. She did a thorough search, but it appeared the helicopter, although sporting a few new holes, hadn't sustained any real damage.

Of course part of her modifications had been to reinforce the steel over the fuel tanks. She didn't plan to go down when something so simple could be improved.

Ice got them back in the air two hours later. The rush of adrenaline had long since disappeared as she headed toward home. While she thought about the men they'd left behind, Levi's stomach growled, and she realized, once again, he'd missed another meal, probably two. Things had been busy this last month.

Ice looked over at him. "Some muffins and apples are in my bag."

Levi reached behind him for her bag and brought it to the front seat. Opening it, he offered her an apple. Together they munched peaceably.

"With any luck we'll get home for the pot roast," she said.

He brightened. "Pot roast? Now that would be good. Seems like all we've been doing is living off of sandwiches since Alfred left. Who knew that man could cook like he does?"

"Or how much we'd miss him when he left." She laughed.

"I'll be happy to be home."

She could feel his pause, then his gaze. "What?" She studied his face. "What aren't you telling me?"

He shrugged. "Did you see the man holding Jimmy?"

She considered what she'd seen. There'd been a lot of action. She'd seen it all—but nothing clearly. She wasn't even sure she'd seen Jimmy down there. And certainly not when anyone had been holding him. "I'm not sure I did."

"It was Rodriguez." Levi's voice was low, calm.

But there was a sense of finality to it. A tone that worried her. After Levi's injury, it had taken him a long time to understand the who and the why of that betrayal. Then he'd gone after the final two men involved. A trip that had been half success and half failure. He'd taken out Herrara, but he'd lost Rodriguez.

Now Rodriguez had surfaced again.

"Why? How could he have known," she exclaimed, "that

you'd be there and when? That makes no sense." She shook her head. "And it can't be good."

"But he did." Levi stared into the blue sky. "I don't know how." He dropped his gaze to his clenched fists, then added, "But I will find out."

THE TRIP HOME to the compound was uneventful. Ice had tried to make the property sound less hostile by calling it the center. But that was too weak a description for Levi. Not when they were fully armed and trained. Nah, in truth, he'd been eyeing a tank on eBay.

His grin fell away as his gaze landed on the two very large black vehicles—SUVs, government issued—parked at the front. That could mean either good or bad news. Ice lowered the helicopter, and he hopped out.

Rhodes stood there, talking with four men Levi didn't know. A passenger door opened, and another man exited the SUV.

A smile broke out on Levi's face. "Commander Jackson. Good to see you again, sir."

Jackson smiled, reached out, and shook Levi's hand. "I'm working for the government now, though not the same type of work. So drop the *commander*." He looked around the compound and smiled. "It's good to see you and your team again. We were in the neighborhood and thought we'd drop off a friend."

Which also meant they wanted to talk without ears. *Interesting.* Levi watched as the passenger door on the far side opened.

Alfred walked around the vehicle. Levi's eyebrows shot up. That man was a mystery in so many ways. He leaves for a family funeral and returns with the brass. A connected man. And a private one.

"Hey, Alfred." Levi reached out and smacked the older man on the shoulder. "We're all glad to have you back. Stone's been handling the office and Ice the kitchen. I'm sure I don't have to tell you how much you've been missed."

Alfred laughed. "It's good to be here. I'll go in and say hi."

"And maybe pick up the pieces," Levi said with a laugh. "The place fell apart with you gone."

Turning back to face Jackson, Levi wondered why the ex-commander was here and what exactly he was doing now. The vehicles had government Secret Service written all over them.

"It's good to be back on my feet again, sir. Even Stone's more or less on his." Behind him he heard the steady *click* of Stone with his racing blade.

"I'm here. I'm here," Stone said in a gruff voice. "Don't you worry about me."

Levi ushered the five men into the compound building. On the main floor they'd set up one room as a big meeting area. He put on a pot of coffee and motioned for everyone to take a seat. He was curious but knew Jackson would talk when he was ready.

While the coffee dripped, Levi sat down directly across from Jackson.

"I didn't expect to see a compound of this size. Or how well prepared you are." Jackson nodded. "You've built a hell of a place here."

"Thank you," Levi said quietly. "Ready for business." Levi waited. No point in rushing the man.

"And I might have need. If not now, then down the

road." He offered a small smile. "I've heard good things about your company."

Alfred walked over, a notepad in one hand and the coffeepot in the other.

Stone took a seat next to Levi, and Rhodes sat on the other side. Ice and Merk stood behind them. Levi nodded his head. "I'm listening."

"We could have need of someone qualified, capable, and not connected to any government agency."

"That's us." Levi leaned back, crossed his arms across his chest, and waited.

"But potentially connected to our problem." Jackson studied Levi as a frown settled on his face. "You know this man I'm hunting." His gaze swept the table. "You all do. He's the one who shot off Stone's leg. And he's back, here in your neighborhood. Potentially part of a terrorist cell."

Ice gasped, her gaze zinging toward Levi.

At those words he slowly sat forward, his tone low. "I just saw him in Mexico ..." He glanced over at Ice. "We barely got out with our lives."

The rest of the men straightened, frowning but silent.

In as few words as possible, Levi explained what he and Ice had just survived. When he was done, the room fell quiet yet again. Levi kept his gaze on the new arrivals.

Jackson eyed him carefully, then gave a slow nod. "That's very interesting. Now how did he know you would be there?"

"No idea," Ice snapped. "We haven't had a chance to find out. But Rodriguez escaped again, the lucky bastard."

"Are you saying he's running a cell around here?" Levi asked. "Because, after today, I'd be more inclined to believe that if he's in the neighborhood, he's more likely after me ..."

and not whatever you think he's doing here. And, if he's involved, he's in charge. Rodriguez was never one to play second fiddle."

"I'm thinking he's killing two birds with one stone." Jackson smiled, but it was a slow twisted version of the real thing. "We think he's aligning himself with a Middle East group. Building an army here on US soil to target US landmarks. He has connections on both sides of the border. About you, I don't know," he admitted. "Rodriguez could also be serious about taking you out—before you become a bigger problem. If you plan to keep going after him, he can't afford to leave you alive."

Silence hung in the room.

Levi knew Jackson was right. But what were the chances that Rodriguez knew Levi was here? Then again they needed to find out how Rodriguez knew Levi and Ice would be at that camp in Mexico too. Wouldn't it have been easier to take out Levi closer to home?

Or, given Rodriguez knew the campsite like he did, was Mexico better because no one would ask questions? Rodriguez could get away with a massacre, and no one would care down there. Unfortunately shit like that happened all the time.

And cells grew. They recruited and farmed out. A good way to keep the action moving without letting anybody know exactly where they were working from. That Rodriguez was involved was more than a mere coincidence. How recent was the intel?

In a low voice Levi said, "We were in Mexico a month ago, following up some information on their location. The data was good, and we took out Herrara, but Rodriguez got away. I never saw or heard about him again until a few hours ago ..." He shook his head, remembering the moment he had laid eyes on Rodriguez holding Jimmy tight. "I couldn't believe it was him at first."

Jackson nodded. "Word is Rodriguez broke free of his connections to run this newer, bigger, shinier operation. He was never strong on loyalty."

"Is this just an information-gathering session?" Stone asked. "Or do we get to kick some ass?"

Levi grinned at the eagerness in Stone's voice.

Jackson shook his head. "Strictly intel."

Stone was chomping at the bit to get out and back into action. Especially involving Rodriguez. They all wanted payback in a big way. Now Levi had more reasons than ever. Too bad he had gone alone with Ice on that routine run. If he'd had Stone as backup, they'd have had a better chance of taking out that asshole permanently.

Jackson continued. "The cell is recruiting people, sending them down to Mexico, doing the training across the border, and then slipping them back into the States to set up the attacks. We haven't any confirmation on this. We just know a recruiter cell is here, doing *some* weapons training but a lot of computer, and by that I mean, hacker training. So we need to know exactly what you can find out."

"Tell us what you've got."

Stone grabbed a notepad and pen. Rhodes grabbed the laptop. Levi, well, he just wanted to listen. Ice stood behind him. He reached up a hand to lace his fingers through hers. He felt her start of surprise but she didn't drop her hand.

"Go ahead, sir," Levi instructed.

What followed was the usual tale of a terrorist finding and setting up camp, and slowly building a relationship with the people around him. The leaders recruiting small numbers, and then they grew larger, gaining—through all kinds of avenues, including social media—young men looking for a cause to call their own.

When Jackson went quiet, Levi asked, "Time frame?"

Jackson's jaw tightened. "Yesterday." He stood up. "When you identify the members of the cell, we need addresses, workplaces, etc."

Levi studied Jackson's face, wondering where this was going. But he decided that, given his current position, he didn't need the details. Sometimes it was better not to know too much.

He stood up, shook Jackson's hand, and walked him and his entourage to their vehicles. The sun was no longer shining, and, once the half-light of evening came on, dark clouds had collected.

The weather wouldn't put a damper on his mood. This was a wonderful turn of events and exactly the type of work they were suited for.

"What do you think?" Ice asked as they watched the twin plumes of dust travel down the road.

Merk's quiet voice answered, "I want to know why they can't do this themselves. He's government, CIA, NSA, FBI ... a spook of some sort. This is well within their area. So why not them? Why us?"

That was a damn good question. Levi had been so surprised at Jackson's visit that he hadn't asked the necessary questions. But Merk was right; Jackson likely had teams to do this type of work. So why weren't they?

"I think this is a test," Rhodes said beside him. "He's figuring out just what we can do on our own."

"No way," Stone said, his arms across his massive chest. "He knows exactly what we're capable of."

"Of what we *were* capable of," Rhodes snapped. "We haven't been tested in our current physical conditions."

Letting his arms drop to his side, Stone gave a snort. "You may doubt yourself, but I know exactly what I am— strong as ever. I didn't need that goddamn leg anyway." He turned and headed back inside.

Levi and Rhodes exchanged looks. Stone was never gonna go down easy. At one point in time he may just have to accept that his body would not be of the same balance and coordination as before. And that would affect his ability to run, climb, and fight.

Then again this was Stone. He might just pull it off.

"On a good note," Ice said, "this is our kind of job. And ..." Her smile was as cold as her name when she added, "even if Jackson is only looking for intel, we might get to take out our mutual enemy."

Levi grinned. There was that. He slung an arm around her shoulders and dropped a kiss on her forehead.

"Does that mean we'll get this week's paycheck after all?" Merk joked from behind them. He pulled his pockets inside out.

Levi winced. "Yeah, Stone couldn't figure out the payroll, but Alfred is back now. It's all good."

"Damn good," Merk said with a grin, flapping his inside-out pockets in the wind. "I'm broke."

Chapter 4

W EARING A HAT for this trip, Levi walked through the hardware store. Supposedly to pick up a hammer. Only a half dozen were at the compound, and there were never enough. Besides, Jackson's man had said the intel showed this location as one of the contacts for the cell. This wasn't a job as much as a casual check. Levi never spent much time in town. There'd not been much opportunity. He'd owned the complex for three months and had moved in, then immediately left for Mexico. Since his return, he'd been busy building, modifying, and dealing with the business.

He wanted to be friendly with the two nearest small towns. The compound was close enough to a city to get all their supplies, so the local towns were more for gas and post office runs. He probably should support them more but hadn't considered it beyond the casual thought. Yet he should cultivate a relationship with the local businesses. Who knew what arrangements they could develop?

The hardware store had no other customers when he entered, the lighting low, the dark instantly making him feel positive about this choice. He rummaged around in the back, looked at framing hammers, and decided on the simple claw type. He picked it up and wandered around the saws and the drills. He really could use another decent drill.

Nobody came to ask him if he needed anything. In fact, besides the single white male at the front counter, the store appeared to be empty. The clerk was watching TV. *Interesting.*

This was a small town, but Levi was used to better service. Still he wandered around, checking out security cameras, windows, and the back rooms. It appeared to be a simple store with parking around the back of the building. Attached to the side was an ice cream shop. From the looks of it, no doorway connected the two. He couldn't get into the back room without raising the clerk's suspicions but suspected the standard office, bathroom, and maybe even a lunchroom would be there. Although that would be a waste; it was likely a storeroom. He wandered up to the front counter, noting the bars on the windows.

"Bars?" he asked with an innocent surprise in his voice. He studied the man's plug piercing—very distinctive. As was the odd freckled pattern on the back of his right hand.

The man looked at the bars and nodded. He stood to ring up the hammer and accepted the cash from Levi, all without saying a word. Not very friendly for someone dealing with the public.

Levi tried again. "Nice place you got here."

The clerk looked at him as if to say, *Who the hell you kidding?* Then handed over the hammer, again without saying a word.

Levi's left brow shot up. "Okay, thanks for the conversation and hammer." He turned and walked back out.

He stood on the front steps and studied the location of the hardware store. Across the road was the only bank in town. It was closed. A dress shop was next to that and some kind of five-and-dime store beside that. Down the road were a take-out Chinese restaurant and a couple other fast-food chains. The streets were empty of all traffic. He wondered how any business survived here.

The main route that used to go through the town had been redirected a couple miles away, turning this into a ghost town. He wandered down to his truck and climbed in. He sat for a moment, waiting to see if any more activity occurred around the hardware store.

The one thing that registered with him inside the store were the lovely surveillance cameras. Very high-tech and way-too-modern security for the age of the building or its lack of valuable contents. He'd kept his hat down, covering his face. He didn't know what kind of computer-scanning software these guys might have, neither did he know what kind of databases they had access to. Terrorists these days seemed to be better hackers than anybody else.

As he sat in his truck, Levi watched the clerk step onto the front stoop and casually look around. Only nothing was casual about his fingers clenched into fists. Levi swore softly. Had he been made? That wouldn't be good.

This wasn't the town nearest to the compound but was damn close enough. The other was in the opposite direction. He watched as the man studied the whole area for a few moments, as if detailing what might have changed since he'd last been out. When he glanced in Levi's direction, he didn't seem to recognize who was behind the windshield of the big truck. Levi's license plate was fully concealed by the car in front, unless the clerk wanted to stroll about.

Instead he pulled out a phone and made a call. Levi turned the engine on as the clerk pivoted and walked back inside the hardware store.

Levi popped his comm device in his ear. "Merk, the

clerk is going inside. Watch your back."

Merk had entered through the store's back door while Levi had been in the front.

No response from Merk.

Using his laptop beside him, Levi quickly noted the incident and the clerk's actions. He'd collected a few photos inside the store and downloaded them to the laptop too.

Merk responded, his voice quiet in Levi's ear. "It's all good. I'm outside again."

Levi grinned. He waited in place until Merk walked around the building at the end of the block. When he hopped into the truck, Levi casually pulled out, making a turn in the middle of the road, heading in the direction he'd come from. "Well?"

Merk shook his head. "Just a storeroom in the rear and it's definitely full of tools. Every kind any carpenter might want. But no power tools and nothing big. And, honest to God, dust was over all of it."

"No restocking in the recent month?"

Merk shook his head. "Not only was it not restocked but the office itself appeared to be unused as well. The whole thing seems to be a front."

"Maybe, but we still have to figure out what's going on and who this place might be connected to." Levi pulled into a fast-food drive-thru and ordered lunch for the two of them. As they waited, he pondered why a terrorist cell was this far out in the middle of nowhere.

As if reading his thoughts, Merk said, "It's really not that far out of nowhere. It's kind of a hidden gem, with highway access to all the major cities. But, when you step off the highway, nobody even knows where you are."

Levi shot him a glance. "You're right."

"Sir, here's your bag."

Levi turned to study the young kid holding out the large bag of food, then retrieved it, passed it to Merk, and waited for the coffees to come. Coffee in hand, Levi drove slowly back onto the main street, his mind churning with options.

"According to some of the locals I spoke with up and down the block, not much is here, with maybe a sleeping sector population of about four thousand people. There used to be a local newspaper, but it shut down when the highway rerouted. Close to half the population moved away a couple years before the new road construction began, and afterward lots of businesses downsized to the skeleton crews they have now due to lack of business." Merk unwrapped a burger and took a big bite.

Levi reached into the bag and pulled out one for himself. A small park was up ahead. He pulled in, parked, and as they ate, they studied the slow meandering river that wound around the town. When he was done, Levi hopped from the truck, tossed the garbage, and walked to the water's edge. The one thing the town did have going for it was the fresh water. It was a good size river, quite accessible, and probably a favorite with the locals during the heat of summer. Levi didn't know if any fish were in there, but it could be an excuse to visit the town or check out the place some more.

He turned to study the parking lot alongside the road where he'd left his ride with Merk. At the far end of the lot was an old beat-up half-ton truck. It almost looked to be one of the original Toyotas. Those suckers seemed to live well past the point in time when everyone else's vehicles died. It also looked like shit, rusted and banged up; probably had to be hot-wired to run. But it obviously worked, as he watched it back up and head toward the highway.

He hadn't seen anybody get in or out. And he'd have noticed. Frowning, he tried to remember the license plate. First two were letters, *LG*, but, other than that, he was lost. He hopped back in his truck and started the engine. Turning to Merk, he said, "You ever seen that truck before?"

Merk already had a notepad in his hand and the letters *LG* written down, adding the rest of the license plate as Levi watched. Merk shook his head. "No. Never. That's not a rig you forget."

Levi didn't have reason to believe anything was wrong though. He drove his truck to the far end of the parking lot where the other vehicle had been. Unable to stop that instinctive prodding, he killed the engine, opened the truck door, and hopped out. Merk joined him. They slowly wandered, studying the trail as they went.

The parking lot was a good twenty yards from the river's edge, a 30 percent slope heading down to the water. Any tracks were long gone. Levi noticed some bent grass, but couldn't be sure it had come from the driver of that vehicle. With his gut still prodding them, the two searched the area to see who and what someone might've been here for. When they found nothing, Levi stood for a long moment and studied the water.

"I just love how after being in the military, doing what we did, now we look at everybody suspiciously."

Merk laughed. "Hell, I was like this before." He slapped Levi on the shoulder and said, "This suits me just fine."

As they turned to the truck, Levi caught a flash on the far side of the river. Instinctively he shoved Merk to the ground and threw himself down beside him.

A hard spit ripped through the air. They flattened lower and rolled in opposite directions. Under the cover of the trees, Merk turned to stare at Levi. His expression was one of shock and anger.

Levi couldn't believe it. Someone had just shot at them. What the hell? Who had done that and why?

"Son of a bitch," Merk swore.

"Any idea what's on that side of the river?" Levi whispered.

They crawled up the hill and sprinted for the truck. Safe now, they turned their attention to where the shot had come from.

A small jetty was out on the far bank of the river with a bridge farther up. Merk reached into the glove box and pulled out a pair of binoculars—the best money could buy.

Having been in the military with good equipment but always knowing the private sector had something a little bit better, Levi hadn't skimped when equipping his company.

With the windows open, they could hear an engine backfire as it raced away on the far side.

"What do you want to bet that was our beat-up truck?"

Merk nodded. "I can't see anything anymore. Let's take a look."

Levi turned on the engine and wasted no time heading to the turnoff taking them on the bridge and across the river. Once on the other side he took another right and followed along the river. They didn't have to go far before the road widened a bit. This wasn't an official parking lot, just one of those gravel shoulders. A few garbage cans dotted the area, but there were no facilities of any kind.

He pulled off to the side and exited the truck, looking for the shooter's vantage point to study the angles of where they had been standing. Levi walked up and down the fifty feet of gravel and found what looked to be the best location for the shooter. Levi dropped his gaze to the ground and studied it. There were lots of tire tracks, but they were faint. It would be hard to discern which tread came from the latest vehicle. The weather had been dry and warm for the last few days. Not the best for picking up tire marks. A single shot had been fired, so not an assault rifle, likely an old hunting one. In which case there would be a shell casing. He stepped a little closer to the green edge and studied the rough grass.

Unless the shooter had picked it up.

"From here it would be an easy shot," Merk said. "So a warning, you think?"

Levi nodded. "It's possible. Or he could have lousy aim. Then again he could have been hunting. I see no evidence left behind."

Back in the truck, he skipped the main road home. The chance of being followed was slim, but today had not exactly been an innocent type of day, so he took a convoluted route … just in case.

At the compound, Levi pulled inside the multiple-bay garage. Hitting the keypad on the side, he waited for the huge gates to close, locking them safely inside. Once he was sure the electronic eyes were up and live, he walked into the building.

"Maybe it's time to find the money to get the towers fully functional," Merk said and followed Levi to the kitchen.

"It definitely is. Bullard will be here in a couple days, so we're waiting for him."

"Not sure that's a good idea any longer." With that laconic comment Merk cocked his head and walked off toward his quarters.

The compound was large enough that each person was

assigned an individual suite. Eventually that would change down the road when they fixed up the apartments, but for right now, the six of them were content with the status quo.

In the kitchen Levi put on coffee. If he could inject his veins with caffeine he would. It seemed his blood was permanently mixed with the dark brew. He waited, staring out into the late afternoon sun, wondering just what the hell had gone wrong.

ICE LET THE curtain drop from her window. She stepped back to study her office, but her mind was on the double gates closing. Levi had looked rattled. Something had obviously unsettled him.

Bullard had devised a brand-new electronic security system. The initial prototype was to be mounted here, and, after watching Levi secure those gates for the first time, she realized Bullard couldn't come fast enough. She left her office and headed to the kitchen. Her wing was on the same floor as Levi's. But she was around the corner and across from him. Levi had the largest room in the house, not that he cared.

But she did. She should be sharing it with him. The damn man was trying too hard to be noble. And she had no plans to let him continue on that path. Her nerves were strung tight as she waited for him to make a decision about them.

Maybe she should just move in. In fact she should have done that upon their arrival here.

Now in the kitchen, Ice poured herself a coffee and turned to study Levi's back. She sat down at the long table meant to seat at least twenty people and said, "So what went wrong?"

He pivoted to study her carefully blank face. "I was just figuring that out."

"Tell me." Ice motioned toward the chair across from her.

She and Levi had been partners in many ways for a long time. They were good together. At least in most areas.

Ice waited for him to begin, not pushing.

Formulating the thoughts in his head first, Levi was extremely methodical. His ability to devise strategies was second to none. His unit had been sent on the most difficult of all missions when they were active SEALs. Most of their ops were so black nobody else understood just when, who, or what they were doing.

They would leave the country and come back, and nobody was ever the wiser. But she knew. Even then she'd been that close to Levi. She understood there was something almost otherworldly about his abilities. And Levi wasn't the only one who had that particular skill. Working as a unit, he and the others were unmatched.

Until something horrible happened and they got themselves blown to shit.

She placed her hand gently across his. "Tell me," she urged.

Squeezing her fingers, he gave a quick nod and explained what he'd seen. She frowned at the description of the clerk at the hardware store. And the shiny and bright new camera system inside. The clerk stepping outside to see where they'd gone. When Levi got to the part where they were shot at, her frown shifted to a glare.

"Why the hell would anybody shoot at you?"

Levi shook his head. "No idea. We didn't raise any

alarms. Yes, the clerk came out on the stoop and made a phone call, but still he needed somebody close by in order for them to line up a shot like that. We hadn't expected to go to the park—it was a casual spontaneous stop. We were there maybe ten, fifteen minutes, that's all. As far as I know, no one should have thought we were suspicious."

"That, in itself, is suspicious," she snapped. "You're new to the town, strangers driving this monster truck and asking questions. They *should be* suspicious. Hell, everybody should. That they weren't is, in itself, suspicious."

He nodded. "You're probably right. The bottom line is, we didn't see anybody acting in a way that stood out as odd or questionable—other than the store clerk."

"Were you close enough to hear any of his conversation?"

"Nope. The clerk did a thorough visual search of the area though."

"Tipping somebody off?"

He raised his gaze to study hers. "That's what I'm thinking."

"The shooter?"

He shrugged. "I'm not sure that's related."

"How the hell could it not be?" She laughed. "Now you have a suspicious storekeeper who immediately calls somebody after you walk out the door. The store has very sophisticated video equipment, possibly audio, and who knows what kind of other software to track who you are. And then, not twenty minutes later, you're shot at." She shook her head. "What's the chance Merk ticked off somebody when he talked to the locals?"

"Anything is possible." Levi gave her a lopsided grin. "It is Merk."

Pushing her chair back, Ice laughed as she stood up. "So true." She walked to the refrigerator and pulled out some of the leftover pot roast, filling a plate and heating it in the microwave. Ice tilted her head to see Levi still hugging his coffee. "I'm glad Alfred is back."

"I think we all are. None of us cook."

The timer on the microwave rang, colliding with a pop from the front corner of the compound. Levi had already left to investigate. As they had a high-voltage line outside, she made a guess that the transformer had blown. But why? Carefully Ice lowered the hot plate to the counter and walked to the window.

Scanning the area, Ice found nothing out of the ordinary, but that didn't mean somebody wasn't skulking around outside. Part of the fence was electric but not all of it. Something they had to fix. Part of Bullard's new setup.

The security lights flickered off.

Quickly she dialed Merk's number.

"What?" he growled.

"Loud pop in front. No more yard lights. Levi's out there alone."

"I'm on it," he said, alarm noted in his voice.

Evening darkness settled. And, with the cloud cover, gloominess filled the air.

With Levi's tale of the recent odd events, the shadowy atmosphere outside added to the eerie effect. Sinister as hell.

Stone hadn't fully healed, and Rhodes was recovering from the shoulder wound, but both needed to be aware of the potential critical situation. It wouldn't matter how injured they were; in the event of an actual attack, they'd step up. Hell, there would be no keeping them down.

Quickly she texted both of them. A second odd shot

split the air.

That did it. As she raced to the back door, her phone buzzed. She answered instantly. Rhodes said, "I'm heading toward you. Stay put."

Outside the back door a large and long veranda wrapped around the side of the house and gave a hell of a view of the hills. Inside the compound proper were all the vehicles and equipment, like her helicopter.

As she watched, a shadow skulked toward one of the big Hummers parked outside. She pulled her handgun free of her shoulder holster and slipped out the back door. That was one of the easy things about fitting into this part of Texas—everybody was armed.

Outside the air was dry. Not a sound could be heard. Normally the night birds sang, and the crickets chirped. But right now the entire place was still. Waiting.

Ice didn't like the feel of it one bit. Sticking close to the side of the building, she crept around to the front of the double garage and stilled. Keeping her eyes on the vehicle she'd seen the man slink toward, suddenly he crept around the front of the truck beside her.

Arms extended, she placed the gun to his head. "Don't move."

Chapter 5

T HE MAN'S ARMS went up slowly, letting her see he had no gun. Was he really not armed? She did a quick search and then pulled his feet out from under him so he dropped to his knees. "Lie down, arms on the ground in front of your head."

Ice fished her phone from her pocket and sent a quick message to Levi. She reached down to the man's pocket and pulled out what she thought was a wallet. Using her cell phone light, she studied the ID. Ice glared at the man. "What are you doing skulking around on private property?"

He jerked to the side, grabbed her leg, and pulled. Expecting it, she held strong, reaching down and hitting him hard in the side of his head with her gun.

He groaned softly and went still.

She stripped off the man's belt and quickly tied up his arms and legs like a calf at the rodeo. He wouldn't get a second chance at her or his escape. Moving quietly she edged up to the front of the Hummer and peered around the side. With one last look at the prone man, she snuck around to the far side and searched between the vehicles for more intruders. At this point she doubted he'd have come alone. Plus, she had received no answers from Levi and Merk. What trouble had they gotten into?

A scraping on the cement sounded behind her. She pivoted and kept low.

"George, where are you?" a man asked in a harsh and unfamiliar whisper.

She bared her teeth and waited. The sound of heavy shuffling came from around the front of the other vehicle. The second man had no idea his friend was down. Good. She'd take them both and haul the rest of her team here. She was the hired pilot, not the muscle. Ready to lunge forward, she froze when a gun pressed against her spine.

"Well, look what we have here."

Shit. She'd been so focused on the man in front of her that she hadn't heard the one creeping up behind her. How many of these assholes were there?

The man in front of her stepped around the truck. "Where is George?"

"Shut up," the man behind her snapped. "We aren't using names, remember?"

She spun, grabbed the long rifle from the man's hands, and smashed the butt into his chin. At the same time she hooked his legs, dropping him to the ground instantly. Ice turned the rifle against his neck then held her handgun on the third man. In a deadly voice, she barked, "Don't move. Raise your hands." The man's arms shot up. Good thing.

At the top of her voice she called out, "Levi?"

No answer.

"Merk, you out there?" she hollered.

Instantly the backdoor opened, and the sound of running footsteps came her way.

"Over here," she yelled, keeping the rifle at the throat of the man on the ground and her handgun pointing at the man standing before her.

Merk appeared magically at her side, assessed the situation, and instantly reached down, punching the man on the ground hard in the jaw, knocking him out. One less invader she had to worry about. She slowly turned to face the third man. Merk walked over, checked him for a weapon, pulled a pair of cuffs from his back pocket, and hooked him up. He shoved the third guy to the ground beside the unconscious man.

"Around the side of the Hummer," she said, "is another."

With eyebrows raised, Merk retrieved the first man. Soon all three were lined up on the ground. Two still unconscious and the third now lying face down. She didn't trust him either, but at least he was cuffed.

Turning, she asked Merk, "Where the hell is Levi?"

"I'm over here," Levi said, his voice low and lethal.

She peered over the hood of the Hummer to see two men walking with their hands in the air and Levi behind them.

When the men appeared in full view, Merk walked over to the side of the building. Hands moving easily, he performed his magic on the control panel. Suddenly the outdoor lights clicked on. She studied the control panel and realized she really didn't understand how a lot of the electronics here worked. But she'd have to learn, and fast.

Next she turned her attention to the two men standing in front of her. "Who the hell are you?" she asked. "What are you doing on our property?"

The first man had his palms open and up, as if to say, *Hey, we're innocent.* Only the words out of his mouth surprised her. "It was supposed to be a lark," he said. "They said you were looking for somebody to test how good your security was." He snorted. "It's pretty darn poor. We jumped the fence in no time."

Levi exchanged a hard glance with Ice.

She snorted. "And yet we caught you."

The second man jumped in. "Sure, but we could slash all the tires in this place or smash a few of those lights, and you'd never get them back on again. Y'all need to fix that."

"We're planning to," Levi said. "But I highly doubt you guys just came here for a lark."

"Well, that and a thousand bucks," the first man sniggered. He motioned at the three men on the ground. "We were all to get two hundred apiece."

"Who's paying you?" Ice asked. She watched the two men exchange a silent glance before turning blank looks her way. Right. They needed a little persuasion. She looked at Merk. "Your turn."

She hated this part, but there was no better way to get a man to talk.

"Have fun." She holstered her handgun and walked away, clapping her hands over her ears. Instantly she could hear the men in the background protesting.

At least until Merk's fist connected, then the protests died.

And the screams began.

Inside she hit the security room and found Stone and Alfred already studying the monitor screens.

"Did you see anything?" she asked.

Stone's huge head nodded slowly. "It's not like any of them made an attempt to hide what they were doing." He brought up the cameras on three corners of the building. He hit Replay on the first, and she could see two of the men scaling the fence and jumping over the side. On the far-side camera, it was the same thing but with only one man. The last two were just as obvious at the middle of the fence.

"They said they were paid a thousand bucks to break in." She shrugged. "They really seem to think it was just a lark."

"And probably was," Stone said. "But we have to ask the bigger question. Why would anybody do that? To test our defenses? To see just how easy it would be to gain access? Or to see how fast we would react?"

"Or ..." Ice mumbled.

"Maybe throw us off the scent," Stone continued, "and, while this distraction was happening, others were doing something else."

Alfred nodded.

Shivers ran down her spine at that thought. "Any sign of more intruders to back up that last theory?"

Stone reached out to tap the first monitor in the series of six. "This camera is blind."

"Shit. I'll go check it out," she said.

"Rhodes went to look, but"—Stone studied his watch—"he should've checked in by now."

"I'm on it." Ice hurried to the door, then paused. "What was his last location?"

"I'll check the other floors," Alfred said as he rushed out, his rapid footsteps clipping against the tile floor.

Stone reached across the desk and punched a code into a small unit on the side. Instantly a light flashed with a corresponding number below it. He lifted it, and they both read the location. "Rhodes is down in the kitchen."

"That could be anything. But I'll go there first. Tell Merk and Levi." Ice cast her mind back to what she'd seen since she had returned to the building. While the men were outside with the first batch of intruders, she hadn't been particularly aware of anything going on inside. She'd made the amateur mistake of assuming the danger was outside. Not any longer.

Moving carefully she slipped her way down to the kitchen again. She saw no one nor signs of anyone having been inside. At the kitchen doorway she stopped and listened. Nothing—the place was silent.

But definitely not empty. Rhodes was at the kitchen table, unconscious over the wooden surface. She raced to his side and checked for a pulse. Thank God, it was there, though barely. Not a good start to their venture. Maybe it was a good thing. They'd gotten soft. As the men had healed, they'd been planning this new life, but from the comforts of home wasn't the same as actually living on the edge of danger again. Previously they were honed to be at their best when they went on a mission, but, back on home ground again, they could relax. With the new company they didn't understand what they'd walked into. There might never be any relaxing; something they hadn't considered.

She tapped her ear comm. "Stone, Rhodes is alive, but he's been hit. He's at the kitchen table."

"An intruder heading toward the inside garage entrance," Stone warned through her crackling headset.

She stopped, reoriented herself, and silently raced forward.

At the garage—really, at this point, this was their work area for the development of machinery—the door was open. She didn't know what this new guy was after. Maybe he was just seeing what was here, but the last thing the team needed was to have somebody checking out their place.

Crouching low, she went through the double doors and hid behind one of the freestanding tool kits. The intruder headed straight for the large truck Levi had driven earlier. *Interesting.*

The guy opened the door and checked inside. He didn't enter or climb in, just merely leaned forward.

What was he looking for? The laptop? Every vehicle was equipped with one, and, although they were still getting some of their systems set up, those were targeted to immediately download any new data to the main computer banks as each of the team came back to base. Then wiped the laptops clean for the next time. So, even if the laptops were stolen, nothing incriminating or confidential would be on them. But that didn't mean the team wanted to give anything away either.

He snagged the laptop and tucked it under his arm.

Along the far side, she lined up a shot, ready to pull the trigger, when the target froze and dropped to the ground. *What the ...?* Voices sounded in the distance. Several men. That should be Levi. Was he bringing the first group of men inside?

The intruder hopped to his feet and ran to the back of the big truck. She didn't take a chance. Lining him up in her sights again, she took the shot. The man dropped, screaming in outrage. The laptop tumbled from his arms and slid across the floor.

In her ear, Stone asked, "Ice?"

"Yeah, I hit him. Turn on the lights, will you? Any more assholes where they don't belong?"

Instantly the huge garage filled with lights.

The man on the ground held his thigh with one hand. But in his other he held an automatic weapon. Of course he did. Whatever happened to carrying a baseball bat?

"Drop the weapon," she snapped.

The intruder sneered. He pointed it in her direction.

She pulled the trigger a second time. His weapon fell to the cement floor while a wild bullet from his gun slammed into the ceiling. The idiot screamed again as his hand oozed blood.

He should have listened to me.

She approached carefully and kicked the weapon out of his reach. "Stone, he's down."

"Merk is on his way toward you. Can you handle him alone until then?"

She laughed. "He's got two bullet holes in him. He's not going anywhere."

"Damn."

The admiration in his voice did her heart good. Stone was never one to give praise, but he didn't stint on it either. And just hearing that tone made her feel better. A lot better.

"Ice, where are you?" Merk's voice rang out behind her.

"Over here." She kept the gun trained on the man swearing at her feet. He glared at her with a darkly veiled promise of retribution. She knew, if he had a chance to come after her, he would. But, for now, with a bullet in his thigh and one hand, he was pretty screwed. She'd deliberately taken out both on the same side to make any other ideas he might have a lot harder.

Merk arrived at her side in seconds. He took one look at the man on the ground and grinned. "Just like old times. Things have been a bit too quiet around here."

Merk picked up the man's weapon and quickly emptied the magazine.

"What is Levi doing?" she asked, as the other team members hadn't moved into the garage. Even after hearing the gunfire.

"One of the men is talking. Apparently somebody knows somebody, who knows somebody, who knows somebody who's got money." Merk snorted. "It's typical. Hey-anyone-know-someone-who-wants-to-make-a-fast-buck line." He shook his head. "And these chumps went for it."

"Not this one." She motioned at the man on the floor. "The others maybe, but this guy headed straight for Levi's truck. Looking for the laptop."

Merk's gaze sharpened with interest. "In that case we need to keep this one." Then his view widened. "Just wait until Rhodes sees the mess in here. You know how he feels about keeping this place clean."

Ice winced at that. "Can't blame me. Better I got blood everywhere than letting this one take the laptop and make a run for it."

"The laptop is probably already clean."

"I'm still not mopping up this mess." She holstered her weapon and walked to the injured man.

"Fuck off," he snapped, twisting in pain.

She examined his leg and his wrist anyway.

Merk stepped on his chest to assist Ice. "Nothing quite like a size fourteen boot to stop your lungs from expanding."

"No doubt." She straightened, then walked over to collect the laptop and return it to the truck. "He'll live. No arterial damage. Bullets went right through."

Then, as if realizing what she'd said, she turned to look at Merk in horror. "If I damaged the cement floor, Rhodes'll think ..."

"Don't worry about it. He gets annoyed about careless shit, but he can see this was necessary." He reached down and hauled the injured man to his feet.

Sweat poured off his face, and, with a sudden jerk upright, all the color washed out of his skin. That's when she realized the man was going into shock.

She walked to the workbench and grabbed one of the stools, bringing it back and shoving it under his butt. "Sit," she ordered. Thankfully he sat and didn't give her any more arguments. "Stone, did you tell Levi who we've got?"

Her earpiece crackled. "He knows." Stone added, "He's got his hands full at the moment."

Right. She needed to finish with this guy and tie him up so he couldn't go anywhere. She opened the medicine cabinet sitting on the shelf. Quickly she bandaged him and placed a tourniquet above the hole in his thigh.

Back at the cabinet, she picked up some wire and quickly ran it around the guy's ankles, tying each securely to the chair legs. She studied his wrists, one bloodied, and wondered about the sensibility of tying them behind him. But he'd been the intruder. He'd been the one spying on them. His injuries could hold for a little while.

She forced herself to be ruthless, grabbed his arms, pulled them together, and quickly tied them up with the wire tight enough that it would cut into his wrists if he struggled. With the snips in her hand, she cut off the excess and returned the snips and wire to the cabinet.

She looked over at Merk. "You okay to stay here with him?"

"He's secure on the chair." He looked at the distance to cross and then back at her. "Want to push him out to where the others are? Then we'll have them all together. Easier to guard that way."

"Good idea." She hit the button to the closest garage door. With Merk pushing their captive along, they headed out across the driveway to where the group of men now waited. Hopefully the team was done using the intruders as punching bags.

She wasn't squeamish, but she liked to think she still had some heart.

LEVI WATCHED THE trio approach. He ran a quick gaze over Ice first, noting her bloody hands and a slight shakiness to her long, lean frame. Everyone saw her as cold. He knew different. The woman was fire on the inside but gave an icy exterior to everyone else.

She also hated violence. They'd both seen more than they should. It hadn't taken a lot of persuasion to convince her to come with him in this new venture. He'd felt guilty for all of ten minutes, then remembered how many times she'd put her life in jeopardy to save somebody else. He knew—one day, one time—she just wouldn't be fast or safe enough, or the gods would be against her. And that he couldn't stand.

While he'd been running the missions with her, he could keep an eye on her. She'd be furious if she knew he thought that way, but it was hard not to when she was the most precious thing in his life. He met her gaze in the harshness of the floodlights. Once again she wore that mantle of professionalism. Like hell. She was anything but a mercenary. Ice was a die-hard true patriot and the only woman he could ever picture as the mother of his children. Too bad he didn't figure that out sooner. Now his weakening aversion to family was a bridge which his injury had stopped him from crossing.

But he needed to.

He refocused on the prisoners again.

DALE MAYER

The man with Ice had double injuries, but this one had a different look. The others were yokels, just guys out for a lark, making some beer money. This one, not so much. Levi turned to the men on the ground already, pointing to the new guy in the chair. "You know this guy?"

The five men nodded. "He's the one dared us to do this. And said he'd make this pot all that much sweeter if we got in and out without getting caught."

Merk snapped, "So how come he wasn't at the fence with you?"

The same guy answered, "He wasn't supposed to come with us at all."

"Shut the hell up, Farraday," one of the other men snarled.

Levi smacked him across the face. "A little too late for that shit."

The man just glared at him. "You got no right to hit us. We've done nothing wrong."

Levi sent a sinister-looking smile the man's way.

The guy instantly fell silent as he caught sight of Levi's face.

"You're trespassing. No one gives a shit if I just pop you off right now."

Eyes wide with fear, the man held up his hands. "No, no."

"Why the hell shouldn't I?" Levi asked. "You're nothing but a lowlife, making money off other people. Spending all your time trespassing, breaking into private property, and stealing. Law's on my side."

"We didn't steal anything," he spat. "It was just a lark. The sheriff will let us off with a warning, that's all."

Merk leaned down and put his handgun right on top of

the guy's kneecap. "But I won't."

The man cried out and screamed, "No, no. I didn't do anything. Don't hurt my leg."

Ice linked her arm into Levi's and tucked him up close. "And then this guy ..." she said with a nudge to the other man she'd brought over. She turned to gaze directly at Levi and added, "He went straight for your truck and then the laptop inside."

Levi's eyebrows shot straight up. "Now that's an interesting twist. Confirms the yokels were a diversion." He pulled out his phone and walked away, calling his friend, a Texas Ranger he'd known for some twenty odd years. "Mike, how are you doing? Got a little problem." Skimming the details, he quickly explained his dilemma.

"I can have the five locals picked up if you want," Mike said. "If you don't want to give them a bullet, turn them into assets. I can scare the crap out of them, but, if you can use them, the opportunity is right there. Fear is a hell of a motivator."

"I'm good with that." Levi looked forward to it.

Mike hesitated for a moment and said, "What are you thinking to do with the sixth man?"

"Oh, you won't be seeing him," Levi said. "I have people who want some time with him."

After a few chuckles, Levi cut off the call. He walked back to the sixth man and took a picture of his face. A click of a button would send it to Jackson. He quickly dialed the number he knew by heart.

Chapter 6

THE NEXT DAY Ice waited at the front door when the
vehicles pulled in. Bullard and his crew had come in a
day early, after all that was happening here. When he hopped
out and opened his arms, she ran into them. Bullard was a
hell of a man and a very good friend. He'd tried to take her
away a long time ago, but she wouldn't go.

Her heart was with Levi, and, although their circumstances were tough, she couldn't leave. Not while she had a
chance to regain what they had. But she knew, if there was
ever a place she'd go to, it would be to Bullard's.

That just made his arrival all that much sweeter ... and
harder.

When she stepped back, she walked to Dave, Bullard's
right-hand man, and gave him a big hug. Finally she turned
and acknowledged the four men who came with them—
Sean, Paul, Jason, and Andrew. She knew them all, not well,
but enough to be on a first-name basis. "About time you got
here. You missed all the fun again."

Bullard laughed. "Not even enough to fly over for. Let's
get some heavy artillery in here. That'd be fun." He stopped
in the middle of the open yard and surveyed the compound.
"Wow. A little too much cement for my liking. The place
really could use some pools and green grass. But, as far as
security, you've got nice bare bones."

Levi walked out and shook Bullard's hand. Ice couldn't help poking the lion as she hooked her arm through Bullard's. He tucked her up close, knowing where her heart lay, even if he wished it were elsewhere. She watched Levi's frown deepen.

Tough shit. Levi needed to do something to change the status quo. She was damn tired of being friend-zoned. She fell into step with them as Levi took Bullard and his men on a tour around the outside. She listened with half an ear as they discussed in great detail where and how the new system could be installed. She expected full training when it was up and running. It would be huge in terms of safekeeping the compound, but she was hoping the applications would be wider spread, as in saving the men when they went into the field.

Next they all checked out the inside. What she loved best. As they entered, she took the lead and quickly showed Bullard's group the hidden staircases, the security control room, and the two escape routes inside and out—only visible if you knew where to look.

In the kitchen, everyone arranged themselves around the table. Alfred brought out coffee and a huge platter of coffee cakes, and she gave a happy sigh.

"Yay to having Alfred home." The others cheered while she got up and brought plates for the treat and spoons for the coffee.

Stone arrived as everyone dug into the cake. He wheeled up to the table with a big grin on his face.

Carrying his coffee, Dave walked over. "What's this I hear about the last prototype not doing its job?"

"Maybe me just doing a little bit too much, too fast," Stone admitted a bit sheepishly. Refusing to look at the others, he added, "Sored up fast. I had to stop using it."

Dave nodded in understanding. "Pressure points are the biggest thing you've got to watch out for. I'd like to take a look. Might be able to help." He pulled up his jeans so Stone could see his.

As she sat beside Dave, Ice could see the blade runner foot of his prosthesis. It had a beautiful etched design on it.

Stone's face lit up like magic. "Maybe after coffee," he said hopefully, then looked around the table at the group of people and added, "Or maybe tomorrow."

Dave sat down beside Stone. Bullard spoke into the sudden silence. "Speaking of which, what the hell happened to your prisoners?"

"Mike let the five yokels off with a warning," Levi explained. "After he showed them proof that we knew exactly where they all lived with their families and where they worked, they were only too happy to be on their way, knowing we could come after them any time if they messed with us again." He gave Bullard a smile, adding, "I wanted to make sure they got the message loud and clear."

"Mike, the Texas Ranger?"

Levi nodded.

"Nice but tough." Bullard smiled.

"Damn right," Levi said. "This close to home you need allies, not enemies."

"I did also mention there might be employment for some people willing to keep an eye out for troublemakers." Levi's grin grew a little wider.

Bullard raised an eyebrow. "Do you think any of them are trustworthy?"

Levi dropped his gaze to his hands, remembering the fear on the men's faces. "Yeah, I think so. Even if it's just a heads-up when a rumor starts."

"Rumors are often the best thing." Bullard studied his friend's face. "And the last man?"

Levi raised his gaze and stared at Bullard. With a lopsided tilt to his lips, Levi said, "He's been handed over for questioning."

A sudden silence overtook the room as Bullard and his men surely were contemplating what that meant, since Levi deliberately hadn't specified to whom. "Sounds like you've got yourself a whole new life again." Bullard nodded. "I approve."

After that, things got to a more businesslike atmosphere. Pretty quickly they split up and headed out to discuss improvements. Ice wanted to go, but, at the same time, she didn't.

Stone and Dave worked themselves free of the group and headed off to the garage or what should be called the R&D room. Stone was a hell of a weapons specialist, and he loved to build prototypes. He and Dave were two peas in a pod.

And just like that Ice found herself all alone in the kitchen. She sat there, studying her coffee cup. It was full—she'd barely sipped it. She hated this sense of disconnection from the others, but, without a doubt, it was there.

When at the top of her field, she had known pressure, stress, knowing one day she might never come home. She'd been lucky in that she always had. And then Levi and his crew had been injured, and she'd been there for him. Kept him safe while he healed.

Then he'd left to take care of business alone, knowing she'd been against him going after his enemies. And she'd been lost until he came back. She hadn't even waited that long, choosing to do the extraction herself.

He'd asked her to join him in this venture, and she'd followed him, with no doubt they'd hit a turning point and that this was a great step for the entire team. Only she didn't have a relationship with Levi anymore. Not the kind she wanted. Just as friends. Both of them so damn loyal to each other it was almost painful to be a part of it without the intimacy ...

Bullard's arrival had just pinpointed how far apart she and Levi really were. And yet how close in other ways.

Unbidden tears came to her eyes. She brushed them aside. It would never do her any good for the men to see her so vulnerable. She dropped her hands to the table and studied her nails absently. So much of her world had changed, shifted. And so much more had fallen away. She was lost. Adrift.

Still she'd gotten herself into this mess. If she didn't like it, she could just pull out. She couldn't go back to the navy. She could fly helicopters anywhere though, if that's what she wanted. Flying was definitely in her blood, but, as she got older, it became less of a necessity. Other issues called to her. The wish for a family was one. She wasn't ready yet, but she'd like to think she would be in a few years, as long as the possibility of children was still on the table. But Levi had made it clear he didn't want any. Ever. Because of his mean, abusive father.

She'd gone through a lot to get to where she was. But it seemed like she was a hell of a long ways from where she really wanted to be.

Even worse, she had no idea where she was going.

Because she couldn't see a future without Levi.

How much longer could she keep this up, waiting for him?

"WHAT THE HELL'S going on between you and Ice?" Bullard asked Levi. "You've still got the cold war happening. What's the deal?"

"You tell me. The only reason you and I are still friends is because you know she's mine." Levi's voice was calm and quiet, but there was no mistaking the coldness behind the words.

"I'll keep my hands off unless I find out you're not treating that girl right. I expected to see her happy and she's not," Bullard snapped. "You better fix it and fast."

Levi did *not* want to discuss this with Bullard. He was a good man, but he also wanted Ice. So far he'd respected Ice's relationship with Levi but for how long? Particularly if she wasn't happy. "Not that easy."

"Hell, yes, it is. Drag her to bed. Most of the problems get solved that way anyway. So much shit that was a big deal before you get into bed is no longer one by the time you get out. You should have solved this a long time ago."

Levi didn't answer. Was Bullard right? Was Ice really sad? Was she so unhappy with Levi? Did she regret leaving the military? He'd known he was asking a lot when he wanted her to come with the team. He had made no promises about their future, but they both knew they belonged together. He didn't know how hard it would be to cross this divide, but, if Bullard was right, if Levi didn't find a way, then it could be over for him and Ice.

And, if it came to that, if he lost her again, that would be one blow he'd never recover from. She'd been the reason he came home after every mission. If she wasn't here anymore ...

He gave himself a mental shake. She'd followed him. She

hadn't argued. She hadn't fought. She hadn't made any conditions. She'd walked away from her career and followed *him*.

Damn. She'd given up everything. He'd given up nothing.

"You figure out how to fix the two of you," Bullard said. "It damn-near breaks my heart to see her like this, without her spark. With that cold and cross temper of hers, the laser gaze that would shut you out, she's the most beautiful woman I know. That edge of hers makes her very special."

"She's no longer in active service, so of course she doesn't have that same edge. None of us do." Levi glanced over at his friend. "Neither do you."

"No, that's very true, but none of us look like we lost our best friend either." With that Bullard walked ahead, and Levi forced his thoughts to the defense system on the outer perimeter. Bullard pointed to where one of the exits from the house itself came out of the tunnel. "Boost the electricity here for communications while traveling in and out of that tunnel."

Levi added that to the notes. So far he had five pages' worth. How long would this take?

"You should get this done in a few days, a week on the outside," Bullard said. "This is a priority. It needs to be done now."

Bullard walked back toward the compound and pointed out how to build supports for the extra thick wiring to electrify the fence. Bullard was a specialist in his field. He knew his job, and Levi was smart enough to listen. He might know how to get into enemy territory, take out the unfriendlies, rescue a hostage, get back out and to home ground in the blink of an eye, but, when it came to making a compound secure, well, that was Bullard's specialty, he was all about tech toys and Levi needed to learn fast.

And Levi wanted what was his to be secure. Everything—and everyone. So far he'd done a hell of a job. That much he knew. He'd put his heart and soul—and every last penny—into this project. Now he had to keep it protected, out of harm's way.

Levi had two men back from a fact-finding mission in Mexico, seeing if any whispers confirmed Rodriguez was still alive. They'd found nothing. But, as soon as the two had landed here, Levi had sent them straight to town to keep an eye on the hardware store. They were suited up with the latest surveillance equipment, compliments of Bullard. They checked in regularly, but, so far, the small town looked normal.

Levi didn't believe that—not for a second.

While Logan and Harrison kept watch, Levi was here with Bullard, planning the modifications to ensure the compound was as impenetrable as he could make it.

He and Bullard walked the ridge on the north side, staring down at the main buildings. From here it was easy to see everything. Something white caught his eye. Several cigarette butts had been tossed and dug into the ground. Unless the culprit was a chain smoker, he, or they, had stood watching the compound for hours.

If he and his people were under surveillance, it could mean a lot of things, and not one of them was good.

He called Bullard over. The two of them studied the debris.

"We didn't see him from here or down below," Bullard said. "So he's been watching and picking his timing." Bullard immediately made plans. "We can attach the crossbeams on the left here to that one there and support cameras up on the side. Maybe mount them at the base of floodlights, and nobody would know they're wired."

That sounded good to Levi. The last thing he wanted to do was think of anybody keeping track of what he was doing, not when it was Levi and his team's job to keep track of what other people were doing.

"My men can start on this right now," Bullard said. "Some of the equipment will need to be ordered, but we can get a lot of this done while we're here."

Levi smiled. Now that was his kind of time frame.

And sure enough, with them all working together, under Bullard's direction, they got the bulk of the job done in three days. At that point they ran out of supplies, and someone had to go to town.

So far, no other discarded cigarettes had showed up. Nothing of interest turned up in town either. And Levi had to ask himself if he'd missed something major.

Chapter 7

ICE HAD BEEN deemed errand runner, so she took the Suburban and headed into town for needed supplies. She didn't mind. She had a lot to think about. Levi, for one, to switch up their relationship. Tossing an idea around for days, which still percolated inside her head, Ice wondered at the sanity of taking such a step.

Yet it was a great idea.

But could she end what she had with Levi? Or would it be the beginning of the rest of their lives? Forcing his hand would at least let her know where she stood.

Going to town gave her time to contemplate. The to-do list was long, and she was going alone as every man was needed for the modifications going on within the compound. Not that she couldn't hold a drill as well as the rest—because she could—but she also welcomed the break from all the testosterone. Security was being beefed up; parts were being flown in from all over the world, and Bullard was in his element.

Levi was scrambling to catch up. He'd been *the man* at the top of the military world, but, in the private sector, things were different. She loved the changes happening to them professionally. She just didn't know what to do about their personal lives, being stuck in one place. Before he'd asked her to join them, she'd been petrified he would take off and leave her behind. Now it felt like their lives were on hold, when they should be sharing one life together.

She parked outside the grocery store and sat in the driver's seat for a moment.

At this point in her life she'd expected to be wearing a ring and discussing a family down the road. Instead she was this well-honed military pilot, born and bred for action. But, since Levi's accident, something else had happened to her. It had been all she could do just to protect the man, and now he didn't need protecting. She wasn't sure he needed her at all.

And that hurt. They'd always been partners, and they still worked well together. The dynamics of their relationship had changed though. She'd never been part of his team before. She'd always been there in the periphery, a specialist in her own area. She'd been the one in command when he'd gone down. She'd made sure he'd stayed safe, had arranged for the new medical facility when they'd been attacked. And then, when he was finally capable, he'd taken off. Not for long though. He received the inheritance. Then, realizing it was perfect for their needs, he'd asked her to come with him. For a month things had been good. Their relationship getting back on its feet. Until the intel had arrived on Herrara.

Levi hadn't walked; but ran after the man who had turned his world upside down. Even though he'd asked her to go with him, she'd been devastated. It had taken her days to pull herself together. Terkel, Merk's brother, had contacted her and told her how Levi would get his ass kicked once more. And she'd stepped in yet again to fly him to safety. If anyone kicked his ass, it would be her. But, of course, she'd flown in and rescued him instead. No way could she leave

Levi's life in the hands of another pilot.

He'd never said a word. Just hugged her tight.

At that point she'd figured they'd be fine. But she'd been shocked and hurt when he'd shown her to her own suite. And never once came knocking …

Instead of grabbing a buggy at the store, she snagged a big flat cart. No point in buying groceries for a day or two; she needed to stock up to feed a near army. Alfred had sent her with a huge list.

One to get the job done as fast as she could, she found an employee to help. Within an hour she was outside again, loading the back of the Suburban. That had gone great, but she had several more stops, which would take a while, plus she had packages to pick up. By the time she was done, she was more than ready to go home.

Ice pulled into Wildon, more truck stop than town, but good enough for her current needs.

After filling the tank, she walked inside to pick up a coffee. Ice was almost home, but she could feel the shakes coming on. She'd skipped lunch, having overeaten Alfred's and Dave's big breakfast.

On her way back to the Suburban, Ice spotted a young woman sitting under a tree. With bright red hair, the woman was hard to miss. Beside her sat a backpack of sorts and some kind of a carry bag. A look of such sadness on her young face damn-near broke Ice's heart.

Making a sudden decision, she walked over, holding the coffee in her hands. As she got closer, she could see the woman was in her late twenties. Her red hair plaited down her back was a bright spot to her appearance.

"Hello," Ice said.

The woman looked over at her. "Hi."

"Are you lost?"

The woman gave a half laugh. "In more ways than one."

Ice smiled; she knew the feeling. "I can relate."

The woman switched her gaze to the Suburban. "You might've been lost at some point in time, but you appear to have found your way now."

Ice shook her head. "Appearances can be deceiving. Do you need a hand?"

The young woman's eyes widened. "Don't we all at some time?"

"Maybe. But I don't right now. My problems have to do with something else."

At that the woman bounded to her feet with a bitter laugh. "Man troubles then. And I've had my full share of those too."

The two studied each other across a three-foot divide.

"I can give you a little money if that would help you get somewhere," Ice offered. She'd never been in this young girl's position, but something about her made Ice's heart ache. The girl looked soft, gentle, innocent.

And Ice was feeling hard, worn down … and old.

The other woman's back straightened, and Ice knew she'd hit a nerve. This woman didn't need or want charity. Before she could respond, Ice added, "Or a job?"

The young woman's mouth opened and closed. She studied Ice curiously. "What kind of job?"

"What skills do you have?"

"Secretarial, accounting." The woman shrugged. "Any kind of office work. I have experience cleaning hotel rooms. I've even done a stint fueling vehicles at a gas station. For the last few years there have been a whole lot of jobs—none of them for very long and none of them paid very well."

"How are you on computers?" Ice couldn't help wondering if maybe they could find a spot for her at the compound. Granted, not a home for waifs, but that didn't mean it wasn't a shelter for those caught in the storm of life. And they did need somebody to help clean and cook, and, if this girl could do office work, that would be a big help. Only the security clearance would be an issue.

"I'm very good with computers. I was working for a company doing forensic accounting." She turned to stare at a point behind Ice's shoulder. "Until something went wrong of course." Her voice ended on a bitter note. "And it's been a downhill slide since."

If she could do that type of work, it would definitely be a plus. What had gone wrong in her life that she was sitting at this crossroad? It could be anything, but some things they couldn't take the chance on. "What happened?"

The woman's gaze flipped back to Ice's face and narrowed as if to say, *Not your business.*

Ice held up a hand. "First, you need to realize I do potentially have a position. But, second, I won't tolerate anything criminal in any way, shape, or form." With a sense of amusement she watched the woman in front of her stiffen in offense.

The redhead snapped, glaring icicles. "I might be in a tough spot right now, but I do know right from wrong, and I choose to walk on the right side."

"My name is Ice. Currently eleven men are back home, five who live there regularly and six visiting right now, although they should be gone in another few days."

"My name is Sienna, and I was raised with four brothers." She spoke drily. "So your men don't scare me."

Ice laughed. "Fine. They are all good men, but they are

on the extreme side for males—except Alfred. Of course that's because the military breeds them that way."

"Two of my brothers are in the navy ... one a SEAL," Sienna said with pride. "So I understand what you mean."

A SEAL? "What's your brother's name?" Ice asked. "And do they walk all over you?"

"Hell, no," she said with spirit. "We were raised to be independent. So when life shifted, I had a hard time going to them for help." She offered a lopsided smile. "His name is Jarrod."

Ice froze. Could it be? Studying Sienna, Ice realized there was a resemblance. Hell, the red hair was one of them. "Jarrod who?"

"Bentley." Sienna looked at Ice curiously. "Do you know him?"

"I do, indeed," Ice said with a smile. "He's a good man." She couldn't leave the sister of any of Levi's SEAL buddies out here. She knew Jarrod, but he and Levi were tight. Ice had to help Sienna. Who knew? Maybe this could turn out to be a good thing. "Have you met any of his friends?"

She nodded. "Yes, several of them."

"Great." Ice wondered if any were the men at home. She hid her smile. It could be interesting times ahead. "Do you have any martial arts or weapons training?" It wasn't imperative that any new hires had that, but it would certainly help. They'd planned to hire from the military but hadn't been able to identify any potential hires yet.

"I have a black belt in karate but never held a weapon in my life."

"Black belt is good." Actually it was damn good. They could teach her how to shoot faster than it took her to get that black belt. "Don't suppose you have any medical training, do you?"

"Are you going to war or something? I have basic first-aid, but that's about it," Sienna said. "War games were my brothers' thing."

Ice laughed. "You never know what we'll need when. Sometimes the work is dangerous."

"What kind of an office do you run?" Sienna turned and stared at Ice. "I'm not up for a dangerous job. I'm looking for safe. Like paper cuts are my maximum pain tolerance."

Ice sent her a laughing glance. "And that's what you'd be doing. But we travel all over the world, and some of our work is dangerous. Always the chance it could follow us home."

"That's the same for any job anywhere. You can never be sure the next person walking into a building won't be a loony tune and shoot up the place or blow it to smithereens."

Ice decided she liked Sienna. She spoke with spirit, and, although she might be down on her luck, she wasn't weak. It would take a strong character to survive the men at the compound. "Then I suggest you get in. You can spend a few days at the compound as my guest and see what you think of it."

Midstep Sienna stopped and looked at Ice suspiciously. "Compound?"

Ice kept walking forward. "That's what we call it. Although I tried to call it the center, the name compound stuck." She shrugged. "We're a private security company, and we take on contracts all over the world. We're all ex-military, so we're heavy into weapons and tactical training."

"Except you?"

"Nope." Ice smiled. "I'm a helicopter pilot first and

foremost." On that cheerful note Ice hit the button to unlock the big Suburban and got in. She cranked the engine while the woman stood in front of her, frowning. Ice could understand.

Sometimes people had to make decisions based on their gut instincts. It said a lot about Bentley's kid sister when she advanced, opened the passenger door, and climbed in.

Ice drove the vehicle to the road and took a left turn. As she went around the corner back onto the main highway, an old beat-up truck pulled behind her. Ice narrowed her gaze, her mind dredging up the description of the truck Levi had seen.

She peered into the rearview mirror and tried to find something identifiable, but the license plate wasn't readable from this distance. The visor was down as well, making it hard to see the driver clearly. If it was the same truck, was this a coincidence? Or was he following her? Ice drove carefully, her mind searching for the best option.

"What's wrong?"

"I'm just curious about the truck behind us. Have you seen it before?" Ice kept her voice casual.

Sienna turned to look through the rear window. "No, I don't think so." She pivoted to face Ice. "Is it a problem?"

"Not likely," Ice said. She shifted lanes, made several turns, weaving through the light traffic, watching to see if the truck followed. It did. "Interesting."

Ice engaged the rearview cameras and recorded the truck as he dipped in and out of sight. She shifted left, then, at the last minute, ripped off to the right and took the immediate ramp heading toward the compound. If he came after her again, she'd head into town and get Logan and Harrison to help.

Instead she could see no sign of him. Keeping an eye out, she slowly drove the long way around before turning into the compound.

Feeling better, she headed in through the gate and pointed out the various buildings to Sienna. Directing the big vehicle to the garage, she pulled up into the empty bay and parked close to the door.

No way in hell would she deal with this load on her own. Ice hopped out, walked around, and waited for Sienna to step down. A little nervously Sienna took in the big machines and the security at the gate before sliding her gaze toward Ice. She could tell Sienna had trepidations, but that was all right; she'd held up so far.

At the sound of footsteps, Ice turned to see Levi walking toward her with a group of men coming up behind.

Ice nodded her head. "Levi, this is Sienna. She's Jarrod Bentley's sister. I offered her a place for a few days and may try her for one of the open positions we currently have. I like the office."

Levi's eyebrows shot up. Ice knew he noted the few bags at Sienna's feet and the force with which she held onto the knapsack, knuckles white and tense. But he didn't argue.

He exchanged a look with Ice and nodded. "I think Stone might be very happy to have you around, Sienna." He held out a hand.

Hesitantly she reached forward and shook it. "Thank you. I appreciate the chance."

Levi's grin flashed. "It's all right. You're in good hands here."

Ice turned back to Bullard and the rest of the men and said, "The vehicle is full. I got everything on the list plus."

Walking over to Levi, she quickly told him about the

truck following her. Then she turned and hooked her arm through Sienna's as she grabbed her bags. "Come on. I'll take you to your room before we introduce you to everybody else."

"There's actually a room for me here?" Sienna asked in surprise. "I can see the place is huge but ..."

As it turned out, Ice didn't get a chance to show Sienna anything. Alfred walked in and quickly took over. While Ice watched in amusement, Sienna was gently cosseted into a cup of tea and a treat before he whisked her away to her new room. In his usual easy manner, Alfred helped make Sienna feel right at home.

LEVI WATCHED THE two women walk away. Ice looked more at peace, happier, as if she'd made some kind of decision. He hoped not because that didn't bode well for him. Not if she had made the decision while he wasn't around. On the other hand, maybe she was just happy to have another woman close by. Ice had never struck him as being the type to have girlfriends, but, as he had a lot of male friends, it made sense she would be missing that.

As for Sienna, he wondered what had put her in Ice's path. Would Ice make a habit of bringing strays home? Still he trusted Ice's judgment. And Sienna looked like she'd shake things up. Besides he'd just shot Jarrod a text, telling him who Ice had run into. Levi expected to hear back any second.

He wondered if Jarrod had any idea his sister was in a bind. If it had been Levi's sister, he'd want another man to help her out, so Levi could do no less for Jarrod. If it happened to work out, maybe Jarrod would join them.

Jarrod had been on the list of men to bring on board from the beginning.

Maybe this was fate.

Levi turned his attention back to the Suburban full of supplies. The men were already unloading the kitchen stuff. He and Bullard got to work collecting the rest of the parts and pieces they needed to complete the security system. This was cutting-edge equipment, and he couldn't wait to try it out. They could keep track of everything within a one-half-mile perimeter of the place, and, if anything moved, deer or jackrabbit, they'd be on it.

His phone rang. Jarrod. With a smile Levi answered, stepping away from the others. "Hey, Jarrod." He quickly explained what little he knew about Sienna.

"Why didn't she tell me what was going on?" Jarrod asked. "She was always so damn independent. Determined to not need anyone."

Hearing the pain in Jarrod's voice, Levi said, "Sorry, Jarrod. Maybe she didn't want to look like a failure. I'll keep her safe here. And it's not charity. I could really use her help," Levi said. "When can you come?"

"I'm leaving for four weeks in the morning. I'll be on your doorstep the day after I return."

Smiling, Levi put away his phone and returned to the unloading.

The two men worked quietly together until Bullard asked, "What did you decide about Ice?"

Levi frowned. He didn't answer. He knew full well, if Bullard tried hard enough, he could possibly take Ice away from here in a heartbeat. Particularly as Levi hadn't expected Ice to be as unhappy as she appeared to be. Damn that woman anyway.

"I don't know what's wrong with her," he admitted softly.

"Have you asked?" Bullard asked. "Ice is a hell of a woman. She needs to be challenged. She's obviously at a crossroads in her life. Maybe it's not the way she thought it would turn out to be."

Again Levi didn't answer. What was there to say? They were just getting busier, with multiple teams operating on separate jobs at the same time. If Ice wanted to go out on missions, she could. If she wanted to stay home and coordinate from here, she could. What he didn't know was what Ice really wanted.

"Not to mention her biological clock is ticking away."

At that Levi shot Bullard a sharp look. What did he know? "Meaning?"

"Most women see themselves having a family at some point in their future. And, over the last several decades, women have been having babies later in life, so Ice has to be considering where she's going from here. She spent a lot of years getting to the top of her game. And then she walked away."

"Not quite. She followed me here," Levi reminded him.

Bullard nodded. "You asked her to come," he said quietly, "and she chose to follow." With a slight hook to his lips, he added, "At least for the moment."

Levi straightened. He knew how close Bullard and Ice were. They always had been. He just didn't know how close *right now*, when Ice was obviously unhappy. He grabbed the last set of boxes and carried them to the workbench. He didn't know what to say. Ice had another option if she didn't want to stay. Bullard was better set up, had more money, with a beautiful place for her to live in security. Levi, on the other hand, had a new not-yet-stable business, was a bit of a mess physically, and was still having nightmares.

All in all, Bullard was a hell of a lot better deal.

Damn.

"You know what to do." Bullard smacked him on the shoulder and turned to walk back out.

Levi's phone rang. Logan, calling from town.

"I'm sending you images from a new arrival. The camera in the hardware store picked it up. I think you might recognize the face." And then his voice disappeared.

His gut knotting, Levi walked to the electronic workbench and hooked up his phone. He could look on the small phone screen, but it was much easier to see the images on the high-tech monitors he used here. They were setting up a large R&D section in the garage workshop, and CAD work was important. That program required decent computers, but, more than that, having these bad-ass monitors meant they could see a pinhead in the middle of the street.

As soon as he had the phone hooked up, with a few buttons the images downloaded onto the main computer connected to the servers inside the house. He clicked on the first one. Instantly the monitor filled with the image of his old nemesis, Rodriguez. Anger mounting, Levi stared at the man laughing back at him.

He snatched up his phone and texted Logan.

Is he still there?

Logan responded immediately.

Not sure at this moment in time. We're running surveillance—haven't seen him come out of the hardware store.

Levi wanted to race over, pull the asshole out of the hardware store, and punch his face into the ground until nothing was left. That man had betrayed Levi's unit and damn-near killed Levi and his men. That they were all up and in ass-kicking shape again was not the point.

Acid churned in his gut at the thought of this man still walking around and how he had now turned up too close to home. When Jackson had first mentioned this cell, it was one thing for Rodriguez to run it from Mexico, not getting his own hands dirty here in the day-to-day terrorist activities. But the asshole was here.

Rhodes, feeling better after having been knocked out, walked up behind Levi and snapped, "Where the hell did that picture come from?"

"Logan just sent it. He's watching the hardware store."

Rhodes unlocked the weapons cabinet.

"Hold on," Levi said. "I feel the same way you do, but we have to make sure we take him—and his whole cell—down." Even if it meant going off script. There was intel gathering then there was problem solving. Levi knew exactly which he was after.

Rhodes turned, but he now wore a shoulder holster and sidearm. As Levi watched, Rhodes tucked a clench piece into an ankle holster. Far from thinking Rhodes was overreacting, Levi approved.

Although Levi would prefer a couple semiautomatic rifles any day, a handgun was elegant and sneaky. It could be hidden in all sorts of places, and, right now, with Rodriguez in town, no good would come out of this. On the other hand, Levi might get that last bit of revenge he'd been looking for. He could finally put down the man like the murdering dog he was.

"What's the plan?" Rhodes asked, standing at Levi's side, his gaze locked on Rodriguez's face.

"Waiting on more intel from Logan," Levi admitted. "Like you, I want to run in there and blow his head apart, but we can't afford to do that. If he's here, he's planning something nasty."

"Agreed, but we also have to move fast. No way in hell is he leaving this town." Rhodes reached out and fiddled with a couple dials, zooming in on the bottom quarter of the image. "Is he carrying some kind of a large bag with him?" Rhodes zoomed in closer to see bits and pieces of what appeared to be a large rifle case.

Levi was stumped. It wasn't like Rodriguez to do his own killings. The weapon could be in exchange for something else, or maybe he decided to do a little bit more hands-on work now. Levi frowned. That was not the Rodriguez he knew. That man hired as many people as he could to keep his hands clean and his dirty work done.

"Looks like he has a new scar across his throat," Rhodes announced. "Hope we're responsible for that."

Levi leaned forward. He could see the scar coming around the left side of Rodriguez's throat on a downward slant. It was nasty looking. The photograph didn't let them see how old the wound was. Levi was not at all bothered to see the man getting a little beat up. After all, they had taken the hit; why shouldn't he?

Inasmuch as they studied the rest of the photograph, it yielded nothing new. He appeared to be standing with the hardware store counter behind him. The camera Merk had placed on the nearby shelf was tiny and actually fit into a hole where a hook belonged to hold up a shelf. So it was limited in scope. But, since it showed the front door, and the second camera showed the back door, it gave them a great deal of information.

Texting Logan, Levi wrote:

Keep an eye on the store. We need to know if he leaves. One of you watch the front, the other rear, and, for God's sake, watch your backs. This guy is the king of bastards.

Levi thought back to how many doors he'd actually seen inside the hardware store. The front and back, yes, but were there any others?

These old buildings didn't exist as far back as any of the world wars. Not like there would've been passageways for smuggling or anything like that close by. He frowned. He didn't know that though. "Rhodes, any smuggling known in this area? We're looking at any kind of underground railroad or bootlegging-type operation. I'm just wondering if some tunnels are there that we aren't aware of."

Rhodes shook his head. "I don't know myself, but I will get on it. However, if that were the case, then we should never have actually seen Rodriguez in the store. I'm sure, with a face like his, he'd want to keep it hidden."

"Except if he knows *we're* here. Plus he doesn't know we hid our cameras inside," Levi snapped. "And he's just arrogant and egotistical enough to think he can get away with anything he wants."

Rhodes nodded. "Think we should get more eyes on the situation?"

Levi studied the monitor. "Yes," he said slowly. "But from the sky."

The two looked at each other, grinned, and raced toward the security room. The computer and security rooms together were one large space with a wall of monitors. They had limited access to satellite imaging. If they wanted, it'd be easy enough to hack into the military databases. But what they'd found out the minute they left the military was how the private sector was already way ahead. Accessing information the government thought was secret and theirs alone was easy—and fun.

Levi had a private investor, a man who'd be forever grateful for the work they'd done saving his daughter from kidnappers in the Middle East. Flanders was one of the wealthiest of all Americans. He owned several communication companies, and he'd given Levi and his group access to some of the best satellite imaging systems.

And then there was Bullard's system.

Not to mention Mason's fiancée, Tesla, who had also devised a pretty amazing software program for the military. Levi had hoped, at one point in time, that Mason would join them and bring Tesla with him. She was one hell of a computer specialist. Just because she created programs for the military didn't mean she couldn't help develop and tweak their system. He'd like to have the best of the best.

That was the thing about SEALs. They were a tight-knit brotherhood, no matter how many years apart they served. One could only be a SEAL for so long before it took its toll. The length of service before that happened varied between five and ten years. Levi knew several who were over five already. And some of those were men he wanted to work for him. He could plan for their arrival down the road.

Mason's close-knit group SEAL unit was the best place to start. They were at the top of their game, and they deserved to be. He'd mentioned it to Evan and Megan already, but they weren't ready to walk away. Levi couldn't blame them. But when any of the unit was ready for a change, he'd be happy to have them join his company.

But he also knew life was a bitch and threw a wrench in everyone's plans at some time. And, if and when it did, he'd be waiting with an irresistible setup.

"Okay, we got satellite feed," Levi said, pulling up a chair and sitting down as Rhodes brought it up on the big screen.

With Stone now standing behind him and Alfred arriving from somewhere, the four men studied the images of the small town. The hardware store was easy to pinpoint because it was the last one on the block; most of Texas had alleys. The storefront looked like every other one in that area.

"Rhodes, any chance of ground-imaging software?" Alfred asked. "It would really help if we had some idea what was below that hardware store."

"Even if we did, it's not likely to show through the building itself. If we were closer, we could do imaging and see who was inside, but even that won't go through the layers beneath. And I highly doubt there's any registered building plans of tunnels." Rhodes snorted. "I sure as hell wouldn't file a plan if I was building a secret passageway underneath."

Alfred reached out and pointed past the hardware store's door to the ice cream shop beside it. "It's a long shot anyone would have spent the money to dig through the limestone, but maybe there's a basement or tunnel. That could explain why they picked this hardware store in this town. Not that we saw anything like that there, but that alone could indicate a connection to the store beside it. While we were busy watching this one, he could have walked out the other."

"It's possible," Levi said, "but, from the outside, the storefronts are very close together. I think we would have seen someone of the same size and build leaving."

"But not at the back door." Rhodes turned to look at Levi. "The rear door of that second building has a porch, and our cameras are not directed that way."

Stone, his voice low, said, "Unless he hasn't left. We're not the only ones who can't stand the man. What if he ran afoul of his new colleagues?"

"Hell, maybe he wasn't supposed to show up here at all. His presence, if noted, is bound to raise alarms."

"It's probably a foolish idea, but it would let us know for sure."

"Search the place?" Rhodes asked. "Logan could handle that alone. He's a hell of a big man."

Levi grinned. Logan held the record for lock-picking over all of them. The man was damn fast. But, if there was something or someone waiting for Logan, Levi couldn't send him in blind or solo.

"Maybe we should search the building beside it first," Rhodes said, "If there's a way through, let's find it from the other side. Not likely to be much in the way of security there."

"Unless you're a terrorist cell using it," Stone said. "In which case there *will* be security."

Although Levi admitted, "Not likely," he still nodded. "Let's get this set up. I want Logan and Harrison to go in tonight."

"I'll run backup," Rhodes said. "A little action would be good."

Levi nodded. "Have them both come home and suit up. This could be a waste of time, but we won't know what we're up against until we get there."

Chapter 8

T HEY HAD LOST their satellite feed, but dinner was a jovial affair.

Alfred had gone all out, barbecuing marinated shish kebabs, served with Caesar salad, baked potatoes, and all the fixings. Sienna helped him in the kitchen, and she appeared to be settling in just fine.

If it kept Ice out of there, she was good with it.

The men were a little overwhelming to a female newcomer, but Alfred would keep everyone in line. Not that they'd overstep the professional lines in the first place, but these were strong, healthy males, and Ice had brought a beautiful young woman into their midst. One related to a friend of many of them. But, of course, there were rules about a SEAL brother's little sister.

Obviously there would be a lot of interest, although she kept to herself.

With Bullard and his men filled in on the developing Rodriguez situation, they were all busy making suggestions. Levi didn't need them, Ice knew, but the camaraderie would do him the most good.

His men all knew what catching Rodriguez would do for him. Levi had healed on many levels, but this one spot just festered with anger and pain.

Sienna sat beside Ice but stayed quiet.

Ice wasn't involved in the actual operation tonight. She would stay at the compound and monitor. Logan and Harrison would be going in fully equipped. A perfect time to test some of their new equipment.

As soon as the food was cleared away, plans were laid out. Dressed in night gear, the guys were to head to town, park on the far side of the river, then make their way across and down the block. None of the stores were open after six, except a Chinese food restaurant, take-out only. Today happened to be the one day of the week it was closed.

No one at the table had firsthand intel about the workings of the ice cream parlor. According to its storefront sign, it would be closed by nightfall too. At no time were any civilians to be put in harm's way. Considering how much damage Rodriguez had done before and the firepower he had available at his fingertips, casualties were all too likely if Levi and his team weren't careful.

Ice went to the control room and set up communications and the new sensors to make sure their gear was working. The men had both cameras set out, which they'd wear to transmit video immediately back to their system. She placed her coffee down and settled in for the wait. The compound was only a few minutes away from town. She had to make sure nothing or nobody followed them home.

Hearing a noise, she turned to see Bullard grab a chair and sit down beside her. He reached over and clasped her hand in his. "How you doing?"

She squeezed his fingers and, at the sight of Levi entering the room, dropped her hand as his gaze instantly locked on their intertwined hands. She smiled at Bullard. "I'm fine."

Levi studied her features, but she refused to look at him and kept her smile pleasant as she brought up the monitors and continued double-checking the equipment.

"Looks like both Logan and Harrison are live," Levi said right as Stone joined them, taking the empty seat on the other side of Ice.

Small talk was over. Instantly all eyes turned to the monitors. She ran through the simple checks with Logan. "All clear. Are you there now?"

The mic was crisp enough that she could hear the snickers, along with his vehicle door shutting. He would cross the bridge and head down the block. Switching to the other microphone, she asked Harrison, "Status?"

"All clear. No traffic, cloud visibility low." There was a smile in his voice when he added, "Perfect."

She knew what he meant. Some nights it just felt like you were moving through the world unseen. And others, it didn't matter how much cloud cover or weather elements were coming into play, you felt like everybody was watching.

"Watch your six," she warned.

A low chuckle came through loud and clear. "Always."

And she heard his door close. She shifted the cameras to watch as he slipped down the bank to the river. From where she sat, she could watch Logan approach the town, already hitting the first building on the other end of the block as he slipped around the corner and headed down the alleyway.

The river was low enough that Harrison could walk across carefully and avoid getting wet. A part of her wanted him to take a full dunk in and go for a swim, but that was just her sense of humor rising. Now on the far side, Harrison raced down the riverbank to come in ahead as Logan approached. As Harrison ran, she watched the distance between the two men get eaten up quickly. Harrison had been a competitive runner in his day. And, if ever a man needed to get from point A to point B fast, it was him. This was hardly a challenge though, nothing but a small-town block. As he made his way up the riverbank and skulked behind several parked vehicles, she switched her attention to Logan.

He approached the ice cream shop. All the lights were off; the Closed sign lit up. She wasn't even sure it had been open today. Everybody in that town appeared to be on their last legs financially. At the same time the businesses were still going. She idly wondered if some private investment groups helped these stores keep up appearances while running as a cover for other activities. It'd be simple enough to do. They could buy everybody out and keep the entire town for their own purposes. She frowned, considering that. If that was the case, other cameras could be up and down the block.

As she watched the screens, she could see when Logan switched on one of the new gadgets Bullard had brought with him. It would pick up bugs and electronic devices active within six feet of the sensor. She whispered, "Keep watch for eyes in the other stores as some group could have bigger hooks there, just using them for cover."

"I thought about that. Not what you call typical towns-folk here." Logan didn't explain as he went up to the porch of the ice cream store. Sure enough the sensor went off. He stayed behind the small porch wall. "Interesting. I have to take this out first." He pulled out a jammer, and they watched while he quickly deactivated the camera.

"Check it again," Ice warned. "Could be more than one system."

At her side Bullard said, "The jammer should've taken out two."

She gave him a surprised look. "Really? It can lock on to

more than one signal once it's marked?"

He nodded. "In the tests we've done so far, yes. It's never been tested on more than two at a time though."

She nodded. Logan had already turned his sensor back on, but all was quiet. He pulled out a simple lockpick, but, instead of going for the door, like she expected, he went for the large window beside him. Within seconds he had the screen off, and, being an old double-pane window, he had one of the windows out as well. With a simple jump he was up and over and inside. "Interesting how they put in that level of security at the door and forget about the window," Logan said.

"Or a second system. If there was one, it would've been wrapped around the windows," Bullard added.

Ice wasn't up on this stuff. She'd always been the eyes in the sky, not connected to the ones on the ground, but, since being here, she'd learned a lot.

She leaned back in her chair, her head coming to rest against somebody she hadn't noticed coming up behind her. Startled, she turned to find Levi, standing there, studying the monitors. But standing close, oh-so-close. Without looking down, he gently squeezed her shoulder. The same fingers stroked her neck to cup her cheek before sliding into her hair and deeper to her scalp.

Warmth flooded her system. God, she missed this. The soothing warmth of his caring touch.

He gently tugged her head backward until it rested against his stomach. "You're fine," he said in a neutral voice. But there was nothing neutral about the caress of his fingers on her cheek.

And she was damn grateful.

That was something else she wasn't used to. In the military, everything was extremely regimented, including behavior between coworkers. Things were relaxed more now, as she'd witnessed before leaving the navy.

Ignoring the feel of Levi's fingers, she focused on the screen—catching a peripheral view of Bullard, still next to her but giving her and Levi some semblance of privacy. Ignoring that too, she watched as Logan's camera did a quick search through the ground level of the ice cream parlor. The retro place dated back to the fifties—probably never been updated. If any of the trendy New York City downtown business people could pick up this whole thing and plunk it down in the middle of their city, they'd make a fortune.

On the other side of her, Stone said, "The place looks to be about 1,800 square feet."

The monitors before them showed the mapping software as it tracked all of Logan's steps and added them to the 3-D diagram pulling up in front of them. The camera was adding information at the same time, letting them know where the walls, the windows, and the furniture were visible. It was as rough as it was crude, but it was fascinating to watch the interior show up with Logan's every step through the store.

"Nothing," he reported. "At least not here." Logan turned and headed back the way he'd come in. "I'll check the back room next."

They watched in silence as the camera spanned the area, finding the bathroom, storeroom, and a small office. It had a similar layout to the hardware store with only a few differences. In the center of the storeroom was a small carpet.

"Logan, move the carpet," someone said.

"I was just getting there." He reached down and tugged the corner of the throw rug off to the side. Sure enough, he found a large trapdoor.

Ice switched her gaze to Harrison's monitor. He now stood outside the hardware store, staring around the corner, hidden from the cameras.

"Harrison, Logan found a trapdoor opening to a lower level in the ice cream shop."

"Got that." Harrison's gaze roamed over the side of the shop. "I don't want to deactivate all the sensors. They are likely hooked up digitally somewhere and would set off a different alarm if disconnected. If it's just for the ice cream shop, chances are good it won't raise the same level." There was silence as he surveyed the area. "The wiring here is new. Looks like it's been recently beefed up."

"Don't touch it. We don't want to set that off," Levi said.

Ice leaned forward. "Is there a second story to that building?"

Harrison's low voice said, "Not a full one. Probably just attic storage, like every place else in this part of the state."

Through the viewfinder of his camera, the people in the control room could see as he scanned the building and the awning.

"I think I can make it up there."

Ice didn't see any way he could. She opened her mouth to say something when she realized he was on the move again. This time he backtracked up several stairs, keeping a very low profile. On the fourth building she could see a dilapidated staircase, which meant people had been living up there at one point in time. He quickly scaled it and ended up on the roof.

With his sensors on, he did a quick scan, but no security measures seemed to be on the roof. Staying low, he walked back cautiously toward the ice cream parlor, stopping to check for bugs or sensors as he reached a new rooftop.

Speaking of which, where the hell was Logan? She moved her gaze to a black screen. She pointed at it. "What's going on there?"

"It's all good," Stone said. "The place is pitch black. But you can see movement."

Stone adjusted the screen darkness, and she could tell what they were actually looking at was gray. And suddenly a much better view popped up.

"Good boy," Levi said with humor. "His night goggles have adjusted to the different lighting now."

Logan was in the basement of the shop, doing a quick search. Shelves lined the bulk of it. It appeared to be one open room with various tables set up.

Ice gasped. "Oh, my God, is that C-4?"

Logan slowly let the camera take it all in. One side was a full-length rifle rack, completely stocked. On one of the tables were boxes and boxes containing more weapons. Someone had been building something, or many things, here, considering the amount of inventory covering the tables.

On the far side, boxes were stacked on the floor. They could all see the stockpile of weapons, chemicals, bomb-making equipment.

She sat back in shock. "Holy shit. Is the compound even safe if that whole lot goes up?"

Bullard shook his head. "Nobody within one hundred miles would be safe if that all goes up." His voice turned hard. "Levi, I sure hope you have somebody you can send this to because we need this taken out and fast."

"And I think I found the connecting door," Logan whispered. He snuck toward the wall on his right, his camera still picking up the dirty cement floor, the different types of wires. And yet, as he arrived at the door, he found a shiny new lock and several bolts on it.

Suddenly Levi reached forward and ordered, "Logan, get out. Now." He switched over to Harrison. "Logan's in trouble. He's in the basement. Get him out *now*."

Ice didn't understand what Levi had just seen, but, with her arms wrapped around her chest, she waited in shock for something to happen. Logan's camera suddenly clicked off, but the audio was still on.

A single gunshot rang out.

"SHIT." LEVI RACED out the door, overturning a chair in his way. He had to get to the hardware store. And fast.

He could hear footsteps racing behind him, voices rising as Harrison called for help on the comm. The last thing Levi needed was to get two men shot. He hit the truck and was out the gate with Rhodes jumping into the passenger side just before Levi slammed on the gas and blasted down the driveway.

They were ten minutes out, but it was still too long. He should've set up another alternate team; Harrison was only a one-man backup. They weren't expecting to find anything, but they should have. Just because it was a sleepy town appearing to be innocent and empty, didn't mean it was— and anything involving Rodriquez was the exact opposite.

"Don't blame yourself. This should've been a no-brainer. A walk through the park. Just info-gathering, like Jackson wanted." Rhodes was busy setting up equipment in the front seat beside him.

Levi didn't waste time talking. The river ran parallel to

the road. The truck hit the bridge at top speed and skidded around the corner. He cut the lights by the time he was on the other side down the alleyway. He was driving fast, passing several stores. He cut the engine and coasted forward.

He pulled up behind the building, four stores down the block from the hardware store.

They were out of the vehicle and slipping down the walls of the back alley. Rhodes was ahead by ten feet. Levi, with his weapon out, pressed his comm device, looking for an update.

Ice's voice whispered in his ear, "Harrison went in after Logan."

"Any word from Logan?"

"No."

"Did you see anything else from his body camera?"

"No," Ice said in low tones. "It's black. Harrison's too."

Levi shook his head and picked up speed. Rhodes gained access to the window. Levi followed. With weapons at the ready, they raced down the stairs where they had last seen Logan disappear. They were prepared for an ambush. Who and what they found when they got there was not what they'd been expecting. He heard Ice's voice gasp in his ear at what she saw from the camera on his own chest.

Both Logan and Harrison were collapsed on the floor. Rhodes did a quick search, but nobody was in the building. At least not down here. Where the hell had their attackers gone? The room was still full of explosives but, by Levi's count, not as full. He frowned and wondered if the plan was to blow the building with his friends inside.

"Damn it. Looks like they've moved out some of the materials. You sure there's nothing on the videos?"

"Everything's black. We can see from your camera, but

that's it."

Rhodes murmured, "Logan's taken a bullet high in the shoulder, missed the heart, but he's losing blood fast."

Levi ran his hands over Harrison, who was lying on the floor in front of them. "Harrison's unconscious but doesn't appear to have been shot. I see a head wound."

Ice whispered sharply in Levi's ear, "We've got activity outside the building. We've hacked into their camera system at the ice cream store, and another vehicle is arriving."

"We have to get the men out of here," Levi snapped. "Tell us where they'll approach from– the hardware store or the ice cream shop. We'll go to the other one."

"No, you won't. Four men are getting out of the truck, two going into each building. Heads up, you've got company."

Levi had already moved. He crouched behind the wall of boxes, his mind racing to find a solution. He had to get both his injured men out safely, plus Rhodes. A ton of firepower was down here. He'd put it to good use himself if he could. He studied the benches around him and glanced over to make sure Rhodes was out of sight. Logan and Harrison still lay in the middle of the floor. Good. The men coming would expect to see them there. And that's when he heard footsteps in the stairwell. The one they hadn't found yet.

Chapter 9

WAS THERE ANYTHING worse than watching your friends and loved ones in danger and not being able to do anything to help them? Ice shook her head.

A second vehicle had headed out from the compound after Levi and Rhodes. As soon as Ice had realized Levi's vehicle was on the road, another team had followed. Some of Bullard's men had wanted in on the action and wouldn't take no for an answer. Typical bad asses couldn't handle the peace and quiet for a few days. Once they got there, the whole block was likely to blow with all that power converging on it.

In the meantime she could only watch the cameras and wait and worry.

Thankfully they'd kept Sienna out of the loop as much as possible. She'd been here earlier, but then Alfred had directed her back to the office afterward. Ice hated to admit it, but she found herself forgetting about the bright redhead. Then again, life had been anything but calm and peaceful.

"How is Sienna doing?" she asked, casting Stone a glance. "She seems to be fitting in well."

"I agree. Sleeping now. Doesn't know anything about this." He shook his head. "Still can't believe she's Jarrod's sister. I wonder what he knows of her scenario."

"Who's to say? She might not have told him anything."

"And that will piss him off. It won't be long before we see him here to check on her."

"Levi heard from him. He's heading overseas tomorrow. It'll have to wait until he's back." She leaned in to peer at the monitors. "Better if she doesn't know about how bad this mess is yet. Jarrod might be good with this, but that doesn't mean she is. Although she likely understands on another level." Ice gave him a worried glance. "How can anyone not?"

"Trust these guys know what they're doing." Stone reached over and patted her hand.

"I know." She nodded. "I've seen them in action before."

Stone laughed. "That you have. And it's no different now."

"Sure it is. They didn't go in prepared for this."

"They're always prepared," Stone deadpanned.

"If that's the case, why the hell did Harrison and Logan get taken down?"

Bullard laughed beside them. "She's got a point."

"Not everyone who is good gets away," she reminded them. "Remember, Levi was betrayed in the first place. Not everything has a happy ending."

On that note Stone nodded soberly. "That's very true. But we have to trust sometimes. Right now men are running to the rescue. They're all trained, and they all know what to do."

Ice slammed down her fist on the table and stood. Her arms then crossed on her chest. She stared out into the night. "That might be. But it still feels like I got the shitty end of the stick." At the sudden silence from the men behind her, she turned and glared. "You know? I kinda wouldn't mind being there to kick some ass myself."

"Ain't that the truth." Stone smiled. When in full bloom, it was beautiful to see.

She snickered. "We need to set up a practice location. I feel like I'm getting rusty without training."

"Or is it you just need a target to let out frustration?" Bullard challenged.

She grinned at her friend who knew her too well for her own good. "That too." She caught sight of the camera, the men racing down the stairs, and pointed to the monitors.

"Here we go," Bullard said.

Ice watched and listened as grunts filled the air, followed by a few thuds and blue language. Although on Levi's side there wasn't much to listen to. He took out the first man instantly. In the background she could hear more grunts and groans as Rhodes took down the second man. The room was dark, the camera swiveling from side to side and then up and down in a crazy motion as Levi fought. Rhodes's camera was even worse.

But suddenly the jerkiness stopped as Rhodes took a deep breath and straightened. "Damn, it took a little longer than I'd hoped."

Levi's chuckle was dry. "Maybe we're all out of practice." He added, "Two men. Both down and secured. Send a team to collect them. Medical attention needed for our two."

Stone answered, "Got it. Two more unfriendlies unaccounted for. Watch your back."

"Rhodes and I are going after them. Using the connecting door into the hardware store."

"Keep the comm lines open and the cameras on," Stone said. "We're recording everything."

"Going silent." Levi's comm went quiet, but his camera kept running the video. The four of them in the control room watched in silence as Levi and Rhodes approached the door, tested it to see if it was unlocked, then Rhodes pulled out his pick and quickly unlocked it.

Both men entered at the same time—one going low, one going high, guns at the ready, sweeping the area in front of them.

The camera swept the apparently empty room slowly. If that was the case, where were the other two men? Nervously Ice watched as Levi did a quick search of the entire area. It was a decent size with several places where people could hide, but it still looked to be empty.

Levi turned suddenly. "Movement in the other room."

Immediately he and Rhodes raced to the doorway and flattened to each side. And waited.

Ice watched, tensing as the seconds ticked by.

Bullard reached out a gentle hand to cover hers, and she jerked back, the first she was aware of how her fingers were clenched into tight balls.

"You really care, don't you?" Bullard asked in low tones.

She glanced over at Stone's blank face, and then, with a shuttered look, she gave Bullard a curt nod. Why was he asking? He knew where her heart lay.

He squeezed her fist gently. "He'll be fine."

Her gaze locked on the screen in front of them. "This is new for me," she admitted. "I'm usually dropping off or picking up, but my focus is on the helicopter and keeping her in the air, not watching the people I care about moving through scenarios where I have no control."

"No. I can see that would be an issue, but you should be getting used to this."

"Maybe I am. But it's not usually Levi I'm watching," she said, her voice dry. "Makes it a little different with it being him."

Bullard chuckled. "That it does." He pulled away his hand, and they both settled back to watch in silence.

Surely this would be over soon.

LEVI DIDN'T KNOW what he expected to see. This was the room that should hold all the answers. But it appeared to be empty. Slowly he straightened as Rhodes was off to one side of an old empty basement.

Shelves on the wall were covered in dust, and Levi took a few steps forward and shone his light into the dark corners. Nothing. He didn't know what he'd heard earlier, but nothing was here now. Rhodes reached out and cupped Levi's shoulder. He turned to see Rhodes pointing at a far corner. Another door. That should lead upstairs to the hardware store.

But the layout of the basement was wrong. Here was a door but no stairwell, which meant it was on the other side of the wall and had to go into the office upstairs. But it didn't, as Rhodes had seen that room and nothing was there. Unless they'd missed another trapdoor.

Then he realized something else. This room was too small. Only about half the size of what it should be.

He turned to look at Rhodes and saw he had already figured it out. With his fingers to his lips, Rhodes slipped over to the door, Levi right behind him. With the lights out they listened. Sounds of people came from the basement underneath the ice cream shop.

He'd already heard from Ice that it was his team. The door in front of them was ajar. Not by much, just enough that somebody on the other side could hear any intruders.

He slipped to the side, and with a nod to Rhodes, they burst through together. Expecting gunfire, they were surprised at silence. Until they turned on their flashlights and saw the storekeeper Levi had spoken with, his body riddled with bullets.

They hadn't heard any shots fired, and, from the dark color of the large pool of blood, it appeared the man had been killed much earlier. This space was smaller than the size of the room they'd just come from. There was a stairway in the middle. If this was the storehouse, it would make more sense. The shelves in this room were empty, but they were *not* covered in dust. So whatever had been on them had been recently removed.

He walked over and bent down beside the body. Not only had the storekeeper been shot, he'd been pulverized with the bullets. This wasn't just an execution; this was an attempt to destroy the man's face. But there was no mistaking the earring plug on the left earlobe or the odd freckle pattern on the back of his right hand. This was the same clerk. Levi went through the man's pockets, but whatever ID he might have had on him had long since been removed.

"Recognize him?" Rhodes asked.

Levi nodded. "The clerk who worked in the hardware store upstairs."

"Well, I guess he's out of a job now," Rhodes said.

Joking in their line of business helped to ease the pain and release some of the stress, not to mention getting the adrenaline back down to something manageable. They stood in the center and studied the small room.

"They're long gone," Levi said. "If it was me, I would be."

"Ready to move upstairs?" Rhodes stood at the bottom

of the steps.

Levi didn't bother answering. He came up behind Rhodes, and together they crept upstairs. As expected, the trapdoor was open. The products on the shelves appeared to be undisturbed. They did a quick sweep of the store, but nobody was here now.

"Stone, how do I get this out of here?" Levi pointed his camera toward the security video system up in the corner.

Stone's voice crackled in his ear. "Check behind the counter, and make sure no timer or some kind of a detonation device is attached. With these guys, we can't take that chance."

Rhodes's voice carried across the store. "Come over here, and take a look at this." Underneath the counter, they saw a monitor system that appeared to be a full computer. The outside camera video was being streamed. Settling his camera on the system so Stone could take a look, Levi asked, "Have you ever seen anything like this, Stone?"

Bullard whispered in Levi's ear. "I've seen something similar. Not exactly the same setup, but this is no good either. That whole place is rigged to blow. If you touch any of the cameras, it'll all explode."

He could hear Ice's voice muttering right on top of Bullard's, making his heart ache and his stomach clench. He couldn't think about those two now. He didn't dare.

Ice's gentle voice said, "An old building like that will take out the ice cream parlor beside you. Wouldn't be at all surprised if it's rigged to take out the whole block."

He exchanged glances with Rhodes. With all the firepower downstairs and next door, it would take out a lot more than just the block.

But he sure as hell hated to leave it.

He studied the wires going to and from. There was no detonator. There was no timer. There was nothing that said this was actually the main location of the triggers. He'd have to find another setup. Bringing up the layout of the store in his mind, he tried to remember how the clerk had reacted when Levi walked in and through the store. The guy kept glancing at the mirror in the far corner. A camera had to be up there, or was there more than that? On a hunch Levi walked over, pulled out a ladder stacked against the wall, and stepped up to take a better look. Once there he could see the flashing light in a watch being used as a timer. Only it wasn't ticking. "Stone, what do you think?"

"A simple setup," Stone said, his voice thoughtful. "We still can't take a chance since we can't see anything else down there. Just because they have one system doesn't mean they don't have a fail-safe."

"What is that likely to be?" Levi asked. With Rhodes at his side the two of them shone their flashlights as they examined the simple bomb. Depending on how it was set, this thing could go off at any time. As he looked at it closer, he realized touching the cameras would likely trigger the bomb. And while they didn't have the ability to take down the cameras, somebody was likely watching them right now.

On instinct he gave the guy on the other side of the digital feed a thumbs-up. Whatever the heck they were up to, they'd done a hell of a job here.

And now they'd know Levi was on to them as well.

Chapter 10

O NE OF BULLARD'S men checked in. At the sound of Dave's voice, Ice leaned closer to Bullard's microphone.

"What have you found, Dave?" Bullard glanced at the monitors, but nothing showed Dave's location. Ice waited and watched while Bullard tried to communicate with his men.

Stone manipulated the dials and buttons on one of the top row monitors and brought up the GPS signal on the truck Dave drove.

"We just passed a black military-looking van parked in the shadows at the end of one of the blocks," Dave responded. "Not on a driveway but pulled off the street, more like an empty lot."

"What?" Bullard asked.

Ice leaned forward. "Dave, can you send two men to check it out?" She looked over at Bullard with an apology for speaking through his set rather than her own. But hers was tuned now for Rhodes and Levi.

Bullard disconnected his headset so the speakers ran through the room as Dave said, "Two men have just been dropped off at the end of the block. They'll trek their way back. We're less than one minute out from the hardware store."

Ice chewed her bottom lip. Damn, she was no good with

electronics or IEDs. They really needed Evan to join the team. He was a specialist in that area. "Remember it's rigged to blow," she warned.

"No worries." Bullard told Ice. "Paul is an IED specialist. I presume he's still in the truck with you, Dave?"

Ice watched the dotted line as it moved on the monitor. Every one of the vehicles on the compound had GPS tracking. Very quickly the vehicles would be lined up outside the store. And that bothered her. *A lot.* "You do realize how many of our men are in danger if that place goes?" She caught sight of Stone's nervous twitch. "Stone?"

He gave a clipped nod. "If they planned to bring everybody in so they could take them all at once, then they've done a pretty decent job of it."

Levi's voice crackled in his headset. "If Paul's here, send a man to keep everybody the hell back. We've got Logan and Harrison loaded into the truck. The two unfriendlies we've taken out have been secured and are now on the back of the truck as well."

"Any sign of the two missing?" Stone asked, his voice hard. Cold. "I can't see a sign of anyone else on the monitors." He shook his head. "Levi, I don't like this at all. Get the hell out of there. Those two men have to be somewhere."

Ice searched the monitors, and they watched Dave's truck pull up close to Levi's. They could only do that and wait.

Bullard turned to Stone and asked, "Do you have satellite imagery here?"

Stone snorted. "In progress. We lost our contact with one and haven't got everything functioning quite at 100 percent yet. We weren't expecting a strike on the home front on day one."

That was a bit of an exaggeration, but Ice knew exactly what he meant. She turned to Bullard. "Do you have it?"

He nodded. "Absolutely. Hard to operate if you don't have eyes in the sky with this."

Ice's gaze went from Stone to Bullard. "Can you log in from here to your system and bring those eyes on this scenario?"

Stone spun in his seat to stare at her. "That's one hell of a damn good idea."

Bullard already worked on the keyboard nearest him. She didn't look too closely. One of the big things about this type of work was security, and that meant not looking over everybody's shoulder.

"Stone, which monitor are you giving me for this?"

Stone got up and fiddled with the equipment. Within seconds the center one in front of Bullard went black before it lit up as a new system came online.

Both Ice and Stone leaned in as Bullard brought up the coordinates of the compound. Instantly Ice could see the outside of their building where the control room was. The darkness, the truck still parked in the compound, the roof. It was cool and a little unnerving. It meant that anybody at any time could keep tabs on them.

She watched and wondered. Bullard quickly changed the satellite focus to the town where most of their men were. To think they were only ten minutes out made her want to jump into the last vehicle and go get them herself. But this sitting by and waiting ... Devastating. Her nerves were stretched thin, and she couldn't stop squeezing and opening her fists to ease the tension.

When a softball landed in her lap, Stone said with a smile, "Squeeze that instead."

She snatched it up and squeezed to her heart's content. The resilience of the ball was enough for her to squeeze as hard as she could without breaking it. She grinned. Perfect.

"There." Bullard leaned forward and tapped the monitor. He zoomed down to check out the vehicles they'd been tracking but couldn't see anyone.

Shit, that meant Dave and Paul went inside. Unless one was waiting in the vehicle. But she knew Dave, and he was never one to step back and let another stay in a dangerous position.

She watched as Bullard suddenly pulled the view back so they could see the entire length of the block again. Then he switched the angle slightly, and the van that Dave had mentioned showed up. Hell, yeah, that was a military-looking vehicle.

They could see Merk approaching from the front and another man had gone around the back of the building and had come up behind the van. She figured that had to be one of Dave's men. But it was hard to keep their eyes on both positions. And, this far apart, they couldn't actually see each other very clearly. The van suddenly turned on flashing lights and ripped forward at a hell of a speed, as if it knew it would be under attack any moment. The two men fired, aiming for the tires. But the vehicle kept on going.

"Any way to get a plate number?" she asked.

The satellite zoomed in as much is it could, and she caught four letters. *LH, B,* and *K.* She quickly wrote them down. Dave's voice filled the air. "Paul has disconnected the timer. Removing the camera system. We'll be out in two minutes."

Bullard asked, "What about the two men you sent after the van? Did you hear back from them?"

"Merk just now checked in. The van left. They took out one tire, but that didn't slow it down."

Specialized tires then, Ice thought. Definitely a military vehicle and looking for trouble. If not looking, ready for trouble. She held her hand to her mouth and whispered, "Levi, you okay?"

"I'm fine." His warm reassuring voice crackled in her ear. "You should have Logan and Harrison coming in any moment."

She shifted her glance to the GPS tracking monitor, and, sure enough, the truck was just a mile away from the front gates. She took off her headset and stood up. "I'm heading to the medical bay. Those two will need help."

Bullard dropped his headset and followed.

Good timing to have him and his men visiting. Bullard was a fully licensed doctor, having training in the military. As he stepped through the doorway, he said, "Stone, it's over to you."

Stone waved them off. "I'll turn on the speakers in the medical room."

"If you need us," Ice said, "just let us know. Bullard could probably handle it all on his own, but, just in case, I want to be there."

"I got this," Stone said. "Go. They're entering the gate now."

Ice, gun at her side, raced straight for the medical clinic. Inside she hit the lights and bolted to the one side door; a large garage door was on the other side. A series of doors kept any kind of danger outside but allowed them access to the patients. By the time the garage door opened, the truck was backing up.

She was grateful to see Harrison walking, a little shaky,

but at least he was ambulatory. Logan on the other hand was bleeding badly.

She got Harrison into the bed beside Logan, had him lie down, and said she could check his head wound when she had a moment. Logan was a priority. With the other two men standing by, she stepped up to assist Bullard. He had already cut away Logan's shirt and was cleaning the wound, ready to go in after the bullet.

Blood pulsed sluggishly from his shoulder. Not good.

She quickly took care of the rest of his shirt, watching as Bullard went to the medical cabinet to pull out anesthesia. He administered a shot, waited all of ten seconds, and tested the area with his fingers. When Logan cried out, Bullard motioned to the driver and Alfred who was now standing at the doorway and said, "Come in and hold him down."

With eyebrows raised, the two men raced in, one on each side, and secured straps around Logan's ankles, hips, and chest. Then they held his head firm.

Ice had seen a lot of surgeries—she'd done a lot of field medicine. But she was damn glad Bullard was here for this one. He went in after that bullet, and he was taking no prisoners. The good news was it appeared to have gone straight in and embedded in the bone. She brought over the X-ray equipment and set it up.

Bullard stepped back, rearranged the angle to find what he wanted to see. Everybody retreated, and within minutes, he had the image he needed.

Then Bullard went to work. She stayed at his side while he cut, stitched muscle and tissue closed, cleaned out the wound before closing up the injury. She kept busy cleaning up after Bullard. But finally he was done. They put a clean bandage on Logan's shoulder, and, now that Bullard had a moment, he set up an IV. She watched him do the last part in surprise.

He glanced over at her and shrugged. "I just wanted to make sure, in case we have to go back in, that I have an easier way to knock him out. This will do it in seconds."

She nodded. That IV provided an instant pathway for nutrients and drugs. She had no problem with it. If they were in a hospital, it would have been set up immediately. Field doctoring, yeah, not as easy.

With Logan resting comfortably, Bullard and Ice switched their attention to Harrison. Not that the head wound was anything to ignore. But thankfully this particular one wasn't terrible. With a few stitches Bullard had the small gash closed.

Bullard patted Harrison on the shoulder and said, "You'll be fine. You'll have a hell of a headache for a few days, but after that, you should be pretty good. No active duty, just lots of rest."

Harrison glared at him. Ice wanted to laugh. "No active duty" was a death sentence to these men. But there was plenty for them to do here now. Harrison was hell on wheels with electronics, so he'd be a good hand to have around.

When she could finally take a breath, she stopped to survey Bullard washing up at the big sink on the side. She smiled. It was not exactly how she'd planned to christen the medical clinic, but there could be worse ways. She walked over, adjusted the thermostat as the other two men brought out blankets and covered up both patients, ignoring Harrison's complaints about not being allowed to go to his room.

She leaned close and whispered into Harrison's ear, "Somebody needs to keep an eye on Logan." She glanced to Logan in the nearby bed, then his injured shoulder, and added, "Please stay here, Harrison, and let us know if things change in Logan's condition."

At that Harrison instantly subsided. Nobody wanted to leave Logan alone. And this was a perfect answer for both of them. Bullard patted her on the shoulder and put Harrison's cell phone within his reach. She tested the Call buttons on both men's beds, making sure they went directly to Stone in the control room, and told Harrison, "I'll get you hot coffee and something to eat."

He reached out and grabbed her hand. "Thanks, Ice."

She shook her head, nodding toward Bullard. "You mean, 'Thank you, Bullard.'" But she squeezed Harrison's hand gently, understanding what he meant, then turned and walked out of the room.

Inside she was shaking. What the hell would she do if Bullard wasn't here next time? She was not a doctor. Sure, she had great medical training, but that was not good enough if somebody needed a real doctor. She could only be expected to do so much here. And, if she'd been alone today, she would have failed.

Bullard reached out and wrapped an arm around her shoulder. "You did great today."

She turned to look up at him, her feet slowing as they made their way back to the control room. "If you hadn't been here, I couldn't have done what you just did."

"And hopefully you would not have needed to. How far away is the closest hospital?"

"Forty minutes, driving like hell. Too far away in a situation like this."

"But, in that case, the men would handle it differently. They'd have phoned for an ambulance and met them halfway. The men would've been stabilized for the trip to the ambulance, and the paramedics would've taken over then. Logan would have been brought into surgery immediately."

"If the hospital wasn't too overrun," she muttered. She held out her hands to see the fine tremor whispering through her fingers. "The adrenaline rush is something else."

Bullard reached across, grabbed her hand gently, and squeezed it. "It's not adrenaline. That's shakiness. It's shock. Get a hot cup of coffee and some food. Then deliver some to Harrison."

She withdrew her fingers and smiled. "I'm taking my coffee straight up to the control room. I need to know Levi is okay."

Bullard nodded in understanding, but she could see the disappointment in his eyes.

She knew what he wanted. But it wasn't anything she could give him. At least not at this point in time. If anything ever happened to Levi, then maybe ... But she couldn't expect Bullard to wait. She wanted him to be happily hooked up now. He was a good man.

In the kitchen she quickly dished up two bowls of the rich beef stew Alfred had simmering on the stove and poured two cups of coffee. She delivered a cup and a bowl to Harrison, and, by the time she made it back to the kitchen, her food was missing. She looked at Alfred and asked, "Did you take the other cup of coffee and bowl of stew?"

"I gave it to Bullard. He's gone to his room with them. He needed to get cleaned up."

She nodded and quickly dished up two bowls of stew and poured two more cups of coffee. "One of these is for Stone," she said. "He's too damn stubborn to come down and get them himself."

Alfred smiled. "He's too scared," he corrected. "He

doesn't want to miss anything and have his friends put in any more danger, not if he can help it."

Chastised, she nodded. "I know." She gave Alfred a small smile and carried the tray to the control room. As she walked in, the first thing out of her mouth was "How is Levi?"

"He's fine," Stone said. "They're all on their way back to base." She set the tray down between the two of them, and his face lit up beautifully. "Oh, nice. I could really use some of this." He looked around hastily. "Unless one of these is for Bullard?"

"Bullard's gone for a shower," she said easily. "He took his coffee with him."

"Shower?" Then his gaze landed on her clothing. She'd yet to change, and he winced. "How is Logan?"

"He's resting comfortably. He has to be watched, of course, but he's holding. He should pull through with no trouble. And Harrison," she added before Stone could ask, "has a minor head wound. We've stitched it up, but he'll have a hell of a headache. But he's fine too. He stayed in the sick bay to keep an eye on Logan."

"Good," Stone said with a sense of satisfaction. "That gives us at least ten maybe fifteen minutes to eat our food and get seconds before the men get back and scarf it all up."

"Chances are the men will say exactly the same thing when they get in and see most of the stew gone." She grinned. At Stone's horrified gaze, she shook her head. "You know Alfred. Of course it's not even close to being gone. He made what looks like enough to feed twenty men down there."

She lifted her spoon and took a sip of the broth. Rich meaty flavor filled her mouth. "Oh, dear God, this is so good. I'm so glad he's home."

Stone picked up his spoon filled with the rich beef mix-
ture and put it in his mouth. Within seconds he was
moaning, enjoying the savory taste. "I hope there is enough
for twenty men. I plan to eat at least enough for ten." That
was the last thing he said until he'd hit the bottom of his
bowl. Then he sat back with a sense of satisfaction and
reached for his coffee. He looked over at Ice and said, "You
know something? For all the ups and downs, headaches, and
problems, life is really not too bad."

She watched the GPS bringing the rest of the men back
into the compound and knew that Levi was safe and sound.
She nodded back. "You're right. Life's not all bad."

LEVI HAD JUST walked into the large bay where they dealt
with electronics when he heard the alarm sounding in the
medical bay. It took him a second to understand what was
happening. He dumped the security system from the store
and ran. When he skidded inside the medical clinic, both
Bullard and Ice were already there. Harrison was sitting up,
pointing at Logan.

"He woke up for a moment and sat up, and then his eyes
rolled back in his head, and he collapsed. It looks like fresh
blood on his bandage."

Levi reached out and gripped Harrison's good shoulder
and told him to ease back. He studied Bullard, who ripped
open the bandage on Logan's other shoulder. Sure enough it
was bleeding. Not badly but enough.

Harrison reached up and rubbed his forehead. "Damn.
If only I caught him earlier. I told him to lie down, don't
move."

"He wouldn't listen anyway," Levi said. "He was still in fight mode so his instinctive reaction would've been to escape." His gaze found the stitches in Harrison's head wound. It looked painful, but they were all used to getting more than their fair share of knocks on the head. "How you doing, Harrison?"

Levi hoped to pull Harrison away from what was going on in the next bed. And it worked. Harrison rolled back slightly, looking up at Levi.

Harrison gave a lopsided grin and said, "Head hurts like a son of a bitch, but it's still working."

Levi nodded. "Good thing. We just brought in the electronics from the store. Their surveillance system was rigged to a bomb. We couldn't find the trigger, but, with some of Dave's men, we disarmed it and brought the whole mess in here to look at."

Harrison brightened. He instantly tried to pull back the blanket and swing his legs to the ground. Levi wasn't having anything to do with that. He pushed Harrison back down. "You need to stay here until your head heals a bit more."

"My head is just fine," Harrison snapped. "And I'll heal much faster if I'm doing something. Those assholes took me out, and I'm looking for a little payback. I might find something in all those electronics, especially from a laptop. Did you bring one?" he asked hopefully.

Levi gave a curt nod. In truth, Harrison was a wizard with that shit. They were all decent, though he had a gift.

But they had a lot of men here right now, and Harrison was injured.

As if seeing Levi's refusal about to come off his lips, Harrison growled in frustration. "Look, let me just come and see. Maybe I can do nothing, and, if my head starts hurting or anything feels wrong, I'll come back and lie down. I only stayed to keep an eye on Logan. And you see how well that went," he said bitterly. "Just let me do something I'm good at."

Levi frowned. Two men down was bad news. He needed them both back up as soon as possible. But he also understood what it was like to feel useless. He'd spent enough months in bed himself. Had to stop sometime. And Harrison had been in bed alongside Levi, Stone, and Rhodes too. They all understood the frustration.

Cautiously Levi said, "Fine. But only for two hours. Then you agree to lie down again."

"Perfect. I can figure out a ton of shit in two hours." Harrison threw back the blankets and cautiously sat up. He lowered himself to the floor and straightened. With a confident smile, he said, "I'm good. Lead the way."

Levi looked at Bullard and caught Ice's glance. Levi asked a soundless question about Logan, and, when she nodded and gave him the thumbs-up that meant Logan would be fine, he could feel the weight of the world roll off his shoulders. He already felt responsible for the injuries that had sent him and his unit onto this path of private security. He didn't want to be responsible for Logan's today as well.

"Let me know of any changes in his condition," he said to the pair still working on the unconscious man. "Harrison's coming to spend a couple hours with us, taking a look at the electronics we brought back from town."

Bullard waved him off, making him feel that much more confident about Logan's condition. Levi turned back to find Harrison already at the doorway, waiting for him impatiently. That was the thing about his men. They were really hard to keep down.

Chapter 11

ICE WATCHED THE two men walk away. She was torn. She
should stay and help Bullard, but she really wanted to be
with Levi. They had so much shit to sort out, and yet, at the
same time, she figured there was almost nothing to discuss
now. So much time had gone by, and neither one of them
even understood anymore what had gone wrong. Given what
they'd all been through, she wasn't sure it mattered either.

"Go." Bullard waved her off in the direction the two
men had gone. "At least if you go, you can keep an eye on
Harrison. If he looks like he's flagging, get his ass back here
to bed."

Ice grinned. "I can do that." She walked to the sink and
washed up. When done, she looked back at Bullard as he
rebandaged Logan. "You'll stay here with him?"

Bullard nodded. "I'll go grab my laptop and sit here with
him for a while. I don't think he'll wake up again but ..." He
shrugged. "Who knows?"

She liked that about Bullard. When he was in doctor
mode, the patients came first.

"I'll check back in an hour or so," she promised.

"Better bring coffee with you then." He disappeared out
one way to retrieve his laptop, and she followed the path Levi
had taken.

Catching up to them, she didn't even know what to call

this room. It was technically a garage though fully wired. It did have huge double bay doors, and connected to the other rooms, but, being full of electronic workstations, it seemed to deserve a better label than "garage."

Harrison sat, his fingers busy on the laptop keyboard. She personally knew very little about bombs and bomb-making equipment, but she knew that, in this line of work, she should become better informed about it. One more thing on her list.

She studied Harrison's color, noting the pallor, but also the glint in his eyes. The excitement and the ability to dig in to find something had caught hold. He'd be fine for a little while longer. She looked at Levi, busy sorting through the equipment they had brought back. In fact the room was almost full of electronics. Dave was here with several of his men. Bullard had only the best working for him. Not knowing quite where to go or what to do, she looked around the room at large and asked. "Did you find anything?"

Levi nodded and pointed at Harrison. "He did."

She walked closer to Harrison and studied the laptop. It was all gibberish to her. "What did you find?"

"The laptop is one of several in a network. So I'm back-tracking. Of course it's bouncing me all over the place now, but I'm pretty damn sure it's not very far away."

"What's not very far away?"

"The system which the laptop is connected to," he said enthusiastically as if that explained it. For her it meant jack shit.

"But then doesn't that mean that it's connected to the van? And that it's somewhere close to us?"

Levi shot her a hard glance. "Maybe, but not necessarily. Have you talked to Stone?"

She shook her head. "No. I've just come from the sick bay. I haven't gotten to Stone yet."

"I'll go," he said. "You keep an eye on Harrison."

"I'm fine," Harrison protested.

"Good," she said, snagging a stool and dragging it closer. "Then you won't mind if I watch and learn."

"That's no problem. You need to learn some of this stuff anyway."

And there followed one of the hardest lessons she'd ever had to listen to. Something about viruses and Trojans and DNS and jumping off points in code that she had never heard before.

She shook her head after he finally wound down. "Do you actually expect me to remember any of that?" she exclaimed in horror.

He laughed. "The more times I say it, the more familiar you'll become with it all. And believe me, I kept it simple this time."

"Nope." She shook her head again. "How about I just watch instead?"

But this time he slowly explained how he did a trace and was tracking the signal back.

"See? They should've hid their signal, but they hadn't disconnected this laptop from the network. So I can trace it back and set up a signal for when it goes live again." Suddenly he leaned forward and cursed. "Goddammit."

"What? What just happened?" She studied the screen, but instead of all the interesting split screens he had up, it was now black. "Where did it all go?"

"The assholes just figured out I was on their tail." He clicked through several screens. "They won't beat me that easily."

She watched as he swore and typed away like a madman. But it was well above her head.

Levi's voice came through the PA system. "Ice, can you come up here to the control room, please?"

"On my way."

She hopped off the bench, studied Harrison once again to see an angry red flush instead of the previous pallor. He was more pissed about what was happening on his laptop than struggling with failing energy. She figured he'd be fine for at least a few minutes. She headed to the control room. It would take at least ten minutes to get to the opposite side of the building. By the time she got there, Stone was acting like Harrison. He was pounding on his keyboard and swearing. She raised her eyebrows and turned to Levi.

"Stone looks like Harrison right now." She added, "Something happened. They figured out he was tracking them, and now he's pissed, trying to work around them."

Levi nodded. "Stone came up against a similar kind of issue on our own system. We need to make sure we're not under attack ourselves. All of our screens have gone black."

Startled, she studied all the monitors, but they were blind; no way to see what was going on outside the building. And that was so not good. "Shit."

"We need to go outside and do a security check," Levi said.

She turned back to the door. "Do you think we might need to hire a few more men? We got Bullard and his men right now, but, when they leave, we'll be very short on staff."

"I know," Levi said in clipped tones as she passed through the doorway, "But we never thought one of the first major hurdles would be an occurrence on our home base."

She followed him down to the armory and grabbed her

gear. He insisted she put on a bulletproof vest, letting her know exactly how serious he figured things would get out there. Great. When she left the military, she figured she was done with war forever. She thought she'd known exactly what being part of this company entailed, but she hadn't really.

Three of Bullard's men came with them. Once outside, they were all headed in opposite directions to check on the cameras and scout the region. If they were coming under attack, they needed to be prepared. The rest of the men were inside on alert. "Did somebody tell Bullard?"

"Alfred is handling that. He's making sure everybody inside is prepped and ready, and Stone is testing the security systems."

"Which way are we taking?" she asked quietly.

"The secret entrance leading up the hill."

"We really need to have better names for these places," she said, heading for the door that would send them toward their destination.

"Lead the way," Levi said. "And you can tell us if anything's been disturbed since you came in."

She nodded. "Will do." They'd already tested the soundproofing in this tunnel. And with small running lights at the bottom edge of the floor, they could move easily. She raced with two sidearms on her hips and her favorite assault rifle in her hands. Once again Ice shook her head at the crazy world she'd been thrown into. She didn't realize she'd said anything out loud until Levi quietly said from behind her, "Do you regret it?"

Without breaking stride, she tossed him a backward glance. "Maybe." She nodded, then couldn't resist adding, even though this was hardly the time or the place, "Depends on if we ever resolve our differences. If this is just me wasting my time here, then I'm not sticking around. However, if this is us building the future, then that's a different story."

She didn't wait to hear his answer but quickly unlocked the tunnel entrance and held up her hand to stop Bullard's men behind them. She slipped outside into the moonlight. The sun would be up soon. They were caught in the time warp between night and morning, not quite dawn but the sky was light enough to see. She didn't move for a minute to allow her eyesight to adjust.

Turning her head, she studied the entrance. She reached up and pushed the button on her comm and said, "All clear."

LEVI HAD NO chance to answer. Her words were like a blow to his heart. Sure they had some problems, but she'd followed him. That had been a statement in itself. But he'd been lax on not picking up the slack. And she was right; after weeks he'd done nothing.

Mostly he did whatever he needed to, usually in response to threats. The hell if he knew about handling this shit. To him it was simple. She'd left the military and followed him here. They were partners. That meant she cared. But it seemed like it was more than that for her. And that's exactly what he wanted.

He also knew that, for him, it could never be over because she was the one, regardless whether she came or left. But to hear her actually say the words was like a spear in his heart. And, of course, like the trip to Mexico … shitty timing.

Using hand signals, he had the men spread out and move swiftly across the ground. They made a full sweep of the area. All their cameras were still intact but not functioning, which was what he expected. There was a good chance the men were tracked back here. With all the tradesmen, cement and army trucks needed to outfit the compound, it wasn't like Levi had been able to hide that they'd moved in. Not to mention having two helicopters. Satellites had picked him up for sure, he knew that, but, whether the locals gave a damn, he didn't know. They'd been as friendly as they could be. Until Rodriguez had shown up. And that was a whole different ball game.

If Rodriguez knew Levi was here, the chances were the compound was about to come under major attack. With everybody stationed on the hillside, checking the roads below from this position, they could see for miles. He had his sensor out, looking for vehicles. And one was beeping. Through his comm device he told Stone, "We have an incoming vehicle picked up by one of our trackers."

"That's theirs. Rhodes put a tracker on it before he went in. I've been watching it approach."

Levi grinned. "Any chance the men got one on the van before it took off?"

"They fired and embedded one in the vehicle, but we can't get it to work. Presumably it was damaged when it went in."

Levi frowned. Those damn things were terrible for that. Too easily damaged. They'd have to devise one of their own. They had the same problem in the military. They really needed a tracker they could shoot from a distance, land softly, and lock on to whatever it was they were firing upon. He sent word to the men outside, alerting them to the oncoming vehicle, about two minutes out.

At the sound of someone approaching, he turned to see

Ice. She dropped down beside him, looking at the road below, then turned to gaze directly in his eyes. He contemplated the look in hers or what it meant until she turned and said, "Incoming."

The vehicle stopped at the side of the road, and four men got out.

Using his night scope, he could see the men were armed and wore dark camouflage. "Heads up. Four unfriendlies on the way."

The three men with Levi acknowledged.

"Hold your positions until we see where they go."

The moon was bright overhead, giving them lots of light to work with. He lined up a scope and watched as the intruders split up. They were taking the same hill from the same side but from different positions. It looked like two of them would come up under Ice.

Beside him, she stretched out and lined up for the shot. "Did you pick out a place for the mass grave yet?" she asked, going for a touch of humor.

He stifled a laugh. That was his girl. The trouble was, the answer to that question was no. Not yet. He hadn't expected this. She looked over at him, and the laughter in her eyes made him realize just how special she truly was. Any other time he'd have leaned forward and kissed her. Wasn't that always the problem? Lousy timing. Never having a chance to do what he really wanted to do.

Instantly he heard one of the men on the comm say, "That better not be what I thought I just heard."

Ice pulled away, her giggles completely overheard, leaving Levi to deal with the fallout. Mumbling an excuse, he turned his attention to the incoming men, but inside he was smiling. This was a good thing and it gave him hope. With a low whisper he said, "Fifty yards and counting."

"I've got one coming up in front of me," said Sean, another of Bullard's men.

The other two on Bullard's team, Jason and Andrew, checked in. Apparently the fourth intruder was coming up between them. Good, all four were covered. What Levi really needed was that vehicle down there.

Apparently Ice had the same idea. They were the closest to it and needed to take out the men, then go snag it, and bring it into the compound where they could dismantle it.

She whispered against his ear, "If we can take out all four men at once, I'll go down. But I'm afraid somebody in that vehicle will drive off at any sign of problems here. Can you take these two while I retrieve the vehicle?"

He reached out and held her down. "No, they'll see you. That'd give us away."

She frowned. "I'd be silent."

He squeezed her shoulder again, and she fell quiet. The first man crested the hill and stopped, surveying the terrain. He was only about ten yards away from them when he glanced over the top. Good. The second man arrived beside him. They both headed toward the other side and would reach the compound in no time.

Moving as quietly as they could, Levi and Ice came up behind them both. Levi jumped his man. Ice didn't bother; she hit hers hard in the back of the neck, and he went down. Instantly they dropped to the ground in the still air around them. No birds flew; no animals cried. They just had two unconscious men on the ground.

They needed the other two taken out just as quietly so they could circle back around after the vehicle.

Levi's communication squawked gently in his ear.

"Number three down."

He looked to the west.

He realized just how well-placed this compound really was. They had the high ground, and, if anybody tried to come up from the side, they still had to come down in full view where anybody in the compound could keep track of them, yet were cut off from their own party on the other side.

"And that was textbook perfect," came in over his earpiece.

With all four intruders accounted for, Levi ordered his men to circle around behind the vehicle. "Beware, there could be a fifth or six man inside."

"Got that."

He turned to look at Ice. "Can you stand watch on the fourth man down? Give me a commentary of what's going on? Jason and Andrew will secure the vehicle."

Soundlessly she got to her feet. Running low to the ground, she crept to the downed man. She spoke into her comm. "I can see the men coming around the vehicle. Still appears to be deserted. There are no lights. The engine is off."

He could see as she dropped out of sight. And then he waited. Were there only four men or had there been more?

The answer came sooner than he thought. Gunfire ripped through the night. Flashes of fire and the sounds of shooting rolled across the hills.

Goddammit. He didn't dare change position. Tense, he waited for one of the men to check in, and then he heard his comm cackle.

"The vehicle is secured. One unfriendly inside. Unfortunately, not possible to take the vehicle and keep him alive."

Right. Ice had not been joking about a mass grave.

Still it was good news. The vehicle was theirs. As he watched, the engine started, and the vehicle trundled closer.

Now to get these scumbags down the hillside … Levi had a few questions he wanted to ask them.

Reaching down, he threw the first man over his shoulder, squatted and dragged the second one under his arm and then flipped him over his other shoulder as well. Thankfully they weren't huge. If they'd been Stone's size, no way Levi would have been able to pack these two. But these guys weren't much bigger than Ice.

He should know. He spent a lot of time unwrapping that package. And that just reminded him. Enough was enough. She was right; they needed to sort out their shit.

Because he was damn tired of sleeping alone.

Chapter 12

B ACK INSIDE, ICE headed first to Logan's side. She wanted to make sure he was still doing okay. At the desk Bullard had his feet up, laptop in his lap, pounding away on the keyboard. "Is he okay?" she asked softly.

Bullard glanced up and smiled. "He's fine, sleeping decently now. By morning he should be a lot better."

"Good."

"I hear you had a successful hunt?"

She grinned. "Yeah, you could say that. Four captured, one dead. The vehicle is now in the garage. We should find out a ton from that."

Bullard jumped to his feet. "Oh, now that's great news. Can I come play too?"

She laughed. "As far as I'm concerned, you can. Check in with Levi though."

He closed his laptop and, before heading for the garage, said, "Where are you going now?"

"Honestly the kitchen."

"And here I thought you'd be off to bed." He gave her a wicked grin and disappeared in the direction of Levi and his men.

In fact that was exactly where she should be going. Still it felt wrong to go to bed while nobody else did. She was part of the team, and one didn't stop until the team did.

Alfred was in the kitchen, making yet another pot of coffee. Seemed as if that was all they drank around this place.

"Alfred, how are you doing?"

"I'm perfectly good." He turned to study her face. Then smiled. "And apparently you are too."

She grinned. "I am. Run down and looking for bed as soon as possible, but, at the moment, I'm holding."

He nodded. "That's all any of us can do."

"It'd be nice if we caught a few hours shut-eye."

"And that's where you're going right now," he said. "We're running shifts of four. Except for Sienna, who doesn't know what's going on, and we'll do our best to keep it that way. When she's up, I'll get her back into the office. Lots of work to keep her busy."

"Isn't that the truth?" Ice snorted. "Do we have that many men left?"

He waved at her with a towel in his hand. "Go. You get some sleep. Move it." She hesitated, but Alfred was insistent. "You've got to be up in four, so move it."

She winced. Four hours was nothing. She raced up to her room and stripped off her clothing, wincing again at the sight of her bloody clothes. She'd just thrown her night gear over them.

Still all had worked out well.

Once down to her skin, she stepped into the hot shower and scrubbed herself clean. The heat, combined with the fact that she would finally hit the bed, just added to her sleepiness. By the time she stepped out from under the hot water, she was exhausted. She wrapped herself in a towel, dried off, and then collapsed on the cool sheets. She pulled the covers over her and was out within minutes.

Four hours later her alarm woke her up. Groggy, she

leaned on her elbow and stared at the clock in disbelief. Surely she'd only been out five minutes. But, no, it read 9:00 a.m. Goddammit. She struggled to her feet and threw her bloody garments into the laundry. Then she carefully folded her night gear to take back down and put away. She should've done that last night. Exhaustion was no excuse.

Dressed in clean clothes and carrying her equipment, she headed downstairs to the kitchen. It looked like she was the only one up. When she had stowed away her gear, she came back into the kitchen to put on yet more coffee.

Somebody else would be up soon. Until then, she needed to know who was where and what was going on. She walked to the intercom and checked the control room. "Who's on duty?"

Stone's tired voice answered her. "I'm still here. Rhodes'll be taking my spot in a few minutes. Then I'm crashing for four."

Ice shook her head. Stone had been up forever. "You do that. You deserve it."

She checked the med bay. There was no sound. Ice had monitors and could click on that room and check on her patients. Sure enough, Logan slept peacefully. No sign of Bullard. That man was likely down for the count too. Swiftly going through the monitor screens, she checked the electronics garage—deeming it the R&D room in her head. And that's where she found several men, including Harrison.

Quickly, Ice poured a cup of coffee and walked down to the bay.

The men looked up when she arrived. Ice raised her coffee cup and said, "More in the kitchen but you only get coffee if you're just arriving for shift. If, however, you're all done and about to be relieved, then no more coffee for you. I expect to see your asses racing out of here and going to bed."

Her gaze turned to Harrison, and she frowned at the exhaustion straining his features. "And, if you don't get your ass out of here fast, I'm taking you back to sick bay."

His lips quirked into a smile. Even at one hundred pounds over her weight, he knew better than to argue with her. "I am tired," he said quietly. "No arguments out of me on that."

She smiled and patted his shoulder, nudging him in the general direction of the door. "Sleep. And don't come back in four hours. Your body needs to heal."

Almost gratefully he stood up carefully, put down the equipment in his hands, and, without another word to anybody, turned, and walked out the door.

She glared at Levi. "Just because you can go all night, and he can when he is healthy, doesn't mean he should when he is injured."

Levi turned to look at the doorway and then winced. "He never said anything, and he appeared to be working strong. It never crossed my mind."

Ice shook her head. "Men," she said in disgust. Ice turned to gaze at all the other guys in the room. "How many are supposed to go down now, and how many of you just arrived?"

Two men held up their hands.

"Did you just arrive?"

They nodded.

"Good, the rest of you go. Minimum four hours down. I'd rather not see any of you back for six."

The other men disappeared, except for Levi and the two new arrivals. Levi stood in front of her, arms crossed, and asked, "Are you really telling me to leave too?"

She snorted. "What would be the point of that? But, if you expect anybody to respect you, you'd better be damn sure you're at the top of your game. Everybody needs sleep sometime. Or have you forgotten that too?"

He glared at her, but, instead of her backing down, she took a step forward and shoved her face into his and added, "Then get your ass upstairs and get some sleep."

Instead of getting angry, Levi grinned, closed the short distance between them, and kissed her full on the lips. "You coming with me?" he asked cheekily.

Her gaze widened. She cast a surprised glance at the two men watching with fascination. Realizing they'd heard him, she glared at them and said, "I'm sure you have something else to do."

With smirks they headed to the door. "Yeah, we'll chase down the coffee you got for yourself."

They disappeared, leaving her and Levi alone.

She turned her attention back to Levi. "And what makes you think you're in any shape to take me to bed?"

"Well, it could be that you're the one who's all rested up and I'm the one that should be just lying there, letting you have your way with me," he said with a grin.

She took a step back, not sure what to make of his teasing manner. After weeks of being amiable friends, this step into lovers' talk was new and heartwarming. But also very exciting.

"What's changed in your world that all of a sudden you think we should be lovers again?"

"I've always thought we should be lovers. You're the one who stepped out of my bed. Remember?"

She nodded. "But that was after you decided I was a little too close to Bullard."

"And you proved my point by leaving my bed."

"No." She shook her head. "It had to do with trust."

"That's not fair. I've always trusted you," he said forcefully. "I'm just not so sure I trust him."

She laughed. "It's a little late, considering you brought him here to help out on the compound."

"That's different." He crossed his arms over his chest. "This is my life but you're my *heart*."

"Levi?" The call came from the other room.

And with that interruption he gave her a curt nod, turned, and walked to the door, leaving her standing there, staring after him with her jaw open. Alfred stretched an arm across her shoulders. "You two really do need to get the hell away from here and sort yourselves out."

She shot him a look. "Wouldn't that be nice?" She picked up her coffee and took a sip. Then remembering all that had happened last night, she turned and asked, "Any news?"

Alfred shook his head. "It's been quiet. No other attempted infiltrations."

"Well, that's something at least." She took another sip and then asked, "What about the men we brought back?"

Alfred smiled and patted her on the cheek. "You slept through it all. They were picked up an hour ago."

She rolled her eyes. "Of course they were. Did we get any information that was useful?"

"No, and none of them were Rodriguez either. Nor did they admit to knowing him or would say what they were doing at the stores. Although an interesting fact is, none of them were the owner of the hardware store or the ice cream shop. According to the government file, they belonged to two separate business owners. However, both are under the umbrella of a larger corporation, SynCorp."

"SynCorp? That could mean anything. It doesn't give us any idea what the business is about."

"That's why they do it, of course."

She nodded. She wanted to ask who had come and picked up their visitors but wasn't sure it was something she really wanted to know. Finally she decided she was all in or all out. "Did Jackson send men to pick up the hostages?"

Alfred gave her a sharp look and a curt nod. "Yes."

"What about the dead man?" She turned to study the hills out behind the windows. She had been kidding when she'd mentioned having a mass graveyard on the property. Now, in the daylight, it didn't seem like such a joke.

"He's with the others. Good riddance," Alfred said with a note of satisfaction. "We need to decide how to legally handle the attacks on the property."

"Levi has an in with the Texas Rangers," she said. "I'm just not sure how the jurisdiction works down here."

With a steely smile Alfred said, "Looks like we'll find out before too long."

She gave a laugh and smacked him gently on the shoulder. "You need a hand in the kitchen? Or is Sienna helping you out?" She glanced around the garage space. "I should go see how she's doing."

"Not to worry. I've been checking in on her on a regular basis. Gave her breakfast and took her up coffee and a snack. It wouldn't hurt if you stopped in and said hi. Although I know your life is a bit on edge right now. We don't need her mixed up in this at the moment."

Of course he'd been looking after Sienna. But still, Ice should see how the woman was doing. This wasn't the welcome she'd planned. Then again, she hadn't really planned for visitors either—friendly or unfriendly—and both types had arrived anyway.

Ice smiled. "I have no idea what's going on with all the electronics here, but it does look like there's less than half of what we brought in last night." She turned toward the windows into the garage bay next door. "And it looks like the vehicle is gone too." Ice frowned and turned to study Alfred's face. "Really? Did they leave us with anything to learn from?"

"That's actually why the men stayed up. They got what they wanted before the equipment was collected."

"Smart." She turned to head back into the main part of the house. "Hope they got what they needed too."

JUST BECAUSE LEVI was tired and his body needed rest did not mean his mind was ready to shut down. Lying in bed after a quick shower, his hands rested under his head on the pillow. Levi stared at the ceiling. He had the largest room in the place—almost an apartment in itself. He chose that deliberately. Not only was it his house, his place, his company, but he had not expected to be here alone. This was meant to be his and Ice's room.

And how the hell would he get her in here now?

He'd been wrong about Bullard. Levi had been wrong about a lot of things in life. But he wasn't about the fact that he and Ice deserved to be together. They were meant to be together. But Bullard was here, and he had made it clear that he'd be ready to take Ice away with him. And if Levi didn't do something fast to make her a happy woman, Levi could consider her as good as gone.

Levi didn't want to believe Bullard would cross that line.

But Levi also knew it had more to do with Ice's decision than Bullard's. Because, regardless of what either of the men said, Ice would make that choice, and it would be rough on the man left behind. In spite of it all, Levi was good friends with Bullard. Levi respected Bullard.

Levi's argument with Ice just before he'd been in the accident had been really shitty timing. It hadn't given them a chance to clear up what was wrong.

And then he'd felt like so much less of a man afterward. One with no future. No good prospects. Although he knew Ice would rip his throat apart for such a sexist remark, he couldn't help thinking that, as the man, he wanted to provide for his family. Ice wanted children one day. He just didn't know if he was capable of giving them to her. He'd sustained an injury to the groin area with some doubt that his sperm count would be normal. He might not be able to produce children.

This relationship would be the death of him. He had no idea what he was supposed to do about this. To him, it was damn simple. So why the hell wasn't she here beside him? With those thoughts twisting through his head, he closed his eyes and fell into a rough asleep.

Just under four hours later he woke up. He already knew he was four minutes early. Too many years in the military to stop that kind of mental training. It was also a godsend. His body hated to wake up to the racket of an alarm. That jerk awake wiped out a good hour of restful sleep.

He dressed quickly and headed downstairs. The fact that he got four hours undisturbed meant nothing had gone wrong. He'd admit he was disappointed he'd lost the vehicle and the bulk of the electronics that went with the weapons to Jackson, but Levi understood exactly why it happened. And he'd been prepared.

Besides, they'd kept detailed images of everything. What he needed to do was find Rodriguez, fast. Before Rodriguez tried to get at Levi again. Because Rodriguez would. There was no doubt on that point.

In the kitchen was the proverbial pot of coffee, which he was grateful to see. He poured himself a cup, then turned around to study the monitors. Rhodes was at the control room on the computers. And it looked like Ice was with him. That was good enough for him.

Levi walked upstairs to see them. He really respected the builder for having built this fortress. And Levi was thankful for it. They still had some modifications and upgrades to make, but, without the plans that had been set into motion decades ago by his uncle, no doubt they would have had much worse casualties than they had last night.

At the doorway to the control room he watched Ice go through the last hours of video, making sure absolutely nothing had been missed. She was like that. She kept track of details like no one else he knew. When she came to an end, he asked, "Satisfied?"

Ice turned, her gaze warming, making the inside of his heart ease back slightly. Surely she cared.

She studied his face, as if checking to see how well rested he looked. Always watching. Always caring for everyone else. Ice would make a hell of a mother.

"Looks like all was quiet," Ice said. "I went back through the video feeds since last evening. I didn't see anything that we missed, so I'm confident we're clear at the moment."

"I still want to walk through it. Make sure they didn't plant anything."

Her eyebrows arched, and she twisted her lips into a

thoughtful frown. "Okay, I'll go with you. I should get up and stretch my legs for a bit."

She turned to Rhodes. "You doing okay here?"

He waved them off silently. She was okay leaving him alone to watch the monitors, knowing the other guys would be here soon anyway. She walked to Levi. He wrapped an arm around her shoulders, and together they stepped out the front door of the house. Outside they stopped, and their eyes adjusted to the bright sunlight. The temperatures were soaring; it would be well in the eighties.

"Let's head up the road a bit."

She didn't argue but stepped forward smartly. He smiled. He could take her out of the military, but it was pretty damn hard to take the military out of her. It was easy to keep pace. She was tall and lean yet still only came to his shoulder. When she wanted to move, she could. They strolled in companionable silence for the next few minutes, came around the corner where the vehicle had been parked last night, about one-quarter mile from the house. He wondered about broaching the subject uppermost in his mind.

"What's that?" She stopped and pointed.

He caught the reflection out of the corner of his eye, grabbed her by the shoulder, and threw them both into the ditch.

Her cry of pain pierced the quiet.

And he knew he had been too late.

Chapter 13

ICE ROLLED OVER and shoved her face into the gravel. Cries were struggling to get out of her throat as pain rippled through her system. She clutched at her arm, feeling the blood coat her fingers. Goddammit, she'd been hit. A sniper had taken her out. Just when they had thought they were out of danger with nobody watching the place.

They were fools. In the background she could hear Levi talking to somebody on the phone. Presumably calling for help. She wasn't badly hurt—but she was angrier than hell.

Levi had thrown her off to the side. Once again keeping her out of danger, protecting her. She should've reacted faster. She should've protected herself. She should've been more aware.

"Don't move," Levi said, his body holding hers close to the ground protectively.

"I wasn't planning on it," she muttered. "He hit me in the arm. But it's not bad."

"How can you tell? You haven't even looked at it yet."

She twisted enough to see his face and then cried out in pain again. His lips came down on hers and stifled the next sound before it could escape. She shuddered under the weight of his body, the caress of his lips. As he went to lift his head, she raised hers, her lips clinging to him. She didn't want to lose the connection. It seemed like so long.

"Shh," he whispered against her lips. "It'll be fine."

She barely understood his words until he reached up and stroked moisture off her eyes. *Only with Levi.* She didn't know, couldn't remember on one hand the number of times she had actually cried. But something about knowing she was safe in his strong arms allowed her to be vulnerable. She knew he'd look after her.

Gasping for breath against the waves of pain, she lay there until her body slowly rebalanced. "I'll be fine," she whispered. "I wish I was home already, but, given that we're not too far away, I can walk back."

"Not happening," Levi whispered. "Men are even now scouring the hills. Someone is coming to collect you."

He didn't move, instead he clasped his arms behind her head and cuddled her close, his body protective above hers. The only way she would get shot at again was if the bullet went through him.

She smiled up at him. "What the hell is wrong with us?" He raised his eyebrows and started to answer, but she reached up and kissed his lips instead. "Look at us. We left the military, set up this company, and are in more danger than ever."

Soberly he stared down at her "Are you sorry? Do you wish you'd never left?" He took a deep breath and added, "Do you want to go back?"

"It's really not the right time to ask me when I'm lying here with a bullet hole in my arm," she said quietly. "No, I don't want to. Like I said, we need to sort this out. I don't feel like I have a future here right now."

"How is it you can't have a future here?" he whispered. "You are the other half of me. This is who we were meant to be."

"So then why are we sleeping in separate rooms?" She searched his eyes, for the truth. "There's a hot and cold element here. Most of the time our relationship is on a cool professional level. Only lately it shifted ... but not enough."

Levi frowned, his brows drawn together.

She wanted to scream. "Look, I know that didn't make a lot of sense, but it's like I'm here, but I don't really have a role. I'm not sure if I am your partner, but I am your partner. I'm not your wife because we're not married. I'm not your lover because we're not lovers. I'm a friend, but that's not the way we're supposed to be."

He lowered his head gently and kissed her. The brush of his lips whispered against hers. "No, you're not my wife because we're not married. Yes, you're my partner because you're my business partner. Yes, you are my friend because we are friends. But you're also so much more. You're the love of my life." He shrugged in disbelief. "How is it you can't know that?"

"How is it I would? You tell me I'm part of this relationship, and that I'm yours, yet you don't take me in your arms and make me yours." She let her voice trail off as she watched his face. Was it really possible that the big silent, strong Levi, the man who did the worst of the missions for the military, was afraid of something? When his eyes dropped and slipped to the side, she knew she was right. But what was he afraid of?

"And how do you think I feel when you throw Bullard at me?" he asked.

He stared into her eyes and this time it was her gaze that lowered.

She could hear sounds of the vehicle coming up behind him from the compound. She knew their time together alone was almost over. Again.

"Bullard is Plan B," she said simply.

"Don't let there be one," he said. "Give me a little longer to make this right."

"And why is it you need time?"

The vehicle pulled up beside them. He looked down at her, back at the men, then at her again, and whispered, "Could you just please give me that little bit?"

She stared into his eyes for as long as they had, and then she nodded. She had to put her plan into effect. Even if it meant the end of them. She couldn't keep going on like this. That's one thing Bullard's arrival had shown her—the status quo had to change, one way or another. "You have twenty-four hours. Or else …"

His gaze narrowed, and his lips thinned. "Don't make threats," he warned.

He slowly backed up and helped her stand. They were behind the protective steel of the big truck.

Quietly she added, "I'm not, but if you don't do something about us, I will." And she turned to let Dave help her into the backseat of the truck.

Levi didn't get in with her. He gave her a hard stare as he closed the door gently behind her. Then he disappeared into the hillside. Ice watched until he was out of sight as Dave turned the big rig around and headed back into the compound.

Rhodes sat beside her. "How bad is it?" he asked.

She gave him a lopsided grin and said, "Bad enough to feel like shit. Not enough to need more than a few days off."

"Bullard will make that decision," Dave said. "And this time you won't be assisting him."

"Then who will?" She snorted. "We're a little short on

medical personnel. Too bad Sienna doesn't have any training."

"It doesn't matter. I do," Dave said.

And sure enough, back in the compound, with their assistance, she hopped out of the truck and carefully walked into the sick bay.

She plastered a smile on her face when she saw Logan was awake. "Now that's a sight to see," she cried out and grabbed his fingers. "How are you feeling?"

His smile lit his face, and then his gaze dropped, seeing blood dripping steadily down her arm. "What the hell happened to you?"

She felt a little on the shaky side. She reached over, grasped the side rail of his bed, and very gently inched her way up and into the second bed Harrison had vacated. "We'll need Bullard here permanently if we keep getting shot at."

"You didn't answer me." Logan sat up slowly to glare at her. "What happened? And are you the only one who got hurt?"

Bullard arrived, rushing into the room and across the floor to her side. The worry in his face eased when he heard her talking normally. She gave them both a rundown of what happened and ended with telling them the rest of the men had gone out looking for the sniper.

"Good." Bullard, in his calm, no fussy way, quickly cut off her sleeve. When he got to where her fingers were pressed against the wound, he said, "You have to remove your hand so I can take a closer look."

She gave him a lazy smile. "I haven't looked at it myself. At the moment it's not hurting at all. The minute I see it, you know it'll make me scream."

Logan reached over and grabbed her dangling hand and held it gently. "And, if you need to scream, we won't tell anyone. Promise."

She laughed. "I think I screamed plenty on the hillside."

"I doubt it. You were still in the war zone. No way you would have made a sound."

She slowly pulled her fingers off her wound, and Bullard cut the shirt up to her shoulder and removed it. The blood continued to ooze, and she knew she should take a look, but, damn it, she hated this part. She turned to glance at her upper arm and could see the blood still running down in a steady stream. The hole in her arm made her gasp in shock. She opened her mouth to speak, but waves of pain crashed in on her, and her stomach heaved.

Bullard reached down and gently examined the back of the arm to see if the bullet had gone through. And the pain hit a crescendo. Greasy waves slammed into her, and her stomach rose up to her throat and filled her head. She collapsed into the bed in a dead faint.

IT WAS EARLY afternoon. Why the hell would anybody set up a sniper shot for that time of day? If it had been Levi, he would have been long gone. But these men were proving to be a different kind of animal altogether.

Four men searched the area, but, so far, they'd found nothing.

Anger still rippled through him. They'd been complacent, thinking everything was fine because they couldn't see anything wrong in their security feeds.

And that was not good. He may not be equipped with a comm or anything else, but he had a cell phone.

He sent a text message for an update on Ice's injury. When there was no immediate response, he shoved his phone back into his pocket and continued to search. It took another ten minutes to make it to where he figured the sniper had been. Staying close to the ground, he studied the area to see what he could find. He checked the position, realized the line-up was wrong, and moved over fifteen feet. There he crouched down to reassess.

Cigarette butts. Again. Same unfiltered brand he'd seen left behind before on the other side of the hill when they'd been reassessing the security of the compound.

So likely the same man watching them.

He picked up several butts and stuffed them into his pocket. They didn't have the capabilities to test for DNA, but he knew who could. If this was Rodriguez, then Jackson would want to know.

He took several long looks around to see if anything else could be found, like shell casings. A good sniper would take them with him. Only it wasn't always possible. And sometimes you just missed one. But it didn't look like that was the case this time.

Taking a seat at the same place where the sniper had been, he studied the area, wondering what the man had been looking for—what he'd seen.

His cell phone beeped.

Pulling it from his pocket, he saw Alfred's message.

The men have checked the area. Cigarette butts, but nothing else is out there.

He quickly texted back.

I'm coming in. How's Ice?

When it came, the response was from Dave.

She's bleeding badly. I'm helping out, but get back here.

The words had him bolting to his feet, racing toward the compound. He slammed into the sick bay.

"Stay back," Bullard roared. "This is a medical area. We need it as sterile as possible."

From the doorway Levi could see the blood dripping in an ever-widening pool. Dave had hooked up an IV, moving the pole to the head of Ice's bed. Bloody clothes were on both sides, and the place looked like a trauma room.

And he guessed that was exactly what it was.

Everyone stood in place, waiting.

Finally Bullard made a loud exclamation. "Got it." He grinned and stepped back slightly. He turned to face Levi. "The bullet nicked a vein. Had to clamp that sucker down and stitch it up." His grin widened. "How's your fresh blood supply?"

And that's when Levi understood something else. In two days, they'd needed Bullard's medical knowledge like he never thought they would. What the hell would they do when he left? His skills were second to none. Whether out in the field or in the hospital, he knew his stuff.

And the only person he could replace Bullard with was another doctor. How the hell would they find one who would be happy to step in when needed, but not miss it otherwise?

Preferably with military experience.

He knew he had to do something ... and fast.

No way could he put his men in danger over and over again and not have the right help here for them when the shit hit the fan.

His gaze locked on Ice's pale face. She looked like her name. Cold. Still. Frozen. His heart seized as he watched Bullard and Dave efficiently bandage up the wound.

He could put her in danger.

Not again.

He'd rather die than see her hurt.

She should go home with Bullard—where she'd be safe.

Chapter 14

CE WOKE UP with a chill. She rolled her head to the side and smiled to see Logan, lying beside her. They were a hell of a pair. She let her gaze roam the room as far as she could see without moving her body. Any kind of movement would hurt like a bitch.

Ice really hated pain, and, for someone who felt that way, she was living with a lot of it.

Still it was imperative no one knew about the internal agony. She'd solve the problem with Levi, somehow. But it wasn't the current priority, given that her arm hurt like hell. Slowly holding her breath, she rolled to her back and was pleasantly surprised when the rest of her body didn't scream at her.

"There you are." Bullard's voice reached across the room to her.

Even though she couldn't see his face, she smiled at his voice. He was a hell of a man. As he loomed over her, she reached up to touch his cheek. "Glad to know you were here. The right man at the right place."

He laughed. "Only not the right man for you?"

She winced. She hadn't planned on bringing that up.

"Just checking," He patted her hand and smiled. "Remember the offer is always open. There is a chance that, one of these days, you'll change your answer."

"What's the question?" Logan asked, then reached up and rubbed the sleep from his eyes. His involuntary cry of pain had Bullard shifting from Ice's bed to his.

She listened with half an ear as Bullard checked Logan over. Her injury appeared to be in the upper arm, but the details of how she got it were a little sketchy.

Still, she remembered enough. The pain was a huge deterrent for trying to recall much more. When he was done with Logan, Bullard turned back to check on her again. She asked, "Did they find him?"

Bullard shook his head. "No. They did a full search of the area and found more cigarette butts of the same kind found on our side of the hill, but no sign of who the sniper was."

"That's what I figured would happen anyway." She turned to study her arm as Bullard gently cut open the bandage. "How bad is it?"

He shrugged. "I've seen a lot worse. You'll do fine. The bleeding stopped. You will feel very tired and weak because you lost a lot of blood. Something you're not equipped for here."

"Is anyone, other than a hospital?"

He turned a smug look her way. "I have a full supply at home."

"Yes." She gave a small laugh. "But the rules in Africa versus the rules here are probably quite different."

"There is that. But I bet you can get some if you needed to."

She nodded. "It's something I have to look into the regulations for. I'm not a nurse. I'm not exactly sure if we're required to get a license for something like that."

"I could get you one." He laughed.

She rolled her eyes. "That figures. Like a lot of things here, it borders on the edge of legal. We've tried hard, but some of the rules just don't fit with the kind of work we've been doing."

After he rebandaged her arm, he brought a glass of water to her. Grateful, she drank quickly. As she handed the glass back, she tried to get up.

"You need to stay in bed, and drink lots of liquids. Your body will replenish your blood supply, but it'll take time. I can transfer you to your room where you will be more comfortable, or you can stay here and keep Logan company. But you are not in any condition to be wandering around the place, getting into the control room, or making any attempt to show up for meals at the table." He narrowed his gaze and wiped off a smile. "Got it?"

She glanced at Logan. "Why can't he go to his room too?"

"I was hoping somebody would campaign for my side." Logan looked over at her gratefully. "I sure wouldn't mind getting back there." He glanced at Bullard. "No offense, Doc."

"None taken." Bullard stood in front of the two of them and tapped his finger on his chin as he contemplated options.

"As long as I can come in and check on you every four hours, I don't have a problem with you both returning to your quarters. However, the minute you refuse to let me enter, give me trouble about checking your wounds, or I see you doing too much, you're back in here. Agreed?"

Logan's face lit up. "Agreed."

"Oh, I definitely agree." Ice's room was much better than this cold clinical space.

She sat up carefully and threw back the covers. Lowering her feet to the floor and putting her weight on them as she stood up, she made use of the handrails on the bed. She was proud of the fact the room only swayed a little. She kept her grip on the steel guards until she thought it was safe to take a step. She took one, then a second. By the time she turned back around, Bullard was there with a sling. "What are you doing getting up without me?" he scolded.

Gently he suspended her arm, taking the weight off her shoulder. Instantly it felt better.

"Keep that on most of the time, even while sleeping."

"Any chance of a shower?" she asked hopefully. She looked down at her bloodstained clothes and knew the rest of her would be covered too. "It would certainly make me feel better if nothing else."

"Not today. You'll have to make do with a washcloth. We'll see how it is in the morning."

Disappointed, she nodded. She was just damn glad to go to her room. Her own bed would feel so much better. She looked over at Logan, sitting up on the edge of the bed, and asked, "Shall we limp away upstairs together?"

He grinned. "Absolutely."

"You're not going without me. And we need to add a wheelchair to the list of supplies. Until then, I'll make sure you get there safely." Bullard walked between the two of them and held out his arms. With both of them holding on gently, they exited the medical bay.

Ice looked behind her and saw the mess. "Sorry I'm not able to help clean this up."

"Not an issue. By the way, Alfred mentioned you were keeping Sienna in the dark about this." He raised an eyebrow at her. "How long do you think that'll work?"

"If we can, it would be best. I'm not sure she'll stay. So why let her in on the secrets or the trauma she might carry away in the form of nightmares for years to come?"

"Makes sense. But she could have helped us through all this." He nodded at the room. "But I guess it might have sent her screaming into the night."

"Exactly."

"Also, in case you get into your own bed today, Alfred has changed your sheets."

Just the sound of that was incredible. All she wanted to do was lie down in her room and go back to sleep. She gritted her teeth and hung on as they slowly made their way to the elevator. This was the first time she realized just how valuable it was.

With a quick glance at Logan, realizing he was in about the same shape, the two exchanged glances and straightened their backs. No way in hell would they let anybody else know how weak they were. They went to Logan's room first.

She dropped her hand from Bullard's arm and said, "I'm not far away. I'll keep going."

"And I will check on you later," Bullard said.

The two men disappeared into Logan's bedroom. Finally alone, Ice had no problem placing a hand on the wall, using it for support as she made her way down to her suite.

Her door was unlocked, probably because of Alfred. She pushed the door open and leaned against the frame for a moment. She just felt so crappy. And this room was very welcoming, but also so damn lonely.

Alfred suddenly appeared at her side. "Do you need help?"

She gave him a small smile. "I should be fine. I'll just rest here for a moment to gather the strength to make my way across to that big bed."

He grinned. "You do that. I brought you extra pillows so you could prop up your arm and maybe sleep on an angle, depending on how the pain level will be."

"Thank you," she said warmly, then made a sudden decision. "There is just one thing about this room."

"Oh?" Alfred leaned against the opposite side of the doorframe, his arms crossed over his chest, that all too observant gaze of his fixed on her face. "What is that?"

Knowing she shouldn't say anything about it but too tired to care, and with her walls completely decimated with the pain and events of the last couple days, she said, "I live here alone. I should be in Levi's room."

An awkward silence passed as he contemplated her words. He looked at the bed, at her, then across the hall to where Levi's room was. "You know something? I think you're correct. And that just might be the best thing to do right now." He grinned. "You shouldn't be alone anyway. So how about I help you into bed, then I will just move your stuff. We won't even tell him."

She dropped her gaze to the floor and then shook her head. "No, that wouldn't be fair. He has to have a choice in the matter."

"Really? And how much have you actually given him already?"

"Lots," she said with spirit. "But he never takes me up on it."

"So then maybe it's time to take things in hand yourself."

She watched his eyes twinkle with sly understanding but also realized he was serious. She glanced at her room and across the hall. And then with gleaming eyes she looked back at him—and nodded. "Lead the way."

LEVI WATCHED THE monitors. Outside of journeying into the kitchen to grab coffee and a fresh bran muffin, he'd been sitting here in the control room for the last couple hours, wondering if the danger level was low enough that they could go back to their normal routine.

However, with the loss of innocence, it meant they could no longer ignore they were targets. If they had to do four-hour shifts until Rodriguez was captured, well, it was a small price to pay to have no one else hurt.

Thinking about that, he decided it was time to check up on Logan and Ice in the sick bay. With any luck they were awake. He'd been in earlier, but they'd both been asleep.

Stone walked in at that time. He looked more rested.

"How are you doing?" Levi asked.

"Better." Stone sat down heavily in the chair. His massive girth—all hard disciplined muscle—made the chair look so damn small. "Had a decent sleep. Could use some food though. Just have to find Alfred for that."

"I swung by the kitchen and grabbed two muffins and a cup of coffee. Life is good, but I'm ready to eat steak, baked potatoes, Caesar salad, and half a chocolate cake, and that's just the appetizers," Levi said with a grin. "What about you?"

"As I'm no longer stuck with office duty, I'm good," Stone said cheerfully. "I'm happy to say, Sienna appears to be whipping that place into shape just fine without me."

Levi laughed. "It looks like she can handle it nicely. I'd like to give her a job if she's a good fit. Jarrod can't come see her for a bit yet, and I'd hate to leave her to her own devices again. She hasn't given us any of her backstory, and I'd like her to feel safe enough to do so."

"Good," Stone said. "Because I'm not going back in the office. So what was that about food?"

"Well, I'll get right on that. But first I need to swing by the sick bay and check on the patients, then I'll find Alfred and see what we have for real meat. A couple of steaks would be a good start."

With a fat grin, Stone added, "With a half-dozen baked potatoes too." He motioned Levi out of the room. "Go find the master of the meals and see that we are fed properly."

With a bark of laughter Levi walked out. This was one thing he never intended to short the men on—real food. It was way too important for all of them.

In the sick bay he stopped in the middle of the room. Both beds were empty, yet the place was dirty with bedding to be changed, so they hadn't been gone long. It surprised him as he didn't think they were in any shape to leave. But it was a really good sign.

Then his heart sank. It was a good sign as long as they left of their own free will, with Bullard's permission. It was not a good one if somebody kidnapped them. He marched to the security logs and brought up the monitors, checking the feed from the sick bay doors. It was the only way intruders could manage to come in. He swung back to the last couple hours and, with relief, saw he had nothing to worry about. So where the hell were they?

As he shut down the monitor, Bullard walked back into the room, his arms full with clean sheets and bedding.

"There you are," Levi said. "I'm surprised to see both of them gone."

Bullard dropped his armload on the closest table and efficiently stripped the sheets off both beds. "I sent them to their rooms on the condition they go to bed and stay there and let me check up on them every four hours. They're not to leave their rooms to do anything that'll cause any further injury."

That news also made Levi feel a lot better. It meant the pair of them were on the mend. And that lightened his mood. "I'll check on them in a few minutes. I'm tracking down Alfred, seeing if we can get some decent meals set up for the next couple days."

"Last I saw him, he was talking to Dave. I think they were planning just that. Dave said he was bored and was looking for a feast. So—"

"It's hardly the right time for a feast, considering we still haven't caught Rodriguez, but the men are looking for some real food."

"Oh my. If Dave's up for a feast, you don't want to be turning him down." The two exchanged smiles. Dave was a wizard in the kitchen.

"You need a hand here or are you okay if I go and talk to the chefs?"

Bullard shrugged. "Go take care of the food. I've got this. There's not much left to do anyway."

Reassured and feeling better on all fronts, Levi headed into the kitchen and found Bullard was right. Dave and Alfred had a notepad out, concocting a dozen dishes.

Levi heard just enough to make his mouth water. He filled his coffee cup, stepped out into the R&D room, as Ice called it, realizing he was avoiding seeing her. There were any number of reasons—she could be sleeping, and she needed to heal. But in reality all he wanted to do was hold her in his arms. She might be better off with Bullard, but, now that Levi had had time to think, he'd be damned if he could let her go that easily. She'd given him an ultimatum and had promptly gotten shot. The time frame didn't matter. She was his. And he'd do everything he could to keep her.

He turned, snagged a second cup of coffee, and walked to her room.

Chapter 15

S HE'D NEVER LOVED anybody but Levi. However, the stalemate hurt so badly.

When she'd been in the military if a woman had come to her with this problem, Ice would have told her exactly what she should do.

It had taken Alfred to help her see this clearly. Well, that was good enough for her.

She sat on the edge of Levi's bed, shaking as Alfred quickly moved over the pillows from her room and helped her get in and lean back against the mahogany headboard. She'd switched out of her bloodied clothes and into her bathrobe.

Then Alfred returned with some of her clothing. Being in the military as long as she had, she'd kept her possessions neat and minimal. It wasn't difficult to pack her up and move her over. With the next load, Alfred brought her toiletries. Then came her PJs. She stared at them. She'd be so much more comfortable in them... but the thought of changing—well, that was too much effort.

She glanced up to see Alfred carrying her empty bags. He stashed them in the closet.

"I think your room is clear." He gave her a conspiratorial smile, then left, gently closing the door behind him.

Alone, she studied the room. Levi's bed was set slightly

back from the main area so he'd have to come all the way in before he'd see her.

And then he'd have to face her, because she wasn't leaving until they settled this. Only she was in no shape to fight.

Maybe it wouldn't be required.

She no longer knew what she wanted. No, that was a lie. She knew exactly what she wanted and that was what Levi and she'd *had* before their devastating argument about children. A hot passionate relationship, a sense of knowing all was well between them. A need to know she was one half of the same special twosome she'd made with him before.

What the hell had happened?

They'd argued over having children. That was before he was injured. Then, when she'd pulled back in the relationship with Levi, Bullard had stepped up. And she'd let him, as a friend.

She'd been confused because Levi hadn't explained why he was so adamant, so against ever having a family. She might have understood if it'd been something to do with the fact that one day he may not come home. That's why so few SEALs were married. Most of them made lousy husbands anyway.

It had all started as a minor argument, something to settle later. But somehow it had become a big deal. Although she'd never thought it would be the end of them. Only then they'd had bigger fights building on that little argument.

Before they had time to fix it, he'd been hurt. And that had changed the relationship even more. Bringing something new into the equation. Something she didn't understand and he wouldn't talk about.

Now the chasm had become too great to easily cross.

Just like that, tears welled up inside and the dam broke.

It seemed like she could do nothing to stop it. She curled up on the bed with just her bathrobe wrapped around her and cried. The tears were for the children she'd never know, for the ache in her heart she could already feel.

She barely heard the door open and didn't hear anybody approach. But when warm, caring arms wrapped around her, picked her up carefully, and held her close, she knew it was Levi.

And she cried that much harder. This was so not her. This was the opposite of how she wanted Levi to see her. But it seemed like she no longer had the same walls nor barriers up. She was broken.

Something inside her screamed for so much more.

But she couldn't stop blubbering. She didn't think she had ever broken down like this before. A lifetime of pain, hurt, and sorrow was just waiting to be free, and, now that the dam was open, it was like she had no control. This was not what he wanted from her. She was Ice. Inside and out— cold, restrained during the day, and fiery in bed but immediately donning the mantle of control afterward.

Surely the pain and drugs were the reason she'd lost control.

Of course there was another trigger too … Bullard had reminded her of his offer to take her away from all this. She appreciated it, a chance to build a life and be happy but she didn't know that she could leave Levi.

And she knew it was still open, which meant it was an option … and that hurt. She hadn't thought it would come to this.

Because it was Levi who held her, she bawled even harder.

"Easy, honey, please don't cry. You'll make yourself

sick."

His hands gently stroked up and down her back, but the way his fingers seemed to hit every rib bone and every vertebrae just reminded her of what she'd lost when she left the military. She thought it would be the opposite. The training had been grueling and maintaining her position stressful. But she'd been in charge. Since walking away to join Levi, it was like her life had spun out of control. She didn't know who she was or where she belonged. And the pounds, never easy to hang on to, just completely fell away. She was a rack of bones now. The problem was, she didn't give a damn. Too much else was going on.

"Easy, baby. Take it easy. Whatever's wrong, we can fix it."

"Fix it?" she cried. "How is that possible when we have no relationship left to even fix?"

"Don't say that." Levi stared down at her, his eyes full of hurt. "Please don't say that. You're my life."

She recognized the note of desperation in his voice. Abruptly she said, "Bullard still wants me to leave with him."

Levi froze, shock rendering his body still. And the look in his eyes ... it damn-near broke her heart.

His voice came out in a gasp of pain as he asked, "Are you leaving?"

"I moved into your room instead," she whispered.

She was instantly crushed against his chest. And it felt so damn good that she ignored the pain.

"I don't think I would survive if you left," he whispered. "You're the reason I come home from every mission."

"We have always had problems," she said, her voice steadying. "We've had them for years."

"Those don't matter. You're the one who left my bed,

but it's like you stepped out of my life and built these walls, putting distance between us. Not the way I wanted it. I don't like this."

She stared into his face. "I need more. Maybe not today or tomorrow, but down the road, I will need more."

"Children?" he asked, his voice gritty with pain. "The doctor said I might not be able to have any."

She reached out to smooth the lines off his face. It wasn't something they'd discussed before. It was, however, something close to his heart. She also knew it made him feel less than a man, and that was not what she was doing here.

"I understand the fear. But even before your accident you didn't want them." She sat up and settled herself on his thighs, holding her injured arm close to her chest. "Now you might not be able to, so you're relieved not to face that burden." She shrugged and looked at him. "It's different for me. I want children. There are no guarantees that either of us *can* have them, but there are other avenues open to us if we want to take them."

"We had a hell of an argument about children before," he admitted. "And then came the accident... We haven't made love since."

"And why is that?"

He turned his gaze to stare at the window. Then he took a stuttering breath. "Maybe you *should* leave with Bullard."

Shocked, she reared back to look at him. Her eyes filled once again with tears and she shook her head. "No. I would give up a lifetime with Bullard if I could just sleep in your arms. But you cut me out. You wouldn't let me hold you during your recovery. Yes, I want children." When she saw him open his mouth to protest, she added, "But you weren't even open to the concept. Before, when you were off on missions all the time, I understood. You didn't want to risk dying and leaving me alone. But it's a chance I would be willing to take. Especially now."

"Why now?" he asked. "What's different about now?"

"Because I almost lost you."

"I might be a horrible father." His voice was dark with pain. "But what I've come to understand is, I'm no longer 100 percent against the idea. You know my childhood was horrific. I'd do anything to avoid another going through what I did."

She reached up and smiled. "No child of yours could ever go through something like that because you would not be your father. No matter how afraid you are of becoming him, it won't happen."

His smile twisted and the vulnerable look deepened. "Are you sure?"

She nodded. "I'm positive. Besides, I'll be there. I'd kick your ass."

He gave a great shout of laughter and wrapped her up in the gentlest of hugs.

LEVI HATED TO see Ice break down.

He hated to see her hurting. But what he really didn't like was to think he was the cause of it. He tilted her chin up gently with his thumb, stroking her cheeks and pulling the last of the wet streaks off her soft skin, then lowered his face and gave her a gentle kiss.

Trust her to take matters in her own hands. If only she'd done it months ago.

It would have saved them a ton of pain, when he hadn't been strong enough to fix this himself.

He gently turned her until she lay on her back. He hated her small cry when he jolted her arm. As she lay there, blonde hair spilling across the pillow, he knew he'd never seen anyone more beautiful. He lowered his head. "You are my world. I don't want you to leave with him. I love you. I always have. You know that."

She pulled his head down for a deep kiss, her good arm wrapping around his neck. The heat burst forth, not just passion, but longing so intense it seemed to swell between the two of them, filling them before cascading through and over them. God, he wanted her. She was the best thing to ever happen to him, and she just proved it yet again tonight. He reached up, sliding his fingers through her hair, massaging her scalp as he kissed away the longing, and the pain and the tears. When she held him close, he knew he was the luckiest man ever.

He slid his hands up under her thin robe to cup her breasts, always a perfect fit for his hands. He shuddered, feeling the nipples harden under his palm, her bare thigh wrapping around his hips. She'd always been hot in bed. He'd never met another woman like her, nor ever wanted another one since.

Even injured she drove him crazy. And somehow she had lost the sling.

She kissed him frantically, her fingers sliding under his shirt, searching for and finding his skin, the scars, and the damaged muscles which she skimmed over as if they didn't bother her.

And why would they? She'd never been concerned with appearances. He was the fool, though a damned grateful one.

As her fingertips slipped inside his belt, reaching for him below, his body was already shuddering, nerve endings warning him this session would be over faster than he'd like.

He rolled to his back and gently helped her straddle his lap—and an alarm shattered their moment.

Ice tumbled to the bed, crying out as she jarred her arm. After a quick glance to make sure she was all right, he sprang for the door.

Damn it. Talk about shitty timing.

Chapter 16

A S SOON AS Levi bolted, Ice struggled into a simple jacket to cover her chest, then put her sling on. She'd managed to pull on her jeans and otherwise finished dressing as she made her way to the control room. If Bullard saw her, he'd throw a fit. But these weren't normal circumstances.

She could sit on a chair and watch the monitors just as well as sitting in her bed. Or rather Levi's.

But she sure wished the damn alarm had rung a few hours later.

Alfred and Stone were already in the control room.

"Oh, no, you don't," Alfred snapped. "Get back to bed."

Dave walked in, looking dashing in a gentleman's smoking coat. She kept her smile to herself and headed for the monitors.

"I'm fine and would rather know what's happening than hiding out and worrying." She patted his shoulder gently with her uninjured hand. "If it's all good, I'll go back to bed." She leaned forward to look at the monitors. "What's going on?"

"Intruder coming in the second garage," Stone said. "Looks to be the only one."

"Who's checking it out?" she asked.

"Levi and Bullard have both gone down. Rhodes and Merk are checking the other entrances." Stone leaned forward to peer closer at the monitor. He reached out and tapped the one on the left. "Appears something is up on the hill."

Everyone leaned closer. "Is it blocking the camera?" she asked. "Or is someone up there?"

"We can't see clearly enough." Stone made a few tweaks on the angles. "We also need to put up firewalls to stop the damn hackers."

"I can help you with that." Dave patted Stone's shoulder. "We'll also make a few adjustments on the camera angles so you don't have that blind spot there. From my point of view, that blockage appears deliberate."

"Do we need to get somebody up there to take a look?" Ice turned to walk back outside. "I'll go."

"Lots of men here. They can take a look," Alfred protested. "You're injured. You need to get back to bed. They can go without you."

She laughed. Considering the recent session with Levi, she felt strong enough to do anything. "How many of them know about the secret exit that opens up to that part of the hillside? I will lead the men, that's all. They can do the rest. I promise. I'll stay at the entrance."

With men at her side, she headed for her gear. Slipping into her boots, she grabbed her vest, carefully slipped her arm out of the sling and put it on. With her good arm, she twisted her hair, gritted her teeth, clipped it up behind her head, and was delighted to realize the pain wasn't as bad as she'd expected.

It had to be Bullard's drugs.

But for the moment, she'd take it.

She grabbed the binoculars and headed down toward the hallway into the two exits. Rhodes was there waiting for her with one of Bullard's men. She gave a clipped nod and moved. "Let's go. Who knows if they've moved?"

Rhodes handed her a headpiece, which she quickly donned. Dropping her voice just above a whisper, she asked, "Stone, can you hear me?"

"Loud and clear." There was a slight crackle to the line, but there wasn't too much interference.

Good. That was a clean reception. She could work with that. "We're leaving the main part of the building now. We may lose some comm as we go through the tunnel."

"Hoping that won't happen," Stone said. "We were aware of that problem and put boosters in. The transmission should hold, so keep talking to me as you move through. Test it as you go."

"Thanks. Can you still see the blockage up on the hillside?" she asked.

"Affirmative."

She picked up the pace, holding her wounded arm to stop some of the jostling motion. "Okay, we're running through the tunnel right now. Turn on the lighting, please." Instantly the stone hallway was flooded with low ambient light.

"Oh, nice." She ran forward for another few minutes, then asked, "Can you still hear me, Stone?"

"Breaking up a little bit but you're coming in loud and clear. Looks like the boosters are working."

"Okay, we're less than thirty feet from the exit. Keep alert, everyone."

Once there she pulled her weapon free of her harness and stepped up to the door. With a nod Rhodes quickly opened the double wooden door, letting a slice of moonlight shine in. She slipped out and went low, sweeping the area.

As she'd promised to stay at the exit, she motioned to the others. Rhodes came behind her and swept high. In the distance she could see something.

Like hell she was staying behind.

Silently the three of them climbed the few feet to the crest of the ridge. What she saw was not what she'd expected. Approaching slowly, she took another couple steps toward the man lying on the ground. If he had a weapon in his hand, she would think he was lining up for a shot; instead he appeared to be motionless.

With Rhodes and Andrew, Bullard's man, covering her actions, she raced forward and held her gun to the man's head, then reached down to check for a pulse.

He was dead.

"Shit."

In her headset, Stone said, "What the hell? You were supposed to stay at the tunnel, damn it. I can see you bending over something. What's going on?"

"It's a dead man."

"You sure he's dead?" Stone asked in alarm. "Can you identify if it's his body that's blocking the camera?"

"Where is the camera?" In the half moonlight she studied the ground—the hidden spot was beyond her. She bent down and lifted the man's head. Using her cell phone's flashlight, she turned to look at the man's features. "It's one of the men who broke into the compound a few days ago."

"What?" Stone asked. "That doesn't make any sense."

"None of this does. But the fact is, we have a dead body on our land."

"Technically," she heard Alfred say, "that's not our land."

She nodded as his words crackled in her ear. "I know

that."

Crouching, she turned to study the rest of the area, but she found no sign of anything else moving. "Stone, do the tapes show how he arrived here?"

"I'm searching through them now," he said. "Give me a minute."

Rhodes and Andrew spread out as they searched the top of the hill, checking over the sides and down.

There were no roads here. So this intruder either came under his own steam or he'd been carried. And he was not small. No, it was probably foolish, but she couldn't help but look up and wonder if he'd been dropped. She hadn't heard a helicopter or plane, but that didn't mean there hadn't been one while they'd been inside. And she'd been otherwise busy ...

She looked down. No way to know how much damage was done to the body in this light. If he'd been dropped, his bones would be smashed to shit.

"Any progress on the intruder?" she asked.

"No, he appears to have taken off."

She shook her head. "I don't like the sound of that."

"None of us do. We're still searching. Looking to see if he left anything behind."

"You mean, besides a dead body?" she asked drily. "Maybe he killed his partners?"

"Possible," Stone said. "We can't afford to make that assumption."

"No assumptions here but it'd be nice to have an answer."

Rhodes approached. "I suggest we take him back into the tunnel. We haven't seen anyone out here, but that doesn't mean there aren't more of them."

"Good idea." She led the way back with the two men carrying the body. Inside she waved the men to go on first, then stepped outside the door and watched to see if anyone, or anything, stirred.

"Stone, can you see anything out there?"

"No, it's all clear."

With one final look, she slipped back inside. "Okay, coming home."

WHERE THE HELL was the intruder? Levi was growing tired of this shit. Not only had this asshole disturbed something very special between him and Ice, but the guy was proving too damn hard to find. With the men all spread out, they were systematically searching the lower floor. Stone said he thought no one was in the house, but that was not enough for Levi. They would check every damn hole to make sure nobody was inside.

They had alarms on the front and back doors, but now they would have them everywhere. Each with its own code so they knew which exit was in use. And, for some reason, the security outside hadn't been organized. Then they'd been running four-hour shifts and hadn't shut down for the night. Normally he'd do the final walk-through the place, but he'd been … busy.

His headset crackled as everyone checked in. No sign of the intruder.

"Damn it," he swore softly. "Where could he have gone?"

"I'm going through the tapes," Stone said. "We'll find him. But you need to get to the med bay and take a look at what Ice has brought home."

Ice? What the hell? She should be in bed. His bed!

He bolted for the medical room. Or had he misunder-stood? Was she back there because she was hurt? Had her stitches ripped open? Or something worse?

At the double doors, he slammed through in a panic—and came to a stop.

Not only was Ice *not* on one of the two beds but she was in combat boots and fully armed, standing over some guy lying down instead.

His gaze swept over the prone man, and Levi realized something else—the man was dead.

Chapter 17

ICE CAUGHT THE flicker in Levi's eyes. She straightened her back and gave him a cool look. She met him halfway. "I'm fine." She nodded toward the man on the bed. "He obviously isn't. However, we found no sign of anyone else around."

"Any idea what happened to him?"

Ice shook her head. "No idea beyond the bullet to his head."

"Right. We need to continue searching the building from top to bottom."

She nodded, and then a thought occurred. She spun to look at the others. "Did anybody check on Sienna?" They all shook their heads. Ice no longer had all her gear on. She walked to the monitors and hit the comm to call the control room. "Stone, have you checked Sienna's room?" She glanced at the men. "We need to make sure she's okay."

"Dave's on his way."

Dropping her hand, she shook her head, not liking any of this one bit. "Something feels seriously wrong." She studied the dead man. He'd been shot in the back of his head. "Levi, do you recognize this man?"

Levi stepped up beside her and looked. "Definitely one of the men who was here the other night."

She turned to look at Levi. "Originally we'd joked about

planning a morgue for this place. Now it looks like we need one. This is getting ridiculous." Her words might've been teasing, but her tone was not. The longer she stood here, the more the itchiness in the back of her head built. "Okay, we have to search every inch of this place. There is something wrong." She pointed to the two men standing across from her. "You two go to the garages and the R&D room. Stay fully armed, and watch your back. I swear to God, someone is inside."

Systematically and fast she and Levi swept the main floor. She studied the tunnel access. The door was slightly ajar. She motioned to Levi. He came up behind her, gun ready, and opened it. Nothing. He turned on the lights but could see nothing. That didn't mean somebody hadn't come in or gone out this way. "We've done one sweep already."

"Not good enough." She motioned toward the pantry and the kitchen and the butler's kitchen too. Basically what that meant was, there were too many places to hide.

She hit the intercom. "All hands on deck. We're assuming an intruder is still inside this building. First floor is clear. We're proceeding to a second-floor sweep."

"Why did you give our position away?" Levi asked. But no anger or disappointment was in his voice, just curiosity.

"Because I want him to find us," she said. "We have to flush him out somehow."

He grinned, his teeth flashing white in the darkness of the room. "I wouldn't expect anyone to try a stunt like this until we were all asleep."

"Except we're running four-hour shifts, so, in actual fact, we were never *all* asleep."

"Which would imply he would know that."

She shrugged. "We'll work to find the nuances of the

how and why later."

In tandem, as they had many times before during practice runs, they again swept through the lower floor of the building, checking out the nooks and crannies, the closets, the hallways. When they were clear, they moved up to the second floor. The other two men checked the garage and did a full sweep outside. She hadn't heard from Stone for a while. They did a full inspection of the second floor, coming up to the control room last. Without any warning, they charged in, guns ready, and found Stone and Alfred, sitting there, watching.

"Hey, guys. It's just us. Were fine. No sign of anyone yet."

Silently the two moved back out to the hallway. As they headed to the stairwell and last bedroom, they were silent. Outside Sienna's room, they found Dave standing guard. "She's fine," he whispered. "She's sleeping like a baby."

Levi nodded and motioned Ice to move ahead of him. They crept up the last staircase together. There wasn't much up here. Her now empty room and Levi's.

With a frown, they glanced at each other and headed toward hers first. They checked out the closets and bathroom, then turned to Levi's suite.

It bothered her to think someone had slipped into that space. It was her space—hers and Levi's—but then again, maybe someone expected her to be there right now. She was injured. What if the sniper knew he'd hit her, and about her relationship with Levi, and expected her to be in his room?

Gearing up for the confrontation, they burst through the door. She went low; Levi high.

Even as pain jarred her system at the movement, she gritted her teeth and charged through it. Things could have been much worse.

With the room open in front of them, they froze. There was nothing to see.

But they had to make sure. They checked the closets and bathroom. Like every other room so far, they found nobody. Back in the hallway again, Levi was already heading to the small door on the side that led to the roof. She'd forgotten about that one and quickly followed him, even though he motioned for her to stay back. Like hell she would. He opened the door, and they crept up the stairs. This compound was unbelievable. There was a rooftop deck, if that was what one wanted to call it. At the top, they pushed open the door slowly and peered out into the night. She hadn't been up here for days.

Weeks actually. In the summer, it would make an awesome retreat in the evenings. However, in the darkness, it gave them a hell of a vantage point to view the compound.

But even here the place was empty.

So where was the intruder?

She lowered her weapon and turned to Levi. "What do you think? Is he long gone?"

"It's possible. I'm worried he might have left bugs behind. Harrison will have to go through the place with the detectors and make sure we're clean."

In her mind she was okay with that idea. The intruder could have left so much worse. But, until they actually checked, there was no way to know. They headed downstairs to their floor. She walked into Levi's room and sat down on the edge of the bed.

She was done.

He stood at the doorway, a worried look on his face. "Are you okay?"

She gave him a lopsided smile and said, "I will be. I'm just tired."

"Did you reinjure yourself?"

Ice shook her head. "No, just tired," she said firmly. Ice waved her good arm at him. "Go. I need to rest."

Undecided he stood in place until she shooed him away several more times.

When he finally did leave, she sank back to the pillows.

"Dear God, I'm glad that's over," she whispered.

Unfortunately he also left the door open. That meant she had to get up again. She struggled to her feet and made her way slowly to the door. Now that he'd gone and the panic was over, she was more tired than she could believe.

She closed the door and turned back to the room. All she wanted was to collapse on her bed.

Except she was no longer alone.

Even worse, she'd left her gun half concealed by blankets on the bed where she'd been sitting.

"Who the hell are you and what do you want?" she asked the gunman standing in front of her.

In her mind she was figuring out where the hell he'd been hiding that they'd missed him. But that wasn't the biggest issue bothering her. It was that this asshole held a Luger in his hand with the casual ease of someone who was used to firearms and had no qualms about using them.

A head shot she would not survive, but a body one she might. She was wearing her vest, but she was definitely not at her strongest to take him down.

And she'd just closed off her one escape route.

The man wore a full face mask and was dressed in dark military garb and combat boots. But something was very unmilitary about his bearing. And the paunch didn't add to the image either.

And then she knew.

"Rodriguez?"

Instead of answering her, he cocked the gun and pointed it at her head.

LEVI HATED TO leave her. Ice had been strong at his side the entire time, and he had forgotten she was wounded. She had never given any sign her injury was holding her back in the least. Until she sat down on the side of the bed. He should have forced her to stop earlier.

But she knew when to quit, and he admired that about her. As he walked down the hallway toward the stairs, he really hated to go.

Dave stood watch over Sienna, and all the other men were busy checking out the security of the entire compound. But what about Ice? Was she safe? She was vulnerable right now. She'd be horrified to even hear him worrying about her.

He continued toward the stairwell and realized he couldn't force himself to. Something was wrong. He stopped and looked back.

And then, incapable of doing anything but following his instincts, he snuck back to his room. Reaching out to open the door—he froze. Instead of turning the knob, he leaned forward and placed his ear against the door.

Voices?

Ice and a man, but not one he recognized.

Anger ripped through his gut. The intruder they were looking for had somehow evaded their best search efforts and had already been inside his bedroom when he'd left Ice alone? And then he remembered the big window and the escape ladder that came down from the roof. The intruder must have been on the roof, then, when they went up, he came down to the room. Goddammit, why hadn't he considered that?

He stared at the double doors and realized he needed several of his men to cover all angles here. If he wanted to be certain Ice got out of this alive, this asshole mustn't. He stepped back several feet and contacted his men. Within seconds the team was mobilized.

Standing ready outside his bedroom, he waited for the signal.

Chapter 18

O F COURSE THIS had to happen when she was already tired and her energy was at the lowest.

"Don't say a word."

Slowly Ice nodded, and the gun lowered away from her head. If he wanted quiet, she'd stay quiet. All she wanted was to go to bed, to lie down. But this asshole could take that as an invitation, and he'd likely shoot as soon as she moved. How long before anybody would notice?

Levi had assumed she'd gone to bed. Everyone else would respect that—nobody would come and check on her. She mentally screamed for Levi to return. And, though they were very close, she didn't think he would be hearing whispers like that anytime soon.

If anybody might actually hear her, it would be Merk or his brother, who had strong instincts that bordered on the supernatural. Only Terkel certainly hadn't phoned today at all to let them know that things would go south.

She considered how to let the others know she was in trouble. There was an intercom in this room, but she hadn't actually pressed the button for anybody to hear her, and it was a good six feet away. She wasn't able to walk over and hit the button and scream for help. Something like that was asking for a bullet.

Rodriguez spoke on his cell phone. But his gaze never

wavered—neither did his gun.

She shifted toward the intercom.

Instantly he raised his weapon and barked, "Stay there."

She stilled; he lowered the gun to the level of her knee-caps, and she froze. That's the last thing she wanted, but it would be effective; she wouldn't be walking anywhere if he shot her leg.

He continued to talk in rapid Spanish. She caught a few odd words but not enough to get the full meaning.

As she stood close to the door, she considered making a break for it. If she could just get outside ... any bullets he fired would likely hit the door, not her.

Outside were two stairwells, one up, the other down. She could also try to make it to her room, but that wouldn't do anything other than pin her in a room across the hall. No gain to be had there.

She thought she heard footsteps outside and tried to hold her breath to hear better, but it was too hard with her heart slamming against her rib cage, blocking out any sounds she might otherwise pick up in the hallway.

Ice glanced around the room and realized she wasn't familiar enough with Levi's room to even know the size and depth of it should she make a run for it. She might reach the bathroom; it would provide a few weapons but not likely enough.

As her gaze swept the windows, she caught sight of something on the side of the big corner window. Rhodes. She almost gasped in surprise. Her gaze quickly zinged back to Rodriguez and was thankful his eyes were fixed on the wall, not her face, as he spoke rapidly into the phone, angrier by the minute.

And that was perfect. She didn't know what the plan

was, but she wanted to be ready. Somehow they knew she wasn't alone. That's when she also realized the curtain fluttered beside Rhodes. This was also how Rodriguez made it in. Likely, when they went to the roof, he came down the outside access and jumped in here. Whether he knew it was the master bedroom or not, it was good luck on his part and terrible on hers.

Now she needed the men to do whatever it was they were planning. Except they needed to know what Rodriguez was up to and with whom first. So once again it was all about timing.

"How many men are here?" Rodriguez asked. "I want to know exactly how many I have to kill."

She shrugged. "We just got a carload of guys a couple days ago, so maybe two dozen."

His face clenched. "You're lying. I haven't seen anywhere near that kind a number."

"It's a big place," she said quietly. "I can't give you a head count because I don't know."

She hoped he would be the same as every other power-hungry, inflated-ego male and consider her useless because she was female. But she didn't look that way, geared up as she was. Then again she wore a sling, so who knew?

He waved his hand, the gun moving as he dismissed her comments. "Of course you have no idea. But you should at least give me a better number than that."

She shrugged. "Like I said, I think there's close to two dozen now, maybe twenty-three." She lowered her eyes and added, "or twenty-four."

He snorted.

Perfect. As far as he was concerned, she was too stupid to count. Good. That gave her a hell of an advantage. All she needed now was an opportunity.

She realized, from the fragments of his conversation, he had men waiting to attack. Probably not very far away.

Rhodes also spoke Spanish so he would understand what was coming.

If she could only get Rodriguez to talk. "It'll take more than a few men to take this place out," she said calmly. "They're all military trained—top of their field ..."

He laughed, but it was a coarse, rough one. "Top of their field? And yet I got in here so easily ..." He smirked at her. "They're nothing but wannabe soldiers. If they were that good, they'd still be in the military. Instead they're just here playing at it." Then he turned idly and said, "In fact, some of them are no longer in any shape to even play."

On that she couldn't even begin to keep quiet. "And whose fault is that?" she cried. "You betrayed them."

"Of course I did. I got a better deal so I took it. That's all there is to it. They shouldn't be upset about that. That's just the way life is when you're arms-dealing."

She shook her head. "I don't believe that. Any one of those kind of men would shoot you in the back if you turn on a deal."

"Exactly," he said with a hard grin. "That's what I did."

"Except you're still walking around free and clear, and the men you betrayed were all injured."

His face muffled with rage as he roared, "And they should've died. They've done nothing but piss me off ever since. They're killing my people, and they were damn good men. They had no right to keep coming after me. It's over. They should've just walked away, been grateful they had their lives."

She scrutinized him, like he was some kind of beetle to

crush under her foot. Was that really what he thought? That after he won whatever small war he'd waged, they should walk away and never think about him again? Apparently that was exactly how he felt. Allowing this cockroach to keep killing other people at a whim was not something the team would let happen. In the meantime she needed to keep Rodriguez distracted.

"And yet you're not in the military anymore, are you?"

He straightened, and this time his voice was cocky and arrogant. "Of course I am. The military is where real men are."

"Then what are you doing here with a cell of terrorists?"

"It's not a cell of terrorists. We're training warriors. More men for the arms race."

Not saying more, he shook his head, as if it was all just way too complicated for her to understand. "Small towns close to the border," he said, "are a great way to find people and make runs back and forth. Training the men and using them in jobs over here makes sense. It just happens to be my bad luck—or not—that you moved into town. A coincidence, or maybe a godsend. I can put you out of your misery now."

"Misery?" she asked in surprise. "Is that what you call it? We came here to build a life. We find out the closest town is infested with terrorists. That's not shitty luck—it's much worse than that."

"It is shitty—for you." He grinned.

The missing spaces and discoloration in his teeth from years of tobacco use made her want to puke.

She didn't know how long it would be, but she sure hoped her men were ready to take out this asshole, unless they were waiting for Rodriguez's team to arrive and get them all at once. She didn't want to be locked up in here alone with him any longer than she had to, but he obviously thought he was safe and wasn't showing any signs of leaving any time soon.

"You look like you're ready to pass out. Go sit over there and be quiet." Once again he waved the Luger, motioning for her to move to one of the big chairs in the sitting area.

She was almost relieved to get off her feet and rest her arm, but she worried she'd be out of sight of Rhodes so he'd have a hard time keeping track of where she was. Still she made her way to the chair as he ordered and sat down carefully. She rearranged her sling to take the weight off her arm, then relaxed back into the chair and watched Rodriguez in front of her. "What's the plan? How many men are you bringing to take down Levi and his crew?"

"Not many. Won't take very many. We might just blow the whole place to shit and hang around to see if anybody crawls out and shoot them."

Her heart froze at that. She'd not be very happy to see this gorgeous place blown to hell. It might be one of the most effective ways but it would attract a lot of attention. "It's a compound. Even if you did manage to flatten it, no guarantee you'd get everybody."

He nodded. "But I've got snipers hitting the hillsides as we speak to take the men out one by one and then come in and do a clean out." He shrugged. "It should be easy. Not to worry. It'll be all over soon."

"Soon?" she mocked. The more information she could get him to spit out, the more Rhodes would be hearing and relating to the others, she hoped.

"That's the trouble with you guys. Totally undisciplined. You've lost whatever military training you had, and that was even a mockery of what real men go through," he snapped. "My men will be here within ten minutes. Guaranteed."

Inside she smiled. That gave her unit an ETA, and, by now, they should be well and truly set up to deal with the approaching threat.

"Then your men must be close," she coaxed. "I thought everybody in this little town was taken out the other day."

He laughed. "What do you know? We own that entire block of stores—not just the two. Typical. You think small. That's why you don't look farther than that," he said. "But we've been planning this for a long time."

"You have?" she asked in disbelief. "I thought you were a new recruit system. It's not like they're your men. You're one of theirs, aren't you?" That remark just seemed to enrage him.

He spat out Spanish, rippling over her head as he stormed toward her. She held up an arm, sinking back on the chair, but she'd take the hit to keep him talking.

Finally he calmed down enough that he stepped back. "Don't you ever insult me like that again."

Instantly she nodded and added, "I won't. I'm sorry."

Mollified he said, "You will pay for that. I'll make you watch as we kill everyone, then we'll deal with you."

Inside she had no doubt exactly what kind of form that threat would take. She just had to keep him calm enough to give Levi time to get here. Rhodes would shoot Rodriguez if he tried anything, but Levi and his team would want the rest of Rodriguez's men too. Just how long would this take?

LEVI CHECKED HIS watch. Two minutes and counting. He had two recovering men handling the control room, and everybody else was all hands on deck. They understood Rodriguez's men were coming and snipers were in the hills.

Thank God, Ice had remained cool and collected and was getting the information they needed. But goddamn him for leaving her alone. That Rodriguez was even now in his bedroom, possibly hurting Ice, was enough to make Levi red with anger, but he didn't dare show weakness. Too many men were counting on him.

The last thing he would do was let this asshole ruin his life any more than he already had. Burn Levi's compound to the ground? No way. Neither would Rodriguez get a chance to hurt any more of his men. This asshole was going to die now.

Logan's voice came quietly in his ear. "One vehicle approaching on the corner. Parking in the ditch, four men disbanding."

Levi nodded. "Understood." Four men. Good. He was afraid they'd be facing a dozen.

"A second vehicle approaching."

"Copy that." He waited to get the numbers. His men could handle the four easily. But depending on how many more were arriving, well, that changed the game.

Levi stood in the hallway, tense, but ready to go in and rescue Ice as soon as he got the word everyone else was in position. They wanted to take them all out, not just Rodriguez. If they didn't end this now, it would be something they'd have to deal with over and over again.

It would never be finished.

Just then a young female voice called out, "Ice, are you there? Where is everyone?"

Levi turned to see Sienna, obviously confused and wondering what was going on, standing in the hallway, hands on her hips, the open elevator door behind her. Levi swore softly. He'd sent Dave out to help against the incoming men. He hadn't considered Sienna might wake up. Now he could use him here—in a big way.

When she saw Levi, she smiled and rushed toward him. "Am I glad to see you." She motioned toward the elevator. "I can't find anybody else. Is Ice here?"

He held a finger up to his lips and motioned toward Ice's old room. He opened the door soundlessly and dragged her inside. "We have a situation." And he quickly explained what was going on.

She gasped in horror. Her eyes were huge, but he saw no signs of panic. "What can I do to help?"

"Stay here and out of sight. We can't have you being used as a weapon too. It's one thing he has Ice, but you're an innocent civilian in all this. We need to keep you out of it."

Sienna glared at him. "I figured some shady stuff was going on these last few days, but I wasn't sure what to do. I really like it here, but it was just too odd. This actually makes sense now. And in that case"—she crossed her arms— "I want to help."

Levi noted the determination in her gaze as she stared back and the complete lack of fear in her face. "Do you know where the control room is?" he asked.

She considered for a moment. "Second floor, first left-hand door off the stairway."

He nodded. "I want you to slip down there and, if the guys have any errands for you to run, then you do that. Both the men in the control room are injured. I don't know if Stone's in there with them or not."

"Stone, he's the big guy?" She slipped her hands through her long hair and twisted and locked it into a bun at the back of her head without a clip.

He didn't understand how she did that, but he really liked the efficient ease of movement she used to get the job done. "Exactly. He's the one missing a leg."

She'd been about to walk toward the front door of the bedroom when she turned and looked at him. "He's missing a leg?"

He watched her face and almost smiled. That was a really good sign. She hadn't even noticed. "Yes."

With the door open, he let her slip out and race to the elevator. He wished he could go with her, but no way was he leaving his bedroom door. He could only hope nobody else was inside the place, and Sienna would be safe that far away.

As soon as the elevator doors closed, he said to Logan, "Sienna is on her way down to you."

"Good," Logan responded. "Harrison decided he was healthy enough to go out and fight. Can't say I'm impressed with being stuck here all alone. Could use the extra set of eyes."

"Okay, let me know she arrived safely."

"Will do," Logan said cheerfully. Levi almost smiled. Add a pretty woman to the mix and every man's spirits rose.

Levi walked down to the end of the hallway, close to twenty feet past his bedroom door, and peered out into the night. He saw a flash of fire from the left-hand side. "Logan, you see that?"

"Yes. We're being fired upon, and we're returning it," Logan said, his voice hard. "Sienna is here. She's sitting down, picking up the monitors with me."

"As soon as you hear it's all clear, let me know. Rhodes, what is the status quo inside my bedroom?"

Levi got no answer. He frowned. There could be several

reasons for that and realized most likely it was the fact that Rhodes couldn't answer without being heard inside the bedroom. As he walked back to the door, he tapped his comm twice and then twice again. This time he received a double tap response in return.

"Good. Rhodes, I'm going in ... three ... two ... one."

And crouching low, he burst into his bedroom ...

Chapter 19

CE THOUGHT SHE was ready. She'd tried to be ready. But she couldn't help the low cry of surprise when the door burst open. Rodriguez spun and fired. But even as he aimed at Levi, his footsteps moved toward her.

Gunshots rang out from both sides of the room.

Rodriguez grabbed for her, but she spun out of the chair and hid behind it. She watched as his body danced in midair, blood spouting from his chest before collapsing—dead on the ground.

She slowly straightened and stepped from behind the chair.

Levi quickly snatched her up in his arms and crushed her against his chest. She cried out as her arm was jarred. But in truth, it was nothing compared to the relief swarming through her. Rhodes had crawled in through the window and stood over Rodriguez. He pulled off the full face mask so they could confirm his identity.

Still within the circle of Levi's arms, Ice turned to look at them. "Did you get what he said about the other teams coming in?"

"Yes, and we have snipers outside picking them off one by one."

"I doubt they got them all," she said, stepping from Levi's embrace. "He sounded way too smart for that. We need to keep an eye on the tunnel, make sure nobody is coming in that way."

She dashed out of the bedroom to the top of the stairs and raced down them two at a time, Levi and Rhodes right behind her. On the main floor, Ice headed to the double doors in the tunnel. Finger to her lips, she then motioned toward the door. It moved slightly.

She stepped back as Levi and Rhodes eased forward. They pulled the door open and out tumbled one man in full night gear, combat ready, and equipped for war.

And he never had a chance to pull a gun. Levi was on him in seconds.

With the man subdued and Ice watching, the two men slipped down the tunnel to make sure nobody else was creeping their way in.

She stood there for not more than five minutes when Dave and one of his men came by and saw her holding a gun on the man on the ground. They quickly stepped in.

They tied him up and dragged him off to the single room they deemed the prisoner's room.

As she watched them go, she realized they still had more modifications to do to the compound. Levi's uncle had done a lot, but he hadn't exactly been considering dead bodies and prisoners. After what they'd been through in the last couple days, she realized they were necessities. Tired but worried, she waited at the double doors for Levi to return.

And he did, ten minutes later. She searched his face. "Well?"

"All clear."

"Any other prisoners?"

Levi threw an arm around her good shoulder and said, "Not alive."

She winced. "We need a very large cooler, and a secure room for prisoners."

"It's already under consideration. I've been talking with Bullard about that. He has plans to convert the cooler rooms to a holding cell for prisoners and likely now a morgue." He glanced around the place. "We have more than enough space for both."

"We'd left off discussing further development on the assumption we'd know what we needed better down the road."

"Right, and we certainly needed more than we thought we would."

He led her back to the med bay. From the doorway she watched as six men were laid out on the ground. "We have to get Rodriguez from the bedroom to this area."

He patted her on the shoulder and said, "I'll go get him right now." Rhodes walked out with him.

She counted the dead bodies and said to Stone, who came in carrying one more man in a fireman's hold, "Are they all accounted for?"

"More on the hill to bring in." He slowly lowered the body to the floor next to the other men. "They're coming in right now."

As she stood and watched, Bullard's men brought in another two bodies and laid them down. She looked at the row of dead men and wondered how the hell Levi would handle this.

At a sound behind her, she stepped out of the way as Levi brought in Rodriguez's body. As soon as he lowered his burden, Levi pulled out his phone and took a picture, first of Rodriguez, and then went down the aisle and took one of each man's face. Then he stepped off to the side and made a call.

With any luck Jackson would have all the bodies collected fast. She glanced at Stone and, just to confirm, she asked, "Do these numbers match those we saw getting out of vehicles?"

"Yes, this is all of them." Stone nodded. "Dave and his men checked both vehicles, and they were empty. They are bringing those here."

With one last glance at the dead men filling the room, she turned and walked out. The last thing she wanted was to deal with the aftermath.

Ice headed into the kitchen to see Alfred busy making a meal for everybody. "Is it really that time already?" After all the bloodshed, she just wasn't sure she could get a bite down.

"The men worked hard, an all-night thing. It's definitely time for them to eat."

Ice poured herself a coffee and sat down at the table. Sure enough, within ten to fifteen minutes, the room filled as the men came to tank up on food.

Even Sienna arrived and joined in. This time she was laughing and joking with Logan and the others. With a shy smile she took her place quite comfortably. Ice didn't know the full story, but, from the sound of it, Sienna had made a place for herself here. And that was good.

The smell of the food hit Ice. Her stomach heaved. She quickly excused herself. Thankfully Levi's room and bed had been cleaned up. She was heading there right now. A place she didn't intend to leave any time soon.

LEVI WATCHED ICE go. Dead tired, she looked shaken. Then, of course, she had reason to be. She'd just been through a hell of an ordeal. She also hadn't been impressed with the idea of food. He, on the other hand, needed to eat. And he proceeded to clean off his plate as fast as he could.

When he was done, he filled up his mug and quickly followed Ice upstairs. By the time he arrived and opened the door without knocking, she was already tucked into bed, her arm in a sling held close to her chest.

But the tears slowly cascading down her cheeks broke his heart. He stripped off his clothes and crawled into bed on the opposite side. He slid across the mattress and slipped his arm around her body, gently pulling her into his embrace.

And he just held her. He knew why the tears were coming, after what she'd been through. He just waited until the storm passed.

Ice was still in her underwear. She'd been trying to undress, he could see that, but at this point, she'd only gotten so far. That he could do for her. Pushing the covers down gently, he quickly unhooked her bra and slipped her arm free of the sling. Her creamy breasts rested freely against her chest. In a smooth motion, he pulled the covers farther down and slipped her panties right off. Then he grabbed the blankets and pulled them back up to her chest.

At least that way she'd sleep peacefully. Nothing worse than being constricted by clothing when you need a good rest.

Throughout his movements, neither said a word. She just let him do what he wanted. Her silence bothered him the most. He slowly rolled her over, being careful to not touch her injured arm, and asked her quietly, "Do you need another painkiller?"

She looked at him with huge tear-washed eyes glazed in pain. "Yes, please."

He hopped up gingerly, so not to jar her arm, and got a glass of water from the bathroom. Back at her bedside he found the bottle of pills on her night table. He popped two out of the container and helped her to sit up so she could swallow them.

"Now rest."

With a grateful smile she leaned against the pillows and closed her eyes. He walked around to his side of the bed and got in, then reached across and turned out the lights. It wasn't exactly how he'd hoped to celebrate the end of a very long but successful day. Still it was more than he'd hoped for even a few days ago. She was beside him in his bed, living in his suite, and he was holding her in his arms.

In truth he was a very lucky man.

Chapter 20

W HEN ICE WOKE, the pain in her arm had diminished, and she was warm and cozy. It was still evening because the light outside the windows was anything but bright.

She shifted to her back and smiled as Levi's arms tightened around her. This was her man. He'd never been shy about saying what he wanted. Until he'd been injured, she'd thought the fight had been about children in their future and Bullard, but she realized it really hadn't been those things at all.

It'd been about fear.

His fear.

And she understood. He'd been afraid he'd die, leaving her alone to raise a family. He'd been afraid he'd be a father like his own had been, and lately afraid about the extent of his injuries. Levi was a man's man. Having always been big, strong, and virile, he'd have a hard time if he was no longer that man.

Only how would he *know* when he hadn't tried?

Because they hadn't slept together since. And, instead of finding out early on and putting it to rest, it had become this huge issue in his head. She loved him no matter what. They'd have to find a way around this point if any of his fears came true, but she highly doubted it. This man was rock hard—all over. And if Rodriguez hadn't disturbed them ...

Just maybe this was the time to take them both over this hump.

With a sexy smile that she knew he couldn't see, her fingers drifted across his huge broad shoulders, the ripped abs, muscled chest, the scars she used to know, each and every one. And a few new ones.

Ice lifted up on her good elbow to look at him. Lowering her head, she smoothed soft lips across his scars. She kissed his collarbone and the hollow beneath it. She stroked his chest and the curve of his neck, the shadow of whiskers overtaking his chin. He lay on his back, napping gently, as she explored the body of the man she loved so well.

With a flick, she tossed off the blankets and sat up so she could admire the beautiful male before her. Then her gaze landed on his hip and thigh at the groin where he'd taken such a heavy blow in the last accident.

Tears came to her eyes.

No wonder he'd been worried.

Ice hesitated to touch the mangled skin but couldn't help herself. She reached out and stroked his hip, her fingers gently soothing over the still pink scars. Dear God, it had been close.

Unable to help herself, Ice reached down and kissed it, her tongue gently stroking the shiny flesh, leaving a trail of kisses across his hip and pelvis. With her head against his belly, she just lay there for a moment holding him close. If she'd lost him ... she wouldn't survive.

And seeing his injuries open like this ... all he'd hidden from her ...

Dear God, it brought it all back again. The fear, the

pain. The shock and horror of the loss.

Instead of tears welling up this time, all she wanted was to hold him close and keep him safe. When he shifted under her, his thighs stretching out and wrapping around her ... she smiled.

Not because of his instinctive leg movements, but because of another one. One between her breasts.

His erection swelled to a hard insistent rod between them.

Perfect. She raised her head and dropped kisses across the breadth of his hips, loving the way they moved underneath her ministrations. She softly ran her hands down his thighs, gently teasing his kneecaps before sliding smoothly to the inside, climbing with slow, gentle strokes as she moved up his inner thighs.

She smiled when she heard his protesting murmur.

He'd always been ticklish.

But he could deal with it. He always had.

Because she loved to tease.

She reached up to caress the soft globes hanging down between his legs. At least they didn't appear to be damaged. She felt a little scar tissue at the top and definitely found a change in the hair pattern from the scars. But, all in all, it didn't look to be that bad. Now.

But what she could see went deeper. There were indents where there should have been muscle. She shook her head, her smile falling away as she slowly sat up, realizing how close he actually came to losing his leg, his genitals, and so much more.

"Don't look. It's ugly." Strong hands reached down to pull her up, but she refused.

Instead she sat back and glared at him. "The scars are

nothing. It's the first time I've seen how badly hurt you were. How much you tried to keep from me." She shook her head. "My God, you could have died."

"But I didn't." His gentle voice reached her ears. "I'm all healed now." There was a bit of a pause, then he added, his tone wry with innuendo, "Obviously."

She smiled in the half light, and, with a wicked smirk, she said, "You know, it's been a long time since I've actually seen this. Maybe I should take a closer look." And she reached out with both hands and wrapped her fingers around his erection.

He gasped and arched his hips, pushing his erection deeper into her hands.

She gave a gentle laugh and stroked and caressed the full length of his shaft. Using her thumb, she gently spread the moisture beading over the head. He groaned. She smiled, then reached down and kissed the ridge, licking, until his cries couldn't be ignored.

"Dear God, Ice, please come to me, please. It's been so long."

"And whose fault is that?" she asked with a gentle smile.

Because of her arm, she shifted up until she was straddling his hips, his shaft between her legs, and she gently rode the full length of him, but refused to take him inside.

His hands reached for her, but she pulled back just out of range. He fell back down, and his eyes burned with passion as he studied her. His voice guttural and deep, he said, "You're so damn beautiful. I thought I'd lost you forever."

She lifted up and positioned his shaft at the heart of her and reached out with her good hand to grasp his.

With her gaze locked on his, she lowered herself down,

hearing his cries deep within his throat, her own welling up. She was almost fully seated when he let go of her hand, cupped her breasts, and then slid his hands to her hips, where he grasped her firmly and lunged upward, placing himself where he belonged—at the heart of her.

She let out a long, slow moan as she was filled to the hilt. Her muscles, not used to such activity any longer, took a moment to adjust to the stretch. She shuddered as her body rejoiced at being one with Levi. Once again being connected to him.

Only very quickly that wasn't enough. She leaned forward, placed her good hand on his shoulder and started to ride.

And she was a natural horsewoman.

With his hands on her hips to hold her close, he let her set the pace. Passion twisted, coiling tighter and tighter within her.

When the tremor erupted deep inside, she arched her back and cried out.

Levi groaned beneath her. "No, no, not yet, not yet."

Grabbing her hips, he surged upward and held her in place as he pounded into her.

She cried out as a kaleidoscope of emotions rippled through her. Beneath her, his body lunged up one final time before he collapsed on the bed, shuddering. She sank down on top of him, their bodies slick with sweat.

"So good," he murmured, his hands running up and down her spine. "God, I missed you."

She propped herself up on her good arm and stared down at him. "So why did you make us wait?"

He closed his eyes for a moment. She reached down and kissed the tip of his nose.

His eyes flew open. "It seemed like I couldn't catch a break or find a way to fix our problems. Then with my injuries, I wasn't the same. Not whole."

She laughed. "You are as healthy and virile as you ever were."

"Maybe. But maybe not," he said in a low voice. "That doesn't mean I can give you children." He groaned. "And I hadn't really realized how I would feel about that until that possibility came up. I do want children. As long as they're yours." He reached up and stroked the side of her face, bringing tears to her eyes.

"If you can't, then that's fine. The important thing is you're alive and healthy and well. And I hadn't realized just how close we came to losing you until I saw the scars. Please don't ever hide something like that from me again. You pushed me away. And that hurt more than anything."

"I wanted you to have the best. I wanted you to have someone whole, healthy. And, if it couldn't be me, then I wanted you to be with Bullard."

She leaned back slightly and said in an accusing voice, "And yet he's the reason why we fought?"

"That was before I got injured," he admitted. "Afterward, then he seemed like the better man for you."

Frowning, she sat back up and slapped him lightly on the chest. Well, that explained a lot of the hot and cold that he had put her through. The mixed messages she'd been getting.

Now she understood.

And none of it mattered.

She loved him. That was the most important thing.

"You're an idiot," she said gently.

"Maybe, but I'm your idiot." He tugged her down close.

"Did you ever think about Mason and his group of Keepers?"

She laughed and snuggled close. "I sure did. But it doesn't apply to us as we've been together since forever."

"But still ..."

"I know. What we have ... it's special. You're a legend in your own right." She leaned over and kissed him. "And in the words of the Keepers—worth keeping."

He pulled her closer and held her against his heart, then whispered, "How about we create our own legend? Our own tale to be told—a legendary love?"

She burrowed against him. She liked that. Liked to think they had their own pathway in this world, unique to them. She tilted her head back and looked up at him.

"Forever?"

The corner of his lips tilted. "Forever," he promised. And kissed her.

Epilogue

THE COMPOUND WAS secure once again. Bullard and his men were gone. Everyone was in clean-up mode. Even the computer system firewalls had been upgraded. Dave had done a bang-up job on that. Bullard had done a final walk-through of the security system with everyone at his side.

They'd all done a great job. Now Stone was compiling a supply list for the compound. He'd already done the R&D room. Bullard had left a list for the medical clinic. Stone needed to check on Alfred's list for the kitchen next. Having that many extra people, they'd cleaned out much of the food supplies. And it had all been worth it. Stone turned and walked into the kitchen.

And stopped at the doorway, a smile on his face. Levi and Ice sat together at the smaller table off to the side. By the window. Holding hands. Their quiet happiness warming his own heart.

Ice had finally melted. And she never looked happier. Levi, well, he looked like he'd won the lottery, and the prize sat in front of him.

Stone was supposed to be tough. Hard. A SEAL. But, watching the two of them, the smiles, that bubble of togetherness—he wanted that. Maybe he always had. But SEALs made lousy husbands. Of course he wasn't a SEAL anymore. He wasn't really a man anymore, at least not the same man he'd been.

But Levi and Ice ... they'll make this place work. They'll make a difference.

Still ... maybe Stone could make a difference too. He wanted that.

Plus ... maybe someday—not anytime soon, of course—he'd find his own special woman ... with the heart of a warrior.

STONE'S SURRENDER

Heroes for Hire, Book 2

Dale Mayer

Chapter 1

"TWO MORE DAMN-CLOSE shots."

Stone Tollard winced, sitting taller in the driver's seat, as Levi swore loud and long into Stone's headset.

The next distinctive *boom* shook their vehicle. Stone turned to look at Ice, riding shotgun beside him.

"Stone, what's your ETA?" Levi's hard voice snagged Stone's attention. Levi and the rest of the unit arrived earlier in another truck and were already situated in town, scoping things out.

At least until Stone swerved to avoid another depression in the road. Likely a land mine again. He checked the laptop monitor mounted before him. Ice's main duty was watching this screen, although she'd rather be flying a helicopter. She nodded for him to continue in the same direction.

Normally this would be a military operation. Yet no one was to know Levi and his unit were in Afghanistan to rescue a senator's daughter—kidnapped by rebels intent on funding their army for another couple years. Not that the senator didn't have the money to pay, because he did; but, as everyone knew, paying was no guarantee of getting the senator's daughter home safe and sound. In the senator's own words, Lissa was a mite too stubborn to listen to anyone—even kidnapping rebels.

The senator knew what Levi could do and also trusted

him to keep this as quiet as possible. On those terms Levi had agreed to take on the job.

Levi's team were all ex-soldiers of some kind and excelled in this stuff, although there was talk of a few other law enforcement types joining them. One of Levi's old friends, Mike, a Texas Ranger, was looking to join up. Stone had no trouble with that because Mike had helped them out before, having access to some information and skills that they wouldn't have otherwise. Stone was all for a global company.

Hell, although the formal name of Levi's company was Legendary Security, privately the team joked their name should be *Heroes for Hire*. Truly sappy. And something to make them all groan. But anything to put a grin on their faces and to turn tough situations into something easier was well worth it.

"Now." Ice's voice rose sharply at the end of the word as she pointed where she wanted Stone to go.

Stone tightened his grip on the wheel and made a sharp left turn and kept going until she told him otherwise. Stone and Levi had learned to listen to Ice a long time ago.

"Straighten up," she said in a calm voice. "You're clear for another hundred yards."

"Jesus, is that all?" he asked.

No way in hell they'd have made it this far if they didn't have that special software. Although military grade, it was an early adaptation of Mason's wife, Tesla's, program. So technically not an illegal copy. More of a prototype, and she'd made a few tweaks to improve its efficiency and accuracy. Stone was damn grateful.

He and Ice would've been blown to shit a long time ago if they didn't have this thing telling them where all the land mines were. They couldn't be positive every single mark on that screen was one, but they sure as hell weren't taking any chances. The program had been developed to forewarn them, and it worked like a charm.

"Stone?" Levi asked impatiently. "ETA? Answer me."

Stone looked at Ice.

She shrugged. "If we could go in a straight line, it would be eight minutes," she said to both men. "Since we're zigzagging across the damn countryside to avoid land mines, double that."

Stone kept his focus on the road, knowing they neared the one-hundred-yard mark, and Ice would fire off another set of instructions soon.

"Clear so far."

He nodded. That meant in ten seconds she would tell him to head in another direction she deemed safe. And he'd follow her order, as he had for years. And it was so much easier now that she and Levi had settled their differences. When they'd been on the outs, it had been tough on everybody. The team could all see what needed to happen, but nobody dared speak to Levi or Ice since both were hotheads.

Stone grinned. Of course he was just a pussycat himself. *Like hell.*

He and Ice drove in silence for another couple minutes, and he was surprised when she didn't tell him to change direction. It also made him extremely uneasy. This was the longest they'd actually driven in a straight line since they'd hit this section of the road. "Is the program still working?"

"It is. And there's one coming up ninety yards to the right. Take a left in four, three, two ..."

The cab was silent except for his heavy breathing as he waited for that final order.

"Now," she snapped.

He jerked the wheel again, making a hard left, and waited for her to tell him to straighten up. That meant heading back to the road when it was clear. But she didn't say anything. He glanced at her quickly and then returned his gaze to the road. The double-cab truck bounced over the heavy countryside, hit a rock, then bounced again. Not a whole lot he could do. The terrain was very rough out here.

"Ice?"

"Get ready," she warned. "When I say so, take a hard right and go forward about ten yards."

"Jesus." He followed her instructions though. It took another five minutes before she had them on the road again. And so it went for the next fifteen miles. At one point it seemed like nothing but land mines were on the road. Finally the small village rose up ahead. Not their final destination but where they would stay for the night. Lissa was being held somewhere within a few miles of this place.

He entered the village very slowly, dust swarming up around them.

Levi's voice crackled in his ear. "Take the second left."

Stone shook his head. There was no left, nor right because there were no damn roads. Just a hodgepodge of makeshift buildings set in the middle of nowhere. How the hell did these people live like this?

Ice lifted her hand and pointed to the left. He followed her instructions and came to a sudden stop inside what appeared to be a shelter of some kind. Instantly the men on the ground covered up the truck with camouflage materials. Stone hopped out and walked over to Rhodes and Merk, standing in front of the truck. For every step Stone took, he heard a *clink, clink, clink.*

Rhodes shook his head and looked down at Stone's foot and leg hidden by his jeans. "That won't work. No way can you sneak up on anybody like that."

"Two screws are loose. I just need a minute to fix it," Stone said.

Merk cleared a spot on the table and said, "Take that thing off, and I'll get to it."

Only ... Stone did things his way. He stood at the table, reached down, pulled up his pant leg, and took off his prosthetic leg. Then he laid it on the clean spot on the table. Instantly a light turned on, giving him visibility as bright as he could get here. Tools were all over the place; few of them belonged to his team. But Stone would use what he could. Quickly checking out the offending joint, he realized one of the bearings was working less than perfectly.

He always carried a repair kit in his pocket, just in case. He pulled that out, quickly changed the seal and replaced the screws, taking great care to oil everything. Soon as he was done, he strapped it on again. This model had a butter-soft leather pad for his stump and was much easier on the scar tissue.

His buddy, Swede, had helped him design a different clip-on system. All in all each new design was getting better and better. None were as good as the flesh-and-blood leg he'd lost, but he was doing just fine.

At least until he was all alone in the dark. Sometimes the waves of depression just couldn't be held back. But those were few and far between, and he sure as hell would never admit those times to anybody else. That would be surrendering, admitting to the weakness within. He'd never done that. Not yet at least, and didn't have any plans to do so in the near future.

He swung around to the others and asked, "What's the plan?"

"You and Ice will take the road up to the rear of the rebel camp on the other side of those hills. We want you to park at the top and be the lookout. Harrison's going with you. Sniper rifles are right over there on the left wall. Ice will run communications from inside the truck. Logan will run comm from down here."

Stone looked over to see Logan's flat glare. "Hey, Logan. Glad it's you this time and not me." Stone grinned at the sour look on his friend's face.

Logan had been shot up pretty good not very long ago, and though he was recovering, his muscles hadn't responded as well as they should have. He was doing physiotherapy and rebuilding his strength again, but that didn't mean he couldn't pack a sniper rifle for hours and still make the shots he needed to.

However, Logan was also a whiz with communications, so this was a perfect fit for him.

It also explained why Ice would be in the truck, communicating with Logan and whoever else was running late, which would in this case, be Levi.

Ice also had been injured—her upper arm—so she'd healed faster than Logan. Another sour point in Logan's life. But he was a good guy, and if need be, he'd pick up that rifle and run through the swamp, desert, or forest or jump out of a plane with the rest of them. Given a chance he'd actually beat them all to the other side. They were a small team, only seven of them at the moment, all having finally moved permanently into the Texas compound. Still they'd done plenty in the military with that many men. Levi expected nothing less from them now.

In fact, he expected a lot more because they weren't constrained by the same rules. Although it also meant he didn't have to follow the same regulations. Sometimes those were a good thing. Levi ran a tight ship, and so far they'd all gotten along just fine.

Levi walked over to Stone as he stood staring at the sniper rifles. "You okay, buddy?"

Stone knew what Levi was asking. "I'm fine. We're good to go."

No need to hash out the fact that this was his first active mission since having his leg blown apart. No way in hell was he getting left behind again. You started that; it never ended. He'd be the one staying with Alfred, the one who kept the compound running and the meals cooking. Plus the team needed Stone. They had so much damn work, they were bringing in more men.

The world was in a sad state of affairs.

"Listen up, everyone," Levi said. "We're out in one hour. Stock up on water because it'll get hot as hell out there today."

Damn. Stone hated the heat. But it didn't matter. This was the job. He'd make sure he was up for it one way or another.

LISSA BRAMPTON CROUCHED behind the door, her ear pressed tight against the wood. She could hear spats of conversation, but didn't understand what was being said. She hadn't been over here long enough to pick up any of the language. Although she'd picked up Spanish and French fairly easily while studying it, she wasn't having the same experience with the Afghan tongues.

But their tone wasn't hard to understand. Something was going on. The men were yelling at one another, and she heard sounds of running feet. Thankfully nobody came in her direction.

She looked at the other two hostages. The three of them had been taken from the refugee camp. A husband and wife, both doctors, and her. Somehow they'd been singled out, probably because they were all Americans.

She didn't know if the kidnappers knew who her father was, but it was likely. She understood the rebels had been asking for a lot of money in order to secure her release, but she also knew the American government's policy was to not pay ransoms to terrorists.

In theory she agreed, but now that her head was on the chopping block, not so much.

She stared down at her hands, not surprised when they clenched into fists yet again. It didn't matter that she'd come to this country of her own free will in the first place. She'd defied her father's wishes and left once again as fast as she could. She had volunteered all over the world, and still couldn't be far enough away from her mother and father. He wasn't an easy man to live with, and watching the relationship between her parents was enough to make anybody flee. He would never change. Her mother would always be this frail, clingy listen-to-your-father-type woman.

Thankfully she had her own condo in a different state. She'd left home as soon as she was old enough.

It didn't matter that inside her head was a brain that supposedly functioned on its own. It also didn't matter that her father had wanted a son; instead he'd gotten Lissa. At least she tried not to make it matter. His attitude toward women was less than inspiring. As his daughter, she was supposed to be a clone of her mother. That wasn't working so well. Lissa had more spine than any other woman she knew. Instead of that being a benefit, all it had done was get her in trouble time and time again.

She reached up and checked out the couple of stitches along her temple. It still hurt like shit. Getting stitches without any anesthesia was not something she'd recommend. But she was grateful to Kevin for putting them in. When they'd been kidnapped, Kevin had been packing up several first aid kits, and those, as well as some of their bags, had been grabbed along with them. He'd managed to keep Susan's bag with them initially, and thankfully it had yielded a small first aid kit.

Lissa turned and contemplated the older woman and her husband. They were in their mid- to late-fifties. Having raised their family, they'd wanted to do more with their skills. So they'd headed out and traveled for the last four years, helping out where and how they could.

Somehow they'd ended up here. Now Susan looked tired, worn out.

Lissa's head pounded, and she was desperately in need of water. But ever since they'd been shoved into this room, they'd been given very little, just enough to stay alive. A bucket was in the far corner, which they had tactically agreed to use for waste, and other than that, not a whole lot was here.

She wasn't into whining, but it had been like this for days.

She walked over to the small window too high to climb up, being a good six to eight feet above ground. She could probably do it with help, but no way would she leave anybody behind. This place was a death trap, and she wasn't like her father.

The beam of sunshine shone on her face where she stood. She didn't need the warmth, but something was just so soothing about being in the sunlight.

Even if just a scrap, she badly needed that piece of hope.

Behind her, Susan whispered, "Do you think we'll ever get out of here?"

And Susan was desperately in need of that ray of hope Lissa had found for herself. With as much conviction as she could, Lissa whispered, "Yes. We will. Rest. Build up your strength. We'll have to draw on it."

And she turned to let the sun shine on her face again. If she stood at the right angle, she could see a distant hilltop. The faraway details were blurry.

Something had changed though. She frowned as she studied the horizon. She had had nothing else to look at in the last few days, so she'd memorized the shape of the landscape in her head. Now an extra shadow fell to the left. And then she caught sight of a flash on the hillside. Was that the rebel leader's men up there? Or was someone, even now, searching for them? Maybe there *was* one advantage to being a senator's daughter.

Just as she decided she should sit down and catch a nap, footsteps raced toward them. She didn't have time to decide if she should hide behind the door and attack, or just fall to the ground and pretend to have passed out from lack of water and food. Suddenly two people were already inside the room.

And screaming at them.

Chapter 2

THE THREE HOSTAGES were grabbed and shoved from the room and down several steps. They were pushed into another room, and the door slammed shut. Not a word was spoken to them; nothing was asked of them.

This room was larger with a door down at the far end; Lissa walked over and opened it. She grinned. She turned to the other two. "It's a bathroom."

Also a hell of a relief because water came from the sink faucet. She walked back into the center of the room to find Kevin standing at the table, then the two women rapidly left.

"They brought us water and food," he said by way of explanation. "Not much of it but enough to keep us alive."

They wanted Susan to eat first as she was in the weakest condition. But Susan wasn't having any of that. She made sure everybody got equal amounts of both, the water and a rice dish of some kind with a little bit of meat and vegetables.

In truth only enough food for one of them. But, like Kevin said, it would keep them alive, which was all that was required at this point. After they ate, Lissa explored the space. It appeared to be identical to what they had had upstairs, but larger.

Still no furniture besides the table, nor blankets or anything to sit on. Just one window, which was slightly bigger than the last.

She took a closer look. They appeared to be on the second floor but still facing the same side of the building. And this time bars were on the windows. Right. No escape that way. But she couldn't help but reach out and give the bars a good shake, just to make sure.

They were solid. And the walls were stone and adobe, traditional native building materials. It would take a grenade or earthquake to make these walls come tumbling down. And considering several floors were above them that would be the worst scenario since they would be flattened inside.

Disgruntled at that concept, she turned to study the rest of the space, but there was nothing more to see. Susan had gone to lie down on the left side of the room, and Kevin held her in his arms. Lissa turned toward the table, but it wouldn't provide much in the way of weaponry either. Simple but old, rickety.

If she were to hit anybody with a piece of it, that would only piss them off, and she'd be in worse shape than ever.

She walked to the door—a big old plank—and studied the hinges. She was surprised this room, like the other, had a door, as mostly just cloth was draped over the openings here. But then this was some kind of a boss's house, and he seemed to expect prisoners here. She reached out and grasped the handle of the door they had been shoved through and pulled it.

Surprise, surprise … The door swung open. Had the serving women not locked it on the way out? Or did the doors not lock?

Instantly two men appeared before her, weapons raised and pointed at her. She held up her hands in apology and pointed to the empty plates on the table. She walked over, grabbed the dishes, held them out, and said, "Please, may we have some more food?"

The two men looked at her with disgust, grabbed them, and left, closing the door tightly behind them. And she somehow knew, even if one had walked away, the other would still be standing guard.

So locks were hardly needed.

Well, she had tried. Just as she decided to lie down also, the door opened again. This time a young girl walked in, carrying a tray with more food. With a smile of thanks, Lissa stepped over to the table and studied the fresh rice and vegetables. More than they had the first time around. Good. Maybe they wouldn't starve yet.

She turned toward Kevin and Susan to see if they wanted any more to eat. Kevin held up his finger to his lips for Lissa to be quiet. She realized Susan had fallen asleep. Also good.

Lissa took a plate with one-third of the food to Kevin. Then she took another for herself. When Susan woke up, some would be there for her to eat. Lissa sat down against the wall across from them and proceeded to fill her tummy. Surprisingly good. But, then again, starvation made anything taste good.

When she finished, she placed her plate on the table and returned to her spot on the floor. It would get cold when night came. But she didn't think blankets would be offered. She'd been cold before, and it was preferable than being hungry.

Feeling a whole lot better, she curled up like Susan and slept.

STONE STUDIED THE layout of the compound below him. He was surprised when they found places like this—a complete oasis compared to the rest of the village on the other side.

Some wealthy man had decided to build himself quite the place here. Large enough to hold an entire village comfortably—nobody would even have to share space, from what Stone could see. Also several good-size trucks drove around, moving inventory from one side of the compound to the other. Stone presumed weapons, considering they needed trucks to move them.

With his scope, Stone estimated the distance to the outside wall to be four hundred yards. Another ten to the inside wall of the actual building. He slowly assessed any weaknesses. His gaze landed on the second-story window, worried about the young woman he'd seen before. She'd been there for a brief moment and then was gone. Now he wondered who she was. But, as she'd been the only blonde he'd seen since they had arrived in this damn country, it was a safe bet that was Lissa Brampton. Intel had said she was here. He was inclined to believe it now.

He had been on enough missions where the data had been wrong so he never trusted it until he could confirm same with his own eyes. What he didn't like was the wind picking up. That made for shitty shots. Not impossible but it just added to the complexity.

A lot of people were in the compound. His team needed to make a diversion, then sneak in for the hostages, and get the hell out of here. The diversion was Levi's job on the far side. All seven members of the team were here, but with only four on the ground, that didn't allow for a lot of cover. Ice was controlling something inside the vehicle that gave them a hell of an advantage though—one of Bullard's new drones.

Those things were something else. The military used them to pick off known terrorist members one at a time all over the world. They were deadly accurate. Stone crept toward the truck where Ice stood. She had two drones set up. It helped that she was the helicopter pilot from hell or maybe she just happened to have a natural aptitude to take to these drones like a boss man. None of the others had the same fine-tuned control she did with them.

"Are you ready?"

She nodded. "Bullard sent instructions on how to muffle the noise ever-so-slightly." She reached down and adjusted something in the rear of the small machine. "Just finished tinkering with it." She glanced at Stone. "Anything from Levi?"

He shook his head. "Not yet."

And all that changed two minutes later.

Ice sent both drones in the sky, directing them around back where Levi was setting up charges on the far side of the wall, hoping the blast would lure everybody over, giving Rhodes and Merk a chance to make their move while Stone and Harrison covered their backs.

Ice tensed beside Stone, watching the screens and controlling two drones at once. She carefully picked off the men on the outside, away from the action.

Stone looked at her with respect. "Two already?" he asked.

She didn't take her eyes off the screens. "Yes."

Then Levi's charges blew. The compound erupted.

The drones were a matte black and, like a bat in the night, were very hard to see until they moved. Plus they hovered at a very unique speed, making them difficult to pinpoint in the night sky.

"Five," she said in a cool tone.

Stone grinned. Maybe he didn't need a sniper rifle after all. He was ready and lined up, but saw no targets. Then he stiffened.

Rhodes and Merk appeared suddenly. With all the gunfire and explosions on the far side, the two of them had scrambled to the side. How did they know where the girl was? But they headed for the blonde he'd seen earlier. Very quickly they had lines thrown up and caught in the bars, and they scaled the wall. Damn, they were good. Something he wasn't sure he'd ever be able to do with his leg now. Well, maybe he could, just not as fast.

He peered through his scope. Harrison scouted the bottom area. Suddenly the bars in the window blew apart, and both men went inside. In Stone's mind, he urged, *Go, go, go.*

The two men disappeared into the room beyond them, then they came out with the blonde and a second woman.

Shit, they weren't expecting a second hostage. When Rhodes and Merk repeated the climb and exited with a man between them, Stone knew things would be a whole lot more difficult than he had originally thought. It was one thing for them to pick up and carry a single woman, but it was another for two men to handle three people.

Just as Rhodes and Merk lowered the rescued guy to the ground, an unfriendly came around the corner. His head exploded even as Stone readied his shot. Damn it. Harrison got him.

There. Stone pulled the trigger, and the second man went down. After that, pick and shoot, pick and shoot.

He kept track of Merk and Rhodes and the hostages' progress but just barely. He could hear Ice swearing behind him and knew she was still at work. A funny poof in the sky went off to the left. He watched as one of the drones blew up. Behind him, Ice said, "Shit."

Hell, he didn't know what she expected. That damn thing had taken out twice as many people as he had, and he was damn good.

His earpiece crackled. "Retreat."

Easy for Levi to say. They now had a total of ten people to extract from this nightmare. Leaving Harrison to give the others cover, Stone and Ice bailed into the same truck. He started the engine to soon be able to gather the hostages. In the darkness he crept down the hill, doing his damnedest to avoid the rocks and trees he'd scoped out earlier.

Almost to the bottom, Merk moved to meet the double-cab truck. Stone picked up a sniper rifle and took several cover shots as the hostages were loaded inside the rear cab. They were parked at a shitty angle, and they still had Levi to find and Harrison to collect. Logan would drive the lead truck, pick up Merk and Rhodes, and then meet up with them soon.

"Drive, Stone," Ice snapped. "I'll take them down."

He transferred the rifle to her. She sat on the open window, firing over the hood of the truck. He drove the vehicle backward and around onto the road and then hightailed it out of there.

Yelling, he asked, "Where's Harrison?"

"He's coming, twenty yards in front of us." She looked around and added, "But where the hell is Levi?"

Stone had no idea.

That happened when people made plans.

They went to shit. Always.

He hit the gas and drove as fast as he could to pick up

Harrison. Stone knew Levi. He'd be here when they least expected him.

Harrison jumped on the running board behind Ice as Stone gunned it. He could feel the tension from everybody in the vehicle. Nobody in the back said a word. Ice never did, but he knew damn well what was on her mind. Levi had to be here somewhere.

They wrapped around the mountain they'd been climbing and headed toward the village. They no longer had a safe place for them. In fact, from the looks of the dust curling up the hillside behind them, they were about to have unwelcome visitors.

Ice opened up the laptop for the minefield software. "I'll navigate. You drive."

His earpiece crackled. "Stone, keep coming. I'm ten yards to the right. Stop and I'll jump on."

Stone had barely hit the brakes when he felt Levi leap into the pickup bed.

Harrison joined him there, yelling at Stone, "Unfriendlies on our ass. Move!"

Stone hit the gas, hating the thought of finding his way at top speeds in the dark.

"Don't worry about it. I got this." Ice barked orders that barely had time to register as she sent them right, then left and right, and left again and now straight forward.

By the time they finally made it to the other side, Stone's adrenaline was running at top speed. A pickup point was ahead, and a vehicle change needed to happen damn fast. Stone hadn't been able to shake the rebels on their ass. In fact, it looked like they'd been following his tail all the way out.

"We've got another minefield ahead," Ice said. "If we do

this correctly, we can take them out at the same time. Take a left now."

Instantly he jerked the truck, hearing a soft gasp from behind him. He ignored it.

"And a right … *now*." Again he jerked the wheel and a land mine went off just behind him.

He glanced at Ice. "That was too close."

She shrugged and grinned at him in the dark. "It was necessary."

He raised his eyebrows but kept on driving until he heard a huge *boom*. Glancing in his rearview mirror, he watched as the truck following them hit a mine full-on. The vehicle was blasted into the air and tumbled before blowing up.

Beside him, Ice closed the laptop and said, "Good job."

Stone laughed. "You mean, *damn* good job."

"Are you people nuts?"

The soft female voice from behind him was the first of the hostages to talk. Stone really hadn't been aware of their presence. What must they have thought of this last hour of panic? He shook his head. Maybe he was crazy, but they'd been smart enough to listen to him and stay quiet. He could appreciate that.

He twisted and gave a quick glance behind him. "You guys okay?" He returned his gaze to the road and asked a second question. "Anybody need medical help?"

"No. Kevin and Susan are doctors themselves," the blonde said. "They're just tired. I'm fine too."

Ice turned to study her. "Melissa Brampton?"

The young woman nodded. "Yes, I'm Lissa."

"Good. Your father's waiting at home for you."

"He actually paid the ransom?"

The shock in her voice made Stone send another quick glance her way in the rearview mirror. She did appear to be in a daze. Whether in shock from the recent events or at the thought that her father might care enough to pay, he wasn't sure.

He decided he'd take one of those doubts out of the question. "Yes, he was quite prepared to pay the ransom. However, the decision was made to come in and rescue you because paying did not guarantee your life."

She nodded silently. "That's what I figured. Never thought he would pay though."

Her words had a slight tone of bitterness that made him and Ice exchange a look.

Then the blonde added, "He was never one to back a losing horse."

Stone didn't know what the hell that meant, but obviously there was some strain in the relationship between father and daughter. Although events like this tended to make even the worst relationships a whole lot better. He wasn't so sure that was the case this time though.

In the rearview mirror he took a long look at her for the first time and was surprised by what he saw. For a woman who had defied her father to come to do good works in a country on the far side of the Earth, a war-torn country at that, he'd expected somebody strong, robust even. Instead she sat tall and lean. Maybe there was a strength to her, but he saw only fragility instead.

What was likely very fair blonde hair under all that grime had been tied in a braid. Her face was covered in dirt, her clothes torn, and she looked like she had just survived a heart-wrenching ordeal. Which, in fact, she had. Yet he could see the strength in her face and her gaze, but physically she was the exact opposite of what he had pictured.

He also wasn't expecting the sucker punch to his gut. Then again he wasn't into showpieces. He liked women with grit, and she appeared to have it, in spades.

Ice's hand whacked him across his arm, making him realize his mind had wandered again. He turned his gaze forward and kept his focus on the road. The last thing he needed was to be sidelined by a woman, full of grit or not.

"Well, he did," Ice snapped in response to Lissa's last two comments. "Although there's no way in hell our team would be looked upon as a losing horse."

Chapter 3

L ISSA DIDN'T KNOW the woman in the front seat of the vehicle. But she was obviously in charge and capable. A part of Lissa felt like she should rebel against that authority; another part told her to just shut up, sit back, and relax. She didn't have to be in control all the time. And she needed to learn to let go more. It seemed like she'd been on the warpath her whole life, ever since she had been old enough to understand that she didn't want to do or follow every dictate sent her way.

Besides, these people had come to rescue her. And had done an admirable job of it so far. She understood they were likely very highly paid for the job, but still she appreciated them. Their lives were in just as much danger as her own at this point.

She closed her eyes and got settled, giving in. With a calm voice she said, "I meant no offense to your team, simply that my father considered *me* to be a losing horse. But my relationship with him is not in question here."

The driver, a huge beef of a man, spoke up quietly. "Ice is just very protective of us. This is what we do."

"And you did it wonderfully. I thank you for saving me," she said without opening her eyes. "I'm just too tired right now to even think straight."

Kevin reached across the backseat and gently patted Lissa

on the shoulder. "We're all very grateful for what you've done. I wasn't sure how much longer my wife would last, to be honest," he admitted. "It's been a tough couple years, but this last week was by far the worst. Of course the kidnapping was the highlight."

Ice turned to stare at them from the front seat. "Week?"

He nodded. "The disruptions at the refugee camp seemed to be getting much worse every day. In fact, we should've known something like this was bound to happen. Not that there were signs, but ... there *were*. You know?"

"Right—the men watching, the extra military weapons showing up, just the ratcheted-up level of fear and tension around the place," Stone said.

Lissa nodded and agreed with him 100 percent. "If we had been smart enough, we would've understood what was going on and left a week ago. Even a few days before would've been lovely." Her lips twisted in a half-sad smile. "Instead we got pulled into this mess. Something I could've done without."

"All three of us could have missed this *opportunity*," Kevin said with a smile. "On the other hand, thanks to your people, we have survived." He glanced outside the windows of the truck and said, "We *are* out of danger now, aren't we?"

"We're never fully out of it," Ice said. "But with every mile we put between them and us, we will be better off."

"We're about an hour away from the vehicle transfer, so just sit back and relax," Stone said. "We'll keep watch."

Lissa turned and looked through the glass windows behind them. "What about the two men in the truck bed? Are they okay?"

"They will be. We're actually meeting another truck up ahead. We'll be shuffling men at that point."

And, about an hour later, Lissa watched as this vehicle then slowed and pulled up beside an older pickup with a man leaning against it, as if waiting for them. Once their truck stopped, the door opened. The man took a look at the backseat and raised his eyebrows. "Three hostages? Are they doing okay?"

Ice nodded. "How are Merk and Rhodes holding up?"

Lissa looked around and realized that the two men who had hauled her from that room weren't actually in the truck she rode in. But she could see them now in the other vehicle. Oh, thank God. As they watched and waited, one of the men in the rear of her pickup hopped out. She only half listened as plans were made.

The last man from the pickup bed came around to the front. She didn't know where these men were born and bred but they were seriously badass-looking dudes. And something about that right now made her feel damn comfortable. It was nice to think she was safe for a change. It seemed like she hadn't felt that way for a long time, if ever in her life.

While she pondered the comparison, the big man got into the front seat with Ice and the driver, who she thought somebody had called Stone. In a way that fit. He had to weigh 250 pounds easy. If not fifty more than that.

She had felt like a Chihuahua, wanting to snap at the Dobermans, the rebels, telling them to keep away. But compared to them, these men were bloody Newfoundlanders, outweighing and outgunning them. She only hoped they were meaner than their dog counterpart.

Being raised by her father with his own Doberman mentality always nipping away at her self-confidence had made her very wary of other men.

Stone turned around to look at her. "Lissa, how are you

doing?"

Just enough real interest in his voice and his gaze had her realizing, even though this might be a job, he was concerned.

She smiled up at him, her first genuine smile in a while, and said, "I'm doing fine, thanks. I'm just so glad to be safe."

He nodded in understanding. "You're still not fully safe yet," he cautioned. "Not until we get you home on American soil."

"Understood." She watched as his gaze traveled to the other two former hostages, a frown developing as he studied Susan. He twisted in his seat to look at Susan's husband.

Kevin said with a smile, "She's just exhausted. We're both doctors, and have been burning the midnight oil for a long time."

Only the big man didn't appear to be appeased. "I know who Lissa is, but I do need to know your names. And nationality."

"Kevin and Susan Salinger, both Americans, born in Kansas. After we became empty-nesters, we decided to find a new purpose in life." With a lopsided smile he said, "Maybe it's time to go home."

"This is Levi and Ice, and I'm your driver, Stone. I'd tell you the names of the other four men in the second truck, but you'll forget and won't have a face to put with them, so we'll do those introductions later. We were actually hired by Lissa's father to bring her home, and you just happened to be in the right place at the right time."

Kevin gave a bark of laughter at that. "While that's a hell of an insight, it's better than being in the wrong place at the wrong time, which is how we felt. We were kidnapped with Lissa." He reached up a hand to shake Levi's and said, "Thank you for being kind enough to pick up two extra people in need."

"No problem and no charge. We're all former US Navy, and this is what we've always done. Now we just do it privately."

He turned around to sit back, facing the front, adding, "There's another stop in about forty-five minutes. We'll grab a bite to eat, take a bathroom break, and switch vehicles. Expect to leave on a flight in six hours, if all goes according to plan."

Lissa really wished he hadn't said the last part but understood his need to clarify. She knew it would be a hell of a long journey; they just had to be patient. She was rather desperate to get home now, but it didn't really matter how much time it took to get there—as long as they escaped from this hellhole.

STONE DROVE STEADILY through the darkness. Even though the mission was a success so far, this was not the time to let down his guard. Too many missions went off the rails because people thought they were safe. He and his team weren't at that point yet.

According to his calculations they were about five minutes out from the rendezvous. He drove onto the side street in front of the large warehouse building and parked, shutting off the lights. There was absolute silence inside the vehicle.

The other half of the team had driven past the warehouse and entered from the far side. One of the rules was to never be in the same place at the same time. Too easy for them all to get taken out. But they had to be close enough to back each other up in case something went wrong.

He glanced at Levi and raised an eyebrow. Even in the half-light he could see Levi's frown.

They waited. Two new vehicles were supposedly standing by for them. Stone checked his watch and realized they were actually two minutes early.

The earphone crackled in his ear. "No activity on the site."

"Silent here."

And they waited.

And waited. At five minutes past the appointed hour, Levi opened the door and slipped out. Ice followed. Stone pulled his handgun free of his holster and laid it on the seat beside him. With those two checking things out, it would be just him and three hostages. Not good odds.

He quickly relayed the change of status to the rest of the team. Better to be safe than sorry.

He could feel the hostages behind him shuffling, looking around, the tension building inside the truck. In as calm a voice as he could, he said, "Nobody else has shown up for the rendezvous. Levi and Ice have gone to check it out."

"And you're expecting trouble, I presume," Lissa said.

"I'm always expecting trouble."

Kevin murmured, "That must be a tough way to live."

Stone shrugged. "I spent a lot of years in the military as part of an elite team doing missions all around the world. Waiting, ready to go in at a moment's notice. From the time we were called up, it was like this every minute until we were home safe and sound." His gaze never stop wandering, checking the area outside the vehicle. He wanted to go in and search, but no way would he leave these people here. But he didn't trust this situation. When things went wrong, they went really wrong in his world. Quietly he ordered, "Sink down."

He quickly ducked below the dashboard.

And they waited. His communication bud crackled again. "One stranger on the left. We're on your right coming up against the side of the truck."

"Understood." He stayed where he was and waited. When shots rang out, he snapped to the people in the backseat, "Stay down."

He crawled out on Levi's side of the truck. Harrison was behind him, on the tailgate. Stone crept forward to peer around.

A second gunshot fired. And then that ever-waiting stillness that came after. Was there another shooter? And who was actually doing the shooting? Merk or someone else? His earpiece crackled. "All clear. One down."

Good.

Except for one thing. Unfriendlies never came alone— they were always with friends.

And this time was no different.

Chapter 4

LISSA CLASPED HER hands over her ears and pinched her lips together to keep the cry of fear from squeaking out. After all they'd been through, she'd hoped to be free of this torment. Instead they were apparently caught up in some other bit of nastiness. The war in Afghanistan had very long-reaching tentacles. She had no idea who was after whom. She prided herself on staying away from politics. Anything in that direction reminded her of her father. She wasn't a child of the sixties and didn't have that whole flower-power thing going on, but she certainly believed in a fair wage for all and wanted to promote peace, not war. She had a hard time with a lot of the political stands taken in her own country right now.

With the presidential election, everything was topsy-turvy. She just wanted the people to get their heads out of the ground and realize something needed to happen to promote the family unit, keep the peace, and do something to help each other. Whatever happened to honesty, ethics, and morals? It seemed like all that had gone by the wayside.

Even manners, such a basic building block of society, were gone. That was partly why she'd been so disillusioned and had allowed her father's final words to send her off—again—overseas. She'd just run out of faith in mankind. And that was hardly fair because a lot of good people were out there. She had met many while doing volunteer work. But there was just something about being in her father's stuffy old house with the windows closed and the maids who never said a word, always silent, always watching. She wondered if they were laughing at her. She didn't even know if they spoke English. Her father was fluent in Spanish, and she wondered if he even paid them a fair wage. She had a hard time with all of it. But at the same time, she knew the maids needed the money to send back home.

Instead of being a win-win situation, to her it was lose-lose on both ends. But there was really no good answer. Frustrated, feeling incapable of changing anything, she'd taken off to the areas she understood.

People who were still focused on the basics of life. Who toiled in the fields all day and broke bread happily as a family at night. Whose only entertainment was storytelling, making simple things with their hands, singing, and dancing. It had been joyous to experience.

She closed her eyes and tried to relax as the men tracked down the rest of their team. She could only hope nobody else would be hurt because of her actions. Her father was right about that. If she hadn't run to help with the refugee camp, nobody would've come after her, putting their own lives in danger. It didn't matter if they were paid or did this on a regular basis. If one of them died, she'd feel terrible.

Way too late for recriminations now. She knew somebody had been shot out there; she just hoped it wasn't one of the rescue team.

On the other hand, if it was one of the enemy, how many more were there?

Susan's tired voice startled her in the silent truck. "What's going on? Where are we?"

She could hear Kevin's low murmur as he tried to comfort his wife. His explanation was done in soft tones, as if that would matter.

The harshness of the scenario had Lissa wanting to run from the truck and do something. Being confined was killing her soul, and bringing up her fear. She used to have panic attacks all the time growing up. But she could lay the blame for that at her father's feet. They began after he locked her in the closet when she wasn't "being good." She thought she had overcome her confined-space issue when she'd finally taken the elevators instead of escalators. It had taken her a long time and a lot of tears and sleepless nights to get to the point where she could now ride them freely. But that didn't mean she liked them.

And now she was in this truck. And although not confined in the same sense of the word, it felt restricting and, even if she left, she had no place to go. She tried to control her breathing, but the panic was setting in. She closed her eyes, clenched her fists, and took great big gulping breaths, but it wasn't enough.

Finally she couldn't stand it. She bolted upright and rolled onto the front seat to push open the passenger door, leaning out, taking in large amounts of fresh air. Behind her she could hear Kevin's shocked gasp. But she couldn't worry about that. She was too busy sucking in oxygen.

As she held the door, the tremors working down her arm made it shake in the night. A strong hand reached up to grip her arm. She didn't know if it was to hold her in place to stop the shaking, or to make her relinquish her hold on the door. No success with the latter. Instead she gripped it like a lifeline.

She didn't have time to react as a face appeared in the

darkness. Instead of being scared, she was relieved to identify Stone, their driver.

He studied her with concern. "You okay?"

She nodded barely. "I just … I just needed fresh air."

But she could tell from the intensity of his gaze that he knew there was more to it. Now that she was no longer alone, and fresh air swooped through the place, she started to relax. She took several more deep breaths, telling her body to calm down, that it would be okay.

When he lifted her hand off the doorframe, she let him. But when he slid his down to hold hers, she froze.

Gently he squeezed her fingers together, a rough thumb stroking up and down on the back of her fingers. "It's okay. Being scared is a normal reaction. You've been through a lot already."

If he only knew. She gave him a slight smile and added, "I could've managed all that. But when you left me locked up in the truck …" She shook her head. "I thought I'd been doing so much better lately, but sometimes being confined gets to me."

He smiled and patted her hand. "I can leave the door slightly ajar if that makes it better, but I can't just stay here."

She tensed at the thought that he was leaving.

Instantly he squeezed her fingers and said, "Don't worry. I'm staying at the side of the vehicle. I'm not leaving you. It's my job to stand guard here."

"My hero," she said with a light groan. But, of course, it was his job. Still it didn't matter; she was such a mess right now she was grateful for anyone's support. She lowered her head to her other arm and just relaxed across the front seat. Her hand was still in his as he gently reassured her that she would be okay.

She thought she was out of the worst of the danger, and it was safe to relax. Then she heard a shout in the distance. Lifting her head, she studied Stone. "What is that?"

He lifted her palm to his lips and dropped a gentle kiss on the back of her hand and said, "Don't worry. It's my men, not the enemy."

In the distance she heard, "Stone?"

Instantly he straightened. He ducked down to look at her and said, "Stay here. I'll be back in two minutes."

She snorted. As if she was going anywhere. No way in hell. She was warm, safe, and dry. And soon this vehicle would get her the hell out of here. But none of that made her feel any better right now.

She pulled her hand in and tucked it against her chest, wondering at his gentle kiss. For such a huge man, the graceful gesture of comfort seemed out of place—and yet not. His actions had been smooth, natural. And that made all the difference.

With her arms tucked up close, she huddled in the front, listening for the men to come back. Only they didn't come anytime soon.

And her return home was to be delayed yet again. She rolled to her back and stared straight up at the ceiling. A chill set in. Likely shock. "Kevin, you doing okay?"

"Susan's asleep again. We're both fine."

But she could hear the underlying worry in his voice. They were all fine. But for how long?

STONE RACED TOWARD the other men, wondering what the hell had gotten into him. Since when did he ever kiss a woman's hand like she was some kind of royalty? It was so not him. But at the time, it seemed to be the best thing to do.

He'd understood the panic attack. Hell, the signs were damn-near impossible to miss. She gulped the air like she was dying. Anything that would help her stay calm and inside was a good thing. He just tossed it off as a casual gesture to make her feel better. Yet he knew it had to be a little bit more than that.

He wasn't sure what the attraction was, but just watching her struggle to control herself added to the admiration he felt already. She hadn't bolted. She'd only opened the truck door enough to get fresh air in. She could have opened the window.

And then he thought about that and stopped, saying to himself, "No, she couldn't have. They were power windows, and I didn't leave the keys in the ignition. So she did what she could."

Smart. He liked that. But not her hero comment. Still he'd take it as a joke as he had no intention of being called a hero. He'd been tagged with that label once too often— relationships where people looked up to him, seeing him as something he wasn't, only to find out he had feet of clay.

Besides he wasn't who he had been anymore either. He was no fool, and that was a fact. Missing a leg was very hard to ignore. He didn't know if Lissa had even noticed, and didn't want to see the look on her face when she finally did. He'd seen a few women's expressions already. Most had been decent about it, but some had twisted their features with revulsion. That had been more than enough for him.

He approached the body on the ground and bent down to take a pulse. Nothing. He glanced at Harrison. "Did you shoot him?"

Harrison nodded and held up another weapon in his hand. "He came up behind me with the gun to my back."

"Right." Stone looked down at the rebel on the ground. "We need to move his body. Anyone can see him here." He glanced around. "Are there others?"

Harrison shook his head. "We've done a full sweep. Levi is talking with Logan right now. We're running behind."

Just as Harrison finished speaking, Levi raced toward them. "We need to move it."

Stone motioned to the body on the ground. "What do we do with him?"

Levi didn't break a sweat as he said, "Leave him there. If we move him, it'll look more suspicious. At this point, I have to say, it's not our problem."

Stone was delighted to find Lissa sitting in the backseat again, staring out the window. He caught her glance and smiled at her encouragingly as he started the engine and turned the vehicle around.

"No vehicle exchange?" she asked quietly.

Levi answered, "No. Change of plans."

"But we'll still make the airport?"

"We'll make it. Don't know if we'll make it in time for your flight though."

Stone watched as she slid lower into the back corner. From the rearview mirror he had a perfect angle to see her as she settled in. With her arms wrapped around her chest and her head resting against the door, it looked like she would try to nap. He highly approved. She'd been running on empty for a long time. Her face was gaunt—he'd felt the bones inside her fingers; the skin over the top of them was sheer, thin. Except for the few calluses where she'd obviously been working hard lately. Overall nothing to take away from the fact that she was very well put together.

But he damn well better keep his mind on the job at hand, not on the curves he could barely see—but had no trouble imagining.

The roads were empty. He drove like crazy to get to the airport on time. When he pulled in, a small plane awaited them, the pilot impatiently stamping his feet at the stairs. Conrad, another friend of Levi's, had been doing flights for them around Europe at odd times. This day he was to take them to London.

"There you are. Finally," he called. "I don't want to have to file another change of flight plan, so let's move it. I've got the paperwork on board." He opened the truck door, motioned them to get out. "Let's go. Let's go. *Let's go.*"

Stone hopped out the driver side and opened the passenger door behind him. Susan, barely awake, was helped to stand up by her husband. But no way could she move very quickly. Nor her husband. Before Stone could make any kind of comment, Levi came around the front of the truck and assessed the situation. He stepped forward quickly, scooping Susan in his arms.

Levi told Kevin, "Come on. Let's go."

Stone checked to see how Lissa was doing. She walked beside them, valiant but tired.

The second truck pulled up beside them, the men getting out and doing a fast sweep. Everyone boarded the plane except for two agents approaching from the small hanger.

Rhodes met the men now responsible for returning the vehicles to the rendezvous point.

Shit went wrong all the time. They had to think on their feet. Plans changed as needed. They were used to it. Inside the plane Stone sat down across from Lissa. This was definitely a no-frills flight. But they would be in London in a few hours. She just needed to hold on a little bit longer.

Levi tucked Susan up against a window seat, and Kevin sat down beside her. They'd barely had a chance to buckle up when Rhodes dashed in to grab his seat.

And the plane began taxiing.

Good. The sooner, the better. Stone watched as the two vehicles they'd driven pulled away, heading back the way they'd come. Now it was just them.

As he looked out the window, it was pitch-black around them. The hangar had no lights and neither did the runway. He shook his head. Typical.

But he also knew Conrad. That man could fly anything anywhere. Just like Ice and her helicopter. Conrad laughed at something Ice said. The two of them were best friends. And at this point, they needed the best they could have. They still weren't out of danger.

Just a few more hours would be good. Stone gazed around the interior of the plane and realized Susan was once again asleep. He studied the color of her face and realized her sleek skin wasn't natural looking. Something was definitely wrong with her. They needed to get her medical attention—and fast. He frowned.

Why hadn't her husband said anything? Did he not know? Was he so stressed that he believed she was just exhausted? Or did he know something more serious was going on but also knew how little anyone could do about it now?

Chapter 5

L ONDON? NOW SHE'D finally traveled to a place she'd always wanted to go, but somehow hadn't reached yet. Of course that was again due to her father. She had really wanted to go to school here, but he'd vetoed it, sending her to a private school in the same state where he lived. He had more control over her there. His donations made a difference and also ensured somebody watched her with a close eye. She'd hated him for that.

The other girls in the school thought it was hilarious. They regularly got her into trouble. Still she had been given some freedom, and her father had left her alone while there. But that watchdog presence had hovered over her future until she could get away.

London was a reminder of the constant battle between her and her father. Only as an adult did she finally break free. When she moved out on her own, she thought he would have a heart attack. Somehow in his mind, she would stay at home until he found the right husband for her.

He'd been introducing her to men for a long time. But they were all his cronies, older men looking for trophy wives. She'd heard her father actually refer to her as a potential up-and-coming one. It made her stomach curdle. She was anything but. As her father had often said, *She looks pretty, but she has a bite. You'll need to control her with a firm hand.*

Was there ever a statement that would send this potential trophy wife screaming in the opposite direction? A firm hand? Yeah, not what she wanted.

She stared out at the huge city below. The bright lights were a godsend. They meant safety to her. They landed, disembarked, and cleared customs at Heathrow with relative ease. Levi had large packets of documentation, and their gun cases were even allowed in. She wondered how many people actually got weapons through high-security places like this. These men had ways and means of accomplishing things she'd never seen.

She walked beside Stone. Since he got on the plane, he hadn't said a word. Just like his namesake, he'd sat there, rigid and unbending. Every once in a while, she watched him massage his left leg. And she wondered if it was an old injury. He was a big man. That body had to be taking a hell of a brutal beating with these kinds of missions. She was sorry if she had added any stress or pain to his life.

She was tall and appreciated tall men. The guy was built like a square tank. She was fairly slim, and this guy would make two of her easily. Still there was something very attractive about that strong silent type. Although, if he would crack a smile every once in a while, she'd appreciate it.

He was quite the protective bulldog at her side. They were catching some attention as they walked as a group. Mostly everybody stepped out of their path to avoid them. Ice and Levi as a couple were very striking, but dressed as they were, it was hardly a relationship-type look for them. All the men of this team were big, fit, and looked ready for any kind of trouble.

The busy airport was suddenly free and clear for them to walk through. She giggled at the thought. She could really use these guys when shopping at the malls.

Stone looked her way, and in a low voice, he asked, "What's so funny?"

She smiled at him. "I was just thinking how helpful it would be to have you guys go shopping with me in the malls. Pathways magically appear when you are around."

His gaze narrowed as he studied the airport, and then his lips quirked. "Not everyone's stupid. They can see danger when it's coming at them."

At that she laughed out loud. "Hell, fear is a big motivating factor for everyone."

He shrugged. "They don't have anything to be afraid of from me."

She shot him a look of straight disbelief. "Surely you are not unaware of how you present yourself. Most people would run away screaming if they were to happen upon you accidentally in the dark."

He frowned and said shortly, "Garbage." He spread his huge mitts and added, "I'm a nice guy. No one needs to be afraid of me."

At that she burst into gales of laughter. The others twisted to look at what the two of them were talking about. She caught sight of Stone as he shrugged his massive shoulders as if to say, *She's just having a moment, so ignore her.* She couldn't stop giggling.

She hooked her arm through his and whispered conspiratorially, "You are scary."

He slanted a gaze her way and said, "You don't appear to be afraid of me."

She patted his forearm and snickered. "That's because I'm not. You're just a gentle giant."

Harrison, who'd been walking on the other side of her,

sniggered. "Oh, that's good. We'll just change your name from Stone to Gentle Giant. No problem," he said. "I totally agree."

"See? Even the guys are on my side on this one." And she snickered again.

She knew Stone didn't know what to make of her. So few big men really understood the impression they gave to others. In his case, he probably thought he was harmless. Unless he was in action. Then that man was all devil. On the other hand, he was on her side, so she had no complaints. He had done a kick-ass job of protecting her so far.

They walked down toward the exit doors. A large group of schoolgirls approached and giggled as they went past. Several were flirting with him. She leaned closer and said, "Ya see? They all want a gentle giant of their own to cuddle up to."

Harrison sniggered again, and she was surprised to see a hint of pink wash up Stone's neck and cheeks. He was embarrassed. How absolutely adorable. She patted his forearm, still holding his arm linked with hers and said, "Don't worry. I'll protect you."

His voice low, he said, "You're having way too much fun with this." He walked faster, with Lissa almost skipping beside him.

It made her feel like a schoolgirl herself as she raced to keep up. "My life's been a bit in the dumps for quite a while. Just a little lighthearted humor to put things in perspective."

He shook his head. "You have a strange outlook on life."

She laughed. "I know you don't appreciate my negativity against my father, but you really have to meet the man."

"What did he do that made you so upset?"

"Well, he locked me in the closet every time he got mad

at me so I now hate confining spaces. Of course you already know about that. How about the fact that he was lining up suitors for the up-and-coming trophy wife who would need a firm hand because she didn't yet have the right attitude?" She couldn't keep the bitterness from her tone.

He straightened and stared down at her in shock. "You serious?"

She nodded. "Every time I came home from college, he always had a new one ready. And the summer before I moved out, he had one coming in every day for a week. Same introductory line every time. I wasn't sure if a bride-price or dowry would be exchanged. My father likes money so maybe a dowry." She studied Stone's face, noting the muscle flicking in the corner of his jaw. "See? Like I said, he's not exactly an angel."

"He is a senator," Stone said cautiously.

"Yep, he is. For eighteen years now. Hopefully he's doing something good for his constituency because his family certainly suffered." Then she gave a mental shrug. "It doesn't matter. It was a long time ago. I walked away and stayed away. I communicate with him and speak with my mom every once in a while. But I don't have a whole lot to do with either of them." She sighed. "Although I owe him my thanks for sending you guys after me."

"When was the last time you went home?"

"Four years ago for Christmas. I was supposed to stay for four days," she said calmly. "I left the same day."

"More suitors?"

"More suitors, even older ones."

"And just how old are we talking?" he asked in a dangerously quiet voice.

"The last two were in their mid-sixties. My father actually thought I should be grateful because then I'd be a widow before too long. With money and freedom to do as I wanted."

"Sounds like a real prize."

"Yeah. I guess some people would call it that."

They walked out into the fresh air. Rain drizzled, soaking through their clothing to their skin. Of course. They were in London.

"Where are we going now?" she asked Stone.

Levi turned to look at her and answered, "To a house for the night, and we'll fly to the States in the morning."

She nodded. Inside her, relief swelled. She wasn't against going home, but she *was* damn tired. Now that they'd made it this far, the pressure was off. "Sounds good to me, especially if this house has hot running water for a shower," she said with a bit of a smile.

"There are showers for everyone."

They gathered inside a large taxi, heading out of the city within minutes. The cab was barely large enough for half of them, since all the men were Stone's size—maybe not that large, but they were certainly big men. Still they squeezed in, and that was what counted.

She tried to settle in the seat, but was pinned between Harrison and Stone—a large thigh on both sides. "God, you guys are like tanks."

Stone tried to move over, but he had no place to go.

She shrugged and said, "Don't worry about it. I'll be fine."

The trip to the house took twenty minutes. By the time they bailed out, she was feeling the effect of all the travel. It was hard even to look around and be excited about where she was. Just a surreal atmosphere to the whole thing.

As much as she'd wanted to keep reminding herself she was safe, she seemed to be more focused on Stone than anything. He was fascinating. Irritating. And yet very comforting. She somehow latched onto him versus any of the others. She didn't know why; maybe because he was the biggest. Maybe she figured he would offer her the best protection.

Of course it was stupid. She did need protection, but with so many men, she doubted anyone could get through. Levi led them up to a brownstone where he gave the door several raps. The door opened almost instantly. The man who stood there was of the same ilk. She recognized a military bearing, but this one was older. She guessed maybe mid-sixties.

They were all ushered inside where jackets and shoes were taken off, and they were led through to the living room. She had never been in one of these townhouses. She looked around curiously. It was sparse but welcoming. With so many of them, they pretty well filled all available seating. The older man motioned to Kevin and Susan first. "Follow me. I'll take you to your room, and you can get settled for the night."

Kevin stood up. "Thank you very much." He turned to Susan. "Come on, honey. Let's get you up to bed."

She gave him a wan smile and allowed him to help her to her feet once again. She even climbed a few steps on the stairway. Lissa winced. Every step looked to be so damn painful. She wanted to ask if one of the men could help Susan but wasn't sure if that was appropriate.

Kevin was slightly older and also suffering the ill effects of their kidnapping, Levi walked over and said something to Kevin.

With a nod, Kevin stepped back and let Levi help Susan. He easily picked her up, ignoring her weak protests, and quickly climbed the stairs, following their host.

As they disappeared from sight, Lissa turned around to see the others staring at her. "What?"

"Is there something seriously wrong with Susan that we don't know about?" Ice asked.

"I'm not sure," Lissa said. "She's always appeared strong and capable until the kidnapping. I don't know if she has a condition that has suddenly taken a downturn or if it's just exhaustion and shock."

"That could be all it is," Ice said. "She's been through a lot."

That seemed to appease everyone, at least for the moment. Their host returned and cast his gaze around the room, smiling at the various men. And stopped, his gaze landing on her. He walked forward and said, "Hi, I'm Charles. And you are?"

Suddenly nervous, she stood up and shook his hand. "My name is Lissa Brampton."

"Pleased to meet you," he said. "I understand you were kidnapped, and Levi and his men rescued you."

"As long as you include Ice in that category, then, yes."

Ice smiled to show him she wasn't really offended.

He tilted his head her way in acknowledgment, then resumed speaking to Lissa. "However, as you guessed, they all have been here many a time and have rooms assigned. I will take you to yours. If you will follow me, please."

She grinned. Stone leaned against the open entryway to the living room. As she walked past him, she said, "I get the shower before you."

"Better save some water," he said. "Tanks like me take a

lot to clean up."

"Better get there fast," she said. "I'm not even sure I remember what hot water feels like."

She followed Charles upstairs, and instead of going left, he took a right. He opened the door to a bedroom that looked out over the backyard. It was a beautiful room with a very Victorian style and a four-poster bed. She stopped and gazed at the bed. "What's wrong with me? This is absolutely gorgeous."

"How very American. Why would anything have to be wrong with you in order to enjoy something our ancestors knew very well how to build and enjoy themselves?" Charles's tone was laughing, yet curious.

She turned and smiled at him. "So true. It's missing a princess dress, and a part of me just seems to think that would be perfect right now. And yet the other part of me says, I should be an adult and let all this go. It's like a dream for a child, and I'm supposed to be all grown-up."

He patted her on the shoulder and said, "No, my dear. It's for discerning people who enjoy the good things in life and who want the very best sleep they can get. Now the bathroom is through there." He motioned to the small door on the far side that she hadn't seen until now. "I understand you have no clothing so we will need to make arrangements for that. However, in the meantime, I'm hoping something in those drawers will fit at least temporarily. Feel free to look."

Walking toward the bedroom door, he added, "Towels are in the bathroom. Please make yourself at home." With a smile he stepped from the room and closed the door behind him.

She did a twirl, then added a little skip and a hop. She

was so damn happy to be here.

This room was fantastic. She couldn't imagine actually having something like this for herself all the time. But for right now, the little girl inside jumped for joy. Her dad would frown and call this frivolous and a waste of money.

She couldn't agree more. And she loved every penny spent on it.

With a huge grin, she headed to the bathroom and the hot water waiting for her. She could finally soak the dried blood off her hair and clean the wound on her forehead. Thankfully it was minor. She didn't know what the hot water system was like here, but she knew one thing. Stone was right. It would take a lot of water to clean his body. She wanted to get in her shower first.

Of course, if she wanted to be frugal and save money for her host, she could have invited Stone to share the shower with her.

That would be fun.

More fun would be the look on his face. Her grin widened. Just the thought of all that heavy muscle was enough to make her body warm. He was deadly.

Since when did she go for the strong silent type?

Since she'd met Stone.

"INTERESTING WOMAN," HARRISON said at Stone's side.

"That she is." Stone turned and faced the rest of the crew. "Are we waiting for anything or can we head to our rooms and grab showers? Of course a change of clothes would be nice."

"Our bags won't be here for a few hours," Levi said. "With any luck they will arrive by the time we wake up in the morning. Charles knows they are on the way." He stood up, reaching out a hand for Ice.

Stone studied the pallor on her face and realized they were all feeling the time change.

"We're heading to bed," Levi said easily. "We'll see you in the morning."

Stone watched as his two best friends headed up the stairs. He was happy for them. They were finally working things out. They'd always been a matched set. But happily for them, they'd become stronger than ever.

What a joy to be with them now. It hadn't been bad before, but it hurt seeing them at a crossroad. The team wanted to help them but was unable to do anything but stand by in silent support and hope they worked their issues out.

Stone wanted to take off his prosthesis and ease up his leg. With a wave at the rest of the guys, he climbed the stairs. They'd all be following him soon enough. He headed into the same room he had had the last time.

Charles was old military. He'd inherited this place from his parents. It hadn't taken long for all his old buddies to find out the space was available for those in need. No questions asked.

Even better, Charles collected great intel for them. He had a lot of connections in London. They often had to call on him for information. Some kind of arrangement had been reached between Levi and Charles; Stone didn't know exactly what it was, but there never seemed to be any hardship, so obviously the agreement worked for them both.

Stone and Levi had been tight in the military; the men in a unit are like none other. Stone considered himself lucky to have been under Levi's command and had never once blamed him for the mess they'd ended up in. Not his fault.

Betrayal happened. In pulling this company together, Levi had breathed new life into his unit. Even bringing Stone in—trusting that he'd get himself on his feet and still be a viable member of the team.

He'd do anything for Levi and the others. But it had been a damn hard fight to get back here. On the outside he seemed like Mr. Invincible. On the inside he knew he was a mess. He walked into his room relieved nobody else would be sharing it with him this time.

He could use the private space. He quickly stripped off his clothing and sat down on the bed. He removed his prosthesis and shuddered with relief. No matter how short or long a time he wore it, it was always a relief to take it off.

In his gear was a salve for the stump, but he'd do without it for the night. He needed a shower first. Standing up, he hopped lightly to the bathroom and stepped inside.

With the hot water pouring down his back, he let his stress ease, and slowly relaxed. Only afterward, standing in front of the mirror and shaving, he thought he heard a knock on his door.

"Hang on," he called. He quickly slipped on his prosthesis and walked to the door, a towel around his waist. He opened it to find Lissa, wearing a robe of some kind.

"Oh, hi." She looked apologetic. "I'm across the hallway. I thought it was your room but wasn't sure."

"You should be sound asleep." He stood quietly studying her.

She winced. "I know, and I hate to bother you, but is there any place to get food?" She leaned forward and said in a low voice, "I have to eat often or my blood sugar drops and I pass out."

"Oh, not good. How bad is it, right now?"

"Bad enough." She looked down toward the stairs. "I was kind of hoping that maybe if you're familiar this area, you knew a place to go and get something to eat. The other problem is, I honestly don't have any money." This time her tone of voice was apologetic, almost ashamed.

He reached out a hand and rubbed her shoulder. "It's all right. I'm sure we can get some food downstairs." He stepped back slightly. "Give me a minute to get changed."

"If you don't mind, I'd appreciate it," she said in a small voice, looking around. "I'd ask Charles, but I don't have a clue where to find him."

"Not to worry. Just give me a minute." He didn't want to close the door in her face, but he was hardly dressed to bring her inside the room.

She stood with her arms wrapped around her chest, but finally she nodded. "Go. I'll be fine."

"I'm not so sure about that," he said, "but I won't be long." He closed the door and walked to where his clothes lay on the ground. He didn't have a spare set, but he gave his a quick shake, slipped on his jeans, put on his T-shirt and shoes, and headed to the doorway. He opened the door and stepped out.

The hallway was empty.

He frowned, hating the instant suspicion. Where was she? Why was she not here? And had something happened to her?

Which was her bedroom? He frowned as he studied the rooms, trying to remember which one was the most unused. She'd said she was across the hallway from him.

He walked there and knocked on the door. No answer.

Dammit, where was she?

Suddenly the door opened in front of him.

And there she was. A bright smile on her face.

277

Chapter 6

LISSA SMILED UP at Stone. "Thank you," she said. "I felt stupid standing in the hallway alone so I went to my room to wait."

"No worries. I was just concerned something had happened to you." He motioned to the stairway. "Shall we?"

She walked down the stairs ahead of him. At the bottom she waited for him to join her. "Where to?"

He motioned to a doorway on the left. "We'll go through here. The kitchen is on the other side."

"Are you sure it's okay if we scavenge for food?" She looked around. "I feel like I'm sneaking around a stranger's house, and that makes me very uncomfortable. Wouldn't it be better to go out and grab a meal?"

He laughed. "It's fine. I'm sure Charles probably hears us even now. He's likely to be in the kitchen, waiting for us."

"Oh, dear. That would make me feel even worse," she exclaimed quietly. "I don't want to disturb the poor man. We already woke him up in the middle of the night to get in."

"Not to worry." Charles suddenly stood in front of them. Dressed in a smoking jacket and pajama pants with big slippers, he looked distinguished and ... adorable.

"I'm sorry if we woke you," she whispered. Not what she wanted to do at all. This had gone from embarrassing to selfish. "We should have just stepped out and found a place to eat."

"That wouldn't have worked. The security is tight in this place." Charles offered a small smile. "I change it regularly so you'd have set off the alarms and woken me anyway." He motioned in front of him. "There are, however, meat pies and multiple other dishes in there."

As they entered the kitchen, he said, "You weren't the only ones hungry." He walked to the fridge. "Some of the men needed to eat before they went to bed as well. In fact, I apologize. I should have offered you something as soon as you arrived. I am sorry for the oversight."

She sat down and watched as he pulled out food from some of the cupboards and fridge. And there was a lot of it. "Do you think we should ask anyone else?" she murmured to Stone. "I would feel bad if others went to bed hungry."

His smile was slow to come but when it did finally shine, it was a thing of beauty.

She forgot to chew she was so enraptured. When she finally remembered, she swallowed hard and said, "You should come with a warning."

He stopped chewing and stared at her.

She laughed. "I guess that surprised you." She nodded her thanks as Charles brought a glass of milk to her. She smiled at the childhood treat. "Are you sure you won't join us, Charles?"

"No, my dear, I ate hours ago."

Of course he did. He ate at a normal mealtime before his company ruined his evening. She forked another bite of meat pie. "This is delicious."

"I'm glad you're enjoying it. It was freshly made today. A touch strong on the nutmeg, do you think?"

"It's wonderful," she murmured around a mouthful of meat and spices wrapped in pastry. "Lovely."

He smiled quietly and cut her a second piece, placing it on her plate without asking.

So focused on her food, she didn't realize when Charles left.

Finally she laid down her fork and leaned back, contented. "That was so good."

Stone was still eating his third piece of meat pie. She watched the big man as he took bite after bite. He was careful and methodical but also showed appreciation for every piece.

He was a fascinating male. She picked up her glass of milk and took a sip, then quickly collected the dishes she'd used and carried them to the sink. She suspected a dishwasher was here, but she'd rather do them by hand. She cleaned up her dishes, then returned for the few Stone had used.

"Are you done?" she asked, studying the empty plate in front of him.

"Stuffed." He lifted his plate and used the table to stand.

Interesting. He'd made several other moves that she'd seen but hadn't really noticed as being different. The little incidences were adding up—in a good way. Then she remembered seeing him limp every so often.

She sat down suddenly. "Are you hurt?"

He frowned. Then shook his head. "I'm fine. Why do you ask?"

When she gazed at his bloody shirt, he smiled and said, "Not to worry. Like you, I don't have clean clothes to change into."

"Right. But something is wrong. I noticed it earlier, but wasn't sure what I was seeing."

"I'm not sure what you're seeing now," he said with a frown furrowing his forehead. "I'm fine."

She bit her lower lip and nodded. If he didn't want to talk, she wasn't going to push it. He was entitled to his secrets. She had a few she didn't want to drag from the closet either.

He stood straight and said, "Are you ready to sleep now?"

"I think so."

He held out his hand.

She placed hers in it and let him lead her to the stairs. "I'm not sure I would have found the kitchen on my own."

"Sure you would have. You traveled halfway around the world to help others. This wouldn't have been a problem."

"Maybe, but that seems a full world away now. Something about being kidnapped has me feeling less confident and secure in my own abilities." She stopped at the top of the stairs and said, "I don't like it."

SOMETHING ABOUT THE tone of her voice made him look at her twice. "Will you be okay tonight?"

She reached out for her bedroom doorknob and said, "I'd be pretty damn sad if I'm in a house with so many men and not consider myself safe. I'm inside, safe, secure, and surrounded by bodyguards."

She tossed him an overly bright smile and walked into her room. "Have a good night. See you in the morning."

She closed the door gently in his face. Frowning, he walked to his bedroom and opened the door. As he went to close it, he found himself studying hers.

Something about this bugged the hell out of him, but he

couldn't figure out what or why. Against his instincts, he went in his room, closed the door behind him, and walked to his bed. Still fully dressed, he lay down on top of the covers, crossing his hands underneath his head, and stared up at the ceiling. She hadn't acted any odder than she had already, and she wasn't all that odd. She was just unique.

He liked unique. But something else was there besides that. So what if she was afraid tonight? She should be fine. Like she said, the house was full of bodyguards. And there was no reason to think anybody was after her anyway.

Eventually he drifted off but found himself unable to get into a deep sleep. He rolled over in time to see his doorknob turn. Instantly he was awake and up. Standing behind the door, hidden from whoever was coming in, he waited.

The door opened just enough that it unlatched. But it moved back and forth ever-so-slightly, as if somebody stood on the other side, deciding if they should open it or not. Then he knew.

In a quiet voice he said, "Lissa?"

Instantly the door opened wide, and she poked her head around. "Are you awake?"

The relief in her voice tugged at his heart. He stepped from behind the door, startling her. She took several steps back into the hallway, but he tugged her forward into his room quickly and closed the door behind her. The last thing he wanted was the rest of the house to be awake and aware. "What's wrong?"

Eyes downcast, she shrugged. He stepped to the side, and the moonlight from the window caught her face, and he could see the shine of her skin. He reached up a hand and stroked the damp tendrils of hair. "You had a nightmare, didn't you?"

She raised her gaze to him, her lower lip trembling, and nodded. "It just seems so unreal," she began. "I couldn't believe all this happened. I had to make sure I wasn't dreaming and that you were actually here. That *somebody* was here."

And he realized they'd made a tactical mistake. They should've had her share a room with Ice.

She wouldn't have been alone then. On the other hand maybe this way he'd benefit too.

He wasn't averse to sharing his bed for the night. Especially if it meant they could both get some decent sleep. He knew that was why he had yet to rest. And he needed to because who knew what tomorrow would bring. He wrapped a gentle arm around her shoulder and tugged her toward the bed.

"You can stay in my bed tonight."

She stopped and looked at him hopefully. "You sure? You don't mind?"

Half in exasperation and half in humor he said, "No, I don't mind. Yes, I'm sure. I offered. And, yes, we're just going to sleep, even though you didn't ask."

He gave her a push toward the bed, and, with a big grin, she rushed to the side he had not been sleeping on, crawling quickly under the covers.

She looked at his still-made side of the bed and asked, "Weren't you sleeping?"

He walked closer and sat down. For the first time he was feeling a little unsure. He shrugged and said, "Trying to."

She patted his shoulder. "That's okay. I'll keep you safe."

He gave a bark of laughter and lay down on top of the covers beside her. "I'd like to see that."

She curled up in a ball beside him and murmured, "You

can get under the covers, you know. You would sleep better if you took off your T-shirt."

He crossed his arms over his belly and said, "I'm fine. Go to sleep."

"You're better than fine, but you'd sleep a whole lot better if you took off the prosthetic limb too." She gave a great big yawn before rolling to face the other side of the room. "I'm beat."

He lay still as her words whispered into his head. Of course she recognized he was missing a leg. Why did that surprise him? Not many people mentioned it, that's why. In fact, no one outside the team and Jackson ever did. But then again, he hung around everybody who knew the details. Not like it was a secret back at the compound. Still, he was relieved that she knew and was okay with it.

As he lay here, he realized he was a fool. The damn thing was chafing his stump, and he really would like to get it off. He waited another few minutes to make sure she was sleeping, then he sat up, pulled off his T-shirt, slipped off his jeans—leaving himself in boxers—and unclipped the prosthesis, dropping it all to the floor. With a quick flick, he had the blankets over him, then he stretched out under the covers.

Much better. With a smile on his face he fell into an easy sleep.

Chapter 7

S HE WOKE ALONE but with a sense of security she hadn't had in a hell of a long time. She turned on her back in the big bed, her hand falling on the warm spot where Stone had lain. She wondered if he'd ever gotten comfortable enough to take off the prosthesis.

She got up, made her side of the bed, and crept to the doorway. Given that she'd spent the night in his room, she didn't want him to be teased by the others or to have anyone get the wrong idea, so she wanted to return to her room without anybody seeing her.

Listening from inside his room, she couldn't hear anyone yet. She opened the door, saw the hallway was empty, and quickly made her way to her room. She went straight to the drawers where Charles had said there would be clothing for her. She could definitely use something clean to wear.

She found jeans, some kind of a yoga-looking pants, T-shirts with long sleeves ... In fact, a whole collection of clothing was here. But nothing in the way of underclothes. Still, probably for the best. She wasn't sure how she felt about wearing somebody else's underwear. She picked a pair of pants and went with a T-shirt that should fit and dressed quickly. Given that she was in London, and, from the window, it was rainy, she found a cardigan that she quickly put on over her T-shirt. She was still adapting to the temperatures.

Although she'd finally slept, she knew she would need a lot more rest. She didn't know what today would bring, and she wanted to be prepared.

She made her way downstairs into the kitchen. The group of men were already seated, enjoying breakfast, including Stone. He patted the seat beside him, and, with a smile, she sat down.

"I'm not sure we should meet again here. Seems like just a few hours." Several people stopped and looked up at her. She winced. "Maybe I wasn't supposed to say anything, but Charles was kind enough to feed me last night."

"Good for Charles," Levi said. "I know most of the men had something to eat before sleeping." He waved at the tableful of food. "Help yourself. Charles is manning the stove. I believe bacon and eggs are coming, if you want some."

And, boy, did she. It might only have been a few hours, but she was starving again. How the hell did that happen?

By the time breakfast was over, she felt comfortable with the group once more. "What's on tap for today?"

"Waiting on the luggage. And then flying home."

"Yay," she said with a smile.

Levi's phone rang, which he answered right away. "What?" His gaze immediately zipped toward Lissa. "Right. We'll bring her in the next couple hours. What about the other luggage?"

She looked around the table quickly and realized Kevin and Susan weren't here. She turned to look at Stone and asked in a very low voice, "Are Susan and Kevin okay?"

He shook his head. "Susan was taken to the hospital this morning. Kevin's with her."

She was stunned at what she'd already missed. She reached for his wrist, twisted it so she could see the time. It was nine o'clock. "Good Lord, when was that?"

"They were gone by six-thirty this morning," he said calmly. "Nothing you could do. She's getting the best care possible. And, yes, you can see them later if the hospital allows."

Levi got off the phone just then and turned to Lissa. "What was in your luggage?"

At the hard tone in his voice, her mouth dropped open. "Just the basics. A couple pairs of pants and shirts, and a hoodie." She raised her hands in an "I don't know" motion, adding, "Toiletries, shampoo, a little bit of makeup, deodorant, and a book. I had an iPod but my cell phone is here with me." She fished it from her pocket and put it on the table. "I don't even know why I keep it. It doesn't work."

Stone immediately picked it up and popped out the battery, checking it. He put it back together and played with its buttons.

"It turns on but won't send or receive, and I can't call out. I should grab my contacts off there before I can't get them any longer. I just need a pen and paper." She watched him for a moment, then shrugged, turning her gaze to Levi. "What's wrong?"

"We have to return to customs. Something suspicious has been found in your luggage. They also want to see anything that you had on you when you came through."

She raised her eyes and froze. "Well, my dirty clothes are still upstairs."

Ice spoke up quietly. "I'm sure it's nothing. We'll head down, clear things up, and carry on. We all need our luggage, but yours came in separately from the refugee camp.

Or did you have a bag at the rebel compound where you were held?"

She shrugged. "Two bags were snatched up with us. One of Susan's and also a bag with first aid kits. But I lost track of both almost immediately. It was all very confusing. I never saw the same person twice, no matter the luggage."

"I have to ask before this gets any further," Levi said in a hard voice. "And you need to tell me right now if you were carrying anything that you shouldn't have been."

She stared at him in surprise and asked cautiously, "Like what?"

"Well, drugs for one."

She sat back, stunned. "I don't do drugs."

"Anything else? Money, weapons?"

"No!" she said in shock. "Nothing like that. I was there to give humanitarian aid, not to run drugs." She shook her head. "It's not like drugs were there anyway. It's not something anyone could get locally. I never saw anything in the clinics where I was working."

Ice asked, "I know this stuff isn't easy to consider, but what about Kevin and Susan?"

Instantly Lissa shook her head. "Oh, no. I never saw them doing anything like that."

Levi straightened from the table and said, "We'll have to deal with this. Not all of us though. Lissa, you and Stone are coming with us, and we'll bring Harrison too. Ice will stay here and await the arrival of the other luggage as well as keep the lines of communication open."

To Lissa that all sounded normal. But the hard glance Levi shot Ice and the blank look on her face said something else entirely.

WHAT THE HELL? Something was going on. Yet, if he could get the others alone, he might be able to find out. But as long as she was beside him, they weren't saying anything. He couldn't blame them if their suspicions fell on her shoulders right now. They had put their necks out to rescue her, but if she was doing something illegal, that could get them all in a shitload of trouble.

He couldn't see it. But he'd been wrong before.

They walked out to the vehicle waiting for them. It wasn't a cab, but the driver obviously was expecting them. In the backseat Stone watched as Lissa nervously clenched her fingers together.

In a low voice she said to him, "I swear I didn't do anything wrong."

He studied the look on her face and what he knew of the tone in her voice. Words might lie, but body language really didn't. It took a consummate professional to pull that off. And he believed her. He reached over and patted her knee gently. "We'll get to the bottom of this. Don't you worry."

She gave a strangled laugh. "How am I not supposed to? They found something in my backpack. Like, what the hell, Stone? Anybody could have put something in my bag. It wasn't even in my possession for the last however long."

"And that's exactly what we'll tell them," Levi said. At least he was no longer the cold stranger she'd seen earlier. Now he looked ready to listen to her.

"Will they believe me?" she asked in a small voice.

"We can vouch for the time you were with us," Levi said with certainty. "And like you said, your bag was not with you for many days. So that will add up to someone else being involved."

"Any chance my passport will be there?"

"No, but we've taken care of that. As soon as we knew where you were, arrangements were made to get you home safely. It would be easier if you had it now, but it's not the end of the world that you don't."

Stone settled back. The traffic was rough outside. He was glad he wasn't driving. If he was forced to navigate these congested streets, he'd like to drive a Hummer. At least then everyone would get the hell out of his way. Instead, the cars were cutting off their driver on a consistent basis.

As he stared out the window, wondering what the hell customs had found in her bags, a small hand worked its way under his palm. He looked at her. She stared out the window, chewing on her bottom lip. Instantly he wrapped her hand in his and gently stroked his thumb across the top, noting how smooth her skin was, how very feminine. His was more of a meat fest. He could crush the bones in her fingers without even thinking about it. "It'll be okay."

When he squeezed her fingers, she squeezed back, never saying a word. She seemed to relax a little bit though.

Once there, they made their way to the customs office. They were met by somebody Levi knew. And then Stone realized Charles was here too. Stone hadn't seen Charles leave the house. Stone frowned and asked Levi, "How the hell did Charles get here?"

"He left ahead of us, heading to the hospital. I called him as soon as we knew there was a problem. He used to work for MI6."

"Well, that's good. Maybe."

They stood and waited until they were led into another room. The four of them sat down in a chair and waited some more. Only Lissa fidgeted, and Stone couldn't blame her.

Finally the door opened, and a man walked in with a file

folder. He sat down at the table opposite them, opened the file, and spread out pictures. It appeared to be photos of clothing, personal effects, and a bag. Lissa leaned forward and said, "That's my bag."

And that started the volley of questions. When had she last seen her bag? Where had she? Did she know who had had contact with it? The questions just went on and on and on.

Finally she threw up her hands and said, "I don't know what else I can tell you. I saw the two bags right after being kidnapped. I thought one was Susan's, but I can't be sure. I never saw it again. As for mine, they were in my quarters in the refugee camp, as far as I know. Again, I was kidnapped and have no idea what happened to anything with us or what was left behind." She shrugged and said, "Honestly I thought I'd never see any of my belongings again. Everything was replaceable."

After that followed a series of questions about her father, family life, business interests, political leanings, and even her religion. With every question she got quieter and quieter.

Stone sympathized, but there was no point in showing that right now. They'd been responsible for entering a foreign country and plucking her from it. This needed to be cleared up right now.

A knock sounded on the door, and without waiting for the okay to enter, the door opened to admit Charles. He came in and handed Levi a stack of documents. "These are her passport and visas—all her documentation." He glanced at Lissa, appearing to note the pallor in her face. "Lissa, I'm afraid that anything in your bag is now forfeit."

"I don't care," she said tiredly. "I don't know what you guys found in my stuff, but I can guarantee you I didn't put any contraband in there."

Abruptly the man on the other side of the table who had been asking so many questions stood and said, "You're all free to go."

Stone wanted to laugh at the sudden sag in her shoulders as she understood that she was no longer being held. He stood and motioned for her to get up. They stepped from the room.

Charles, now with them, said, "I suggest we take her somewhere so she can grab some clothing and see if we can get you all on the same flight this afternoon."

"I don't really care about new clothing. Please, can I just go home?"

Stone reached up and rubbed her shoulder. "Soon. Very soon."

But he doubted it would be soon enough to suit her.

Chapter 8

F OR SOME REASON she hadn't expected they would be
flying commercial, although she wasn't sure what other
options there were. The large group was spread out up and
down the rows of seats. She'd been afraid she would get
stuck beside one of the other men, but she felt luck was on
her side that she was sitting beside Stone. As she glanced at
his bland face, she thought maybe that had nothing to do
with it.

As the plane taxied down the runway, she leaned over
and said, "Thank you."

"You're welcome."

From the twinkle she saw in his eye, she knew he understood what she was thanking him for.

He really was a nice man. She also knew she wouldn't be
completely relaxed until they cleared customs in the States,
and she was free and clear.

They'd opted not to go shopping in London, so she was
still wearing the clothes Charles generously donated to the
cause. She made a mental note to send him something nice
as a thank you when she got home.

Not exactly how she thought her first trip to London
would go. But after that customs visit, she was a whole lot
less inclined to return.

She leaned back in her seat and closed her eyes. It would

be a long flight home.

Although it was, it wasn't as bad as she thought. She copied her contact list off her phone onto a napkin. Then it didn't matter if she couldn't use this phone; she could still contact her friends when she got a replacement. With the flight attendants coming up and down the aisle with coffee, drinks, and snacks, along with Stone beside her the whole way, the trip was actually fairly fast. They landed in New York, and just like that, they cleared customs.

When she finally stood on the other side of customs, she beamed with joy. "Wow, that went a lot better than I thought it would."

"Not everything is full of those bumps in life," Ice said. "Sometimes things actually go smoothly."

It hadn't occurred to Lissa to ask what they were doing after getting her here. She turned to study Stone and felt her heart jerk. "Am I saying good-bye to you guys here?"

"Three of the unit will be heading back to base," Levi said. "Four of us are taking you home."

"And whose home would that be? My home or my parents'?"

Everyone stopped. Levi said in a conversational tone that ended with a question, "Your father said you lived at his home. In Colorado."

"Of course he did. Whereas I actually have a townhouse in the suburbs of Houston, Texas."

Silence.

"In that case," Levi said slowly, "I'm hoping we can get your cooperation to visit your parents so we can complete this, and then we'll see about getting you to Texas."

"Are the tickets already booked for Colorado?"

"Yes. Like I said, for the four of us. The rest of the crew

is going home."

"And where's home for the rest of you?" she asked curiously. And as hard as she tried not to, her gaze drifted toward Stone.

His lips quirked. "Texas."

She beamed. "Perfect. So can I go home with you guys, please?" she asked in a pleading tone. "I don't want to stay at my parents' place any longer than I have to. I can pay you back the ticket price."

At that, Levi nodded. "We can change yours so you travel with us all the way there." He smiled. "Your father is paying for these flights though."

"Then don't tell him one of those is for me. He'll cancel it before we ever get out of the house if he knows."

They landed in Denver and were still in the airport several hours later.

She wondered if she'd ever get to her home. Each leg of this journey was taking more out of her. It felt like soon there'd be nothing left of her.

Standing in the airport lobby, she recognized the limousine as it pulled up in front of the wall of doors.

"Typical, Father." She got in the back with the others.

The trip was less than twenty minutes, but it helped that there was mostly no traffic. As they pulled up to the family home, she studied the austereness of the residence. An imposing big brick structure with nothing to soften the heavy lines. "He really should move to London. That would suit him."

The driver, a man she didn't know, came around to open the door for her. She waited until they'd all exited the limo before walking up to the front door.

It opened before they made it to the porch.

Her father stood in the doorway, his arms crossed as he glared at her. She stepped forward in front of the team and said, "Hello, Father."

"There you are. Are you done causing trouble?"

She heard the hisses of surprise behind her. But it would take a lot for her father's words to hurt her anymore. "As I didn't ask to be kidnapped, nor did I do anything to cause this, I hardly think it's fair that you blame me for it." She motioned at the open doors behind him. "Are we going in, or am I saying good-bye right here?"

His eyebrows soared, and the anger in his face dropped away. "What do you mean? You're leaving? You can't leave now," he protested. Still he glared at the others, then stepped back from the doorway. "Come in. Come in."

Levi entered first, and the others followed.

Lissa stood outside on the big porch and wondered if there was any way to disappear. But with her father glaring at her, and Stone standing there waiting, she didn't think so.

Oh, well, might as well face the music right now rather than later.

They walked into the living room. As Lissa stepped around in front of the others, she caught sight of her mother sitting beside the fireplace, poised perfectly, as if for photographs. But so not as a mother greeting a daughter who had just returned from a harrowing kidnapping experience.

Lissa stepped into the middle of the room and said, "Hello, Mother. You're looking well."

Her mother stood and smiled prettily. "Thank you. You're looking better than I expected, but oh, dear, stitches. You know that will leave a scar," she said reprovingly.

"I'm fine, thank you. No need to worry now that I'm home safe."

There, the polite conversation was done. Maybe she could leave now. As she glanced around, she caught sight of Stone's frown. She slightly rolled her eyes as if to say, *I told you so.*

"She was very brave and handled herself well under the circumstances," Stone said in a low voice.

Her mother gave a delicate shudder. "She goes on these excursions, putting herself in danger, and it's very trying for us all."

This time Lissa did roll her eyes. Of course it was trying for everyone but more so for Lissa, not her mother. All it did was interrupt her mother's schedule and force her to adjust.

Her father who had left, reappeared suddenly. He handed an envelope to Levi. "A bonus. And you have my deepest thanks for rescuing my daughter."

The two men shook hands. In her father's typical style, he completely passed over Ice who stood at Levi's side as he proceeded to shake Harrison and Stone's hands.

Her eyes twinkling, she prodded her father. "Don't forget about Ice, Dad. She's one of the main members of their unit."

Her father looked startled at the comment or maybe at the unusual name but moved in front of her, appearing to be amiable about shaking her hand too.

Ice glanced at Lissa, a glint of humor in her eye as she said, "Lovely to have met you, Lissa. You've been very brave throughout this whole event."

"That's a good one. I survived. That's about all I can say. Except that I wouldn't have without you guys. I'll miss you," she admitted warmly.

She heard her mother's disdainful sniffle behind her. Lissa stiffened at the rebuke, and her gaze caught Stone's once again.

This group was more her kind of people. She was a misfit in her family and always had been. She turned to her father and said, "Now what, Father?" He'd always orchestrated her life. She had no doubt he'd planned her return down to the smallest detail.

"I'm sure you're tired. Go to your room and rest," he said in a tone that brooked no argument. "We'll talk in the morning."

She knew how that worked. Instantly she ran up the stairs. The obedient returning daughter. *Like hell.*

Thankfully, she knew this house well. She heard her father at the front door saying good-bye to the team and realized she had no time.

She just hoped they could stall long enough so she could sneak out the rear and come around to the front without being seen. They knew she had a ticket booked to go home to Texas with them. She did not want to miss that flight. Nor did she want to stay here.

At the top of stairs was the fire escape out the back. She was on that, skittering down as fast as she could. Hitting the ground running, she came around to the side of the property. The limo was already driving around the circular drive that would take the big vehicle to the main road.

She cut a corner across the front yard and dashed into the center of the road.

She didn't dare look at the front door to see if her father was still standing there. She was counting on the fact that he would not watch the vehicle leave.

The black limousine hit the brakes. Thankfully, he hadn't been going very fast so the squeal wasn't enough to raise alarms inside the house. The driver frowned as he looked through the windshield.

The rear passenger door opened, and Stone stepped out, a hard look on his face. "Are you nuts? That's a great way to get yourself killed."

She dashed to his side, reaching up to kiss him on the cheek. "I missed you too."

She dove inside the vehicle and sat on the front seat facing them, then pounded the glass lightly to tell the driver to move. With an impudent grin, she glanced at the others. "So, what did you think of my father?"

STONE KEPT HIS thoughts to himself. A lot of comments rolled around in his head, but his mother had taught him a few simple commands to follow in life. One of them was if he couldn't say anything nice, don't say anything at all.

And there was nothing nice about his thoughts right now.

In fact, if he had Lissa's father in front of him, Stone would be hard pressed to hold his fists back. And as for that doll of a mother ...

Well, he had no words.

Apparently nobody else in the vehicle could voice their feelings either because complete silence reigned.

Lissa laughed. "That's all right. It's exactly how I feel too."

She settled down into the vehicle and tucked her knees up against her chest. She stared out the window, watching as the miles passed. Stone studied her features, but they were blank, as if she herself didn't know what to think. He sensed a finality in her and wondered if she'd ever return to her parents' house.

"What will your father do to you for sneaking out?" Ice asked.

Lissa turned to her. "Who said I had to sneak?" She turned her gaze back out the window for a long time. Then she said, "I have no idea. He should be used to me fighting his dictates, but he always seems surprised when he gives orders and I refuse."

"Why not stay a little while with your parents?" Harrison asked. "I don't mean any offense. I just have trouble with you not wanting to at least reassure them that you're okay after what you've been through."

"And I did that," she said quietly. "As you can see, it's not like they wanted to spend any time with me. I was ordered to my room to stay for the night. Father would speak with me in the morning, when he had time. But what I can tell you from past experience is, he would order me to his office the next day, and he would give me a complete dressing down for my actions. After that I'd be ordered back to my room. I did not need to listen to that again."

Harrison nodded. "As long as you know for sure that's what would happen."

"What about your mother? Has she ever intervened?" Ice asked. "I don't have a mother or haven't for a long time, but my father and I are close. I can't imagine not having the kind of relationship that we have."

"I can't imagine having what you must have," Lissa said. "Honestly, I don't know anything other than our cold existence. I was never hugged or held, except by my nannies. I wasn't allowed to eat at the same dinner table until I was *old enough*. I went to boarding school because it was more convenient for them, so they didn't have to drive me anywhere or deal with me on weekends."

She glanced from one face to the other and finally landed on Stone. "It wasn't so bad," she said quietly. "I made friends in school. Every once in a while I would go to their place for holidays." She turned to stare out the window again. "In fact, it was nicer at boarding school than it was at home."

Stone stared down at his open hands resting on his lap. They were open to prevent him from clenching them into fists and pounding something. The only thing available to pound was the vehicle, and he didn't want to end up dealing with her father over that.

Chapter 9

B Y THE TIME they got on to the next flight, she was too tired to talk. Stone once again sat beside her, and she made absolutely no apologies for curling up and resting her head against his broad shoulder and closing her eyes.

The only thing that bothered her was her heart taking on the fear of the approaching good-bye.

She was not looking forward to that.

Somehow she had become accustomed to being with Stone, but she didn't get close to people easily. And yet somehow she felt attached to him. He'd also been there with her for the last couple days, and she would find it very hard to let him go. Yet he had a life. *Remember*, she told herself, *she was just a job*. Although they might both live in Texas, that didn't mean he was interested.

"Wake up, Lissa."

She straightened and stared at him blurry eyed. "Are we landing now?"

He nodded. "Will be. We started our descent. We'll be down in ten minutes."

She nodded and reached up to cover her mouth with her hand as she yawned. "Oh, man, am I tired."

"It's been a long trip home," he said. "You'll need a couple days to relax."

"I still have to get home," she said. "That means trying

to find a taxi at this hour. And I don't think I have keys to my house anymore."

"Didn't you hide a set?" he asked with one eyebrow raised.

"No. I left the spares with Marge so she could get in and check my mail." She made a face. "Now to find a way to break in. Part of me wants to say I hope I left a window open, but another knows damn well I better not have." She slumped into a chair, depressed as all hell now. "Goddammit."

"Don't worry about it. We'll figure it out."

"You mean, I'll have to. You'll head off to your home, back to your job. Me? I need to go home and find a way to start my life all over again." She hated the note of bitterness in her tone, but right now, a little bit too much had happened over an incredibly long series of days. All she wanted was to go home and crash on her bed. The fact that she probably couldn't even get into her own house ... Talk about a grand finale. And yet, because of him, she had a life. She needed to stop whining and appreciate what she had.

"I'm not leaving you after all that we've done so far. I need to be sure you'll be okay," he said in exasperation. "You are just over an hour's drive from my home. I'll take you to your place first. We'll see if we can get you inside. If not, we'll look at other options."

Feeling shaky but relieved, she threw her arms around him and gave him a big hug. "Thank you so much. I have to admit I was feeling really nervous about this last bit. And I shouldn't be," she exclaimed. "I finally get to go home."

He reached out and grabbed her hand. "Hold that thought. We'll get you there probably in about an hour and a half, depending on how much trouble we have getting off the airplane. But considering the minimal baggage you have, there should be absolutely no problem."

She stood outside the airport exit not knowing what to do. For the first damn time in a long while she was home. The team was in sight, and she didn't want to be separated. Nerves? Or just plain fear? She didn't know.

She turned to glance behind her. Stone was talking with the others. Finally some kind of an agreement was made. Some shoulder slapping, smiles, and then the other three turned in another direction.

Stone came toward her. "Okay, we have two vehicles here. They will take one and go home, and I will take you to your place and then go home myself."

She watched the other three retreat, feeling a sadness she hadn't expected. "You sure it's okay with them? Shouldn't you be going home with them?"

"Actually they were all coming with me," he said. "But as this should be a simple trip to get you into your house, they decided to go home themselves." He wrapped an arm around her shoulders as they walked to the parking lot. "I'll keep them updated. If there's any difficulty, they'll be here."

It took a moment, which she put down to tiredness, before the statement actually penetrated her foggy brain. "What do you mean by 'difficulty'?"

"I don't mean anything."

Before too long, he had her safely ensconced inside the passenger seat of a jeep. She laughed when she got in. "I always wanted to ride in one of these but never have."

"You have a car?"

"Yes." She winced. "I have a Toyota Prius."

"Interesting choice."

"Well, I do care about the environment, and my daddy

was extremely against it." She laughed. "As I look back at my life, it seems like everything I've done has been to spite him." She gave her head a shake. "Definitely time to grow up."

"There's time for that," he said comfortably. "If you had stayed at your parents' house last night, what would you be facing now? And how much trouble would you have getting home to your own place now?"

"I don't have any money on me so I couldn't have gotten here without your help. God knows Father wouldn't have helped me. But, once I'm here, there's a telephone. Father can call me, but he does have friends in town who often come by to make sure I'm okay." She shrugged. "It's like he can't quite let go of that bit of control."

"He's a father," Stone said.

"That he is, but I doubt that has anything to do with it," she said quietly. She didn't mean to be mysterious, but there was just no understanding her father.

"Have they always been well-off?"

She nodded. "Old money, blue blood, and married wealthy. They did all the expected things. They even had a child. Unfortunately I seem to be the one part of their life that didn't turn out the way they expected."

Up ahead was the exit from the airport. "I need a few directions," he said.

"Oh, sorry. I am really tired. Take a left here. We're taking the Aberdeen exit about five minutes down the road."

"I know the area."

"Do you?"

He nodded. "I've spent a lot of years in Texas for one reason or another."

She studied his craggy features and said, "You know so much about me, and I don't know anything about you."

"Not a whole lot to know."

"The military is an interesting choice."

"Mom died of cancer six months before I enlisted. At that point I was lost. I was looking for a family. I signed up for BUD/S training and surprised myself by actually succeeding." He laughed. "At the time I felt I had found my perfect place.

"What is Buds?"

"Basic Underwater Demolition/SEAL training."

"But?"

"But what?"

"You said you thought you had found your perfect place *until ...*"

He turned to look at her. "Until we were on a mission and somebody betrayed us. We all took some pretty heavy physical damage. My unit, all four of us, had to leave the military because of it. I am the only one who lost a limb. Levi and I were hurt the worst. Rhodes and Merk had an easier time of it but not by much. Still we all survived and that's what counts"

He patted the dashboard. "But Levi was never anybody to stay down long. He'd always had it in the back of his head that, when his time was up in the military, he'd set up a private company and continue doing what we always did so well. So here we are."

"You don't have any family?"

"Only the family I work with."

Somehow that seemed really sad to her. Then again, how many times in her life had she wished to be an orphan? Maybe he had the better deal after all.

They turned off the highway, and she directed him through the small town toward her place. She was getting her second wind.

When they pulled into the driveway of her building, she smiled. The pretty Victorian look had always appealed to her. This place had seemed perfect for her at the time. And, in a way, maybe it still was. Except that, for some reason, she never spent any time here. She could change that now. Her traveling bug had certainly disappeared.

"Is this the place?" Stone turned to look at her.

"It certainly is." She hopped out and ran up to the front door. Sure enough it was locked. Although why she thought it wouldn't be, she had no idea. She ran down the stairs to Stone and said, "Let's check the back door."

He followed at a much slower pace. As she went around the building, she kept up a running stream of commentary about the place. "I bought it a couple years ago. At the time I really liked the pretty look to the place. It's just I haven't stayed here longer than a few months." She shrugged. "I've been traveling so much that it has not really ever seemed like home." She turned to look at him and froze.

His features had gone hard, a glint of steel to his gaze.

She reached out for his arm and stepped really close. "What the hell's the matter?"

He lifted an arm and pointed to the back door and the kitchen windows. "You tell me."

She turned to look at her kitchen and realized the windows were smashed in on both sides. The door, although closed, looked like it could flap in the wind. "Oh, my God! My place has been broken into."

"Did you have some kind of arrangement with the management to rent it out while you were gone?"

She shook her head. "No, I never wanted strangers in my house." She didn't make a move to get closer to the building.

Instead she just stood, clutching his arm. "This makes no sense."

"Why is that?" he said in a drily. "Tough times, small town, and an empty house for months on end ... I'm surprised it wasn't broken into before."

She turned to face him. "My friend Marge should have stopped by last night and checked it. She's been coming by once a week to collect my mail and to make sure the place was okay. She comes every Sunday night like clockwork."

"Can you check to see when she was here last?"

"I could, but she's sleeping right now, and I don't have a phone anymore," she said. "Why?"

"Just to make sure we have the correct time frame. It seems suspicious that you left this place empty for what, six months? Considering your friend was here recently, we have to assume she'd have noticed this damage, so it must have happened after her last trip here. We'll need to contact her next to confirm she came last night but if so ..."

"Eight months," she corrected.

"Right, for eight months. So we have to consider the possibility that now, on the day that you actually arrive here, your place is broken into."

Slowly her gaze went from the house to him, then back again. "Oh, my God! You think it's related, don't you?"

"LET'S JUST SAY it's not a coincidence I'm comfortable with," he said. "We had trouble with the London airport. Now you come home, and your place has been broken into. Not last week, but just now within roughly twenty-four hours of your return. Until we can confirm, we can consider this a working theory."

"Someone wants to scare me off?" She waved to her house. "It's not like I have much in valuables. I have a few pieces of secondhand furniture and some personal stuff. That's about it."

"*Hmm,*" was all he said, but his mind was churning. "Let's go take a look inside and see how bad the damage is."

He led the way, his boots crunching on the glass scattered on the steps. He reached into his pocket and pulled out a glove. Gently he opened the kitchen door. The screen came toward him easily enough, and she realized the exterior kitchen door had actually been broken in two.

He stepped inside and motioned for her to follow. "Don't touch anything," he warned.

"I won't," she muttered.

Beside him were the remains of a kitchen table and four chairs, all smashed to smithereens. He could hear her gasp in shock as they walked through the place. The contents of the cupboards looked to have been tossed; the fridge door was ajar, but even that looked to have been checked out. He walked toward the living room and stood stock-still.

Coming up behind him, she let out a gasp of outrage. "Oh, my God," she cried. "There was no need to destroy everything."

"This wasn't a normal burglary," he said. "Looks like they were searching for something."

"Or they were vandals," she snapped, "who just wanted to ruin things because they could."

He didn't say anything to that, but, as far as he was concerned, this looked like a whole lot more than a bunch of teenage hoods trying to make an impression.

He led the way upstairs and walked into her bedroom, finding exactly the same thing.

She pushed past him into the center of the room and stopped. Tears sprang to her eyes, and she put a hand to her temple. "Why?" she cried. "Why would anyone do this?"

Stone had more than a few ideas, but he didn't think she was ready to hear them. "I know it's a disaster, but can you possibly see if there's anything missing?"

She glanced at him to see if he was serious.

He nodded. "Yes, I'm serious."

She opened her arms wide. "I haven't been here for eight months. How am I supposed to remember what might've been here?"

"Were there any special mementos? Any money, jewelry, anything valuable at all?"

She shook her head. "Everything I have that is along that line is in a safety deposit box at the bank," she said. "I meant it when I said I was never here." She turned to study her bed. Not only had the bedding been slashed, the mattresses had been upended and apparently the tops cut open. "There was nothing here to find."

He waited while she walked through the room, talking out loud.

"This doesn't make any sense. This is more than the work of vandals. What could they possibly have been looking for?" She turned to him. "And why now?"

He kept silent, waiting. She'd get there eventually.

"No one knew I was coming home," she said, waving her arms. "So this couldn't be timed."

"Your dad said you were living at home with them." Stone shrugged. "But, after Levi called your father, we changed your flight."

"But, if no one knew about the side trip to Denver and just assumed I was coming straight home, I'd have been here when this happened." Her voice rose at the end to almost a shriek.

Stone nodded. "If you're thinking that somebody from London might've known and then set this off, I don't think so."

She stared at him. "Somebody had to know I was coming home." She shook her head. "That's just too bizarre. The timing's too tight. It's just too much to expect that somebody would've been logging on and searching the airline passenger list, deciding whether I'd be here, and then when I'm not, they tear my house apart," she said. "Or did they think I had come home and then left again?"

Stone froze. "Maybe they did think you would be here. And maybe they also thought you would be bringing something home with you."

She spun around and stared at him in shock. "Oh, my God! The drugs?"

"If it's drugs that were actually seized in England." He pulled out his phone. "I think we better ask Levi to check that out a little closer."

Chapter 10

L ISSA SAT INSIDE the jeep once again. With her arms wrapped tightly around her chest, she tried to find some logical explanation for what had happened to her place. All she could come up with was vandals out having a "fun" night. And that was a terrible thought. But the alternative was so much worse ... to think someone was waiting for her to come home ... and specifically targeting her.

Stone stood outside the jeep, talking on the phone. She didn't bother listening. He'd been on the phone for at least fifteen minutes. The conversation seemed to be doing a roundabout. He'd obviously caught Levi before he got into bed, and the two of them were hashing out the same old thing from different angles. Finally the driver side door opened, and Stone sat down behind the wheel.

She didn't know what kind of a solution he would find; she just hoped he had found one. She wasn't ignorant of the fact that this was really her problem. But, if connected to the overseas mess, maybe he'd stick around a little longer and help her out. She'd pushed the bonds of a few days' friendship already way too far.

He turned on the engine and put the jeep into reverse.

"Where are we going?"

"You're heading to my place, the team's place," he corrected. "We all need some sleep, and then tomorrow we can all sit down and sort this out."

She looked at the road ahead, twisting to take one last look at her property. It might look pretty on the outside, but something was rotten on the inside. She no longer wanted anything to do with it. "Shouldn't we call the police?"

"We will do that in the morning."

She had to be satisfied with that. She was too tired for much else. A tremor ran through her, she felt almost a disconnect from everything going on. Why was this not over? All she'd wanted to do was go home. Instead, it wasn't even habitable. "I'll have to call the insurance company."

"Yes, you will. But again, tomorrow. Let's get through tonight, rest, and recharge. In the morning we'll figure this out."

But just because he said it didn't mean her mind would shut down. Had somebody expected her to bring something back? Had they torn her place apart looking for it? But since she hadn't brought anything, if she'd been home last night, chances were it wouldn't have worked out so well for her. Although theoretically she understood all that, it just seemed so far-fetched.

If it had happened over in Afghanistan—absolutely. She'd believe anything about those people. She'd been kicked, smacked, and hit. But it had never happened on American soil. She considered her home safe.

She stared down at her clenched fists and forced herself to open them. She'd come home expecting to feel safe, to have forgotten, left behind all the bad stuff. Instead she felt cheated, violated.

She was still running on adrenaline and fear. And with no end in sight. "Do you think anybody was still there? Watching us?" She turned to catch his gaze as he stared at her, a hard look in his eyes.

"Why would you ask that?"

She shrugged. "They went to a lot of trouble. Maybe they were waiting around, watching for me." At her words, a tremor rippled down her body. She stuffed her fist into her mouth to hold back a cry.

He reached across and gently clasped her knee. "Don't even think like that. We didn't see anybody. The place was empty."

"But was it really? We didn't look inside the closets. We didn't look under the destroyed bed, what they left of it. It would make sense that they wouldn't jump me if they saw you there." She waved her hand at his body. "You're the size of a bloody tank. Unless they had weapons, they wouldn't want to take you on." She studied his face and added, "And thank you, by the way."

He gave a strangled exclamation. "What are you talking about? Why are you thanking me?"

"I'm thanking you for bringing me home. Because I can't imagine if I'd gone into that nightmare on my own."

He held out his hand, palm up, and just waited. She didn't hesitate. She slipped her hand into his and squeezed his long fingers tight. "I just can't get it out of my head. What if I had come home and interrupted them?" She began to cry.

He squeezed her hand gently. "It didn't happen. It won't."

He dropped her hand to shift gears and took a corner on the road. Thankfully, they were deserted. She was pretty damn sure he wasn't going anywhere close to the speed limit.

"This is the kind of work you do all the time? How do you sleep at night? After your injuries, weren't you always afraid of it happening again? Didn't you wake up in the middle night screaming with the instant replay happening over and over again?"

He nodded. "Absolutely. It's like a nightmare that never ends. But eventually it eases. The power of it diminishes. Sometimes you're really lucky, and it doesn't come at all."

She realized she had unnerved him. She reached across and gently patted his thigh. "I'm sorry. I didn't mean to bring back bad memories."

He laughed. "Don't worry about me."

She studied him. There was an aspect of his personality he hadn't shared, and he likely wasn't ready to. Maybe because she was a female. Giving into her feelings was a lot easier. She turned to him and said, "Do you ever just surrender? To feelings of fear, of the emotions?"

"Never." His tone was hard and clipped.

She snuggled closer to the door, giving him a little more space. She hadn't meant to pry, didn't mean to prod, but it seemed inevitable. "I'm sorry," she said in a small voice. "It's none of my business. I didn't mean to open old wounds."

"You worry too much."

She didn't. But she wouldn't say another word. It was the least she could do for him. They drove silently for another forty-five minutes. She lost track of the turns he made, even the direction they traveled. She realized just how much trust she'd put in him. He brought her safely out of that horrific terrorist's home in Afghanistan, and now, here in Texas, he was still looking after her. They finally drove into a very large compound. The gates closing behind the jeep caused her to jump. She couldn't quite hold back her gasp of surprise.

"Don't worry about it. It's not locking us in. It's locking

the world out."

He turned off the jeep and hopped down. She opened her door and slid to the ground. A huge home with turrets stood before them with more buildings on both sides. She didn't know what to think. As he walked around the jeep toward her, she said, "What kind of a place is this? It's huge."

"It's home." To him it was that simple.

She'd either get used to it or she wouldn't, but she'd long lost the opportunity to escape. No way was she scaling the gate and fences around her. Then she realized she didn't have to. He stood there with his hand out, waiting, always giving her a chance to say no, or to trust. She put her hand in his once again and said, "Well, I've trusted you so far."

He tucked her hand into his and headed toward one of the doors. As they stepped on a rubber mat, the double doors opened up, and he led her inside.

SHE'D BEEN THROUGH a lot. He would have understood if she'd refused to come into the compound. But he had driven straight in and closed the gates behind them. At this point, he was too damn tired to give an explanation. They were here; they were safe, and the rest of it could be dealt with tomorrow.

But he had to get her inside and set up in a bedroom first. He hoped someone had designated one for her. This house had lots of rooms, some stupid amount, like thirty-two of them. But they weren't all ready and set up with furniture and beds. He'd move her into his bed again tonight if need be. But it would be different in this location.

Still, if that was what was required, then that was what he'd do. She snuggled close as they entered. He couldn't blame her. She didn't know who she could trust. As long as she trusted him, they'd be fine.

Throwing his arm around her shoulders, he didn't give her any option but to keep moving at his pace. He kept going, straight to the stairs. He could've taken the elevator but that would probably be a bit much for her to handle at the moment. The stairs were close. Besides, he remembered her in the truck gasping for air. Claustrophobic.

He led her up the first flight, then the second. His bedroom was the second door, and one of the spare rooms was beside his. The others were on the same floor but down the other wings. At the spare room he opened it up and hit the lights, thankful a made-up bed was ready for her.

"This is yours for the night." He motioned toward the bathroom on the right side of the room and saw a set a towels sitting on the bed. "I suggest you get some sleep, and we'll talk in the morning." He turned to leave, hating the fatigue dragging him down.

One of the things he wanted to do right now was kick that prosthesis across the far side of the room and ease the load on the stump. He knew it would be inflamed. He'd been on it too much. Just as he reached the doorway, he heard her cry out, "Wait."

He spun to look at her. "What's the matter?"

She whispered, "Could you show me where you're sleeping so I know I'm not totally alone?"

He curled a finger and waited until she walked over to him before he said, "This is your door and"—he pointed at the number sixteen, then to the door next to hers with the number seventeen on it—"that's my door."

He walked over and pushed it open, turned on the light, and said, "It's almost a mirror image, and that's where I'm sleeping." He nudged her into her room and pulled the door almost closed. "Get some sleep. Everything will look much better in the morning."

He tugged the door closed. He called out, "Good night," then walked into his room and closed his door firmly. He knew that she'd hear the *click*.

He was too damn tired for anything other than walking over to the bed and stripping down. There he removed his prosthetic leg and laid it down on the floor beside the bed and crashed heavily on the covers. The throbbing in his leg slowly eased. He knew he should put cream on it tonight, but he was too damn tired. The one thing he did do was take a couple muscle relaxants. That was about the extent of what he could handle. And now he hoped he could actually crash.

Everything hurt. He rolled over, closed his eyes, and tried to fall asleep.

Just as he started to fade, he remembered her words. Surrender? Hell, no. He wasn't even sure he knew what that meant. And then he drifted off to sleep.

The door opening woke him up a few minutes later. He bolted upright, and then he knew. "Lissa?"

The door opened wider, and she peered around the corner. He would not be sleeping alone tonight. Internally he was glad. It was important that she be the one to make the decision. He reached across to the inside of his bed and pulled the covers over toward him.

She slipped inside his room quietly, clicked the door closed, and then ran to his bed. She tucked up underneath his sheets and whispered, "Thank you."

He shuffled slightly so he could wrap an arm around her and pulled her up against his big chest. "You're welcome. Now go to sleep."

And just like the last time, she drifted off like a baby. And just like before, he had a hard time.

How was he supposed to sleep with an angel in his arms? Even exhausted, the last remnants of fear still clinging to her, she smelled wonderful. And she felt even better. Lean, long, she fit him like a charm. But the sense of fragility no longer surrounded her.

And that was a good thing. He avoided tiny women. He was a big guy and had always been afraid of hurting them. She wasn't tiny, but she was damn slim.

Still he'd seen her inner spirit, strength, and determination that she had used to get through these last two days. He smiled and pulled her close, whispering, "What am I going to do with you?" And when she answered, he thought he must've heard it wrong because he knew she was asleep. He'd heard her snore gently for a few moments.

She'd been asleep; he'd been sure of it. But he'd also have sworn he heard her say, "Love me. Just love me."

Pleased at the idea, but knowing she was dreaming, he closed his eyes and drifted toward sleep. He took that thought with him. Was love even possible? What he held in his arms right now was just so damn special, he'd do anything to not lose it.

Maybe dreams did come true. He'd never been a dreaming kind of guy, and lately he'd had only nightmares in his world, but maybe, just maybe that was changing.

Chapter 11

L ISSA WOKE WITH a start. She lay still, figuring out what was wrong. Or maybe what was seriously right. A man's arms were wrapped around her, holding her close. By just the size of him alone, she knew it had to be Stone. She could feel the soft rise and fall of his chest behind her, the gust of warm breath as it wafted somewhere in the vicinity of her head. She smiled and snuggled closer.

With her eyes closed, she just enjoyed the sensation of being held in someone's embrace. It had been a long time since she'd had a serious relationship. She'd had a few short-term flings in the meantime, but nothing that counted. And overseas she had always been too afraid of the rules of foreign countries to get involved.

Now there was Stone. She never wanted to leave. But this was his home, his space.

Which reminded her of her home, or rather what was left of it. The windows alone could be several thousand dollars to fix. The doors, all the furnishings inside, those were definitely an insurance claim. Almost everything had to be replaced, she knew, and it would be a big job.

She couldn't live there anytime soon. She hadn't for a long time, which meant she must find another place.

She needed to call Marge and let her know. Lissa didn't want her friend and neighbor to show up unexpectedly and see the house like it was.

Add that to the other list of things to do. Plus she had to get a phone—to call the police, the insurance company, and her friend. All of this was a bitter note to herself.

Yet instinct was saying, *Don't move. Enjoy the moment with Stone. Reality will interfere soon enough.* Her exposed shoulders were slightly chilled. She reached up and tugged the covers higher and snuggled a little deeper underneath. She loved the wash of warm air as the blankets closed around her. Somehow she'd caught a bit of a chill with all the traveling. She didn't feel sick—just not quite 100 percent.

"You okay?"

The deep slumber of his voice rolled over her. She patted his forearm wrapped around her chest and said, "Yes. Just cold."

Instantly he shifted her into a deeper embrace, as if he could impart the necessary heat she needed. And, in fact, he could. Just amazing. Like being surrounded by an oven. Being a big man especially, his body was a furnace.

Her eyes drifted closed, and she relaxed. She'd gone to bed too tired to even think about all the events. Now, of course, her mind wouldn't shut off.

Was there a connection between whatever had been put in her luggage and the search of her house? She knew what the answer was. How could there not be? Two strange incidences countries apart and she was the common denominator.

Outside the bedroom door in the hallway she could hear footsteps. She froze. Was somebody likely to come into Stone's bedroom? Would they check out her room and realize she was missing?

She chewed her bottom lip, wondering if she had put

him in a tough spot. And yet, for all that she might, she couldn't feel sorry about where she was right now. For she had been somewhat afraid to be in that room across the hall, a strange bed in a strange bedroom in a strange house. Arriving the way they had, as the minutes ticked by, her fears had gotten worse. And she'd been too tired to work her way through it, so she just came right to Stone. Like a homing pigeon.

"Relax."

His hand reached down and grabbed hers, making her realize she'd been gently petting his forearm.

When he murmured to her, she smiled. Who'd have thought this guy could be ticklish. She pivoted gently in his arms until she was across his chest, her head tucked up on his shoulder. She let her arm drape across his body. He shifted to give her more room, then wrapped his arms around her again. Perfect.

She dropped a kiss on his chest. It just seemed the right thing to do at the time. Besides, if this led to something so much more, she was totally okay with that. Like she'd said, it had been a long time.

To that end, she pushed herself up on her elbow and looked down at him. In the early morning light, he stared at her. A question was in his eyes. She gave him an impish smile and said in response, "Do we have time?"

He slipped a hand up her ribs and along her shoulder, his big thumb reaching to stroke across her cheeks.

But the frown forming in his expression had her narrowing her gaze at him, and she said, "Don't even begin to ask me if I'm sure I want this."

Reaching up to cup his cheek and chin, she slid her fingertips across his lips, and he kissed the tip of one finger. She smiled. "Of all the things I have been through these last few days," she said, "this is the only one that feels right."

And she lowered her head and kissed him gently, just a light exploratory taste.

She draped herself across him, dropping several tiny little kisses on his nose, cheeks, chin, then to his lips. This time she slipped her tongue between his and kissed him for real. There was just something about him she couldn't get enough of. This wasn't her normal behavior, the last two days either. Now that she tasted him, well, she just couldn't get enough.

Stone reached up with both hands, and before she realized what was happening, she'd been rolled over to lie flat on her back.

"There might be time," he whispered.

His lips trailed across her cheeks, warm air from his breathing washed over her. She shivered as tremors rippled down her body. She stretched and laughed, wrapping her arms around his neck.

"But I have no intention of taking a shortcut regardless," he whispered.

He lowered his head and kissed her—a deep, drugging one that seemed to pull at the muscles at the heart of her. She moaned and held him close. When she felt his erection against her, she shifted enough so she could press her pelvis up tight and cuddle him closer. She felt his gasp, but she'd covered his lips with her own, inhaling it, taking and accepting it, and giving it back to him in yet another kiss. He slid his hands down to come up underneath her T-shirt and cupped her breasts.

She made a small cry and arched her back, pressing her breasts into his hands. Her shirt disappeared somehow, and the blankets were pushed away. She could feel the cool air, but she didn't care because her body burned for more.

When he lowered his head and suckled her nipple, taking it deep into his mouth, she twisted and cried out, "Stone, dear God."

He murmured something she couldn't hear but didn't care. His hands, fingers, and mouth were busy caressing, stroking, and tending to the fire within. No embers, but a pure flash fire of heat. Stone. She wanted him. She wanted this. She tried to tug him over her, but he wasn't moving.

Instead he lowered his head straight down to her hip bones, her pelvis. She sat up and tried to tug him higher to kiss him, but it was like trying to move a mountain. When he slid two fingers between her legs, she fell back, crying out, her hips arching up.

She was already wet, waiting, and hot.

He retreated, then slid one finger inside, and she whimpered. "Please, please."

He slipped in a second finger and she realized he was making sure there was room.

She gave a broken laugh. "I won't break."

He lifted his head. Trailing a path with kisses up to her breast, he stopped to feast for a second while his fingers gently teased her. She shuddered, mindless at the gentleness of his hands.

"You sure?" And then he kissed her, his tongue diving deep inside her mouth as he moved on top of her.

When he pushed inside, she wondered if he really was too big. The man was massive, but she didn't expect that part of him to be any larger than normal. She held her breath, and he plunged deep.

She moaned half in pain, half in joy. She wasn't just filled, more like almost being impaled. And yet it felt so damn good. How could anything like this be wrong? And yet she couldn't move as he held her in place.

His arms wrapped around her body, holding her against him. His arms kept her where he wanted her. She tried to stretch, to move, but she really had no place to go.

He tilted her chin and dropped a kiss on her lips. "Still okay?"

She gave a slow, sexy smile, then said, "I am for the moment. If you don't start moving soon, you won't be."

He gave a soft laugh and slowly withdrew, then plunged again. With each one, she was rocked slightly in the bed, and as he withdrew, she cried out, afraid he'd take off and leave her. With his hands holding her hips firm, he drove them both forward.

She twisted, higher and higher, twisting, crying, finally she was pleading, "Stone, please finish this."

He bent over her, raising himself up slightly, holding her head with his hands, his hips moving forward, driving, plunging, taking them toward the end they both wanted.

Her climax ripped through her.

She shook and trembled beneath him. A growl tore free of his throat as his body shuddered over her; something she'd never heard from any other man before. She held Stone close until finally he collapsed beside her, still shaking. After a long moment he wrapped his arms around her and tucked her up close.

This was not what she'd expected, but dammit, she'd take all she could get.

She yawned and snuggled close. "Any chance of a couple minutes of sleep?" she asked.

"Sleep. You'll be fine."

She closed her eyes but not before she slid her arms

around him and held him tight. Dear God, she was getting way too attached to this man. Especially now. Just as she drifted off, she heard the same question he had asked the previous night.

"What am I going to do with you?"

And she answered the same way she had before. "Love me. Just love me."

She closed her eyes and slept.

SO HE HADN'T imagined that response. And she hadn't been dreaming ... Stone couldn't quite believe this woman in his arms—so accepting, gracious, and caring—was here with him. He didn't want to be a hero to her, but he'd known ever since she had first tucked up close to him, that she'd stick by him like glue. He'd wanted her to be able to sleep last night and had been surprised, but also secretly overjoyed, when she'd come to him, again and again. Nice to know that somebody actually cared for him. Sometimes he felt like he was doomed to be alone. But, when he had turned to look at her this morning, she was right here, waiting for him. In more ways than one.

He let his hands slide down her back as he considered the complications.

And there were several.

First, he wasn't exactly ready for a relationship. Not that he was against it; he just hadn't expected to meet a woman anytime soon and even if he did, he figured the artificial leg would be a deterrent. He also realized that she had never asked about it and as yet, hadn't seen the ugly scarring or what he actually looked like when he stood up on just one leg. He knew that would be a shock. Hell, it still was for him every day.

He'd been told by a lot of people that some women just wouldn't care. He was willing to believe that. He just wasn't to believe that would be the case with Lissa. She'd been raised among the wealthy; she'd had the best of everything. Maybe not a great family but she certainly hadn't suffered on a monetary level. She was used to getting her own way and doing what she wanted. That was evident by her turning up her nose to her father at every turn. She showed no fear of reprisals or accountability. And that last one bothered him a lot. He hadn't expected her to end up in his bed, and he could almost hear the others telling him, "Stone, hell, no. Not only is she a case, but she's one that's got some severe complications."

He still didn't understand what had gone on in London. Customs had finally let her go, but he wasn't sure exactly what the issue was. The word "drugs" had been bantered about. He just didn't understand the where, how, or what. Her bag hadn't even been with her. So, therefore, it could've been anybody's actions that led to finding drugs in her bag. And he wasn't even worrying about that part until he had ended up at her house, and then it became an unpleasant reality. What it really meant was … trouble. Something he didn't need in his life right now.

If she was completely innocent, this wasn't something she needed either.

He heard footsteps, followed by the soft tap on his door. When it came again, he knew what the message was. He frowned down at the sleeping beauty in his arms and wondered if he could sneak out without waking her. She should be exhausted. He'd caught six hours of sleep and that would likely be all he got.

That knock had been Rhodes. Stone's presence was required at a meeting downstairs. Soon. Shifting gently, he rolled her on her side, watched until she curled into a ball, covered her up, and then gently eased his weight off the bed. He stood at the side, holding his breath, waiting to see how she'd react.

He needn't have worried; she just snuggled deeper into the covers. He put on his prosthesis first, then quickly dressed. He'd like to shower, but there was just no time. At the doorway he gave her one last glance, realized she was still asleep and likely to be out for hours. He opened the door and slipped out.

He followed the smell of fresh coffee to the kitchen. When he walked in, there was an awkward silence. He ignored it as he headed to the coffeepot and took out his cup. When he turned and studied the table, he realized they all waited for him to say something. He lifted his cup and said, "Good morning."

He kept his voice bland, his face neutral—in no way giving any indication what he'd been doing for the last hour.

Besides, from the look on their faces, they already knew.

Levi walked in just then, stopped when he saw Stone, and said, "Good, you're up. Let's get moving."

Chapter 12

L ISSA WOKE UP and realized she was alone and still was too damn tired. She rolled over and curled up to sleep. After the second time, she sat up in the big bed and stretched. She felt so good. Hard to believe she had slept with Stone all night, well, except for a little bit of activity between the sheets. She grinned. And that, of course, had been the best of all. She threw back the covers and slid her legs over the side of the bed.

Standing up, she realized her clothes had been collected nicely at the bottom of it.

As if he'd walked around and gathered her clothes into a pile. That was sweet of him. She shook her head. Who knew clean clothes would be something that she'd crave? Should she stay here or go into the other bedroom? None of her belongings were over there. Hell, she hadn't even gotten undressed in there. She'd lain down on top of that bed and knew she'd never be able to sleep alone.

With that thought in mind, she would stay where she was. She walked into the bathroom, loving the masculine smell of the small room, and stepped under the shower. She'd have to apologize and thank him afterward for letting her use his shampoo because she was desperately in need of getting clean again. She quickly scrubbed down and turned off the water.

When she stepped from the shower with a towel wrapped around her, she heard a noise in the bedroom. She froze.

"Lissa, it's me."

She smiled. "Okay, I'll be out in a second."

She didn't have a toothbrush or hairbrush, but he had a comb on the side of the sink, so she rubbed her hair with the towel, picked up the comb, and quickly tamed her long hair. Then she wove it into a single braid down her back. She flipped it to hang over one shoulder.

Stepping from the bathroom, she joined Stone in the bedroom. He stood beside the window, but the look on his face was not one she'd been hoping to see.

Instantly she apologized. "I'm sorry. I hope it's okay that I used the shower."

She clutched the towel to her chest and wished she was fully dressed already. She collected her pile of clothes and said, "You want me to go to my room?"

"Of course not. Get dressed. I brought you some coffee. We need to talk, and the rest of the team needs to discuss what we'll do from here with you."

Her eyebrows shot up into her hairline. "This involves the rest of them?" She slowly sorted through her clothes as she thought about that. "Just how many people are in the team?"

He laughed. "Just a few more than you've already met. Not to worry." He walked into the bathroom and closed the door. She felt unaccountably pleased to have a few moments of privacy.

She dropped the towel and dressed quickly, figuring he'd given her time on purpose. She'd take the moment as a gift. She wasn't usually self-conscious, but an awkward morning-after scenario was happening here, and she didn't like it. By the time he came out, she was trying to pull her T-shirt down over her still-damp body.

He quickly helped her move the cotton from her sticky skin, unrolling it so it would lie flat. She tossed him a bright smile. "Thank you."

"Don't thank me. If we had been thinking at all, we'd have grabbed you some more clothes last night from your house."

She said glumly, "I considered that this morning myself. It's not that far away, but I can last in these a little longer." She shrugged and picked up the damp towel, went into the bathroom, and hung it up. "I'm sorry. I also used a little bit of your shampoo too," she said self-consciously. "I hope you don't mind. I can always buy you a new bottle."

He laughed and held out his hand. "Stop. It's all good."

"Really?" She studied his face intently, then decided he was being honest. With a beaming smile she reached out for his hand and said, "Thank heavens for that. I was kind of hoping you weren't a stickler for things like that, but ... you never know with different people."

"Absolutely you don't know. Come on. Let's get you some breakfast."

She dropped his hand and went to the night table, where she spied the coffee he'd brought her. "I'm not letting the coffee you brought me go cold." She took a deep sip and then moaned with joy. "Is there anything better than waking up to a fresh cup of coffee?"

He walked over, leaned closer, and whispered, "Yes. Waking up to you and hot coffee. Something I didn't get a chance to do this morning."

She could feel the color wash over her face, but smiled at

his compliment.

He reached out and grabbed her hand and said, "Now can we go?"

With her cup only half full, she walked carefully at his side as they exited the bedroom, heading to the hallway. It was the first time she'd actually had a chance to look around.

"This place is huge," she exclaimed. "It's like a fortress."

"Almost," Stone explained. "It is a very safe compound with lots of housing set apart for the unit."

"Unit?"

He turned to look down at her with a smile on his face. "We were all in the military together." He shrugged. "For the four of us who came here and started this originally, it still feels like we're doing the same job."

"If you helped people in the military, then you *are* still," she said, "because you certainly were a huge help to me and the others."

They walked around a corner to another long hallway, where he stopped and pointed to a double-wide staircase. She shook her head. "This place is really grand," she said. "By the way, any update on Kevin and Susan?"

Stone shook his head. "Not yet, but I'm not sure anybody called to get one."

"What about Charles? Has Levi spoken to him yet?" She bounced lightly down the stairs at his side.

She marveled at the big stone construction of the building. Part cement—or maybe stone and cement. She didn't know. But very imposing. The place looked like it had been built to last. And she really appreciated that.

As he came to the bottom of the stairs to another hallway on their right, he motioned for her to carry on in that direction. "You're coming too, aren't you?" She frowned at him. "No way are you leaving me all alone here."

"I wasn't," he said with a smirk. "I was going to tell Levi that you are up."

"No need. I'm here."

Levi's voice washed over her. She spun around to see the big man coming from an office that she hadn't seen on the far side. She gave him a bright smile. "Hi. Thank you so much for letting me stay here last night. Honestly I wouldn't have known where to go or what to do if Stone hadn't been with me."

Levi's gaze lifted and crossed with Stone's. She could feel some kind of hidden communication going on. She didn't want to be *that girl*. She stepped in between them, effectively breaking their eye contact, and said, "Your hospitality is much appreciated. Obviously I'll try to get home and sort out my place as quickly as I can."

He nodded in the direction they were headed. "Come on. Let's get you some more coffee and breakfast. We need to discuss what happened at your place."

She walked into the kitchen with them, shocked when half a dozen men got to their feet, several nodding their heads. "Good morning, ma'am."

She winced at the *ma'am* part. "For those of you who don't remember or didn't know, my name is Lissa. Nice to see you again."

She sat down where Stone motioned and studied the plates in front of the others. She didn't know if they had a chef, but if she could get a plate like they had for herself, she would be very grateful. It seemed like forever since she'd eaten.

Charles had fed them in England, and they'd eaten on the plane, but that'd been because she'd needed the food, not because she'd enjoyed it. This looked like food she could enjoy.

Another man walked into the dining room, a stranger— older, distinguished, and in some ways he reminded her of Charles. He looked at her and smiled. "I'm Alfred. You must be Lissa." He added, "Do you want tea and toast or would you prefer a plate, like the boys?"

She grinned. "If possible, I'd love a plate."

"Good. Be back in a minute."

At that she settled down and realized that somebody had refilled her coffee cup. She turned to glance around and saw Stone replacing the coffeepot on the machine sitting on a sideboard. She grinned at him as he turned to face her. "Thanks, Stone."

He sat down beside her without a word, ever that strong, silent, supportive presence.

The silence around the table grew awkward.

She sat quietly and sipped her coffee, not knowing what to say. Finally, Alfred returned with the plate of twisted sausages and hash browns. "Thank you, Alfred," she said warmly. "This looks wonderful."

And then, completely ignoring the rest of the men, she picked up her knife and fork and dug in. The food was so good. She was starving.

When she plowed through the plate without slowing down, Stone chuckled at her side. "I had no idea you were that hungry."

She cast him a sideways glance and said, "Superhigh metabolism. Can't keep any weight on, and I eat a lot." She picked up a particularly decent-size bite of potatoes and sausage and popped them into her mouth.

Stone said, "Interesting. You don't have either of your

parents' physical traits."

"You noticed that, did you?" She swallowed the rest of the bite and added, "Growing up, I wondered if I even belonged to them. But ... alas I do."

"You know that for sure?" Stone asked, a frown on his face and his tone darkening.

"Yes," she said. "My father insisted on a DNA test when I was born." She grinned at the unusual silence. "Much to his disgust, I'm his." The silence continued. She laughed. "Don't worry about it. At least he knows, as do I." She shrugged as if to say, *What can you do?* She polished off the rest of the food on her plate and sat back with a sigh of satisfaction. "Oh, my God, if you guys ever decide you don't need Alfred ..."

"Fat chance," Stone said with a grin. "And you're not the first one to try to steal him from us."

"I wouldn't steal him, maybe just borrow him for a day or two." She rubbed her tummy and pushed her plate away slightly. "If everybody's done eating," she whispered to Stone, "I'll do the dishes."

Before she even got the words out, Alfred arrived and collected all the plates and cutlery. Stone laughed. "Sometimes he asks for help. The rest of the time he's got it in hand. A commercial-size dishwasher is in there, so usually he's fine."

She nodded and picked up her coffee cup. She expected the discussion about her situation to start soon. She looked at Levi and decided to open it herself. "So, now that I have a full tummy, what was the conversation you wanted to get into this morning?"

He studied her over the rim of his cup. "We've circled back to the theory somebody broke into your house last night looking for what they had smuggled in your backpack, hoping you would bring it into the country."

She froze, slowly lowering her coffee cup. "Right, we're back to that." She turned to face Stone. "It would make so much sense."

"It would, in a way, explain how they knew whatever was in your backpack *was* there," he said. "Because, of course, they were the ones to do it."

She frowned as she worked her way through that. "That would imply they actually knew who I was and were aware I was coming home." She turned her gaze to Levi. "How is that possible? Unless they found out while we were in England?"

"That's what we wanted to ask. How many people knew where you lived? How many did you work with in the refugee camp? Did you get to know any of them well enough to discuss your home life, and would they have had access to your bags?"

She shook her head. "Lots knew I lived in Texas, but few knew exactly where." Her gaze drifted from one stern male face to the next. Where was Ice? Then again it was a huge place, she could be anywhere. Lissa said, "I mean, my bags were always in my room. There wasn't anything you could call a lock on the door. We had a safe where we kept our passports and wallets with our IDs and cash," she added. "But how very presumptuous for people to think I'd be able to bring something back into the country and then for them to come get it from me." She locked her gaze with Levi's. "Besides, didn't they say 'drugs?'"

Levi nodded. "Yes, but a rare form of opium. The British are analyzing it right now in their lab."

Her eyebrows shot up. "Opium? How much was there?"

Levi shrugged. "Enough worth getting out of the country."

"Jesus," she whispered.

TRY AS HE might, Stone couldn't hear any sign of deception in her voice. And he had spent plenty of time learning all the ways people could hide a lie. He was generally a very good judge of character, but he knew he was off his game with her. Nothing like sleeping with a woman to affect your perceptions. And, if she was hiding something, coming to his bed last night would just have been another good way to throw everything off. He hated even thinking that way but hard not to under these circumstances. He glanced at Levi, whose one eyebrow was slightly elevated.

Levi shook his head, a tiny perceptible movement, confirming that he hadn't heard or seen anything either.

That made Stone feel better. As much fun as last night and this morning had been, he'd hate to think he'd been hoodwinked as part of a plan. But she wasn't off the hook yet.

"So what do we do now?" Lissa asked. Her voice trembled, and she'd shifted ever-so-slightly on the bench seat, moving closer to Stone. Her hands wrapped on her coffee cup trembled slightly. Those types of reactions were hard to fake.

Words were one thing, but the physical reactions didn't lie. Also very hard to train someone to produce fake body language.

"Make sure your home is safe and that whoever seems to be following you doesn't return," Levi said.

"And why would he?" she cried out in shock. "Surely, if

he didn't find what he was looking for, he wouldn't come back."

Stone hated to say it, but she needed to understand the danger. "Because he might come looking for you to get the answers he wants."

She turned her head slowly to stare at him, her body slumping. "I don't have any for him. How could I possibly convince anybody I don't know anything about something when I don't know anything about it?" Her voice rose at the end. She reached up a shaky hand and rubbed her temple. "I hate to say it, but maybe I should stay with my parents."

"That might work temporarily, or he might decide to follow you there," Levi said in his no-nonsense tone.

All the color drained from her face. "I can't put them in danger. They didn't do anything to deserve this."

Harrison spoke from across the table. "Did you?"

Stone could see the confusion in her eyes before she turned to stare at Harrison and asked, "Did I do what?

"Do you deserve this?"

She shook her head slowly. "No, of course not. I didn't do this. I didn't do anything. I went over there to help people, to get away from my family. I thought I was doing something useful. And then it all blew up."

"Right." Levi stood up. "You"—he pointed at Lissa—"Stone, Harrison, and I will head to your house now. You can collect a bag of necessities and come back here and stay with us for a few days. I'll call the police. Get this in motion. They will need to make a full report, might check for fingerprints, but I doubt they'd find any—other than yours and Stone's at this point."

"I wore gloves," Stone said.

She stood up. "Thank you," she said sincerely. "I appreciate that. Why wouldn't there be any fingerprints?"

Stone answered for Levi. "Because it was too professional a job. They wouldn't have left fingerprints behind. That's a rookie mistake."

She turned to stare at him. "Professional?" She shuddered. "We're not talking assassins or mercenaries or anything like that, are we?"

"We have no idea what we're dealing with. So let's not jump to any conclusions," Levi said, walking toward the kitchen entrance. "Let's find out the facts first."

With a long face she said, "I'd love to find the facts. So far I don't know anything."

Stone reached up and patted her shoulder. He was delighted—internally—at the idea of her staying with them for a few more days. He'd had worse assignments; keeping a close eye on her had a lot of perks. He just wished they could clear her of all wrongdoings. Then he could really enjoy being with her. It wouldn't feel like he'd crossed the line. Levi hadn't said anything, but Stone knew what Levi was thinking—what they were all thinking.

Stone wanted to believe she was who she portrayed herself to be. But, after being betrayed once, trust was a little harder for the team to give. Stone didn't know what she'd get from this by lying, so, for the moment, he'd give her the benefit of the doubt—and watch his back.

Chapter 13

THE DRIVE BACK to her house was faster this time. In fact, in daylight, it was a fascinating trip. She'd never been to this corner of Texas before. The compound seemed to encompass a small valley with ridges around two sides of it. As they drove out, the big gates locked and secured the property behind them.

She wondered at their need to always have the gates closed. She turned to Stone and asked, "Have you been attacked in there or something? I just wondered why you keep it locked, especially during the daytime."

"We have actually," he admitted. "But hopefully not again." He turned to look out the window. "And we don't always keep it locked up."

End of conversation. *Right.* She stayed quiet for the rest of the trip until they hit the small town where her home was. As they drove into the cul-de-sac and up to her place, she knew the front, which appeared undamaged, hid what was so much worse in the back, especially in the cold, harsh reality of day. Like a facade, it hid the evil that lurked beneath.

And somehow she'd gotten caught up in it.

They exited the truck in silence. She watched as Levi studied her townhome and then every other one on the block. One large row-house complex. Twelve in this unit. She had the end one. Beside her was a fence and then a large playground. She stepped forward and led the way around the rear.

She braced herself but couldn't hold back the gasp, still was shocked to see it again. She stepped out of the way as Levi gave the place a solid once-over from the outside. She had no idea what he thought he was looking for.

He obviously noted the busted doors, pushed them open, and stepped inside. She waited for Harrison to join him. Stone, however, wouldn't let her stand outside alone. He motioned for her to follow the other two.

She frowned up at him. "What if I don't want to go in?"

He shrugged. "Then I'll stay out here with you." He turned to look at the busted windows and said, "I thought you wanted to come."

"I did," she said quietly, then admitted, "but that doesn't mean I'm up for going back inside." Before she'd said her last word, he'd held out his hand. Always offering support. Always offering security. She'd do a lot to have a man like this.

She reached out and gripped his fingers, hard. "What if they came back?"

"Chances are, we won't know. They made such a mess the first time," he said with a mocking laugh.

"If they were watching us," she argued, "then they would know if I went inside."

"And, if they are watching you, they would know you brought nothing in. And that we weren't here long enough for you to do very much."

"Good point." Feeling better, she ended up dropping his fingers and walking inside; then she headed straight for the stairs. As she climbed, she realized that the other two men had stopped and watched her silently. She shivered. She really wanted them to believe her. But this was still hanging over her head.

A new feeling for her. She wasn't used to being under suspicion. Well, other than from her father.

At the bedroom doorway she stopped and studied the mess. She couldn't possibly know for sure, like Stone had said, but it didn't appear to be any different than when she'd left in the wee hours of the morning. Only now it looked harsher. In the bright light the damage, the mess, and the work ahead seemed even more depressing.

On the far left side, she spied her large traveling bag. More like a beach bag but with a zipper—so she sometimes used it as a carry-on for a flight. She carefully picked her way through the mess and grabbed the bag. She upended it to make sure it was empty, then walked over to the dresser. She'd been gone a long time and had taken the bare necessities with her. She hadn't even lived in this house for much more than four months before she had left it, so the drawers weren't very full. But she did have a few changes of clothes. She quickly packed up what was in her drawers, then turned to the closet and winced.

Some of the clothing had just been tossed on the floor, but a lot of it appeared to have been ripped. She didn't understand that part. It was more vindictive. Like a woman who hated another. But she honestly couldn't think of any woman who hated her so much. She hadn't cultivated many friends over the last ten years.

She picked through the closet, making a pile of usable clothing. She found a couple cardigans, a simple dress, several blouses, and skirts. If she took the skirts, she would need shoes. She wasn't sure any of those were wearable either.

Stone spoke from behind her. She turned with a pair of sandals she'd forgotten she owned in her hands as he said, "You finding what you need?"

"I'm finding what's left that's still usable. Why would they possibly want to rip my clothing?" She held up an evening dress where the shoulder pads had been opened.

He frowned. "We're back to considering they thought you might've hidden whatever they're looking for."

She stared at the shoulder pads, then back at him. "If that's true, then what they're looking for is damn small."

"We knew that, but we didn't know how small."

As she watched, his gaze wandered to her bag, mostly filled now with the least-damaged clothing left in her bedroom.

"Is that all you have?"

She nodded. "A lot of it has been destroyed, and I didn't have very much to begin with. Plus, I've been traveling." She turned toward the closet and spied an old purse. She crowed with delight. "Oh, perfect." She snagged it, walking carefully through the mess. Taking it over beside her other bag, she dumped the contents of the purse on the bed, delighted to find a little bit of her makeup and a hairbrush. She beamed. "Oh, to know how to appreciate the simple things in life." She picked up the hairbrush, waved it at him. "Now I don't have to borrow your comb anymore."

He shook his head. "Glad you're happy with the simple things."

"Oh, I am."

She gave her bedroom one last walk-through, packing away as much as she could. Scouring through the mess, she found a scarf she'd always loved, and a pair of socks rolled off to the side. She snagged those up too. Then she headed to the bathroom. Some things should be left in there, but, as she walked into the small room, she realized her intruder had been before her here as well. The contents of the cabinets below the sink had been emptied—no longer usable.

"Looks like they opened everything and dumped it on the floor." She stood in the doorway, her expression full of dismay. "I don't understand that mind-set."

Stone made his way behind her and studied the mess. "That will take work to clean up."

She turned to face him, appalled. "My God! Do I have to do all that?"

"Your insurance should take care of it. But we have to get the police report filed first."

As if they'd heard his words, she could hear a vehicle driving up, parking in the driveway. She glanced out the window and saw a cruiser. Two local policemen got out, walking to the front door. She quickly grabbed her bag and made her way down the stairs. She dumped the bag in the front hallway and opened the door. The first man tilted his head at her and said, "Ma'am, we heard there was a break-in."

She made a face. "There are break-ins, and then there is this break-in," she said. "Yes, it's been broken into, but the entire place has been trashed." She stepped back and motioned for them to enter. "Come on in."

They entered, took one look at the living room, and shook their heads. They silently walked through the entire house. She didn't even follow. What was the point? Stone had stayed at the top of the stairs, and she saw Levi and Harrison leaning against the hallway wall, watching the uniformed guys quietly. The new arrivals just nodded at the other men.

She wondered at the lack of friendliness on all five male faces. Was that standard or just something very male? She walked to the library, wondering if anything else could be salvaged, but there was really nothing. The room was cold and empty. She checked the downstairs bathroom and then went into the kitchen. She'd hardly even cooked here. Everything was of decent quality, but nothing held memories that she wanted to hang on to. Systematically she went through the cupboards to see if she'd forgotten anything. She opened one cabinet and found her keys. Pulling them out, she stared down at one of them.

"What do they open?" Stone asked at her side.

"This is my spare house key. This is my spare car key. I parked my car at Marge's place. Why would I want to leave it here all the time without anybody living here?" She pulled up the other key and frowned. "I think this is my safety deposit box key, but I'm not sure why it would be here."

"Where else would it be?

"In my purse." She turned to study the rest of the room.

"Except that you left the country for eight months, so would you have taken it with you? Why not leave it here with all the rest?"

"That's sensible. And it's likely what I did. I don't re-member exactly. Such a long time ago."

She pocketed all the keys and continued to rummage through the kitchen. But it was virtually empty. At the entryway closet she opened the door, happy to see two of her jackets still there, apparently not cut or destroyed in any way. She slipped one over her shoulders and the other she packed in her bag. She picked up her purse and plopped her keys into it.

Turning to Stone, she said, "Any chance of a trip to the

bank so I can get money and new bank cards?"

He nodded. "We can do that. But we have to deal with the police first."

"Right." She turned to the policemen who were now in the living room and asked, "What do I need to do?"

"Come on down to the station and file a report."

The second man, who'd been quiet so far, looked at her and said, "Do you have insurance?"

She nodded. "I haven't been home for eight months because I traveled to Afghanistan. I set up special insurance just for that reason."

"Good. They won't be very happy with you."

She winced. Between the broken windows, damaged floors, contents strewn about, this would be a pretty big bill. On the other hand, it wouldn't be hers. That worked for her.

Her parents may be megarich, but she wasn't; yet she was well-off. Enough to ride through this mess if she had to.

WHILE LISSA CHATTED with the two cops, Stone headed over to the guys. It had been interesting to watch what she considered worth saving. She had collected clothing and a few articles from the bathroom but not much. Yet she'd been delighted when her old purse had yielded a bit of makeup. She picked up no valuables. She collected no mementos. In the kitchen, she collected her keys, but that was it. Straightforward, no-nonsense, common sense woman. He liked it.

And he liked her.

He walked over to Levi and said, "Let's take her to the police station so she can get that process started. Then we'll go to the bank so she can get money and new bank cards."

She had mentioned she'd stored her vehicle at a friend's.

He glanced around the room and asked, "The same friend who's been keeping an eye on the place has your car?" Stone asked Lissa loudly. When she nodded, he added, "While we're here, we'll need to talk with her and see what we can find out."

Lissa added, "She doesn't live in my complex, but she's not far."

Levi's phone rang just then. Stone waited patiently after he heard the name Kevin. He watched as his friend's face hardened. Harrison walked closer, sensing something going on. When Levi got off the phone, he pocketed it and said, "Kevin's gone missing."

The three men exchanged a hard look. "Missing, as in possibly dead, or as in he slipped out of the country?" Harrison asked.

Levi's glare deepened. "Either or both. No one knows anything at the moment."

"And Susan?" Stone asked.

Levi shrugged. "That's likely the reason he's gone AWOL. She passed away last night."

"What? I thought she was just worn out." Stone hated to hear that. Sure she'd been tired and not looking very good, but he didn't think she had been that bad. But once she'd been hospitalized, the team had lost touch as to the updates. He'd have to tell Lissa; the news would be upsetting.

Harrison brought up a point that Stone had completely overlooked. "When did he go missing?" Harrison asked in a slow, drawling voice. "Interesting that he does and Lissa's place is broken into. Because Kevin could easily have been smuggling something into the country and using her as his mule."

The three men stood in silence, contemplating the possibility.

"Interesting thought," said Levi. "We'll keep it in mind. The question is, after Kevin's wife died, what happened to him and his plans?"

"And that's the problem. It's supposition. We have no way to know. Too many plausible excuses here." Harrison headed toward the back door. "We need to find out the truth."

As they walked toward the vehicle, Levi's phone rang again. He glanced down at the number and frowned. Then he walked several steps away from everybody and answered it.

Lissa walked up behind Stone. They were both just far enough away that they couldn't hear Levi's conversation.

"What's the matter?" she asked him.

"I'm not sure."

Whoever Levi was talking to was really pissing him off. His back was rigid, and his free hand was clenched into a fist before he shoved it into his pocket. Finally Levi put away his phone and stood for a long moment before walking off into the distance. Then he spun on his heels and said, "Lissa, that was your father."

She cringed instinctively, her hand grabbing Stone's. Then she straightened, lifted her chin, and said, "What did he want?"

"His bonus back."

She gasped. "That's not fair. You had nothing to do with me leaving."

"Your father seems to feel we did," he said in a laconic tone. "Even though you didn't get into the limo at the same time we did, and he saw you go upstairs. However, the driver would've known exactly who took you to the airport."

She glared at him. "Let me borrow your phone so I can talk to him."

"No, that's not happening. You want to pick a fight with your father, you do it on your time and your phone." And he turned and walked over to the truck to get in.

She swallowed hard. Stone grinned down at her. "Don't worry about it. That's between Levi and your father. Levi's too cagey to let it go down like this."

"Maybe. But I don't want him to lose out because of me," she said forcefully. "My father wouldn't even miss that little bit of change he handed out. And you guys have been so helpful that I feel like I should be paying you for this, but I don't have any money at the moment." She stopped and looked at Stone. "Am I paying you for this?"

"You're not. I'll talk to Levi and see what the deal is. But, if he didn't mention anything upfront, he certainly wouldn't be charging you on the sly. Levi's too honorable for anything less." Stone motioned toward the truck. "Get in."

She hopped in. Both Levi and Harrison were in the front; she and Stone were in the back again. "I'm sorry, Levi. My father can be very difficult."

"Well, he's about to learn I can be too. Somebody set you up. And, like I told him, for all I know he's the one who did it."

Stone laughed. "I bet he backed off on threatening to pull the bonus check after that."

"He didn't back off much. But, from his reaction, I don't think he was involved. He's also horrified to think that his daughter is involved in some kind of smuggling operation."

Stone watched Lissa slump into the corner.

"But I'm not," she said defiantly. "I have nothing to do with this."

"Then let's find a way to prove it."

Chapter 14

FOR A DAY that had kicked off pretty damn decently in Stone's bed, it was rapidly going downhill. Still she made it through the filing of the report at the station, then, at the bank, she got money and ordered replacement cards. She was also relieved to see that no unexplained withdrawals had showed up on her bank account, at least as far she could tell.

After all, if somebody had gone through her house, maybe they'd also wanted her money. But, with that out of the way, she had to admit to feeling much better.

Once again outside, the men leaning against the truck, she realized what she really needed was to get her wheels again.

She stood in front of them and asked, "If I could ask for one more favor ... could I get a ride to my friend's house where I can pick up my car?" She pulled her car keys from her purse and said, "That way I can be mobile again. You wouldn't have to run me all over the place."

The men exchanged glances, then Levi gave a curt shake of his head. "You have to get insurance on your vehicle so you can drive it again."

"Right." She'd forgotten about that. "I seem to have forgotten the simple basics of living here." She reached up and rubbed her temple. "I'd like to just go home and take a nap.

But ..."

She caught the way Stone looked at her, then realized she had no home. She was hopefully still allowed to go to Levi's place ...

But they'd done so much for her, she hated to impose. She straightened her back. "Look, I can go to my friend's house and stay there," she said. "I haven't spoken with her yet, as I don't have a phone, but I'm sure it would be okay with her."

"Let's get your phone first," Stone said. "Then we'll run past the house and see about getting your car. Right now you can't make a good decision about what you want to do."

She smiled up at him. "Thank you for being very kind."

He rolled his eyes. "I haven't done anything anyone else wouldn't have done. Come on. Let's get into the truck. Hopefully we can grab a new phone for you someplace."

Once in the vehicle, the discussion was about cell phone plans. As it happened, a phone store was at the end of the block. Levi quickly pulled up, and they walked in. Within twenty minutes she had a new cell phone and a new number.

She grinned, almost doing a happy dance. "I forgot how good it felt to be connected. This last week has been kind of tough," she admitted. "I didn't have Internet most of the time I was over there, and those of us who had cell phones, they didn't work, except for Kevin's. Mine worked for the first bit, but then the battery died, and the charger didn't fit the electric plug-in. The outlet kept shorting and ..." She shrugged. "The end result was, my phone was useless for most of the time. I'd check it every once in a while, but ... Kevin ended up giving me his old cell after he bought a new phone on one of his trips. Of course it wasn't reliable either. Hence, why he got a new one, but it was something."

"Trips? What kind of trips?" Levi asked.

"It's kind of hard to explain because I really don't know the details," she said. "I was there in a different capacity than they were. I was just there a volunteer to help out. I didn't get paid, but got room and board. I paid for my own travel. Of course most of the people got reimbursed for their travel costs if they needed it. In Susan's and Kevin's case, because they were both doctors, they were on a medical program. He was coming to Texas soon for a conference, but I guess that's out now."

She frowned. "And they went around helping in other refugee camps. I saw them come and go for a while, and then they were stationed at the same one I was at for the last few months. But still they flew in and out, getting medical supplies and trying to drum up financial support. Maybe just some R&R for them." She shrugged. "I don't really know all the details. Volunteering was a chance to be somebody I wasn't. A chance to let all my history fall away and just help others. I didn't ask questions, and very few people asked any of me."

She stared out the window as the truck rumbled toward her friend's house. "It was a different lifestyle. A chance to step out of the regular world and be someone new."

"And who were you over there?" Stone asked curiously.

She smiled. "I was nobody. Exactly how I wanted it. My father wasn't a senator. My mother wasn't one of the ladies of the clubs. I was just me. I slept on bunk beds, cleaned up in the kitchens, and gave children hugs. I was a volunteer who did anything and everything. Sometimes I did clerical work assisted in the medical rooms, others I helped in the kitchen." She smiled with the memories. "It didn't matter to me. I was happy to pitch in wherever."

"What kind of training do you have?" Harrison asked. "You said something about boarding school and college."

"Yes. And again my father decreed I become an art major. I actually went into business." She smiled at the surprised look on their faces. "Just because I don't like my father's money doesn't mean I don't like it as a whole." She upped the wattage of her smile. "And I do like to look after money. If nothing else, the business degree gave me the ability to handle what I do have."

"And do you have money?" Harrison asked. "Normally we wouldn't ask that, but considering you were kidnapped, who your father is, and how you are avoiding him ..."

"My grandmother was very wealthy. She left me a trust fund."

Harrison snorted. "Lucky you."

"Actually I can now say you're right. It is lucky me." She turned to gaze at the scene traveling past the windows. "For a long time though I didn't see the value. I do now."

Stone's quiet voice reached her. "Sometimes, through the hardest adversity, we truly understand what's important."

She turned and looked at him, her eyes getting misty. He'd been to hell and back and survived. She could do no less. "I'm not as good a person as you are," she said, "but I'm trying."

His eyebrows shot up in surprise. "What makes you think I'm a good person?"

She laughed. "Stone, I've said it before and will again—you're a gentle giant with a big heart."

HE REALLY SHOULDN'T let her get away with calling him that. It would completely ruin his image. He was a badass, always had been, planned to always be one. But in quiet moments, he would allow that he could be warm and fuzzy inside.

Probably not a good thing. He caught sight of Harrison's grin and realized that, as far as the guys were concerned, that nickname would stick. Okay, so he was gentle and big, and maybe he was packing ten pounds too much, but it was all muscle.

And he'd stand by that any day.

Of course he also dropped thirty pounds when he lost his leg. The doctors had been good to him. And he'd be the first to say it could have been so much worse. He had a few other injuries, but they'd all healed. Physiotherapy had helped. Yet how damned amazingly hard it had been to relearn how to walk when he didn't have a foot. Something so simple and yet so damn precious.

Finally, with all the errands done, they dropped her off at her friend's house. She pointed to the car in the driveway, set off to one side. A small bright-red Prius.

He grinned. Figured she'd pick something like that. Bright but not flashy but definitely a statement. He slid from the truck on his side and waited for her to come around, and together they walked up to the front door. She'd already pulled her keys from her purse and flicked the unlock button at the Audi. Instantly they both heard the locks unlock with a *click*.

"How nice to have wheels again." At the front door she knocked and waited for her friend to answer. But none came. She pulled out her new phone, added her friend's name, and quickly dialed the number.

He glanced at Levi and Harrison, but they weren't going anywhere. Not until they knew she had either a place to stay or her wheels to follow them to the compound.

She knocked again and held the phone to her ear as she tried to call her friend inside. Stone crossed his arms, wondering if she might be out. He walked around to the side and peered in the living room window. What he saw made his heart freeze. He immediately made a slashing move toward the men in the truck. He grabbed Lissa's hand and dragged her to the truck, ignoring her protests. He shoved her into the backseat and barked, "Stay here."

The others were already out of the truck. They headed around to the rear of the house. Stone went to the front, checked the lock on the door, and realized there wasn't one. He pushed open the door, making sure he was hidden from view. When he heard the signal from the back door, he entered.

He went in low, weapon raised. The living room had been trashed, similar to Lissa's house. But no one was in the house. He quickly made his way to the back room and around to the kitchen. The others were there, standing, staring.

A woman a few years older than Lissa's age was tied to a chair. Blood no longer dripped from her dead body.

She'd been shot in the head. But it didn't look like the killing had happened quickly as evidenced by the blood on her wrists and beaten face. Her feet had been tied to the chair legs, and she looked like she'd been here for a while.

He turned, grim-faced, to the guys and said, "This woman was supposed to have checked on Lissa's house the same day we flew in."

"Are we thinking somebody, while watching the house waiting for Lissa to come home, instead saw this girl?" Harrison turned to study the rest of the kitchen. "And followed her here and beat her up, looking for information? The poor girl didn't know anything."

"And that's when they shot her," Levi said.

"Oh, my God."

Stone spun to see Lissa standing in the doorway, both hands clasped over her mouth, tears in her eyes as she stared in horror at her friend.

He raced to her side. "Damn, I told you to stay in the truck."

She turned her face toward him, and crumpled into his arms.

He held her close and spoke to the other two. "We need to do a sweep of the house," he said in a low voice. "Just because she's dead doesn't mean they didn't stay here."

Both men disappeared through the doorway. Stone held Lissa close. He rubbed her back and shoulders and dropped a kiss on her forehead beside the stitches. They needed to get those removed soon. "I'm so sorry, sweetheart. I was hoping to save you from seeing this."

She shook her head. "She's dead because of me, isn't she?"

How could he answer that? Probably, yes. And yet Lissa wasn't to blame. He led her through the front door, onto the small porch, and made her sit down on the steps. "Look, you need to stay here. We can't contaminate the scene. We need to make sure whoever did this isn't still here nor won't return. I need to trust you. Can you stay here for me?"

He could see the shaking start. But no way could he help her. Right now they had to make sure the place was safe.

He reached out and gently stroked her head. "Lissa?"

"It's okay. I'll be fine," she whispered. "I promise I'll stay here."

With that vow Stone went back into the house and raced upstairs. In the master bedroom he stopped to see it had been completely destroyed. Even worse than Lissa's. Both Levi and Harrison were poking through the mess. "Anything?"

"Not that we can see. It's similar to Lissa's house. Everything destroyed as if they were searching for something. But this room seems to have received particular attention."

He looked around. "It's pretty darn hard to imagine why though. And if they found anything, there's no way to know."

"Considering the disaster here, I'm guessing they didn't."

Harrison kicked a drawer and shrugged. "This just looks like rage again."

They both stared at Stone. "You think she would know anything about the contents of this room?"

"She might, but she's been gone for eight months, so who knows what or how it's changed since then."

"Right."

"We need to call the police again," Stone said. "This could be enough to finish her."

"They'll ask more questions, but that's all," Harrison said. "Where is she staying tonight?"

"She's coming home with us," Levi said. "Til we get to the bottom of this, she needs to stay somewhere safe."

Stone nodded. "I agree, but we also can't forget the fact that we've now shown up at these two locations. If anybody's watching these houses, they may very well be following us to the compound."

"Which is exactly why, as soon as we left this morning, it went on lockdown," Levi said calmly. "Ice is watching. She'll know if anyone is hanging around."

"Good. Let's get this show on the road then. The sooner we're home safe and sound, the better."

Chapter 15

S HE WAS NUMB, just not enough. She could still feel the waves of grief as they roared through her system. This was so not fair. Marge had never done anything to hurt anyone. In fact, she'd been such a good friend to keep an eye out on her place. Lissa understood it was a case of being in the wrong place at the wrong time, but she'd seen what they'd done to her friend. It terrified her. Marge had been a hell of a nice person.

What would these men do to Lissa if they caught her?

Even as she considered that, her body made a small cry of protest. She couldn't think of that right now. First she had to face the police again. This interrogation would be a little deeper, longer, and harder.

But the men stood by her side and explained what was going on. That helped. She couldn't imagine being a woman alone trying to do this. It just looked a whole lot like rage and jealousy from the condition of Marge's bedroom.

Until the police had the autopsy report on Marge, Levi couldn't prove that Lissa was out of the country at the time of Marge's death.

When they could, it'd be a small relief, considering her best friend was dead. She curled up in the front seat as Stone drove her now-insured car. Not a long drive, yet part of her wished it was a much longer one. She just wanted the world to go away. So she could try to forget what had happened. To pretend Marge—that bright, beautiful young woman—was still alive and laughing.

No wonder she hadn't answered her phone. She couldn't.

Lissa didn't want to return to the compound. Everyone around her was dying. She didn't want anyone else to get hurt. She tried to tell Levi to leave her alone, that she was nothing but bad news for his team and home. That whoever had done this to Marge would come after them for helping her.

He held up his hand and said, "Don't ever say that again. From now on, Stone will look after you."

And she'd fallen silent and let Stone lead her around like the lamb she'd become.

Dear God, she hoped her parents didn't find out about this. It would just give her father even more ammunition for years to come. He'd then tell her how she was such a wreck that she was destroying the lives of everybody around her. He'd told her that once before, and it had hurt so badly.

Only now, as she stared down at her long history with her father and this recent event, did she realize maybe he was right. She was always making impulsive decisions—though she thought for the right reasons. But currently, with such a fallout as this, she wondered if maybe he'd been right all along.

"Don't try to think," Stone said quietly in the darkness. "Just relax. It'll take time to get over this."

"I don't think time can help much," she murmured painfully. "She was a really beautiful person."

He reached across and grabbed her fingers, interlacing them with his. "I'm sure she was. So you'll need to grieve for her loss, and then we'll honor her life and find a way to make her passing a little easier on you."

She didn't think such a thing was possible. But she knew people lost someone special all the time. She'd just been blessed to not experience that until now.

It hurt too much.

Instantly a wave of grief washed over her and brought the tears dripping down her cheeks again. Surely no more were left inside? She hadn't cried since forever, barely making it through the police interviews. She was actually afraid they'd ask her to go to the hospital to see somebody, get counseling—and that wasn't happening.

The car slowed unexpectedly. She peered in front of them and realized they were already at the compound. Stone drove her car in and parked around the side, out of sight with the other vehicles, blocking it from view. Levi and Harrison drove up behind them and parked the truck, damn-near blocking the car from moving anywhere.

Her mind was fuzzy. She thought she understood their reasoning but wasn't sure anything mattered anymore. They were trying to protect her, and she was beyond caring. So many people hurt. It should have been her.

Stone got out and came around to open the door for her, helping her to her feet. Instead of trying to push her inside, he just held her close. She burrowed into his arms and clasped her hands behind his back.

She couldn't think of another time in her life that she had had somebody to just hold on to. Someone who was willing to help her through a tough patch in her life. Someone so very special to her.

Also, something she couldn't afford to get used to. They hadn't spoken about anything personal between the two of them. She was in no shape right now to even consider something like a relationship, but she knew she wanted to keep him in her life if at all possible.

She had no idea how she'd fit into something like the ex-military unit living at this compound. They had a good thing here. The only couple appeared to be Levi and Ice, and Lissa didn't know the details behind them either.

Finally she stepped back and gave Stone a watery-eyed smile and said, "Thanks. Any chance I can go lie down?"

He slipped an arm around her shoulders and kept her close. "Good suggestion. Come on. Let's get you into bed. You didn't get a lot of sleep last night and have had nothing but shocks ever since."

Just the thought of nearing a bed was enough to keep her putting one foot in front of the other. She let him lead her where he would. When she realized she was standing beside the same bed she'd awakened in this morning, her heart melted a little bit more. "Are you sure?"

He laid her purse and bag down on the floor beside the night table and turned to look at her, asking, "Am I sure about what?"

She paused before answering. This was his bed, his bedroom. "I kind of pushed the limit by coming in here last night. Are you sure you want me to stay here with you?"

"I thought we were past that stage actually," he said with a smile. "You shouldn't be alone right now. So I'm totally fine with this. But maybe I should be asking if you're okay with it?"

He waited for her to answer.

Inside she was torn up with grief and with all her emotions, it was like she had no filters anymore. She didn't know what to say or how to say it. At first she was afraid it would come out wrong and then realized she just didn't give a damn anymore. She slipped her arms around his shoulders and said, "There's nothing I want more."

She just hugged him and held on tight. She didn't even understand how, but, a few minutes later, she was lifted and placed on the cool sheets, completely naked, with the blankets tucked up over her from her shoulders down. A gentle kiss was dropped on her temple.

But somehow, in her foggy mind, she realized he had made the impossible happen. "You're a miracle, you know that?"

"No," he whispered. "I'm not. I'm just a man."

And he disappeared from the room.

She lay in the half cloudy space that she'd entered and felt the waves rise once again. And she gave into them, letting the tears flow and the sobs ripple through her as she cried herself to sleep.

THEY HAD BIGGER problems now. Stone closed the door quietly behind him, his heart aching at her sobs. But he couldn't help her or hold her right now. He had to let the storm fly through her system and come out the other side, where she could slowly piece her life together again.

It wasn't just the loss of her friend that gave her that guilty feeling but believing she was somehow responsible for the murder of her friend. Because their association *had* likely gotten the young Marge killed. It would be hard to dissuade Lissa from believing she wasn't responsible. That none of this was her fault would take a lot for her to believe right now.

He walked into the kitchen, headed straight for the coffeepot. After pouring himself a big mug, he leaned against the counter, facing the group collected around the table.

"How is she?" Ice asked. "That's got to be a tough shock for her."

"She's crying right now. Should be asleep in minutes." He shrugged and sat down heavily at the table. "She's in shock. Overwhelmed with grief. And horrified that she's responsible for Marge's death."

The others nodded. They understood.

"Anything unusual happening here today, Ice?" Stone asked. "Any sign somebody is watching the place or that we brought anybody here?"

"Not so far." She glanced at Logan. "You've been watching the monitors. Any alerts?"

Logan shook his head. "Not yet. But, if they saw the number of us and the sheer size of the place, I wouldn't expect them to do anything stupid. They might just hang around and check out the place for a while. Lay low and make a plan."

Levi nodded. "But I'm not sure this was as organized and as professional a job as we would've done."

"Why would they murder the woman?" Harrison asked, anger threading through his voice. "And I think the damage to her place was more for show than anything. When they finally believed she didn't know anything about Lissa and didn't have anything of hers, they shot her." He stared down at his coffee cup. "The rest was just for staging."

"Can anybody come up with any other explanation than Lissa being used as a mule to smuggle something across the borders?" Ice asked. "We've certainly seen it happen before. But never with this kind of an end result."

"In this case, she didn't have the bag. If she did, then maybe it warranted this kind of attention but she didn't ..."

Stone said.

"Nothing else makes any sense," Ice added.

"We'll figure it out. But it never seems to make sense until the very end." Levi stood and refilled his coffee cup. "I also spoke to Charles."

The others turned to look at him.

Harrison asked, "What about Kevin?"

"No sign of him." Levi shrugged. "And we still don't know if that's ominous or not. Or maybe he didn't give a shit." He turned to look at Ice. "Although, from what we saw in Afghanistan, he appeared to be a very caring husband. So the other alternative is, he's lying somewhere dead in an alleyway."

Ice winced. "Did Charles do a background check on Kevin and Susan?"

"He's looking into it now. But, so far, nothing's showing up."

"Have you considered that they were the ones doing the smuggling? Or that they were also targeted for smuggling?" Stone asked. "We brought three people back with us. We were only expected to bring one. And we got all three through customs at Heathrow."

"I was wondering about that." Levi sat down on the bench. "But getting information on Kevin and Susan is turning out to be hard to do. Charles is the best man for that job, and he is struggling."

"What do we do from here?" Stone asked.

Levi turned to stare at Harrison. "Okay, well, I think Merk has a few connections with mercenaries, as do you, Harrison. Maybe send out feelers and see if somebody knows anything about the job."

Harrison nodded. "I'll try. This isn't exactly a typical job though."

"I know. I'll also contact a few of our old brass and see if anybody can get a line on what happened at customs," Ice said. "Maybe a little bit more information was being withheld."

Harrison smiled. "Sometimes honey works better than lemons."

Ice stood up and patted Harrison on the shoulder. "I'll do that now. I'll be in the office if anyone needs me."

Stone stood up. "I'll check on Lissa, then see if I can grab some sleep." He stood up and walked to the doorway. He knew the others were watching him. He turned at the last minute and said, "I did check out her car." He stopped and shoved his fingers in his pockets. He pulled out the contents of the glove box and dropped it on the kitchen table. "I don't think any of this means anything, but I haven't had a chance to check. Remember, she's been gone eight months."

"Do we know that for sure? Anyone?" Harrison asked. "Not trying to be a shithead here but, at least, confirm she has been out of country for that long."

"I'll do it," Levi said. "We can find that out pretty damn fast."

Stone nodded. "If you check further, prove she's legit. Because I hate to say it, but I'm falling hard. Make sure I've got a soft place to land, not another nasty betrayal after Rodriguez. I lost a leg to that one. I don't want to lose my heart to her."

With those harsh words he turned and walked out, leaving the men to stare in his wake.

Chapter 16

S HE FELT THE heat soak through her chilled body and bones until it became a burning furnace where she had been added to the hellfires of the damned.

"Easy, Lissa. Stop crying, honey. You'll make yourself sick."

Internally she knew she was already. Something was wrong with her. People didn't love her like they did other people. Something just wasn't right with her world. Why did shit like this keep happening?

But she also realized that the man speaking was Stone, and he was really worried about her. He held her tight against his chest, and that was the source of the furnace. She opened her watery eyes and wiped at her tears, trying to dry them enough to see him through the waterfall. "I'll be fine," she sobbed. "It's just so hard right now."

He dropped his head and kissed her deeply. She wrapped her arms around his neck and whispered, "Make me forget. Just for a moment, help me forget."

He rolled her to her back and positioned himself right between her thighs. Dear God, exactly where she wanted him to be. He kissed, stroked, and caressed her, all while her emotions were jumbled, mixed, and torn. But it wasn't long before she twisted beneath him. When he finally entered her body, she welcomed him with all her heart. She wrapped her legs around his hips as high as she could go, and she hung on for the ride. A journey to remember. He didn't just stop at one climax. He rode her right through and drove her off the cliff again and then again. By the time she lay boneless in his arms, with him sated at her side, she knew she'd died and gone to heaven. For real this time.

"Do you believe in heaven?" she whispered. "I desperately want to believe that Marge is someplace better."

"I believe there is something else beyond us all," he whispered against her ear, rocking her in place. "And you know that she's there. Hold that thought. Believe it."

She smiled because he understood. Even if she didn't for herself, she knew Marge had believed it. She'd been a staunch Protestant, and a firm believer that she would go to heaven. In her heart, Lissa knew if there was a heaven, Marge was knocking on the front door right now and that there'd be no problem letting her friend in. She was one of the good people in the world.

"Now go to sleep." He shifted her body slightly so she could curl up, spooned next to him like the previous night.

And with his arm wrapped around her body, his hand cupping her breast, she snuggled deeper and smiled. "What if I don't want to?" His chuckle rippled through her back, making her body vibrate on the bed. She laughed as she rolled over. "Okay, you're right. I am tired. But maybe in the morning?" she asked hopefully.

Warm lips nudged her neck and ear. "I'd be happy to oblige now, but in theory, you should be too tired to do anything but sleep."

With a little wiggle to a better position, she shifted closer to the growing ridge at her hips. When he shifted, lifted her thigh and slipped inside, she gasped and arched.

"Oh, dear God," she whispered.

"Okay?"

"Better than," she cried out on a whimper.

With his hands on her hips, he moved slowly in and out, not doing anything more than enjoying the moment, and the sensation of being one with each other.

The climax when it came, took her by surprise.

Big waves of peace. Not ripping through her. Not exploding inside. Instead a gentle wash of sensation that rolled over and through her with joy.

Tremors still surged through her when she closed her eyes and dropped off to sleep.

Something about him was so damn caring.

"I could love him," she whispered to herself. "I really could."

And she smiled as she drifted off.

COULD SHE? THAT was something he wanted but hadn't exactly expected. This had all happened fast. Too fast. Maybe. And maybe not.

She was special. He had never denied that. But he hadn't expected to feel what he was. Or to experience the depths of her emotions either. But no doubt, this would be a connection he'd miss.

He held her close against him and let sleep take him too.

He had no idea what was going on in this world, but he needed to be fresh and ready for anything.

When the alarm ripped through the compound several hours later, he bolted awake and stood, ready for whatever danger was present. Turning, he was quick to get his prosthesis on and then dressed. By the time he looked at the bed, Lissa was sitting up with the bedcovers clutched to her chest, staring at him in shock.

"What was that?" she asked.

"An intruder alert. Stay here. I'll be back as soon as I can."

"Oh, hell, no." She bounced out the other side of the bed and jumped into her clothes.

A sight he would've enjoyed any other time but not now as he was exposed.

She turned to look at him as she watched him pull his pants up over his prosthetic leg.

Hardly any light filtered into the room, but enough was here that he knew she'd see some of it. But what she said afterward surprised him.

"The next time we go to bed, I want to explore your body. It seems like you're always taking care of me. But you're so big and beautiful, I really want to appreciate yours too."

And damn if he didn't feel an erection coming on. Just the thought was so damn enticing. He brushed it all aside and said, "Next time."

And now he'd do his damnedest to make sure that there was one because that thought would keep him on the edge, and full of anticipation, until it happened.

But first they had a problem on the compound.

He slipped over to the door and held out his hand. "You're to stay with me. No going off in any other direction. I need to know exactly where you are at all times." In his other hand he held his handgun.

She looked at it and swallowed. "It's likely to be them, isn't it?"

"I sure as hell hope it is. I'm more than ready to beat

these assholes to the ground."

"Me too. Lead the way," she said with a smile.

He opened the door and peered around the edge of the doorframe into the darkened hallway. With his hand firmly grasping hers, he led her to the stairs.

For better or worse, he'd rather have her at his side than anywhere else.

Now to find out what the problem was.

Chapter 17

W ITH HER HEART pounding, she followed Stone into the dark hallway. She had no idea what time it was, but moonlight came in the window at the end of the hallway so she'd estimate two in the morning. She called that the witching hour. That's when every asshole came out to do their dirty work. And for all the nerves rippling through her chest, closing in tight against her, she felt fine because she was with Stone.

With the grip of his fingers on her hand, she knew he had no intention of letting her go. And that meant she was exactly where she wanted to be. Of course the circumstances could be different, but she was damn glad she wasn't alone.

Downstairs on the main floor Levi stood in the center of the lobby, searching in all four directions as if looking for something to indicate where the trouble was. Just as suddenly as it had started, the loud clashing alarm stopped.

Silence reigned. Normally she'd be delighted, but right now, she just took that as another bad sign. She felt Stone's hand tighten on hers.

He gave her a quick reassuring smile, brought her hand up to his, and dropped a kiss along her knuckles. Instantly her stress eased.

If he wasn't worried, then she would let him handle this. Apparently it was what he did. She trusted him. So far he hadn't let her down. Neither did she want anything to happen to him. He was a hell of a good man.

He led her toward the kitchen, and they stopped just short of the doorway. He peered around the corner and then took her inside. In a low whisper, he said, "Rhodes, what's up?"

When Rhodes turned around, she gasped. She hadn't seen the silent figure against the wall between the two windows. She couldn't get any closer to Stone, but she tried. In the dark, Rhodes looked to be one big scary-ass dude. And she realized she was snuggling up to Stone, who was one of the baddest-looking dudes she'd ever met.

Rhodes's low whisper finally penetrated her mind. "No sign of an intruder in the house, nor did I see anyone in the yard. But something tripped the alarm."

Stone nodded. "Haven't had it tripped accidentally by animals since we fixed the height."

"Doesn't mean it couldn't be something bigger though."

"Who's in the control room?"

"Ice, and Levi's heading there."

"I'll take Lissa up and leave her with them and come back down. We can do a full sweep together."

"Make it fast," Rhodes said. "Don't like sitting here. I'll check to make sure we don't have any of our weaknesses compromised."

Lissa was still trying to figure out what that last part actually meant when Stone led her to the hall and then the stairway. He never said a word as he took her to the top floor. She hadn't been up here yet. He brought her down to a simple door that could've been a bedroom or closet for how innocuous it looked. He knocked once, then twice, then again. Without making a sound, it opened under his hand.

Ice stood there. She glanced from Stone to Lissa. Then she opened the door wider. "Come in, Lissa. Grab a chair over by the corner if you like."

She turned toward Stone as Lissa made her way inside the small room full of computers and monitors—as in one hell of a security system. In the background she heard Ice say to Stone, "Looks like somebody tried to climb the fence at the top of the ridge."

"I'll go check it out," Stone said. "Just keep watch. Let's make sure that wasn't a decoy."

"So far there's no sign of anything else outside," Levi said. "Merk went down to check out the two entrances."

"Send Harrison with him then," Ice said. "Everybody needs to be in twos right now."

Stone frowned. "We're a little short on men for that."

Ice turned a pained gaze on him. Lissa was surprised he didn't melt. Ice might be less than half Stone's weight, but something was just so damn commanding about her.

Their voices dropped into a hushed whisper, then Stone left. The door closed as silently as it had opened, and Ice returned to her chair in front of the monitors.

There wasn't a whole lot for Lissa to do or say, so she stayed quiet and watched. She'd never seen a system like this. Not only was it massive, but it appeared to be cutting edge. On the monitors she could see various sites outside—the buildings in the compound—as well as rooms inside the house.

She had no idea where Stone was actually going. She studied the monitors, hoping to catch sight of him.

Then she gasped and leaned forward. A man dressed in black with a weapon of some sort, appeared to be on the ground by the fence. In a low voice she asked, "Is that

Stone?"

"No," Levi's voice was curt. He picked up a headset, put it on his head, and said, "Stone, can you hear me?"

She watched anxiously as the man on the ground lined up a rifle. Shit. Pointing at somebody or at the house itself. Either way was bad news. Stone was going out there, and he was unprepared. She clenched her hands into fists as Levi continued trying to raise Stone.

Levi switched to calling someone else.

There was only silence.

"Logan, we've got a sniper on the top fourth corner. He's taking aim. Stone went out alone."

Then Levi's hands fell to work on the keyboard. Apparently whoever was on the other end of the communication line had answered. She could hardly sit in the chair. To know Stone was walking into an ambush was more than she could stand. She jumped up and walked to the window, like that would help, as if she could see something and yell at him.

Instantly Ice snapped, "Sit down."

She turned back, not quite understanding, and then realized if she was in the window, she was a target too. Quickly she moved behind the stone wall and slowly sank to the floor. And then the shakes came.

She wrapped her arms around her knees and tucked them up close to her chest.

"Just stay where you are. You'll be fine," Levi said.

"Or you can go back to the chair. Just don't stand in the window where your reflection will show. Enough targets to keep track of right now. We don't need you getting hit by a sniper," Ice said.

Lissa raised her gaze to stare at Ice, who was doing a

damn good job of modeling her name. "How can you guys be so calm?" she cried in a low voice. "When you talk about snipers, shooting, and killing people, you don't even blink," she finished weakly.

"We're used to it. This is what we do." Ice's focus never left the monitors in front of her.

Lissa watched Ice as she clicked on a few keys, and something shifted on the screen, but Lissa hadn't really realized what had been there so didn't understand what was there now. It was confusing, but at the same time, almost awe-inspiring.

"We'll look after you," Levi said. "You'll be fine."

"I'll be fine?" she cried out. "I don't give a damn about me. What about Stone? He went out into an ambush."

Both Ice and Levi turned to look at her. And maybe it was her imagination, but she thought she saw approval in both their expressions.

Maybe it was just what she had wanted to see. She lifted her head, her gaze to the monitor, and gasped. She pointed. "I just saw a flash."

And realized that the sniper had fired. Most likely on Stone.

STONE REALIZED ALMOST instantly that his comm unit was out. Although a problem, not a major one. He could hear the tapping of Morse code on his headset. And that was good enough for him. He listened to the series of dots and dashes. A sniper was on the hill.

Stone changed directions and came around the back, creeping up the hill on the far side so he could see where the sniper hid. Stone lay down flat on the ground and studied the layout. They'd all done extensive night training here to make sure they knew every inch of this section. As Harrison said, the weaknesses were the ones that got you. And Stone had no intention of letting an asshole like this get into their place.

The sniper made no sense. He was taking a hell of a chance. Probably not a professional as much as a hired gun. For some, the distinction was nonexistent, but for Stone, it was major. Professionals were soldiers with lots of arms and military tactical training. A hired gun was somebody who would pick up a gun and shoot. Often they were damn good too.

But they didn't have the same background or discipline as the mercenaries. Stone heard a *ping*. Flattened on the ground as he was, it came nowhere near him, but gave him enough data to see where the shooter was. Stone picked up his night goggles and checked out the sniper, realizing Levi had been right. Black jeans, black T-shirt, and what looked like a hunting rifle. Not a professional, mercenary, or terrorist. They'd have better weapons.

So who the hell was this and why? Stone studied the layout and the man's exit avenues. With any luck, Harrison could set up on the one, and Stone the other. Between them, they'd pull this guy off his perch and bring him in. To that end, Stone shifted down the hill as quietly as possible.

There had been no rain in a long time; the ground was dusty. Both good and bad. It made for a smoother walk but left a trail. He went from peak to peak, saw a little bit of wild grass, and made his way over to it. He tested his comm system again and found it now worked. He sent a message to Harrison, telling him where everything was happening. They could use a few more men just in case. He didn't know how fast this shooter could run. It would be easy enough to end up in a long-distance pursuit. Something Stone didn't want.

Not when weapons were involved.

The sniper would have a vehicle somewhere close. It needed to be found and guarded. If the other men on his team used the hidden passageway, that would take them out around the corner of the road and effectively pin anybody between them. It would extend to the far ridges too.

A passageway they needed to complete fast. This was the second time the compound had come under siege in as many months. Sure they'd had half a dozen other jobs in the meantime, but this wasn't cool.

The compound was meant to be home. To be safe and secure. There'd been talk about some of the men moving out, living in the closest town, and that was always an option. Levi was also talking about bringing in contract men that they all trusted but who would live in various parts of the country. That was also good. But nothing quite like the tightness of the unit who lived or fought together.

From his new vantage point, Stone lifted his weapon, lined up a shot, and slammed a bullet into the fence post in front of the man's head.

His cry echoed across the valley. Realizing he'd been found out, the man ran straight downhill. He made no attempt to hide his tracks. This was a flat-out race for freedom. Only Stone was already halfway down the hill himself.

"Stone, I see him," Logan snapped in his earpiece. "I'm on the road. I should be able to cut him off."

"You do that. I'll meet you at the far side on the compound. Let's make sure this asshole doesn't get away." Harrison's voice disappeared as quickly as it came.

Stone grinned. This shooter had no idea what he was up against. They were effectively boxing him in. Pretty damn soon they'd have him. As Stone watched, he saw the headlights shine over the compound as Logan drove out of the gates. He quickly made his way across the low ridge, so he could see down the other side. Sure enough an old beat-up truck sat below, Logan driving toward it. The sniper was farther out than Logan; but Harrison would grab the intruder soon. So which direction would the man take? Stone hoped the sniper would break toward Stone. He wanted to get his hands on him.

Knowing Levi was watching the situation, Stone considered the possibilities. "Levi, I need you to be ready." And he quickly explained the options for the sniper.

"Got it," Levi said calmly. "Rhodes and Merk are searching outside the compound. Rhodes is in front of the compound, Merk the opposite side."

Perfect. Stone squatted down and watched. He'd have to make a decision as soon as the man came around the bend. And sure enough, the sniper caught sight of Logan pulling up behind his truck. He hit the brakes and came to a complete stop.

Which way would the shooter go?

Stone grinned with anticipation. *Let him come to me, please.* The sniper broke to the right—in line with Stone's path.

Chapter 18

W HEN THE ACTION started, Lissa bolted to the chair beside Levi. "Oh, my God! He got him," Lissa cheered.

"Of course he did," Ice said complacently. "Stone's big, but he moves like a panther. And he is very good at strategy."

"I believe you," Lissa said. "I've never seen the warrior in him quite like this. Sure, in Afghanistan, he was there and played a huge part in getting us out, but I think Merk and Rhodes were actually in the room and blew the window bars off." She sat back, relief washing through her. "It is something to see Stone in action."

"He's a good man." Levi stood up, took off his headset, patted Ice on the shoulder, and turned, walking out of the room, closing the door quietly behind him.

As Lissa watched on the monitor, she could see Stone shepherding his prisoner to the truck where Logan was. It took a few minutes, but then both vehicles were driven into the compound, convoy style. She realized that's where Levi had gone. To handle business down in the yard.

"I wondered if Stone's leg would've affected him," she admitted. "We haven't really talked about his disability, but, from watching him on that hillside, I'd never have known."

Ice laughed. "He's very determined not to let it make a difference in his life. When it first happened, we were all stunned, and then immediately we remembered this was Stone. That man can handle anything," she admitted. "Only that wasn't fair, because he still had to adjust. It didn't matter how capable, good, or awesome he was, he still lost a major part of his body, and it will take time to deal with the fallout."

"More time than anyone really realizes, I think," Lissa said. "The stump is a bit puffy-looking. And sometimes he hisses when he puts on the prosthesis."

Ice turned to study Lissa's face. "He gets sidelined if he does too much. He's actually been forced into office duty because he stayed on it longer than he should," she said with a smile. "I know he still pushes it, but it's way better than it used to be."

"He needs a better design for the leg." Lissa studied Ice. "Does he have a physiotherapist or specialist who works with him?"

"Of course. Plus, many doctors and engineers. The problem is taking his leg to a whole new level." At that Ice laughed. "And that means a lot more going on in that replacement leg than normal."

"A whole new level?" Lissa wasn't sure if she should ask.

She'd seen the man in action. She almost couldn't imagine. But then she thought about how alert he always was, how aware and protective. And that he carried a weapon with confidence, almost like it was a part of him. And what a liability not having that leg could be, but he'd turned it into the opposite.

"Oh, I know." She grinned. "He's trying to figure out how to turn it into a weapon."

Ice stood up and laughed. "I see you're getting to know him."

"In many ways, yes, but not anywhere near enough," Lissa admitted.

Ice walked to the door. Before she opened it, she turned and said, "Make sure if you walk down that path, you're prepared to go the distance." She studied Lissa's face for a long moment. "He was betrayed before. A mistake that cost him his leg. The guy is due for some good times, not more hard ones."

Ice turned and opened the door for someone, somehow knowing he stood on the other side.

Alfred walked in with a tray in his hands. "Coffee and a treat, ladies."

Lissa jumped to her feet and ran over. "Oh, my goodness, how did you know?"

"How did I know you would be starving? Because I noticed how much you eat at any one time." He grinned. "Ice is the same way. So I brought double portions for both of you." He walked over and set the tray down on the small table. "Looks like it'll be a very early morning here. The prisoner has just been brought into the compound. You're staying here?"

"Yes." Lissa glanced at Ice and then at Alfred. "I'll stay here until Stone's free."

"I'll tell him." Alfred walked out the door, closing it quietly behind him.

Lissa suddenly wondered at his question. "Does that make me a prisoner?" she asked slowly.

Ice turned to stare at her. "No," Ice said calmly. "It means you're always to be with someone. Never alone."

"Oh," Lissa said in a small voice. "Because I can't be trusted?" She'd really rather know how the land lay on that topic. If she wasn't welcome, she didn't want to be here.

But Ice's response surprised her. She laughed freely, the light sound tinkling around the room. "Good Lord, no. If we didn't trust you, you wouldn't be within one hundred miles of here. It's because you're a target and we have to make sure we keep you safe."

"Oh. Okay, that's much better." She reached for a huge muffin and took a bite.

Ice stared at her. "You know, very few people would think that being a target was much better than not being trusted."

"Maybe it's because they don't have my father. He never trusted me to do anything, nor my word," she mumbled around her bite. "Gives one a complex, you know?"

"I'm sure it does. But it's well past time to leave behind your father and whatever influence he had over you and begin a new life. You've been your own person for a long time. Don't stop now."

Lissa stared at the very intuitive woman. "You're right, you know?"

Ice nodded. "Yep, I am." She picked up one of the other muffins on the plate and said, "We see it all the time in the military. As a child, you join a family unit. Then grow and mature, gaining confidence and separating. In your case, you needed to leave to achieve that. Maybe you did that years ago. I don't know, but, with all this chaos going on, knowing that someone is trying to hurt you, it does make you want to revert back to being a little girl, looking for your parents to take care of you. However ..."

"However, as they barely ever took care of me before, my fallback plan isn't working." Lissa studied the muffin in her hand, but her thoughts were on her past as she thought about Ice's words because that was exactly what had happened. "I just don't want to have transference issues from my father to Stone," she admitted quietly. "I really like Stone, but I don't want to put that burden on anybody. And in my next relationship, I want a partner, not a father figure."

"Damn good thing," Ice said cheerfully. "Stone is nobody's idea of a father figure. He's a hell of a good man. But he also needs a partner. He doesn't need somebody that he's forced to look after. A limpet attached to his side for him to be the big bad hero. That man lives that same scenario. He needs somebody who can walk beside him and hold him when he needs it, help him make decisions when they have to be made. Not just someone looking at him to create the world she wants to live in. Relationships are all about both people making their lives work together."

How very perceptive of the woman. It said a lot about her relationship with Levi. They looked great together physically, and yet that affection and caring obviously went deep between them.

"You're right. But Stone is a big presence to live up to. I'm not sure I'm good enough," she admitted quietly. "That's been a problem for me since forever. Men who are bigger than life and expect more than I can give. Men who give decrees, and expect people to follow them, and do it so perfectly they're never disappointed."

"Stone's not like that. He's not like your father in any way. And that's something you need to separate out very clearly. They always say women marry their fathers. But I also happen to think we marry the qualities we like in our fathers and we're happy to ditch the parts we don't want. If your father was an alcoholic, it doesn't mean you have to marry one. But, if your father was a very generous, caring animal lover, maybe that's the part of him you want to take forward into your next relationship. It's all about balance. And when things go off balance, it gets very hellish."

"And you're speaking from experience, I presume."

"I am. Thankfully most of that's in the past. Relationships aren't too much work when you're with the right person, but they are something that you work at."

"Oh, I like that phrase. No one ever explained it in that way." Lissa reached for a second muffin. She ate half of it in silence as she thought about Ice's words. "Does everybody live here in the compound?"

Ice shot her a look and then nodded. "Lately everybody does. Several apartments are being outfitted and some of the men will move into those instead of the rooms. But like everything else, it's a work in progress."

There was silence for a few moments as Ice's gaze moved constantly from the monitors to Lissa and back. "What's worrying you?"

"My relationship with Stone actually." Lissa shrugged. "You know, there's the normal dating thing, and then the nights over at various places, followed by the living together." She laughed. "We sort of skipped all the other parts and just jumped into the last. I'm afraid I've intruded in some way."

"So maybe rather than worry, you should talk to Stone about taking some time out just for the two of you to go to a movie or for a meal, even take a picnic out in the blue yonder and just discuss things."

Lissa brightened at that idea. "Actually that sounds lovely." Her mind was spinning. Possibilities wafted in and out. Because that was exactly what she needed—time with Stone.

Then Ice burst her bubble. "You'll have to wait until this problem is solved," Ice reminded her. "No taking off just the two of you when we have snipers following us to the house."

"Right." Reality crashed in once again.

HE DIDN'T KNOW if it was by accident or deliberate that he could overhear parts of the conversation through Ice's headset, but thankfully his comm unit worked just fine now. Either way Stone was damn grateful for the opportunity to hear the girls talk. It surprised him, but it also made him feel a whole lot better about Lissa. And Ice was right; he and Lissa needed time together to talk. But reality was a bitch, and right now Levi was questioning a sniper sitting in a chair inside the compound.

"Is there any point asking more questions when the asshole isn't answering?" Stone asked Levi. "Why not call the authorities? They're just a phone call away."

Merk and Rhodes remained silent but gave a small nod Levi's way.

Harrison snorted. "Screw that. Without answers, we'll just dig a ditch out back and dump him in. Remember that comment about a mass grave? We really need to work on that."

From the looks of the man sitting in the chair he was of Mexican descent, likely a rebel from across the border needing the money and so he took on the job. He'd talk if they forced it out of him, but they probably couldn't trust what came from his mouth.

Suddenly Stone was sick of the whole mess. He looked at Levi and said, "Just kill the asshole. None of it matters anyway."

Levi turned, walked to the bench, and picked up a handgun. He checked that it was loaded and turned around to face the man in the chair.

Something about Stone's voice or Levi's actions said they meant business and really didn't give a shit if the shooter lived or died because all of a sudden, the man took notice.

"No, wait."

Levi stopped and looked at him. But a bored look was on his face, as if to say, *Make it good or else.* "I'm listening. Better be something worthwhile. I've already lost enough sleep this night."

"I got a phone call. The person asked me to check out the property."

"Who called you, when, and why?" Levi crossed his arms over his chest and leaned back against the workbench.

"I don't know the man's name. We don't ask questions like that. He said there'd be cash for the information, if it was any good." The man spread his hands. "Cash is a little thin on the ground these days. I needed the money."

"What information were you supposed to give him?"

"He wanted to know how many people were here and the kind of setup you had. He understood this was a large property, and I needed to drive partway and walk the rest. But I couldn't get any closer without being seen."

The man's face oozed earnestness. Stone tended to believe him.

"How were you to get the information to him, and where was your money to be sent?" Levi asked.

Stone walked from one side to the other, his mind busy. No renovations had been done lately, though they were gearing up to do two more apartments. But they hadn't had any workmen in recently. They didn't even get mail delivered here. Everything was picked up in town. On purpose. Everybody who came through the gates to this place had to be vetted and security here had to be tight. They'd been busy with jobs of their own.

The odd person drove down the road, saw the locked gates, turned, and left again. And there had been a couple of those.

They could check the camera feed to get the vehicles' license plates. That was a hell of a damn good idea.

Isolation wasn't everything, but it sure removed a lot of variables in a situation like this.

To Levi, Stone said, "I'll go check out the surveillance cameras. See if we've had any 'lost' vehicles around lately. Might have been the man who called him."

"Good idea. In the meantime, I'll get the rest of the information out of this asshole."

Chapter 19

W HEN THE KNOCK sounded on the door, Lissa already knew who stood there. She could see his face from the hallway monitors. That was how Ice had seen Alfred arrive earlier. Lissa looked at Ice and asked, "Can I open it?"

Ice nodded, her gaze never leaving the monitors in front of her. Lissa opened the door and smiled up at Stone. She stepped back so he could enter.

He came in, his voice low when he asked, "How are you doing?"

She beamed. "I'm fine, thanks. How are you? You're the one who went out there after that man."

He let that roll off his shoulders with a shrug and proceeded to pull up a chair beside Ice. "Ice, do you have the video feed for the last few days? Maybe go back as far as a week. We're looking for any vehicles that came to the compound and turned around, as if expecting something else to be here. You know, like if the person was lost. We want the license plates and if we can, pictures of the driver. Somehow someone knew we were here. And if they followed us in, they would have known it was one way."

"Unless they use Google Earth," Lissa said, listening to the conversation with interest. "I do that all the time. It would've shown the road stops and that a big compound was here."

Ice turned the monitor setup to run the feed, then hit Start. Lissa and Stone sat side by side and watched as it ran in Fast Forward. They slowed the video as a car drove up six days ago with an older couple in it. They got out and stared, then shrugged, turned the car around, and headed into town.

"I presume they were just lost?" Lissa said.

"Probably."

It also made sense if it was an older couple. She turned her head to watch the feed moving again.

Two days ago a truck came in, pulled up at the curve before the gate, and parked. For ten minutes the driver sat and surveyed the compound. Stone leaned in, then quickly adjusted the monitor to get a close-up. He froze. "That's him," he snapped. "That's the guy we're holding downstairs."

"I thought you said you were looking for somebody different?"

"That's what he said."

"Is it possible somebody else came by earlier than a week ago?" Lissa asked.

"Sure, we get people all the time," Ice said. "But if this relates to you, then it happened since we rescued you from Afghanistan."

"Oh." She had forgotten about that. "So maybe we should run the last day and a half and see if there was a second vehicle?"

Stone hit the button, and the feed continued. On the other side of them, having marked down the date and time stamp, Ice brought up a different feed from the ridge. Lissa's gaze went from one side to the other, trying to take it all in. As soon as they ran through the rest of the time and realized no other vehicles had showed up on the one monitor, they shifted to the other she had set up and hit Play. Sure enough a truck turned around without coming into the compound and headed back the way it came. They could only watch his tracks for a few miles before the feed lost sight of it.

Stone stood up to study the man's face clearly on the feed.

"Could you positively identify the driver from that monitor image? I can make barely make out his features." Lissa asked. "Or is it possible it just looks like him?" With the two of them staring at her, Lissa shrugged. "I'm just wondering if you mistook the identity of the driver, and there are actually two people."

"I suspect it's the same driver both times," Stone said. "And he's trying to throw us offtrack by making it seem like there's somebody else. I do think he was probably contacted and hired for this job, yet that person did not come here himself." Stone walked to the doorway. "He wouldn't take that step if he were trying to stay hidden."

That made a strange kind of sense to her too. She hopped up to her feet impulsively and said, "Can I come with you?"

He turned to her, looked over at Ice, and then nodded. "We got the culprit downstairs," he said. He held out his hand. "You might as well come and see if you recognize him."

"No reason why I would," she said as she left the room.

Stone closed the door securely behind them, leaving Ice locked in again.

"Is there always somebody in that room?" Lissa asked.

"No, but when we're having security issues, like we are right now, then somebody is always tracking."

She nodded. "That actually makes me feel a lot better."

"It doesn't necessarily take people to keep the entire system running," he said quietly. "It runs automatically twenty-four hours a day. But it doesn't send out alerts if somebody is seen, so we need to be watching the monitors to see an intruder in real time. However, the feeds are always there to refer back to every day, and you can bet we do check."

"I hadn't considered that your job might be this dangerous," she said. "I figured this was all just because of me."

He laughed. "It might be right now," he said, "but this place was attacked a month ago, and that had nothing to do with you."

"So you're in danger living here?"

As he was several steps ahead of her, he stopped, turned to look at her, and said, "No, absolutely not. This is probably the safest place any of us could be right now."

She nodded, but it was hard to equate. "My life used to be very calm and quiet," she said. "Never any of this danger or secrecy."

"Most of the time we don't have any either. But it's our job in the private security business to handle trouble all over the world and we try to make sure we don't bring those problems home." He stepped in front of her, still standing on the stairs, and said, "Don't forget. We were all well-trained in the military and we're good at what we do. There'll always be assholes out there. And there'll always be a need for people like us to stand up for the little people."

She smiled. "You really are heroes, aren't you?"

He laughed. "Yes, *heroes for hire*."

"Oh, my gosh, that's a great name."

He turned to look at her, his eyebrows raised, and said, "Hell, no. We don't see ourselves as heroes. We're just men."

"Men with a very particular skill set," she argued. "If you

were to advertise, oh my, you would make a killing."

His voice still teasing but with a cooler tone, he said, "Not happening."

She'd been so engrossed in the conversation that she didn't notice where he was taking her. She stopped in the doorway to see the rest of the men gathered around somebody seated on a chair. And she realized this was the man who'd shot at Stone.

Suddenly rage washed over her. She walked right up to him, hefted her arm back, and smacked him hard across the face. She could hear the gasps from the other men and heard Stone say, "Whoa, easy there."

But instead of listening, she shoved her face into the stranger's and said, "And that's for trying to shoot one of the guys." Then she stepped back to stand beside Stone, linking her arm with his. Under her breath she muttered, "Asshole."

The other men took one look at the intruder in the chair, back to her, then to the shooter again—and they grinned.

NOW SHE'D DONE it. Stone wanted to roll his eyes, but inside he was grinning too. It took a lot of gumption to stand up to somebody like that, and to think she'd done it in his defense was just great.

But he also knew the guys would never let him live this down. He glared at them, his gaze flicking from Rhodes's big smirk to Merk's grin to Levi's cold and hard face though his eyes twinkled. Nobody had missed it. Even Logan and Harrison were coughing and holding their hands to their mouths.

The intruder just stared at her in shock. "I didn't shoot

at nobody, bitch."

She gasped and stepped forward, her hand swinging behind her again. Stone quickly grabbed her and pulled her to his side. "It's okay, honey. We'll deal with him."

"But he's lying," she said in outrage. "I saw him shoot at you. Asshole."

This time the man just shut up and glared at her.

Stone instinctively stepped in front of her, blocking her from the man's rage. "We already know what you did. I wanted to see if she could identify you, see if any shared history had brought you into her life."

"I don't give a shit about the bitch." The man spat in the ground. "A bullet would be the best answer for her." This time Stone's fist came out and slammed into the man's jaw.

Instead of snapping back as he'd done from Lissa's slap, the man's head lolled to the side. Stone had knocked him unconscious.

"Stone, we weren't quite done talking to him," Levi said in exasperation.

Splash.

Everybody swore and stepped back as a bucket of ice-cold water rained over the intruder's face. They turned to glare at Lissa, standing, holding the empty bucket in her hand. She said, "Now Stone can go at him again."

And sure enough the intruder shook his head as he came back to consciousness. The men just looked at Stone, back to her, then shook their heads.

"Wow, you got a live one this time," Merk told Stone.

"This time?" She jutted her jaw out at Merk, who immediately wiped the smile off his face. "I'm the last one," she snapped. She turned back toward Stone, who was studying her as if he didn't know what to make of her. She grinned.

"You might have a history, honey, but I'm your future. Get used to it." She reached up and placed a kiss on his chin, which was as high up as she could reach, then turned to glare at the others and snapped, "And don't any of you be forgetting that."

She turned and stormed out.

Stone watched her go. He couldn't believe what she'd done or said. But at the same time, both had made him smile. Then he laughed. Great big belly ones that rolled through the massive garage. When he finally calmed down, the others still stood in the circle, around the intruder, but stared at Stone. He grinned, his chuckles still escaping, and said, "Don't look at me for answers. I don't have any. She's something I've never seen before."

"You can say that again," Levi said. "You sure you're up for that?"

But Stone couldn't take the grin off his face, nor did he want to squelch the joy running through his system. It seemed like he had lived such a serious and dark life for so long that she was a breath of fresh air. With Lissa being unpredictable and definitely unique, maybe he wasn't quite sure he was up for it, but he'd be damned if he would walk away from the opportunity.

"I better be," he said with a smile. "Otherwise she'll eat me alive."

At that the whole group burst into laughter.

Chapter 20

LISSA DIDN'T KNOW why the hell she'd shared her expectations. It was stupid as hell. She and Stone were too far away from anything like a relationship-status declaration. What the hell did she do? It just made no sense.

She blamed the asshole in the chair. She'd seen red when she realized he'd been the one who had shot at Stone. And when he blacked out, she just wanted to hit him again. So she tossed the water on him. But all she'd really done was give the rest of the guys a laugh.

She lifted a shaky hand to her brow and wished she had some self-control. She really was a stupid, impulsive fool. Her father was right. He kept telling her, *You have to stop and think about the repercussions of your actions.* It seemed like that was all she'd ever heard growing up. Apparently it hadn't done any good because here she was, still being foolish.

She walked into the kitchen and sat down at the table where she could just be alone for a moment—only to realize she wasn't. A cup of coffee was placed in front of her. She turned to look at Alfred. "Thank you," she said sadly. "I really don't belong here, do I?"

His eyebrows shot up, and he walked around the table, pulled the chair out across from her, and sat down. "Why would you say that?"

"If you'd seen what I just did ..." She shook her head. "I'm a fool."

"And sometimes we all need that breath of fresh air," Alfred said. "Just because you're different doesn't mean you don't fit in."

She looked at him blankly.

"These guys have way-too-much military training, discipline, and regimentation in their world. They need laughter, light, and some sunshine. It's very important."

She looked at him and wondered if he was just trying to make her feel better. "It's been way too fast and easy. Well, okay, maybe not that last one, but definitely been the first."

"What, you and Stone?"

She nodded. "He probably thinks I'm an idiot."

"Stone's always had to be strong and tough," Alfred said quietly. "It's expected of him. To think that you are somebody he's attracted to, that just makes my heart warm and gives me hope for his future."

She looked at him curiously. "Why?"

"Because it means it's something that he really wants in his life. He wants happiness, laughter. The four men that started all this—Rhodes, Merk, Levi, and Stone—they did some of the ugliest, deepest, darkest, nastiest jobs the military could throw at them. They always came through with flying colors, except for the last mission," he said. "It changes a person to see and do all that. Stone doesn't have to live on that level of darkness anymore, but it'll take somebody like you to pull him into the light."

She drummed her fingers on her cheek as she studied Alfred's face. "Stone seems so strong and independent. So capable of being alone. It makes me feel like there isn't any room for me."

This time Alfred's smile, when it came, was slow and gentle. "It's not that there's no place for you. But he's been locked in tight to keep the world out. Hard to do but they all had to, and it'll take somebody very special to make a place for herself inside their circle."

"How does Ice fit into this?"

"She was the helicopter pilot who rescued them on their last SEAL mission," Alfred admitted. "Levi and Ice have finally got their issues worked out."

"I can't imagine Ice ever not having a place in that circle. They respect and like her."

"But that's also because she knows that's where she belongs. Imagine if one of them tried to tell her that she didn't."

Lissa grinned. "There'd be fireworks."

"Exactly." Alfred stood up from the chair and said, "Think about that." He picked up his coffee and walked away.

She stared after him, wondering if he was right. But in order for her to have that self-confidence, to feel she was exactly where she belonged, she had to know they could do nothing to move her out. She had to acknowledge that on an inside level.

But that meant she also had to connect with Stone a whole lot more. Although he had let her in, sometimes ... she didn't know if that was something he regretted. They hadn't had a chance to find out, all because this asshole had come into their lives.

So effectively the shooter was stopping her from having a future with Stone, and that just made her angry all over again.

And yet it wasn't just him. It was this whole mess. She

got up with her cup of coffee and sauntered to the room where the men were talking with the intruder. She didn't let him see her, in case the flow of words stopped when he caught sight of her. He obviously didn't like women, especially her.

And maybe she should start there.

When a lull in conversation came, she stepped around Stone, her hand automatically reaching up to clamp onto his elbow. She asked the intruder, "Why don't you like me?"

The intruder's face shut down, and he spat in her direction.

She felt Stone go rigid under her hand. She patted his big forearm and said gently, "It's okay. He obviously doesn't know me."

The intruder snapped, "And I wouldn't want to. You're nothing but a rich trust-fund bitch."

"Interesting." She studied the other men, realized they agreed. So this guy actually knew her, or about her.

"Is that the fuel your employer used to make you do this? Learning to hate somebody who has more money and was born with a silver spoon in her mouth? Someone useless, who doesn't understand the struggle, how you had to claw your way through life to get to where you are?"

He glared at her. "Exactly. People like you. Useless, can't do anything, born with money, die with money. You don't know what it's like for the rest of us."

She nodded. "Nothing I say will change your view of me. But it's interesting that that was the tool used to help you target me. I'm one of many so I would still like to know, why me?"

He snorted. "That's easy. Because even though you're a rich bitch, you figured you could cheat the system. But when you get into bed with the bad boys, you sure as hell better do the job or pay the price." He grinned. "In this case you didn't do the job but you took the money. So you're paying the price."

"Okay, I can see that would be your take on it. By the way, what exactly is the job I was supposed to do?"

"You were supposed to bring that shit into the country and hand it over. You were well-paid for the job. Now you'll pay for screwing them over."

"I wasn't paid for anything," she protested. She could sense the attention of all the men circling the two of them. But she also knew she didn't dare break eye contact because the shooter was finally talking.

"And what exactly was I supposed to bring over?" She kept her voice light and conversational. But it was hard because she was finally getting to the crux of the matter.

He snorted. "They didn't tell me exactly. But I understand it was some kind of experimental drug."

She turned to stare at Stone, then back at the intruder. "You do realize all my luggage was seized in the London airport, including that experimental drug, right?"

He frowned. "Heathrow?"

She nodded. "Yes, Heathrow. We flew back via London before we came here. All my luggage was taken, and I never had any of it to bring with me."

The intruder stared at her in shock, and then he laughed. "Oh, that's rich. Now there's nothing to save your sorry white hide." And he laughed some more. "Not while the drug companies are after you."

OVER BRUNCH THE topic was discussed at length. But the

one conclusion they'd all confirmed was that somebody had slipped the drugs into her bags, which were then seized at Heathrow. And whoever had slipped them in was expecting delivery here in the USA. With the drugs gone, and this person waiting for them, Lissa, as well as Levi's team, had a problem.

The intruder had given them only a little more, but had confirmed they were looking for medicine grade pharmaceuticals. With that information, Stone had a good idea what was going on, but needed proof. And he needed to get his hands on Kevin. There were more than a few questions he wanted to ask.

"It also means somebody from the refugee, or terrorist, camp, put the drugs into my bag," she said.

Stone stared down at her plate. She was hardly eating. It had been a pretty nerve-racking morning. He nudged her gently. "Eat up."

She nodded and lifted another bite to her mouth. She turned to Levi and asked, "Did you ever hear from Charles?"

"Just a couple messages. I have to call him back as soon as we're finished here." He smiled at her. "It's been a little busy this morning."

"Did you get an update on Kevin?"

He shook his head. "No, but I will be sure to ask Charles."

She nodded and kept quiet but wasn't eating again. She was toying with the food on her plate.

That worried Stone more than anything. He'd seen this girl eat. He polished off his plate and asked, "What's bothering you?"

"I'm worried that the same person who's behind all this may have killed Kevin ... and Susan."

Silence sat heavy in the room. Stone turned his gaze to the others. No wonder Lissa was worried. She'd worked with the two of them for months.

"I wasn't going to bring that up," she said quietly. "But I also have to consider they may have killed Marge."

"Are you thinking they saw or knew who might've put this into your luggage? Otherwise why kill them?"

"Or because the bad guys put it into their luggage too," she said. Tears filled her eyes. "There's just so much death right now, it seems like a logical link to wonder if maybe they weren't the first two deaths. Then Marge."

Levi nodded, quickly emptied his coffee cup, and stood up. "Time for me to check in with Charles." And he walked out.

Ice had already finished eating. She got up and walked off with him.

Lissa looked at Stone. "It's hard to think others were killed or hurt because of this."

"Whether they did or didn't, it is not your fault. The fact is that sometimes assholes move people around in this world like a chess game to take out good ones. It still doesn't mean you're responsible. But it does mean we have to do everything we can to make sure you are not next."

She wrapped her arms around her chest and nodded.

"And for that to happen, you have to eat." He nodded at her half-empty plate. "Finish this up, and I'll take you to get a nap again."

Her tone was dry but her words were teasing as she said, "There's the Stone I know. Always trying to get me into bed."

Stone glanced at the guys remaining in the room. Lissa had pretty much blown any cover their relationship had had with her speech earlier. He might as well be equally honest here. "I'm pretty sure it's the other way around." He laughed. "There's a lot worse things for me to do than that."

She quickly polished off her meal and stood up. He nodded to the rest of the crew and led her from the room. Upstairs on the second floor, he took her to his room and got her settled into bed. "Do you want me to stay here, or will you be okay?"

She smiled. "I'll be fine. There's a ton of people around this place."

"That there is. That doesn't mean they'll be watching out for you though. We can't always see when somebody's in trouble."

"Outside of this nightmare, I'll be fine." She curled deeper into the covers and closed her eyes.

He waited for a few minutes to make sure she actually drifted off. When he figured she was under, he walked to the door and took a last look. As a precaution he pulled out his keys and locked the door. At least she'd be locked in. She could get out if she wanted to, but it would be damn hard for anybody else to get in.

Then he headed to the office. Ice and Levi were both here. Levi was on a call to Charles.

Stone looked around and asked, "Whatever happened to Sienna?"

Ice never lifted her head from the paperwork in front of her. "She had a few things to settle up before moving here full time. She's expected next week."

"For real?" Stone was happy to hear that. She was a nice girl. She helped to improve the balance of the testosterone around the compound. It might also give Lissa a friend.

"Yes. Alfred drove her to the airport while we were in

Afghanistan."

"I must be really out of it, considering I didn't notice she was gone until now. That makes me feel like an idiot."

"Charles has news." Levi announced putting his phone down on the desk. "Kevin and Susan were almost destitute. Medical bills to the tune of hundreds of thousands of dollars, and their house in France has a second mortgage."

"Which is motive right there," Stone said.

"I've been trying to track his phone, but it's off or dead. Or he's ditched it," Ice said quietly. "There's something not right about him."

"Charles had another tidbit ..."

Stone turned to look at Levi. "What?"

"The initial tox report on Susan said an experimental drug was used on her, and not one they'd ever seen before."

"Interesting. It definitely fits." Stone thought about what such a drug could mean. "I wonder what the cause of death will end up being."

"Cardiac arrest at the moment," Levi said. "I spoke to Merk earlier, and he's found nothing on his pipeline. Neither has Rhodes so far."

"I'm not surprised," Ice said. "Once we get into the pharmaceutical market that opens the world up for suspects."

"Charles mentioned a company called Narque Ltd. It's well-known for being on the shady side of the law."

"Harold Jorgenson runs that outfit." Ice smiled at the look of surprise on their faces. "I've heard my father cuss about him and his company in the past. Jorgenson's reputation is pretty ugly."

"Right. So we need to send a message. Let them know Susan is dead and Kevin is missing. There is no drug or money." Stone nodded. "Easy, right?"

"Actually it might be." Ice turned to Levi. "Call Bullard."

Levi's eyebrows shot up. "Good idea." He was already making the call.

Stone walked over and sat on a spare chair. "I hardly know Sienna."

At that, Ice lifted her head and smirked. "I think you've got another girl on your brain, Stone. Sienna just didn't quite make the cut."

"She's a nice girl, but I think she's much more Rhodes's style."

Ice tilted her head to the side and looked at him. "Interesting. Why him?"

He shrugged. "There's a chemistry there."

Ice nodded. "You saw that, did you?"

"Oh, yeah, I saw it. I think everybody did."

"Just because there's chemistry doesn't mean it's right."

Stone stopped and studied her for a moment. "Is that directed at me or Rhodes?"

She raised that flat gaze of hers to him and added, "Whichever fits."

He studied her for a long moment. "Do you have a problem with Lissa?" He'd really rather know up front because if he did start a relationship—hell, he was well past the starting point, but if something was developing here, they all lived in close quarters.

She shook her head. "No, actually I really like her. She's got gumption. And that's worth a lot. But she's also a softy. And you have the power to break her heart."

He winced. "Did you ever consider that maybe she has the power to break mine?"

At that Ice smiled. And when she did, it was easy to see

the goddess within. In a soft, gentle voice she said, "That's how it's supposed to be."

Levi finished his call and turned to join them again. "Bullard knows Jorgenson. He'll make the call but can't promise anything."

"Good enough. We've done what we can for now. This might get him off our backs." Stone shrugged. "And it might not. If Kevin is still alive, he better have the goods, all their money, or one hell of a good hiding place to live the rest of his life."

Stone agreed with a short nod, then studied Levi a moment and said, "I know it's really early yet regarding my relationship with Lissa, but aren't a couple of the rooms being rehabbed into apartments?"

Levi nodded. "And one of them was slated for you, no doubt about that. I don't know what she does, or if she even needs to do anything jobwise, but that's something that'll have to be considered as well." He studied Stone. "Are you sure you're ready for this? You barely know her."

"I know. And maybe not, but let's be prepared just in case it does work out. Besides, she needs a place to stay in the meantime. After this is over, who knows?" Stone stared off in the distance. It *was* fast. But it was also something he didn't want to *not* be ready for. He nodded. "I don't know the truth about her financial situation either. But she'll have to make some decisions about that herself." He settled down in the chair between the two of them. "I actually find myself in a position I hadn't expected to be in."

"She's young, but not that much," Ice said quietly. "Remember, it's only girls who would be upset by the amputation. For a woman, it wouldn't even make her blink."

Maybe for the first time Stone believed that.

He thought back to most of the women he'd spent time with, not just over the last year but decade. They'd all been short-term relationships. More of a good time, not a long-term type of thing. Although they might consider it fun having sex with a one-legged man, he really didn't see any of them handling it for any length of time.

That didn't say much about his judgment where women were concerned. And yet ... this situation was very different. He was pretty sure Lissa had noticed his leg at the beginning. Yet, in bed, she didn't seem to care.

Chapter 21

WHEN LISSA WOKE up the next time, it was like a homecoming. She'd been in Stone's bed just long enough now that it felt right. She was also in no rush to leave. As matter of fact, she wished she could have what she'd called a pyjama day in which she didn't have to get dressed but could just laze around in bed the whole day. Seemed like a long time since her life had been calm enough to allow for something like that. Memories came flashing back about the sniper and all the security crap that had gone on here of late.

She shuffled around to sit up and lean back against the headboard. She reached for her new phone. She'd been asleep for hours according to the time.

She studied her phone and then decided to try a couple people she knew from the refugee camp. She pulled out the napkin she'd written all her contacts on and saw Kevin's name.

She really needed to put them into her phone. She quickly dialed his number. It was a long shot. Half of the people involved in this nightmare expected Kevin to be dead. But she always had hope. Maybe it had just gotten to be too much, and he had walked away.

Hell, she could see that happening at any time.

If she'd just lost her husband, was stuck in a foreign country, and didn't have a way to handle any of the logistics involved in dealing with the police investigation, or burying her spouse, she could see being so stressed she might just walk away. And they could all be looking for a boogeyman.

The phone rang and rang and just as she went to shut it off, a man picked up and said, "Hello?"

She grinned. "Kevin?"

"Yes, who's this?"

She bounced in her bed, shuffling higher against the headboard. "It's Lissa," she cried. "Oh, my God! I finally reached you."

But an odd silence fell on the other end of the phone. And then the man said in a hard tone, "I'm sorry. Wrong number. Don't call here again."

And he hung up.

She stared in shock. "I could swear that was his voice. And he said yes to his name," she said out loud to herself. She stared down at the phone but didn't know what to do. And then she realized she had to tell someone. She slipped out of bed, phone in hand, and headed up to the control room. She didn't know if Stone would be there, but she was sure somebody would be at the monitors.

She hoped so. She gave a quick rap on the door. She didn't remember the specific number Stone had used earlier, but if they were watching the monitors, somebody would see her here.

Stone opened the door with a big smile on his face and said, "That was a short nap. I didn't expect you up so soon."

"I had a wonderful one though." She smiled at him. "Look, something odd just happened. I don't know if it means anything, but I thought I should tell somebody."

He opened the door. "Come inside."

Ice was there, as well as Levi.

She held out her phone and quickly explained. Levi slowly straightened in his chair and said quietly, "Did you recognize his voice?"

Instantly she nodded. "I've spoken to him several times on the phone over the past months," she said. "Even though it's a different phone with more background noise, I still recognized his voice."

"Interesting." Stone brought up the last number she dialed and held it for Ice to see. She wrote it down and then quickly did something on the keyboard.

Lissa looked over and asked, "What are you doing with it, Ice?"

"A search to see if I can find out who owns it."

"Do you think it was him and he just didn't want to acknowledge you?" Stone asked at her side.

It was a rhetorical question as she already knew that's exactly what he had done. "I don't understand why though."

Silence.

Her gaze went from one face to the next. "You think he's involved?"

"We don't think anything at this point," Stone said reassuringly. "But it would be nice to ask him some questions and clear up some issues."

She thought about that and realized she'd like to ask Kevin some of those same ones herself. "Okay, that makes sense. I imagine he'll be doing his damnedest to get another phone as soon as possible if he is involved."

"Of course. We'll do what we can right now. See if we can find out what country he was in when he answered." That came from Ice. "That will tell us a little more."

"Can you do that?"

"I'll make a couple calls. Run down what I can." She

reached for a phone and within seconds spoke to whoever answered the other end.

Stone motioned the two of them out of the small room. Hard for Ice to have a conversation on the phone with other people talking. He shut the door and said, "Not to worry, Lissa. We'll figure this out. How about you go to the kitchen and see if there is any coffee?"

"Sure, that might be nice. If you've got a few minutes, come join me?" she asked Stone.

"I've definitely got some. Has there been any contact from the insurance company yet? Do you need to go to town for anything else?"

"Honestly, I keep my phone off most of the time. I really don't want to deal with very much more right now."

"You just turned it on to call Kevin?"

They walked down the hallway toward the kitchen. "I was planning on contacting some of the other people in the refugee camp. I made a lot of friends there." She looked at him and added, "I remembered that I copied all the numbers down from my old phone while we were on the plane to London." They walked into the kitchen, and she finished with, "I saw Kevin's number and just dialed."

"Nice," he said in an admiring voice.

She shook her head. "I should have tried earlier."

He laughed. "Good job anyway."

In the kitchen he poured two cups of coffee. With her at his side they walked to the small table in front of the windows and sat down.

They hadn't been here for more than a few minutes when Stone's phone went off. He pulled it out and said, "It's Ice. She needs to see me for a few minutes."

Lissa waved him off. "Go. I'll be fine here." He stood

and looked at her. She smiled up at him. "Go."

"Okay, I won't be long." Leaving his coffee cup behind, he strode quickly from the room.

She pulled out her cell and took a look at it, then brought out the napkin with the rest of the numbers on it. It was almost the same as the last one, just updated. She entered the numbers. She put in her father, mother, and then her lawyer's. That was always a good one to put in there. With a smirk she continued to enter the rest. When Marge's came up, she froze as grief overwhelmed her once again.

Surely Kevin couldn't be involved in something so horrible. He was a doctor. He was all about healing, not killing people. And even if he had needed a drug or ingredients to make something of his own creation, why wouldn't he have made alternate plans before?

Maybe Susan had had something to do with it. Lissa considered her quick decline. The fact that the couple's luggage hadn't been with them had Susan asking about it a lot. They had been told it was coming, but it never did.

And Lissa's mind made a giant leap. Maybe it was a good kind of drug. Maybe Susan had a particular disease and the drug kept it at bay. But the minute she couldn't get the next dose, she'd gone downhill quickly—within days. When they had no access to their luggage. By the time they had reached England, still without it, within twenty-four hours she was taken to the hospital. That would also explain why Kevin had disappeared. Because if anybody knew about the drugs, they would've questioned him.

And that meant Lissa needed to talk to the others again. She stood up, grabbed her coffee, and turned around, only to see Stone walk back in again. "There you are," she cried.

He raised his eyebrows. "I was only gone a couple minutes."

She nodded. "I've thought of something else. What's the chance Susan was using the drugs that customs found in my luggage? And without it, she died."

He froze—his mind churning through the possibility. And then with a quick nod he said, "I'll be back in another minute." At the doorway he turned, stopped, and said, "Stay here."

With a laugh she sat down and took another sip. But inside she was feeling much better. They were on the right track. If they could just get a few answers, they could put this to rest. No reason for anybody to still be coming after her.

She looked at the phone, wanting to say something to Kevin. He probably didn't know her luggage never made it to her. If he had been in contact with anybody from Charles's, then he would know the luggage was being held in customs. And now that Susan was dead, what was the point?

Unless the drug had been successful at doing what it was intended to, which is prolonging life and delaying the onset of the disease.

She opened her phone and quickly dialed Kevin again. This time when it rang, it went immediately to voicemail. A computer-automated voice that left no names. She said quickly, "Kevin, my luggage didn't come with me to the States. It was seized by the British authorities. If you're looking for something, I don't have it."

And she hung up, she realized her hands were trembling.

"That's an interesting message," Stone said, standing beside her. He leaned against the wall, his arms crossed over his chest. "Why would you do that?"

She twisted in her seat to face him. "I didn't want him to

think if he hid something in my luggage, there was any chance I still had it."

"Because that also sounded as if you were telling him you lost the package."

Her jaw dropped. "What?" Then she understood and bolted to her feet. "Oh, my God! You can't think I actually knew I was carrying this drug."

"No. It never crossed my mind until I just heard that message you left."

She shook her head emphatically. "I was only trying to tell him to lay off. That if he had hidden something with me, I don't have it."

"Unless he sent it to you another way. More of it perhaps." Stone's intense gaze studied her.

She frowned. "What do you mean, sent it to me?"

He shrugged.

She stared. "He could have, but it would still be sitting in the post office because I haven't been there to grab my mail for the last eight months."

"I thought Marge picked up your mail?"

Lissa frowned and said, "Yes, she did collect what was in the house, but parcels would still be at the post office, wouldn't they?"

"Unless she picked up the notice and took it in to retrieve the packages for you."

"But she'd have to have my ID," she protested.

"Or *somebody* would have to."

She sat back in shock. "Hang on a minute. Are you saying it's possible Marge picked up the mail that could have had a parcel pickup notice in it? And the killer grabbed it and got the package? Or the notice is still sitting in Marge's house?"

Silence came first, then he gave a clipped nod.

"I need my mail anyway. Can we go back and see?" she asked.

"We'll go now." Stone checked his watch and said, "We have a couple hours still left in the business day. I'll tell the others."

She sat quietly. Her thoughts were confused. Did Stone trust her? Or was she really a suspect? And if so, did they actually have any kind of relationship, or was she just fooling herself? Was this some kind of a ploy for her to be kept under close watch in case she slipped up? "In which case, in their minds, I just slipped up," she muttered.

With a heavy heart she walked back to the room she'd just woken up in and grabbed her purse. She caught sight of her single bag of belongings from the day before. She'd added bits and pieces to it and realized how easy it would be to just take it with her right now. She could stay at a hotel overnight. She didn't need to remain here. In fact it was probably better if she left now.

In which case, she should drive her own vehicle so she had her wheels too.

Stone walked into the room behind her. "You ready?"

She turned and picked up the bag of her belongings and said a defiant, "Yes."

At her tone his gaze went to the bag and then to her. "Are you moving out?"

"That's probably a good idea, considering you don't trust me." She took several steps toward the doorway, but he stepped in front of her, crossing his arms, blocking her way.

"And," she added, "maybe you *never* did." She waved her arms around the room behind her. "Maybe this has all been just a sham, making sure you stuck close to *the suspect.*"

The look on his face went from shock to incredulous and then he broke into boisterous laughter. He stepped forward, took the bag from her hand, and tossed it on the bed. Then he wrapped his arms around her and tucked her up against his chest.

"I might do a lot of things in the name of getting the job done in order to save somebody else's life," he said, "but I've never slept with anyone because of that. And I wouldn't. Yes, you threw me with that message, but your explanation is also reasonable. These are tough times right now, and we have to consider all possibilities. No, I never thought you were guilty. And, no, I do not think you are now."

She looped her hands behind his back. "You're making me crazy," she wailed. "I used to have a normal life."

He stepped back, then used a finger to tilt up her chin, and said, "You've never had one. But hopefully, when this mess dies down, you'll find out what having one actually means."

HE SHOULDN'T HAVE laughed at her. That wasn't fair. But she'd gotten so defensive, and he realized how she must've taken his questioning earlier. Of course they were going to hurt. But nothing she had said afterward caused concern. He'd always known she was innocent. It just shocked him when he heard the message.

Now he had to do his best to make her believe him, because he did trust her. When he'd first met her, he'd been worried about her lack of interest where her father was concerned for her actions. As if there would be no reprisals. But Stone had come to understand and realized he'd been wrong. She was many things, but unconcerned and heartless weren't two of them.

He reached out and grabbed her hand and said, "Let's go. We don't have too much time to hit the post office before it closes. Have you considered calling the refugee camp to see if any parcels were sent to you there?" He shrugged. "But would anybody have done that without you knowing?"

"Maybe, but I don't know why." She turned her back on him.

"But then it would also mean somebody understood you would be going home, or that someone would be collecting your mail for you."

"Or they thought the latter, and then when we were kidnapped and eventually returned home, they realized there was a change of plans because I was now here."

He studied her face as they walked to the front door. "That's possible." He motioned to the big truck. "We'll take this. Can you call them when we're driving?"

"Sure." As he took them out of the compound and headed toward town, she asked, "Do we need to get permission to go into Marge's house?"

"Levi's working on that." He grinned at the look on her face.

But of course Levi was. They had to look at all angles. They worked with the law, not against it. Unless they were forced to.

His phone rang as he turned onto the main highway. He pulled it from his pocket and clipped it on the dashboard. After pressing the button, he said, "Hey, Levi. What's up?"

"The police say you can go to Marge's. They're okay with her taking any mail that might be there as long as her name is on it. An officer will meet you. Don't enter until he arrives."

"Okay. That's fine. We'll wait for him."

"Also keep an eye out. We're waiting for the officers to transfer our prisoner. You should pass them soon. Can you call me when you see them?"

"Will do."

Stone drove on. Just on the outside of the town's limit, he passed a big black smoke-windowed SUV. He waved at the driver, then leaned across to push Levi's number on his phone. When he answered, Stone said, "Just passed a vehicle now, Levi."

"Thanks. Where are you?"

"At the town's limit."

"Okay, so he's ten minutes out." They could hear Levi talking to somebody in the background. He came back on again and said, "Be careful in town." Then he hung up.

Stone stared at the windshield. He knew exactly what Levi's last words meant, but was hoping Lissa didn't.

He should've known better.

Chapter 22

S HE DIDN'T WANT to ask what particular danger they were facing in town. Her imagination had been running for days as it was. She didn't need any other fuel for that fire. But with Stone beside her, she felt quite confident they'd handle whatever it was.

Hating that sense of impending doom, and being incapable of doing anything about it, she brought out her phone and called the main office in the refugee camp. She hoped Cindy still worked there. They'd been good friends, often spending a fair bit of time together.

"Hello?"

Lissa grinned. "Cindy? Is that you? This is Lissa."

Shocked surprise was followed by an explosive exclamation. "Oh, my God! Lissa, are you all right? We were so worried about you after the kidnapping. We got word you'd been rescued, but that must have been terrible," she cried.

"That's one of the reasons I'm calling," Lissa said. "I wanted to let you know I'm okay. We were rescued from the terrorists, flown to England, now I'm back in the States. All safe and sound."

"Oh, thank God! That was so terrible. We were in shock for days."

"Did you ever increase security after we were kidnapped?"

"Oh, yes, big time. Are Kevin and Susan both okay?" she asked.

"Unfortunately, Susan didn't make it." Lissa's voice dropped in pain. "We got as far as England, but then she died in the hospital there. It looked like she was quite sick. It was something that maybe she didn't know about."

"Oh, no. That's so sad. She was definitely sick. Kevin said she was undergoing constant treatments for some kind of a blood disease."

"Oh, dear. I'm so sorry to hear that. How is it that I didn't know?"

"The only reason I knew was sometimes I had to get Kevin some of the drugs for her. They were really expensive."

"That must've been fun to source out of Afghanistan."

Cindy laughed. "Mostly just mailing stuff to their addresses at one of his houses. And then the drugs were there waiting for them when they got in."

And that brought up a whole mess of new questions. "I didn't even know they had houses." She turned to study Stone, who was paying attention to the road and her conversation.

"I used to mail them out to France and England. They have a house in both places, or that was my understanding."

"Did you send any out recently for him, like before we were kidnapped?"

"Just one to the States." Cindy stopped. Then she said, "I remember now. The last parcel I sent was for you."

"Oh, I totally forgot about the parcel mailed for me." But she turned to look at Stone and shook her head as if to make sure he believed her.

"You probably don't remember because Kevin actually asked me to send it to you for safekeeping. They were coming over for the conference in Houston this week. Remember?"

"Right. With everything going on, it slipped my mind."

"Now that Susan's gone, he may not attend anyway."

"Right, I can ask him. If he wants me to send the box somewhere else, I can do that too."

"When you talk to Kevin, give my condolences. Susan was such a sweetheart."

"That she was."

Lissa hung up after that. Then shared with Stone what was up.

"Interesting. I wonder if that parcel has even arrived yet. It's good news for us if it hasn't."

He pulled the truck up to a stop light. He glanced both ways and then made a left turn. They pulled up in front of Marge's house so fast, she hadn't even realized they were that close.

One of the local officers stood outside waiting for them. They walked up to him slowly. Lissa hooked her arm through Stone's, grateful he was here with her at this house. She did not want to walk in there alone, nor see the devastation again. She knew Marge's body had been taken to the morgue, but she doubted anybody had cleaned up.

She wasn't sure who was responsible for such a thing.

Hopefully the insurance company would step in. She paused at the front door and took a deep breath. It took a moment for her gaze to go past the devastation the intruder had wrought and to think logically about where Marge would've put her mail.

"She said it was in a basket," Lissa said to Stone. They walked in the living room and looked for one on the floor or shelves, but they didn't find anything. They proceeded to the kitchen and took a look around.

On the counter against the rear kitchen door was a small basket with mail in it. Stone lifted it up for her to take a look.

"It seems to be a mix of hers and mine." She kept her eyes averted from the bloodstains on the kitchen floor; the chair appeared to still be in the same position where Marge had been tied up. Lissa went through the mail and pulled out fourteen pieces with her name. Nothing noting parcels waited for her anywhere.

They continued to look through the cupboards for anything else, but it made sense that the basket was where she kept all of it. They replaced it, then turned to the deputy and showed him the mail she had pulled out. She offered her ID to prove who she was, and he let them walk out with it. When they got back into the truck, she rolled down the window and took several deep gulping breaths.

"You okay?"

"I'm not sure I will ever be," she whispered. "Just being in that house—I'd almost blocked it out, but seeing it all over again…"

She felt his hand wrap around hers. He stroked her fingers for a long moment before laying her hand down on her thigh. He cranked the engine. "How do you feel about running past your house? We can check to see if any mail may have arrived today, or since Marge's last visit."

"We might as well. It's on the way to the post office anyway."

"Good enough."

When they pulled up in front of her house five minutes later, her heart sank. This was the last place she wanted to be. On the other hand, with a fast in and out, they might be lucky to find what they were looking for.

Only she stood in the living room fifteen minutes later and realized there was no easy way. They hadn't found anything here. Mail or otherwise.

"Can we leave now?" she asked. She made her way to the front door and opened it. She couldn't wait to get the hell out of here. As far she was concerned, she was never coming back.

He came up behind her, leaving the house together and closing the door. Hearing the door lock, she walked down the steps to the truck. "Do you think anyone's watching us?"

"I don't think so right now. But we will always proceed with caution, with the assumption that it's possible."

They drove down the street to the post office and parked. She sat in the truck for a few minutes, just staring at the front door of the building. "So do I just ask if there is a parcel for me?"

"Does that bother you?"

She shrugged. "It seems odd. Aren't I supposed to have a notice or something?"

He laughed. "I'll do the talking."

"Good." She laughed too. "I like that idea." She hopped out of the truck and fell into step beside him. Inside he headed straight for the front counter.

Without preamble he said, "Good afternoon. Lissa, here," he turned and tugged her forward, wrapping his arm around her shoulder, "just came back from eight months of traveling. She was expecting a parcel, but we haven't seen any sign of it yet. Her friend was collecting her mail, but she has been well, you might have heard, but she was murdered. Her place was trashed. So we have no way of knowing if a notice was left for her to pick up or not." He gave the clerk that damn heartbreaker smile.

The older woman melted. She turned to Lissa. "Oh, you poor dear. What's the last name? I'll go check."

"Brampton," she said quietly. "And thank you."

"No problem. The mail was late today so we have quite a few parcels to sort through." She disappeared into a room in the back.

Stone and Lissa stood silently and waited in the empty store. It was almost closing time.

When the lady didn't return right away, Lissa paced impatiently.

"Well, we found your parcel." The woman came out, carrying a small box. "If you have your ID available, I can confirm it's yours."

Lissa already had it out. The woman checked it, then handed over the box. "There you go."

"While we're here, maybe we can do a change of address form to forward her mail."

"Of course." The postal worker slapped a form down in front of Stone. "Just fill this form out and give it back to me for six months of forwarding."

And then they were done.

As they walked to the truck, the lady walked behind them and locked the post office door.

"Good timing," Stone said as they climbed into the truck.

Lissa didn't say anything. She was still working through his request for the change of address form—and the one he'd written down. It only made sense, considering she wasn't returning to her place and didn't have Marge to pick up any missed mail anymore. It still felt strange. Like a seal of acceptance on her living arrangements with the team, with

Stone.

"You recognize the package?"

She stared down at the simple brown cardboard box. Her name was on the front, but no identifying marks were on it. She checked all the other sides, but nothing indicated where it had come from, other than the stamp that said it was from Afghanistan.

"It's just as Cindy said. But I have no idea what it is." She turned to look at him. "You want to open it here or take it home?"

"Why don't we head down to the coffee shop, and we'll take a look there and then drive home."

HE KNEW HE'D made the right decision by suggesting coffee at the place at the end of the block. It was hardly a date, but it was a few minutes non-work-related away from the others. He had jumped forward and stepped on her toes about forwarding her mail to the compound. But she hadn't protested, although she'd been silent while they were in the truck.

He pulled in and parked, then led her to a small booth at the far end of the restaurant. He ordered coffee for them. "Do you need anything to eat?"

She shook her head. "Alfred's got a big dinner happening. We have time for coffee, but that's about it."

Right. They were working on Alfred's time frame here too. Stone checked his watch and said, "We have half an hour." He brought out his pocketknife and offered it to her.

She shook her head and moved the box closer to him. "For all I know that stuff will explode."

For the merest second, he hesitated and she burst into

cheerful laughter.

He grinned and gently slit the tape open. Flipping open the box, he pulled out another small one with the logo affixed of a very popular and expensive brand-name perfume. Frowning and yet wondering at the same time if this Kevin guy was seriously brilliant or stupid, Stone opened it and found the perfume.

He carefully lifted the bottle from the box and noted the seal around the neck but on closer examination, found it was actually tape, it was well-done.

Replacing the bottle inside, he then repackaged it in the mailing box. He kept it close as he lifted his coffee cup and took a sip, eyeing her over the rim.

He asked the questions burning in the back of his mind. "Where do you see yourself in six months? What do you see yourself doing?"

Startled, she put her cup down and lifted her head to stare at him. "You serious?"

"Yes, I am." And he waited.

"You know, that's not the thing I expected you to ask about." She nudged her chin toward the box. "That's what I was waiting on."

He shrugged. "It's pretty obvious what it is, where it came from, and how it got here. The right answers will come in time." He lowered his cup and added, "What I don't know is what you want. Do you want to go to a friend's house? Be with your family? Or somewhere else? What do you want for yourself?"

"And if I don't have an answer for you?" she asked curiously.

He waited for a moment and then asked, "Don't you have any idea?"

This wasn't exactly going the way he wanted it to. But then they had been falling into a relationship, and he wanted to know that she was invested in this. When he'd seen her grab her bag, ready to move out today, it almost broke his heart. That's when he realized he needed to do something to at least know where he was headed with her.

He didn't want to just travel aimlessly forward into a relationship not really founded on anything other than circumstances. He wanted to know where they stood.

The door to the café opened with force. He glanced over, noting that most of the tables were empty, and caught sight of the man's face and stiffened.

Lissa spun around in her seat and gasped. "Kevin?"

Chapter 23

LISSA STARED IN shock as Kevin walked in the diner and sat down beside her. Then she felt the cold metal of a gun barrel against her ribs, but he never even looked at her. He kept his gaze on Stone. Smart man. Stone would rip him limb by limb for this.

"I'd say it's good to see you, Kevin, but obviously it isn't," she said caustically. "Did you kill your wife?" For the first time she saw a pained look cross his face.

The gun barrel jammed harder into her ribs. "No, you did."

She gasped. "I had nothing to do with it. You can't blame that on me." She shoved her face into his, ignoring the gun barrel's pressure against her ribs. "Besides, it's because of me that you and your wife were rescued."

He glared right back at her. "I needed Susan's bag. The one the kidnappers grabbed. If we'd been able to keep it with us, she'd be alive right now."

She thought about it. "You knew the drugs were in there."

"Of course. It went everywhere with us. Until the kidnapping," he said bitterly.

"But then why do you want it now? And why send it to me?" She motioned to the box. "What difference does it make now? She's dead."

"But I'm not," he spat. "And I have the same damn disease."

"Oh, no!" She stared at him in horror. "Why aren't you getting help then?"

"Have you any idea what that costs? It's not tens of thousands of dollars but hundreds for the treatment. And we don't have any health insurance. We spent the last decade traveling around the world helping people. Keeping everyone else alive. When it came to getting help for ourselves, nobody would cover us. Susan was already sick, and I was showing signs. No insurance company would give us the coverage for pre-existing conditions, for the medicine we needed to keep ourselves alive so we could continue to help others. When it came down to it, nobody cared," he said bitterly. "There's only one treatment, and it was made in Europe. Damn expensive and hard to get a hold of, but I kept digging and digging. Finally I understood how to make it. I have a degree in chemistry and enough knowledge of the body and its systems to create my own. It took several tries, but we had nothing to lose. We were dying anyway. Finally, I found the one that worked. We knew it was no cure, but it slowed the progression." He shrugged. "That was as much as we could hope for. We were looking at having another thirty-plus years this way."

"But that's wonderful. You can make the medicine, save yourself, and give it to the world so others can be helped."

"Anyone who wants it will have to pay for it." He glared at her. "Do you know what it's like to beg for just the basics of a health-care program? It's disgusting. We spent years helping others, and yet nobody would do the same for us. That's what I take away from this. If somebody else wants that goddamn medicine, then they'll have to pay for the treatment."

Not liking what she heard, she sat back. Before her was not the same man she'd worked with for months. Instead she was seeing the bitter hard result of a man who'd fought and lost a war and his wife as a result. "I'm so sorry about Susan," she said. "I had no idea she was sick." She nodded at the box with the perfume in it. "Take it. Take it and go."

"It's not that simple anymore." He turned his fury to Stone. "You involved these men."

"*I* didn't involve anyone. My father hired them to rescue us. We went to the airport to collect our bags, only to be told they were caught up in customs because they found something odd. *Your* drug concoction," she said accusingly.

"Yes, and, if those bags had cleared, I wouldn't have needed the stuff I sent you." He shrugged. "I sent a shipment to my house in France, but it was seized as well. The French officials want to talk to me about it," he said bitterly. "And to top it all off, we've already been paid for the product. And now they want the goods. They want *all* of them."

"But they can't have the stuff from England because it's already been destroyed, and you can't access the shipment in France," Stone said calmly. "So you have this, and nothing else."

Lissa cried out, "Give them what you have and tell them you can make more."

"No. I need this bottle for myself, to stay alive," he snapped, reaching out and snagging up the medicine. "I only came here to get it from your house. You wouldn't even be there, so no harm to anyone. The dealers were supposed to get this, but I can't afford to let them have it now. It will kill me if I do. And they will kill me if I don't. I have to run before they find me. At least until I can collect the ingredients to make more, and that's not so easy to do," he finished in frustration. "It's illegal to import the ingredients. Better I go to the Middle East for them."

"They've already found you, haven't they?" Stone asked.

Lissa stared at Stone. "What do you mean?"

Her gaze went from one to the other. "Stone?"

"Kevin didn't kill Marge. Neither did he trash your place." Stone leaned forward, his face hard. "So someone else knew he was coming here, and he's been one step ahead of Kevin, and been here the whole time." He waited a long moment, then snapped, "Right?"

Kevin frowned. "Yes, damn it. I had told the boss, Harold Jorgenson, about the stash I'd mailed here because I thought I had the other shipments. It would have been so different if I hadn't. He was supposed to keep his eye on the house for it. When Marge showed up to collect the mail, I told him to follow and find out where she lived so he could search her house, but he wasn't supposed to hurt anyone."

"A little late for that, considering Marge is dead," Stone said in a hard voice. "Of course Narque Ltd. has a long history that the authorities are very interested in. We've picked up several minor-league henchmen but there's no guarantee someone higher up the food chain doesn't still want your ass."

Kevin looked slightly relieved, but he didn't ease up the pressure of the gun on her ribs.

She studied his face. "This has been a shit show for days, Kevin. What do you need to do to get out of trouble?"

He turned to her, a light in his eye. "I need money, lots of it. I have to pay them back."

"Just make more and give it to them. Tell them you need another week."

Stone added, "Or however long it takes. If you give them a bit of this supply for them to test, then it will hold them off for a little longer."

"And if you have any of the money left, give him some until you get the rest of the drug made up."

He curled his lip at her.

"Money is not so easily found or handed over." He sneered.

"What choice do you have?" she asked quietly. "You've lost Susan already."

"And Susan failed awfully quickly," Stone added. "Maybe she wasn't reacting the way you thought she would, or maybe the drug doesn't work the way you thought it did."

"That's because she didn't get the next dose," he said in frustration. "If we'd just had that, she would've been fine."

"Are you sure about that?" Because the more she thought about it, the more Lissa wondered if the drug worked at all. Maybe Susan was dying regardless of whatever drug he'd given her. Although Lissa had no proof. "Does it really work?"

He froze.

She leaned forward in shock. "Oh, my God! You took money and promised delivery for a drug that doesn't work."

"It does," he insisted. "It's just Susan was getting accustomed to it. We needed to switch up the dosage and frequency, but we didn't have any more of the drug to do so." He stared out the window, pain in his gaze. "The drug kept her alive for this last year. But like all medication, the body adjusts. I just needed more time. She'd improved so much …"

"Or it needed more testing and you ran out of both money and time." Stone leaned forward. "Isn't that correct?"

Kevin leaned forward, and the two men glared at each other.

Then suddenly Kevin slumped in his seat. He pulled the gun from her ribs and tucked it into his pocket. "What am I going to do?"

STONE STUDIED THE man across the table from him. Stone hated the fact that Kevin sat beside Lissa. That was the last time Stone would let her sit on the opposite side of the table. It left opportunities like this one. Anger burned inside him for Kevin pulling a gun on Lissa in the first place.

But right now they had to decide how to get out of this mess. "How did you find us?"

With a blank look, Kevin shrugged. "They've been watching for you. They told me to come in and get the drug."

Damn. Stone was afraid of something like that. "Let's get to the compound. Levi can figure this out."

For a moment Kevin looked hopeful, then his face fell. "No, I can't do that."

Stone stood up. He motioned toward the door. "Then I'm taking Lissa home."

Thankfully, all the fight seemed to have left Kevin. He stood up meekly, pocketed the bottle, and walked ahead of them to the front door of the restaurant. Stone held it open with one hand for Lissa. He tossed the empty packaging in a trash can behind the door.

As he stepped out, he heard two hard spits. Kevin's body jerked before collapsing to his knees.

A man raced away from Kevin. The bottle in his hand. He dove into a sedan as it accelerated past the café. Almost for good measure they fired once more. But Stone was already on the move, sending Lissa to the ground and covering her body with his while pushing Kevin all the way to the ground.

Stone felt his shoulder jerk, then heard the vehicle as it screamed off in the distance.

He rolled off Lissa, still swearing a blue streak. Lissa sat up and screamed.

"How bad are you hurt?" she cried. "Oh, my God, they can't keep getting away with this."

"I'm fine, it's just my shoulder." He sat up and glared at the neat hole in his shirt now soaked in blood. "Damn it. I liked this shirt."

She froze, leaned closer, and said, "You really are fine?" Then she grinned. "Well, that was one way to end this."

"Glad you are enjoying yourself." Stone pulled his phone from his pocket and tossed it to her. "Call Levi. Give him an update. Kevin is dead, and the shooter has the medicine. Have Levi let Bullard know too. They were after Kevin all along. Hopefully this ends it. We'll let the authorities deal with Narque Ltd."

In the distance they could hear sirens. Someone had called the cops, so that was done. He lay back on the grass and groaned softly. "This isn't how I had planned our evening."

She kneeled down beside him, ending her call. "Levi and crew are on their way." She picked up his hand. "How did you want it to go?"

He gave a strangled laugh. "I'd planned to discuss our future over coffee and then maybe continue it a little later in bed."

She leaned over and stared into his eyes. "Is that what

you meant about *where do I see myself in six months?*"

"Yes," he whispered. "But you weren't ready to open up."

"I wasn't exactly sure what you were talking about." She kissed him gently on the lips. "But now that I know ..."

"What do you know?"

"That I want to spend the next six months—per my new address notification—with you. Getting to know you, spending my days and my nights with you ..."

He reached up and grabbed her hand. "You have to realize that sometimes my work is dangerous."

"I know." She placed a finger on his lips. "Apparently sometimes mine is too."

"Are you prepared for that?"

"Of course not," she said smoothly. "Who is, until it happens? But what I can tell you is I want to try."

"Are you sure?"

"Absolutely." She grinned and lowered her head. "Surely, with a bum wing, you'll spend the next couple days in bed, right? We do have lots to talk about."

They did at that, and he realized he'd finally found someone he could be himself with. Not just on the good days but on the darker ones too, when life looked gloomy and lonely. It would take a lot for him to open up, but for the first time, he could see himself doing it. Surrendering to what he had with Lissa—in all ways.

A few days in bed? Hell, yes.

"And lots of other things to do?" He grinned at her. "Depending on what you want of course."

"I want one thing and one thing only." She leaned in closer. She whispered against his ear, her warm breath stroking along his neck, sending shudders down his big frame. "Love me, just love me."

His gaze widened, and he twisted so he could see into her eyes, and saw the truth. "That part," he whispered, his heart in his throat, "I can do easily. In fact I already do."

She dropped her forehead gently to his, tears glistening in her eyes. "Thank God. I hated to think I was in this alone."

"I was lost from the start," he murmured. Damn his shoulder. All he wanted to do was hold her close—all night long.

He knew he didn't need it, but he'd do his darnedest to stretch his healing into several days, just so he could stay with her. The guys would understand. They'd bug him about it, but they'd do what they could to give him the time. Life had never looked better.

Epilogue

MERK WOULD MOVE out. That's all there was to it. Or he would insist on every job Levi had out of the damn state—better yet, the country.

The compound had turned into *The Love Boat* on land. Sickening.

There were way too many loving looks and hugging moments for Merk to handle as a single guy. And he knew Sienna had felt the heat too, as had Rhodes. So, okay, Merk wasn't as bad off as he originally thought but still, Legendary Security was getting a name for itself, and he wasn't sure this angle was the type Levi had intended.

He walked past Lissa and Stone sitting at the kitchen table, heads bent together as they made plans. Merk gave a happy sigh. Okay, he was glad for the big guy. Stone had had a much larger hurdle, maybe more than any of them, to finding a permanent relationship. Then again, Lissa was special. And from day one she'd had eyes only for Stone.

They looked so right together.

So did Levi and Ice. Hard to imagine any two people more suited to each other. He knew Mason's unit had been given the moniker Keepers, much to the men's chagrin, but it was seriously true. Now what was Levi doing here? Instead of their nickname, *Heroes for Hire*, it seemed *Heroes for the Heart* sounded a whole lot more appropriate.

Merk shook his head and walked to the living room. Alone, again. He sighed. Sometimes he wished for what the two couples at the compound had, but he had no idea who would be a perfect match for him. He'd had many relationships, but none had worked out.

Then again he had no illusions as to what they were all about. He'd been married once. Not that it counted. How long did a marriage have to last to count? Not that it mattered either; his was over a long time ago. But he'd learned his lesson—and he had no intention of making that mistake again.

Not in this lifetime.

MERK'S MISTAKE

Heroes for Hire, Book 3

Dale Mayer

Chapter 1

"**T**HIS IS IT, girl," she said to herself. With a last look around, Katina Marshal took a deep breath and slipped into her car. She jammed the keys into the ignition and started the engine. Wanting her actions to look as normal as possible, she pulled into traffic at a sedate pace and stayed in her lane. She couldn't help studying the rearview mirror to see if she was followed.

Ever since she'd seen the damning information, she'd been planning this for days, subconsciously for weeks, if not longer. Now that it was upon her, her palms sweated profusely, and her heart slammed against her chest.

Everything rode on this escape.

Her gaze darted to the mirror on the passenger side, a frown forming on her forehead as she watched a black car switching lanes to tuck up behind her. Shit. She studied the driver's features, but couldn't see him clear enough. Her breath whooshed out; then, in a sudden move, she shifted to the left lane and slowed. A car honked behind her, but she ignored it.

The car shot past her. With a sigh of relief she picked up speed and blended into the traffic. She had no final destination in mind, just heading west. Away from Houston, from her best friend. Leaving Anna was the hardest thing to do. Katina wasn't tied to her old home or the city, but Anna...

well, Katina also didn't dare put her in danger by stopping to say good-bye.

If only she'd connected with Merk. She'd called him several times but so far, got no answer. She laughed bitterly. "As if he'd help."

Katina knew it was foolish to think of him in that light, but it was hard not to. He held a special place in her heart, plus, he'd been heading for special military training after leaving her. Maybe, just maybe, he'd know how to handle trouble. Like *big* trouble.

And maybe she was just an idiot.

Better to hit the highway and keep running. The people after her would give up soon enough.

Wouldn't they?

Unable to help herself, she reached for her phone and called Merk once more.

Please let him answer.

TWO DAYS TRAVELING to safely deliver one prisoner to Washington and then a shorter trip home, Merk Armand had had enough of airports for the moment. The last trip hadn't been bad, just not short enough. He'd been ready to come home days ago. He located his truck in long-term parking, unlocked the door, and hopped in, instinctively reaching for his cell phone still in the glove box where he'd left it. Found four messages, but didn't recognize the number.

All from the same person. Someone he'd thought to never hear from again.

And his ex-wife, Katina. He was surprised to hear her voice. He called the number but got no answer.

"Damn it." He was too tired for this, but worry niggled at him. He called an hour later when he hit his bedroom. Again no answer.

First thing in the morning he called once more. Still nothing. Worried now, he looked up her number in his cell phone and tried that one. Out of service. So much for that idea. Determined to put her calls out of his mind, he walked toward the garage door, heading into town for supplies. A full day of errand running. Oh, joy. But it was necessary. The men were doing upgrades on the compound, and having just got back, Merk was the one with the most flexible time to handle this.

Just as he stepped into the garage, his cell phone rang. He pulled it out. Katina again. He quickly answered it. "Hello? Katina?"

Only a strange static answered him. Damn it. He disconnected, then quickly hit Redial. No answer. Frowning, he turned back to the group working in the garage, their R&D room, and said, "I've got the list but don't expect me back anytime soon after you and Ice added half a dozen more things to my day."

Merk walked to the truck, one of several company vehicles that Levi had picked up. The company Levi had created with Ice was doing extremely well. But it also meant they had teams moving in and out all across the country, depending on what their current projects were. Sometimes it was simple security detail, like Logan's job in California right now, leading a team of bodyguards for a big-name singer.

Merk gave a shudder at that thought. Not that he couldn't do the job; it just wouldn't be his first choice. He was a people person in small groups, not large crowds like that. And when he led a security detail, he wanted free rein to do what was necessary. Not maximum force, but some. And Logan's hands would be more or less tied.

Although being in California right now would not be a good idea. Merk needed to figure out these weird calls from his ex-wife. Not that the term *wife* actually applied here. They'd known each other for only a few hours when they decided marriage was a great idea. Part of the reason for hooking up in the beginning was they were both from Houston, and it had blown up from there. But then what did he expect of a wild party weekend in Vegas? He wasn't ashamed of it, but neither was he proud. One of those chapters of his life he'd like to call closed.

He'd been young and stupid. His last fling before he headed into BUD/S training. A bunch of them had gone down to Vegas for the week, and he'd fallen in lust and celebrated by getting thoroughly drunk. The cold hard reality had hit them both in the morning around the same time as their hangovers.

Only years later did he realize he'd been dating other women who looked exactly like her. Katina had been small with long blonde hair—not plain, not gorgeous, but when she smiled, her whole face lit up. And he'd been instantly enthralled. Enough that he'd bought a marriage license right then and there. Sure the margaritas might have had something to do with that—at least with them following through on it. Tequila was always a shit drink for him, allowing him to indulge without showing signs, then knocking him silly when he hit the worm at the bottom. They had one hell of a night and had both woken up the next morning in shock and horror.

It was almost funny, laughable really, at how quickly they'd gotten dressed, sat down over coffee, and figured out how they'd undo the mess. When they finished the research, grabbed the paperwork, and filled it out, they still had to wait one year to file for the no-contest divorce. But they'd done what they could at the time. He'd left for his training the same day.

In a way that got him through the horrible nightmare of training too. Nothing like seeing yourself as the fool you really are and knowing you need to change. It had helped him to dig within, make it through some of the deepest, darkest times to find himself. He'd been a different man ever since. And he had never heard from Katina after the filing.

Until now. He had no idea why she was calling. Getting out of the compound for the day would be perfect.

He waited for Stone to move his truck, but he stood in the doorway talking to Ice and Levi. Stone was moving his new girlfriend, Lissa, into the compound. Lissa was a dear. And she'd been to hell and back. Merk had had a hand in her rescue in Afghanistan, but as it sometimes did, the war had followed them home. Her place had been thoroughly trashed, though it was all good now. Between the insurance estimates and the work getting done, they'd spent a lot of days traveling back and forth to her townhome.

But today was their move-in day to a new apartment for them in the compound. As Merk watched Stone hop into the truck and drive away, Merk muttered, "Jesus, has it only been six weeks since we met her? Seems like we've known her forever."

He pulled out of the compound, hit the gas as he reached the main road, and sped toward Houston. He laughed as he passed the small town only minutes from home—and the scene of a pretty dramatic incident of late. All in all, Levi and the new company had had a baptism by fire. Merk reached over and hit the radio button to see what music he could drum up down here. It was country, and he was just not into that sad twang.

After the divorce, he'd stuck to very simple relationships. One big mistake in his life was enough. Seeing Ice and Levi finally work through their shit and become that perfect couple would've been nauseating if they didn't have everybody else wanting the same thing for themselves too. Ice and Levi were devoted to each other.

And now there was Stone, finally surrendering from his hard stance of nothing long-term, only amplified after losing his leg. He'd fallen hard for Lissa.

Merk felt like the two women had turned their matchmaking gazes on everybody else in the compound. And Merk just shook his head, his hands raised in protest, saying, "Don't look at me. Don't look at me."

Merk drove up the ramp and hit the main freeway. It was a nice drive, and he liked being on the open road. Twenty minutes from the city, his phone rang. He had forgotten to hook it up on the dash. He quickly placed it on the holder so he could talk hands-free and said, "Hello." In the background was a weird crackling noise. And more static. He repeated, "Hello, who's this?"

Then came a voice that, although he hadn't heard it in ten years, was impossible to mistake. "Merk, it's me. Katina."

"Hey, I've been calling you." He grinned. "What the hell are you doing contacting me after all this time? Are the divorce papers wrong or something?"

He wished he could take those words back. It had been a joke of a marriage. Wouldn't it be stupid if the divorce were too?

"No, nothing like that," she said hurriedly. "I'm in trouble."

He frowned. "What kind?"

What he knew or remembered of Katina was just a college girl in Vegas for a fun weekend. She'd knocked him flat right at the beginning. But she wasn't the kind of girl to get into trouble.

"I need your help, please."

"If I can," he said cautiously. "What's this all about?"

"I'm in Houston right now. I need to talk with you."

"I'm almost fifteen minutes out. I can meet you for lunch if you want."

Inside he was wondering what the hell he was doing. She might be a slice of his past, but a door he probably should keep closed.

"Joe's Bar and Grill on Main Street. You know it?" she said as her voice rose in a panic, rushed as if she was afraid she'd run out of time before he agreed.

"No, but I can find it." He entered the city limits, hating the traffic pulling up on all sides of him. He vaguely knew where Main Street was, but it was still an hour away from lunchtime.

"Meet me at noon." And she hung up.

Worried, curious, and frustrated. Yeah, that was about the state of affairs in his head. It gave him less than an hour to get a couple stops out of the way and then head there for lunch. He hadn't even planned on stopping for food, but obviously his day was shot to shit already, so what the hell.

By the time he pulled up to Joe's Bar and Grill and parked in the back, he was running ten minutes behind. He'd called her to let her know he would be late but got no answer. And no voice mail. He walked into the smoky bar in a shady part of town, wondering what the hell she was doing down here.

The clean, wholesome college girl hoping to celebrate her twenty-first birthday in style that he remembered would never be caught dead in a place like this.

Then he had to stop himself. Hell, they had been in an Elvis Presley Wedding Chapel together. So maybe this wasn't as far off as he thought. He took a seat by a window and ordered a beer. There had to be something good to this day, so he'd take it now in liquid form.

He didn't allow himself to drink very much. They always had to be ready to head out on the next mission. And being bright-eyed, bushy-tailed, and with all their mental faculties and physical prowess intact meant not letting themselves get shit-faced. Besides, Vegas was always in the back of his mind.

Merk waited ten minutes, slowly sipping his drink, wondering what the hell was going on. But he saw no sign of her. He could see the traffic on Main Street, but not the back of the building, and instinct told him he needed to switch sides. What if she was out back waiting, not wanting to come in? If she was in trouble, it complicated all kinds of things.

He ordered a coffee and told the bartender to deliver it to the other side of the bar. Casually, trying not to draw attention to himself, he sat where he could stare out at the parking lot. No one was there. Thinking he'd been stood up, he finished his coffee and got to his feet. If she needed help, it was either too damn late or she'd had second thoughts.

The too-damn-late part was worrisome, because it could mean her trouble had found her a whole lot faster than she'd expected. He walked back outside and stood next to the doorway.

"I don't have time for this shit. My day is full already."

He headed around back to the parking lot when he thought he saw her standing by a small red car.

His footsteps slowed as he studied her. Size and shape was about right, but he hadn't seen her in eleven years and she wasn't facing him. She was also too far away to get a really good look. Determined to get to the bottom of this, if one was to be found, he walked toward her. She looked around fearfully, and he realized maybe she hadn't expected him to go inside the building and had been waiting in the parking lot for him. She took one look at him and bolted.

"Katina?"

She came to a stuttering stop, turned, and called out, "Merk?"

Her voice said she hadn't recognized him any easier than he had her. He nodded. Relief washed over her face, and she ran back toward him.

A van raced into the parking lot between them and stopped. Two men got out, grabbed Katina, and threw her inside. He barely had time to register what had happened before the van drove right past him. He tried to jump on board, but the vehicle was moving too fast. As he went down and rolled, trying to catch sight of the license plate, he realized there wasn't one.

He was in his truck, the engine roaring, and out of the parking lot in a flash. He knew all too well how easy it was to kidnap women and how absolutely impossible to find them most of the time.

Chapter 2

S HE WAS SUCH a fool.

Why had she run away from him? But he was big, and his hair was cropped short, and she had barely recognized him. Hell, even now she wasn't sure it was him. For all she knew, a complete stranger had nodded at her, thinking she was talking to him. But he'd called her name. It had to have been him. Only, instead of running toward him, she'd run away. Now look what the hell happened. Her one chance of freedom was gone. She'd been flung into the back of a van, a hood quickly pulled over her head, and then tied up.

She hadn't even caught a decent glimpse of the two men who had grabbed her. The vehicle moved in a crazy, erratic pattern that rolled her from side to side. Someone booted her hard, making her roll over the other way. It was all she could do to stifle her sobs.

She'd been threatened, told to stop, and to hand over what she'd taken. But none of the choices had been much of an option.

Where was she supposed to go now? These people had long arms and a lot of resources. And for their crimes, they wouldn't stop until they tossed her lifeless body into a river. Or worse, put cement shoes on her and dropped her in the ocean alive. She was pretty sure it had happened to a few other people who had crossed their path. Only she had no proof. How the hell could she get out of this?

She didn't cry often, and she sure as hell wouldn't now. She was too damn mad. At herself, at Merk.

Why the hell hadn't he been there earlier? Then she realized he had come from around the building. As if toward his vehicle with his keys in his hands. Had he been waiting for her in front? Or even inside? Had she told him to wait outside or inside? She no longer remembered.

She wasn't acting or thinking clearly anymore. Panic had overtaken her world. And now she could barely breathe.

The vehicle took a hard left, and she was flung to the side once more. She slammed her back into something again. She couldn't hold back the moan.

"Stupid bitch, stay where you are."

How the hell was she supposed to do that when they were driving like crazy men? Why *were* they driving like that? It would bring attention to them. She stifled back a gasp of hope. Unless they already had unwanted attention. Was it possible Merk had given chase? Was he even now calling for help? Please let him be calling the police. It was the only way she would get out of this mess. She should have done that first, but was afraid the men after her had connections high up in law enforcement. She didn't know who to trust.

So she had called Merk. His had been the first to come to her mind when she realized she was in deep trouble. Maybe, just maybe, he had become a SEAL—one of the few goals he'd shared with her in his drunken haze. She understood the stats that almost nobody made it through the training, and she really didn't know who he was personally. But she'd hoped ... Damn, she'd hoped he'd be here for her.

She closed her eyes and forced herself to breathe as naturally as she could. With the hood over her head it was hard, but she didn't want to hyperventilate, and she could feel the dizziness starting. And then the din around her set in.

"Lose the bastard."

"I'm trying to. What do you think I've been doing for the last ten minutes?"

"Farting around. Get rid of him."

Another voice kicked in. "And if you can't, pull over and let me drive. I'll shake this asshole."

She smiled. So maybe calling Merk hadn't been the biggest mistake she'd ever made. It is possible she would get lucky and somebody would help her—for once.

The vehicle turned yet another corner, tires squealing, men swearing, and then came music to her ears—sirens. And now they were really cussing.

"Move it, move it."

"Fuck that shit. We can't have the cops coming down on us. Get the hell out of here."

"I am. Just give me a minute. I can get to the tunnels and lose them there."

"You can't go in there the wrong way, damn it. Oh, shit!"

Instead of shouting, there was silence. But the vehicle hurtled at top speed, and she realized they would likely end up in a major crash. And if she wasn't lucky, she would die in this damn tin box. She'd be okay if they all did, only she wasn't up for going under at this point in time.

Still, she was incapable of doing anything about it. She was trying, but her feet were bound and her hands tied up behind her with some heavy rope, though the knots around her feet were unraveling with all her rolling around. Then came more shouting.

"Watch out."

"Holy shit, that was close."

The vehicle swerved and wavered as the sirens behind them grew nearer, louder. She had no idea where the hell Merk was in all this. She didn't want him to get in trouble, or hurt, but she sure hoped he hadn't left her.

The sirens were a huge sign. Only the vehicle's momentum never stopped. It was a Monday, and she knew the traffic had been heavy before they put the bag over her head. This *was* Houston. But the van still zigzagged through vehicles while pulling off this escape. In her world of darkness she could hear metal crunch against metal as cars slammed together, punctuated by screaming brakes, then impact sounds. Suddenly, they were out of the darkness and back into daylight. Even with the hood over her head she could sense the difference in the light around her.

"Take a left. The auction yard is just ahead."

The van turned that way, follow by a hard right, then the driver hit the brakes so fast she was flung forward. She slammed into something sharp. She cried out in pain. Her leg, shit, it was injured. Hopefully not bad enough to stop her from running because if she got a chance, she was out of here. She lay on the floor, gasping for breath. Grateful they had stopped that suicidal run, at the same time her ears were alert, searching for the sirens.

But found only silence. Her shoulders sagged as she realized they'd actually done the impossible. They'd escaped. From the police and Merk, she was still a captive. The door opened, and she was grabbed, tossed to the ground outside. She cried out as she landed, her injured leg slamming onto the hard dirt.

"What you want to do with her?"

"Keep her with us. We need new wheels. Pick out something from the lot and hotwire it. We'll throw her in the back again."

And that's when she realized she could see ever-so-slightly through the hood they'd placed over her head. Some burlap sack. Like so much of the shit made today, lacking textile quality. The holes were wider than normal. She watched the men spread out, she counted four, looking for another set of wheels.

She was in a used car lot or junkyard. Vehicles were everywhere. What a perfect place to hide the van. At the same time, maybe she could get herself out of here too.

She sat up, kicked the now loosened rope off her legs, hopped to her feet, and turned to look around, anxious to find any place to hide. She darted in between the first row of cars. The men had gone to the left; she went right.

And she just kept on running. Twenty yards later she tripped and fell, hitting the ground hard, her face going into the dirt. She sat up, spitting, but at least the fall had loosened her hands. With her arms free, she quickly took the hood off her head. She could see where she was clearly now. A main road was not far away.

Staying low, ducking between the vehicles, she ran and kept going until she reached a gate. But she couldn't open it. She didn't know how they got into this place, but the wire atop the fence could be electrified.

She kept following along the perimeter, looking for the gate they had come in through. And then she heard one gunshot in the distance. She clapped a hand over her mouth to hold back her cries and slid under a vehicle. If nothing else she could hide. After the weapon had fired, she heard sounds of a car racing up and down the rows. And men shouting.

Followed by blessed silence. She lay under the vehicle, gasping for air, trying not to cry out loud. But the sobs still came out. Where had they gone? And why? Was she safe?

Had they all left? Or was someone still waiting for her?

Sirens came screaming toward the lot. And then all hell broke loose. For sure she knew the men who'd kidnapped her were gone. She didn't know who had been shot, but knew there was a chance that right now she was safe. Or she could get the next bullet.

Within minutes she heard someone calling. "Katina, are you here?"

"Katina?" another man called.

"Katina, where are you? Are you hurt?"

All unfamiliar voices. And she realized they were systematically searching for her. She couldn't see them yet, so she waited. But even if they were policemen, could she trust them? Then she heard a voice that made her heart swell with joy.

"Katina, its Merk. Where the hell are you?"

In the silence that followed, she could almost hear him growling. He was so close.

"I saw the car leave, and you weren't in it, so I know you're here somewhere. Are you hurt? We'll search this place from top to bottom, but if you can hear me, make a sound or let us know where you are."

"Here," she cried out. "Merk, is that you?"

And suddenly there he was, his face just inches away from hers as he crouched down beside the car she was under.

And he grinned. "There you are. Can you get out? Are you hurt?"

She dragged herself along the ground until she was clear of the vehicle, then Merk snatched her up into his arms and turned around, calling out, "She's here."

Carrying her, he walked to a dozen policemen and their vehicles. The men quickly surrounded them. She couldn't stop crying. God, she hated that. In times of stress it was such a relief to cry, but at the same time, it made her look so damn ... female.

Merk asked again, "Are you badly hurt?"

She raised her hand to touch his face, whispering, "I think I'm okay. My thigh hurts, but not too bad."

"We have an ambulance coming," one of the policemen said. "Blood's coming from the back of her leg. She should be checked out."

"Do you know where they were taking you?" Merk asked in a hard voice.

She shook her head as her sobs kept erupting. "No," she said. "I have no idea."

"Why did they kidnap you? Did you recognize those men?"

"No," she whispered. Now, she realized, she was safe. "I've never seen them before."

She opened her mouth to tell them more and held back. Her gaze caught sight of a dead man on the ground. She closed her mouth, then whispered, "Was he the driver? I heard the shot but didn't know who'd been hit."

"We're not sure who he was. I was hoping you could tell us," one of the cops said.

Wide eyed, she shook her head. "I had a hood over my head most of the time. I never had a chance to see anyone."

Merk squeezed her against his chest, and she could feel that insistent gaze as he stared down at her. She opened her eyes to see him, then she made a tiny, hardly perceptible, nod to the men around them. Instantly Merk understood.

She had no idea how, but he did.

Thankfully, the ambulance arrived. Merk carried her over.

She gripped Merk's hand tight and whispered, "Please, I don't want to go to the hospital."

"Depends on how bad it is."

"It's not. I'm good." She turned to stare at him, willing him to understand. "I will die in the hospital."

She consented to having the EMTs check her out. As she sat on the edge of the ambulance, the coroner arrived for the dead man. She stared blindly out at the yard; emergency vehicles were everywhere. Over a trailer was a sign. Action Auctions. She shuddered. What a great place to switch out vehicles.

The EMTs did what they could and one said, "She should get checked at the ER."

She hopped to her feet, crying out, "No." She took a few steps experimentally, and although she winced, the pain wasn't bad. "Nothing's broken. I'll go home and see my doctor. If I need painkillers or something, he'll get me the prescription."

The EMTs told her it was her choice. Merk led her back to his big truck, and she smiled. It was as badass as he was. When she went to open the door, his big hand got there first. He opened it, gently lifted her up, and placed her on the passenger seat.

"Stay here."

He closed the door, but just before it shut, she stuck her head out and said, "What will you say to the police?"

He gave her a reassuring look. "That we'll come down and give a statement."

Disappointed, she slumped in her seat. Not what she

had expected. There would be a hell of an investigation over this.

The trouble was, she didn't dare tell any of them the truth.

MERK HAD NO idea what the hell was going on. But she obviously felt other police were, or could be, involved, and she was just as terrified about the hospital. He wasn't sure what to do with her, but she couldn't be left alone right now. He needed to get her away somewhere private to find out what was happening.

After assuring the cops he'd bring her to the police station later this afternoon once he had a chance to calm her down, they let him go. The police had other things to do as well, and she needed to rest a bit. Maybe he'd take her to the doctor first. His plans for the day had completely changed, and mentally he prioritized the rest of it.

The cops grumbled until he handed over his card and said, "Contact Levi if you got a problem with this, but I personally promise she will be there."

"She should still go to the hospital," one of them said. "That cut's pretty deep."

Merk nodded. "She's hoping to see her doctor. I'll get her checked out first, then we'll be in." As he walked away, he said, "If you guys aren't there, who do we report to at the station?"

One of the men stepped forward and said, "I'll open the file on this one." He handed over his ID and said, "Contact me when you arrive. I'll be there in a couple hours. We'll do a thorough search of this place, especially looking for the getaway van, to see if they left anything behind."

"Good enough."

Merk walked back to the truck, happy to see she hadn't left, but noticed she'd slipped down, as if not wanting anybody to see her. He hopped up in the truck, turned on the engine, and slowly reversed out of the auction yard. As far as a hiding place went, this was a damn good spot.

"Wait."

He hit the brakes. "What?"

She pointed. "There. Isn't that the van they kidnapped me in?"

He parked, jumped down, and walked to the vehicle. It blended in with the others perfectly, as if it belonged. He checked the back for a license plate and realized she was right. There wasn't one.

Opening the side door, he took a quick look, then reached for the glove box. No papers anywhere. He quickly wrote down the VIN number and then called the cops over. When the police arrived, he explained this had been the vehicle they'd been chasing down.

The men went to work. When he got into the truck, he turned to her and said, "Anything else?"

She shook her head. "No. Please, can we just get the hell away from here?"

He nodded, and this time when he exited the auction yard, he kept going.

Chapter 3

"**C**AN YOU DRIVE me to my car, please? I really want my wheels back."

She sat curled up in the corner on the far side of his truck. She stared at his profile, wondering how he'd become such a big man. It seemed like the man she had married had almost been a boy compared to who sat beside her now. He was a hell of a lot more attractive and powerful-looking now too. How could that be? Seemed people got worse when you hadn't seen them for a decade or so. Instead he'd gotten seriously better. He was sexy as hell.

She shook her head. Even back then she knew how to pick them.

"When will you tell me what the hell's going on?"

"It's better if I don't say anything," she said hurriedly. "These guys have obviously proven they will do anything they can to shut me up, and I don't want you to get hurt."

His head spun toward her, his glare hard, the glint lethal. "Don't even play that shit game with me. You're in trouble, and I am one of the few people on this goddamn planet who can help you. So just shut the hell up with that kind of talk, and tell me what's going on."

They were almost at the rear of the pub now. "I need to get my car, give a statement, and have my leg looked after," she said. "After all that, if I have any energy left, I'll tell you."

On that note he drove right through the parking lot. "So we'll go to the police first." He glanced over and saw the look on her face. "No, change that. Clinic first to get you treated, the police second, and then back here for your car."

She glared at him. "You didn't used to be so high-handed."

"And you didn't used to be so stupid." He glared at her. "You really think I'd let you run off with these men after you? Like hell."

"This is big," she protested. "Like, really big."

"Good," he snapped. "Because I do big, so just get used to it."

She subsided into silence, wondering how her life had gotten so crazy. But it didn't matter now because he had just pulled up beside a clinic and parked. He got out, but when he slanted a gaze at her, she realized he was still pissed.

She watched as he walked around and opened the passenger door. Although he might be angry, it wasn't directed at her.

He held out a hand and said, "Take it easy getting down."

With his help she got out of the truck. Her first step brought a cry to her lips. She limped forward, murmuring, "Thank you."

But he didn't drop her hand. Instead he led her inside the front door of the building. Thankfully, it wasn't very busy. She had to wonder if she'd won the lottery on that note.

Once inside, she had her leg cleaned, the doctor put a couple stitches in, bandaged it, and she was back outside in less than ninety minutes.

She shook her head. "Was it because of your presence

that we got in and out so fast?" she added with a note of humor.

"Maybe." He shrugged. "I didn't give a shit as long as you were taken care of." He helped her back into the truck and walked to the driver's side.

She watched as he hopped in easily. "Now where?" she asked.

"Police station. Let's get that damn statement down so we can be done with all the necessities."

As much as she wasn't looking forward to it, she knew he was right.

Besides he wasn't giving her much choice.

Finding parking at the police station, now that was a different story. She hadn't quite understood when they got to the clinic why it was so empty. But when they had arrived at the station, she figured it had been because three-quarters of the damn town was here. Merk still somehow pulled off a miracle locating an empty spot in the far corner. Her leg was damn sore though, so the walk wasn't something she appreciated, but this had to get done.

"I'd offer to carry you now, but chances are you wouldn't want that," Merk said at her side.

She shot him a look. "I don't remember you carrying me over the threshold way back when."

He let out a bark of laughter and said, "I wondered if we would bring up that point in our lives." In a move that shocked a squeal from her, he stooped and picked her up, carrying her around to the front of the station. "You're due one trip over the threshold now since I missed an opportunity way back when."

"You were probably too drunk," she said, a smile on her face.

"And, therefore, chances are *you* were too drunk to re-member anyway," he reminded her.

And without another word that settled them back down, both knowing where they'd been, what they'd done, and surprised to find themselves in today's situation.

She still wondered at the impulse to call him when she'd been in trouble. But as it turned out, it had been the best decision she'd made in a long time.

Inside, he set her down near the chairs as they had to wait. Finally, the detective came out and took them to his desk. She wrapped her arms around her chest and tried to answer the questions calmly. She wasn't sure she should say very much though, so a few times she hedged, giving only half answers. She'd been warned not to go to the police, so she didn't really understand what she was supposed to do now. Given a choice, she wouldn't have come to give a statement at any time.

She'd been willing to run halfway across the country, and still planned to, if she could get back to her wheels. Her apartment was gone; she'd been living in a hotel for the last few nights, and they'd still found her. They'd even called her cell phone. The policeman's questions kept coming, but she fell into monotone and monosyllabic answers. "I'm sorry. I'm just so tired, and the pain is really kicking in," she whispered.

The police officer looked at her in sympathy. He printed off her statement, then handed it to her for her signature. "There you go. If you can wait a few more minutes, we have to ask your friend some questions," he said. "Then you can both go home."

"Sure," she said with a faint smile.

Her leg throbbed. They'd given her a shot when they

put the stitches in, but it was wearing off. She thought she had a prescription in her pocket because the doctor had handed her a piece of paper, but hadn't looked at it. She'd just shoved it in a crumpled ball into the corner of her jacket pocket. She rarely took drugs, knowing she would be sleepy and therefore too tired to drive if needed. But right now … she wished she had them.

She listened as Merk gave his answers, then realized he did exactly as she had. He was hedging. Giving half-truths, not exactly lying, but not giving everything. And with that one little act she trusted him all the more.

How stupid was that? But he was covering her ass as well as his, and she appreciated that. When he was finally done and signed his statement, he stood up and reached out a hand for her.

By the time they stood outside, she wasn't sure she could stand much longer—not to mention drive. Besides, her car was a standard.

And for some reason that truth hadn't kicked in until she looked at his truck. She stared at it in dismay. "I don't know if I can drive."

"Doesn't matter because you're not trying."

"I can't just leave it in the parking lot. It'll get towed."

"I've got that figured out."

He half boosted her into the seat and closed the door on her. By the time he got around to his side and hopped in, she was busy asking, "What do you mean by that?"

But he didn't answer. Instead he left the lot and drove back to the pub where her car was parked.

That's when she remembered something else he had said. "I'm sorry for messing up your day."

He grimaced. "I had a full list of errands, but I'm not

too optimistic about getting any of it done."

"I'm so sorry."

He shrugged. "I still have to pick up a bunch of supplies, but the rest may have to wait until tomorrow or the next day." He glanced up and down the street as if sorting out where they were. "We'll deal with those issues once we address your car."

She leaned her head back and wondered what the hell that meant, but she felt just shitty enough not to give a damn until he pulled into the rear of the pub and parked behind her car.

He reached out a hand and said, "Where are the keys?"

She stared at him blankly. "Why do you want them?"

He motioned toward a man standing before them. "This is Levi. He'll drive your car back."

"Back where?"

Merk gave her a hard stare and said, "Back to the compound where I live."

She opened her mouth to protest, then realized she really had no option. She couldn't drive; she was in shitty shape. She really needed somebody to take charge, at least for a few hours. She dug into her pocket and handed over her keys. Then she watched while Merk hopped from the truck to speak to the big man in front of them.

The discussion lasted about ten minutes with various hand movements she couldn't make heads or tails of. Finally, Merk climbed back into the truck and said, "Good. He'll help pick up the supplies I came into town for."

"You're not making any sense. He had to get into town somehow, and if he's driving my car, how is his own getting home?"

Merk laughed. "Lay your head back and go to sleep. If

you were feeling normal, you'd know that answer."

They drove past another big truck almost identical to Merk's. A beautiful blonde was at the wheel. Merk nodded lightly; she waved, and they carried on. Instantly a stab of jealousy fired through Katina. Who the hell was that woman?

MERK DIDN'T HAVE a clue what was going on in Katina's life, but something sure as hell was. He wanted to question her, but she was in no shape right now. Her eyes were fuzzy with pain, her body hunched into the corner, and her arms were across her chest. She should be asleep in a few minutes.

But he had lots of stops to make. He'd split up the load with Levi, but they were running out of time before the businesses closed. Still he would grab what he could, and then he'd return to the compound. He shook his head. Who'd have thought his day would end this way?

He hadn't seen her in eleven years. And out of the blue, she called asking for help.

Well, before she could leave the compound, he would learn a whole lot more about this trouble she was in because he'd seen her get snatched. This was no simple hit. No stranger abduction. She'd been targeted. And he wanted to know why. That they'd shot one of their own men and left him behind told Merk a much bigger issue was going on. Also she didn't speak truthfully to the cops. So either she didn't want them involved or didn't trust them.

Not that Merk didn't either, but he'd been burned and betrayed himself. His whole unit had, so he'd given only minimal information in his statement. It was just as important to understand who your enemy was. And at this point, he had no clue. When he stopped at his third store, he raced inside to pick up the materials for Stone's latest prototype, returned to the truck, and tossed the items behind the seat. He realized she'd finally given up the ghost and had fallen asleep. He stopped and studied her features for a long moment, then reached out a finger and stroked her cheek.

In a low voice he murmured, "I wonder what trouble you've gotten yourself in, Katina. But if you think you can just tease me with little bits and pieces, you're damn wrong. I will get to the bottom of this, with or without your permission." He settled into his seat, buckled up, and turned on the engine.

He'd never backed down from a fight yet. And when those men had kidnapped Katina, he wanted nothing more than to get his hands on them.

Chapter 4

S HE WOKE UP when the truck came to a sudden stop. She sat up, groggy, and stared as they passed through a huge metal gate into a large fenced area with several buildings. Several other trucks were parked outside, just like the one she was in.

She turned toward Merk and said, "Where are we?"

"Hey, how are you feeling?"

"Better," she admitted. "But you're not answering my question." She gazed around and realized another vehicle came up behind them. They parked alongside her car. She turned again with a questioning look at Merk. "Is this the compound you were talking about?"

"Yes, it's where I live and work."

She studied the layout. It was huge. Her gaze went straight back to the man who got out of her car. He was as big as Merk, if not bigger. And stunning. But more than that, he carried himself like Merk. The same air of can-do attitude and controlled power.

From around the building, the blonde goddess walked toward the other man, and with a smile, he wrapped an arm around her shoulders, and they went into the large building together.

Abruptly Katina told Merk, "I want my keys."

"You can have them." Merk opened his truck door,

hopped out, and walked around to open her door. "Let's get you down and then inside." He stepped back slightly to give her a bit of room. "Then I have to unload the truck."

She slid to the ground without his help and winced only a little as her feet slammed to the ground. The pain wasn't too bad. She took a few experimental steps and realized that, although it hurt, it wasn't crippling. "Feels much better," she said to him, already grabbing things from his vehicle. "I can go home on my own now."

"You could, but you have to go inside and ask for your keys back." He turned and walked away from her, his arms full.

"Or you can get them for me," she called, standing beside her car, "and save me some steps."

"If it hurts that much, then you can't drive anyway."

The door to the house slammed behind him. She glared at it. She wasn't walking in there. She didn't know anybody here. She turned and leaned against her car and waited for him to come back out. It took about five minutes, then he arrived whistling.

Nice that he was happy. She asked, "Did you get my keys?"

"I did." He tossed the keys in the air and then while she watched, caught and shoved them into his jeans pocket.

"That's not fair," she protested. "Give me my keys."

"If you think you're driving away with that leg, you're wrong."

She glared at him. "Who died and made you boss?"

He turned and pinned her with a look. "You did the minute you called me for help." He took a step toward her, and in a low voice, said, "Now get used to it. I'm here to help and I'm not walking away. No matter what you say or how you try to push me away."

Shit. Now what the hell would she do?

When he came back out for the third round of goods from the truck, he stopped and said, "You ready to go inside and meet the others now?" She crossed her arms over her chest and said, "And if I don't want to?"

He shrugged. "Well, they're waiting for you, but if you don't want to be social, that's okay. You can stay out here. It'll get mighty cold soon though. Inside it's nice and warm with hot food and coffee." As he walked away again, his arms once again full of the truck's contents, he called back, "We might all be warriors, but we don't bite off innocent heads."

She glared at the door and thought about how helpful he had been otherwise. He was right. She'd called, and he'd come running. He'd saved her life. Going in and socializing for a few moments, well, it was the least she could do.

Fine.

When he came out the next time, she stood almost at the doorway. He stopped when he saw her and smiled. "Glad to see you're being reasonable." He motioned to the truck. She waited until he picked up the remaining boxes and walked toward her. She held the door open for him, and he walked in, unconcerned if she followed or not.

He was making her crazy again. He'd been like that eleven years ago, and they'd only known each other for a day.

She followed him in. He took a left and laid all the boxes in the middle of the room. She turned and looked at the contents in fascination. Like a huge garage but with workbenches and more, as if they did some fancy development work here.

As he walked toward her again, she eyed him carefully and asked, "Just exactly what do you do for a living?"

"Private security," he said simply.

"Oh."

He took her hand and said, "Come on."

He walked with her into what appeared to be a kitchen with a long bench. In the center of the room were at least half a dozen people.

She stood awkwardly beside Merk as the goddess-looking woman turned and saw her. "Hello, my name's Ice. Who are you?"

And the words that flew from her mouth were not what she had ever expected to say. "Merk's wife."

The room froze.

And then she realized what she'd said. "Ex-wife. I'm Merk's ex-wife," she said hurriedly. "My name is Katina Marshal."

"Welcome, Katina. We made a place for you at the table, so come and sit down." In a smooth voice Ice turned to Merk and said, a twinkle shining in her eyes, "Merk, get your wife a coffee."

Katina winced. "Sorry, Merk."

With an irritable shrug, he said, "They were bound to find out sometime. So, whatever."

But would they? If they were surprised, it meant he hadn't told them about what happened eleven years ago. When Katina finally sat, Merk handed her a large cup of coffee. Black just the way she liked. She wondered at that. She had remembered all kinds of little things about him too. Deciding not to bring it up, she huddled over the cup and blew on the top. She'd really like to drink it, but it was hot.

When they were all seated, that air of expectation hung over the table. She looked at Merk and shrugged.

He just said, "You brought it up. You explain."

Her eyebrows shot up toward her hairline. "I would rather we not have to. Isn't it obvious? We were married. Now we're divorced. It's a closed book."

"How long ago was this?" Ice asked curiously. "I've known Merk for a long time."

Katina laughed. "When we were both dumb and stupid. As in Vegas stupid, eleven years ago."

That startled a laugh out of everyone at the table. Merk just rolled his eyes. She grinned. "Hey, the Elvis Presley Wedding Chapel was damn good that night."

"Yeah, how many margaritas did it take for that to look good?" Merk teased her.

Under the glare of fascination from everybody around them, she shrugged and confessed, "I don't remember." That brought everybody into full gales of laughter.

Sheepishly she grinned and said, "Still, when I ran into trouble, I knew exactly who to call." She looked across at Merk and said, "Thank you for saving my life today."

As a conversation stopper, it was a killer. Complete silence swept through the room.

"YOU'RE WELCOME." MERK studied Katina across the table. It was a weird bridge across time. That same simple honesty had caught and held on to him the first time he'd met her. He even remembered what it was—something to do with standing before a card table in Vegas and her turning to him and saying she didn't even know how to play. He'd taught her right then and there. Of course, before the end of the night, they'd been teaching each other plenty. "You ready to tell us what this is all about?"

She stared down at her coffee cup, afraid to lift her gaze

to the others. "I don't know any of you. If you're all part of this private security company, maybe you can handle yourselves…better than I can obviously. But this is very dangerous. I don't want to put anybody else in the crosshairs."

Ice reached an arm across to Katina's shoulder and gave her a gentle hug. "I wouldn't worry about that. We've taken on some of the most dangerous jobs in the world."

Merk watched as Katina studied Ice's face, then she looked at him for confirmation. He nodded his head. "We're all ex-military," he said. "Levi formed this company with Ice, and we're still doing what we did before, only privately now."

Katina slowly relaxed, like the starch had gone out of her shirt. "I really was right to call you, wasn't I?"

He nodded. "Although I'm curious as to why you did. We haven't spoken in over ten years."

"You were headed for special military training after Vegas. Did you go?"

He nodded. "I did indeed."

"And I was hoping that, if you had, maybe you'd know what I was supposed to do"

"That's where I met a lot of these people. But now it's time for you to come clean. Just what the hell have you gotten yourself into?"

She glanced around the table and said, "Some of it's a little bit personal, so just bear with me." She glanced over at Merk, then dropped her gaze quickly.

He leaned forward and laid his hand out on the table. She stretched across and placed hers on it. Just as she had eleven years ago. He marveled at how small and yet capable that hand was.

She took a deep breath and said, "When I got back from Vegas, the ink wasn't dry on my wedding certificate, was even less so on our divorce papers, which we had to wait one year to file," she said, interjecting a note of humor.

"I took stock of my life. I'd gone to Vegas to celebrate my twenty-first birthday and didn't really like what I did while I was under the influence. I hadn't been much of a drinker but of course, turning twenty-one was a big deal. When I went home, I completed college and got an associate's degree in bookkeeping. I decided I wanted to do more, so I got my accounting degree. I worked for several small companies initially. And then finally, about four years ago, I was hired to work for Bristol and Partners, Ltd., a real estate property management company with an office in Houston."

She glanced around the table, wondering if anyone knew the name. Some people nodded and she continued.

"At first everything seemed to be simple and normal. Of course, I was in a junior accounting position, and we had several senior accountants in the company as it was a large business, with many locations nationwide. In this last year I was moving up the ranks. About four months ago, one of the accountants took an extended leave and I was asked to step in temporarily until she got back on her feet."

She stopped talking. Merk gently stroked her fingers and said in a low voice, "It's okay. Tell us the rest."

She shrugged. "Well, once I did, everything went downhill."

Chapter 5

S HE REALLY SHOULDN'T tell them more. She looked around at all the hard-looking men and even stone-cold Ice—aptly named—beside her. She had no idea who they all were, although quick introductions had been made. Making the wrong decision here could get someone killed. Merk squeezed her fingers in that indomitable way and said, "Continue."

"Well, I imagine you can guess the rest," she said. "I found a few discrepancies, shall I say." She waved her free hand in the air dismissively and said, "Not anything major but just a little bit more than I was comfortable with, and I didn't quite know how to handle it. I sat on the information for a while and then decided to see if the original accountant had just made a simple bookkeeping error, because that certainly can happen, particularly when we're talking about large sums of money. When I backtracked, I found a few other things wrong."

"Big-dollar figures?" Ice asked.

"Yes. Tens of millions of dollars."

They all nodded as if they had expected that.

Katina continued. "If I'd followed the company line, maybe nothing would have happened with this. I was supposed to go to my boss and tell him what I'd found. Let him deal with it." She broke off again.

"But you didn't?" Merk asked.

She shook her head. "No, and what I did was probably worse. I have copies of everything I saw."

They all straightened up.

She winced. "I was afraid I would get blamed for this misallocation. It would have been so easy to frame me for some of this, after doing the woman's job for months." She shook her head, knowing some of this was definitely jail-type stuff. White-collar crime it might be, but a lot of money was being moved. "I didn't want to take the fall for it."

"That's certainly understandable," Merk said. "But in all seriousness, if you have that information, it's very important that you hand it over to the authorities."

"I know that." She stared down at her coffee and wondered if they believed her, if she should tell them the rest. But if she didn't, how else did she explain why she hadn't already told the police when she'd been at the station today?

"Tell us the rest," Merk said firmly. "We can't help if we don't know all of it. You can't keep something like this to yourself. It'll eat you inside out."

She lifted her head and let her gaze slip around the group. Her stare stopped at a new arrival in the doorway. This woman didn't have the same look as Ice at all. A second joined her. She looked about as hard as a cotton ball.

Katina frowned and tilted her head toward the doorway. Merk turned and said, "Sienna, Lissa, come join us."

Lissa said, "We don't want to disturb you. It sounds like it might be personal."

Stone, the largest man in the room—and that said a lot—stood up and reached out a hand. She walked over, grabbed it, and he tugged her into a spot at the table beside him. "This is a mix of business and personal." He grinned.

"Merk's ex-wife has come to him for help."

Lissa spun round and gasped. "You're laughing about that? She's in trouble. You have to help her. You did me."

As if he got the rise out of her he wanted, Stone turned toward the group as he draped his huge arm around her shoulders. "That's what we're discussing, whether we can do anything. To decide wisely, we need the rest of the story. So sit quietly. Let's listen." His focus zinged over to Katina. "The floor is yours again."

Katina dropped her gaze to the table, barely hiding her worry. Really she could do nothing else but ask for help. She had to tell somebody. Shit, she didn't know why she trusted these people, but they looked capable of handling anything.

She looked up to find Merk studying her carefully. "I found a notebook in the accountant's drawers. Like a code book. I didn't understand it all, well any of it actually as it wasn't standard accounting procedures," she said. "I found a list of names—or short forms of them—and beside a couple were written the word *cop*. So I'm assuming some policemen are involved in this mess, but I don't know who or which ones, or how high ranking they are. Presumably those on the lower end don't have the kind of money for what's going on here."

She reached up and pinched the bridge of her nose. "But that's my personal judgment. A lot of people have money we don't know about. Just because they don't work in a high-paying job, doesn't mean they don't have extensive portfolios."

"Do you remember the names?"

"They weren't complete, just short forms. Like … *TMET14—cop*." She glanced around to see if that made sense to anybody, but blank faces stared back at her. "Like I said, I don't know what it means, or if her usage of the word *cop* means something else entirely, like an acronym of some sort."

"Good reason to be worried about the authorities involved," Levi said.

She asked, "Am I just paranoid?" Her gaze circled the room, hoping someone had an answer.

Ice snorted. "You were snatched in a parking lot. They tied you up, threw you in the back of a van, with the kidnappers proceeding in a high-speed car chase to evade Merk and the cops. And you're making light of it or dismissing it as just your imagination?"

Laid out that way, it made her sound foolish. "Not until after I got the phone calls and emails did I get really worried."

"Whoa. What emails? What phone calls?" Merk asked. "Let's go back to where you found this information. Exactly what did you do and what happened from that time? And how long ago was this?"

"A couple months ago, I found the first entry that didn't make any sense. I knew I was really onto something seriously crooked last month though." She stared at Merk, gaining strength from the support in his gaze. "I didn't do anything for the longest time because I'd never been in this situation before and didn't know what to do. But then I heard rumors that the accountant was returning since she had recovered from some car accident. That's when I knew I had to act because I wouldn't have access to any of this information again.

"So one day I'd been complaining at work about having a hectic week—on purpose, to give myself a cover story to stay late in the office," she said with a sigh. "Instead I copied and saved as much of the information as I could to a USB key without raising any alarms."

"And you didn't tell anyone?" Levi asked.

She shook her head. "No, again I didn't know who to tell. I was afraid to go to the wrong person. Or, if I went in and made a full disclosure, this huge internal investigation would go nowhere, but I'd be blamed. Or maybe my company would fold, and they'd come after me." She leaned forward slightly, looking at their faces. "At no time did I think I was in serious danger because honestly, I didn't think anybody knew what I had found."

Merk said, "But somebody obviously did."

She shrugged. "I guess, but I don't know how they would've." She clasped her hands together and continued the story. "The accountant came back, and I returned to my normal position. But I had all this information, and I retained her login so if I needed to, I could go back in. But I was pretty sure the accountant would change it her first day back." Then Katina stopped. Expectation hung in the air around her. "I wanted to see if she had deleted the information, because if so, I wasn't sure anything I had would stand up in its place. In fact, I didn't want to login again at all because I had no business in that corner of the world in terms of the company files."

She fell silent.

"But you did anyway," Merk said drily. "Didn't you realize that would likely trigger somebody's interest? It's one thing when you were filling in at her desk—although that kind of extracurricular activity shouldn't have been allowed either—but if you had gone in after the accountant was back, and she had changed her login, they would know somebody else was accessing the information."

"I *know* that. I didn't do it again," she reassured him. "The only reason I had access to those files was because she kept it on the company network, not her private computer. I have access to the network to do my own job and so when working in her files, I found the login to her protected ones. Once I realized what was going on, then I went looking for more and…found it."

Everyone sat back and stared at her. She shrugged. "However, afterward it seemed as if I was suddenly under somebody's watchful eye. I'd get called to the head office a little more often. When I got up and went for coffee breaks, I felt like people were watching me. When I went to the lunchroom, almost always somebody would be there, suddenly sitting with me—where in the past I would be alone. Nobody before had ever given a shit about who I was, where I was, or what I was doing." She winced. "For a long time I thought I was imagining things."

"Is there any chance, because of your new position, that others wanted to get closer to you?" Lissa asked curiously. "The higher up the food chain you move, the more others want to rub off some of that shaker-mover energy from you."

"Oh, now that's an interesting idea," Sienna said.

Katina looked at the two women and realized just how different their mind-sets were from the men. These two weren't military, but were more in tune with the popular or common man.

"I never considered that," Katina admitted. "I suppose it's a possibility. People were certainly friendlier after I took over the top accountant position. But as it's not something that I would do, it never occurred to me somebody else would."

"Did anybody at work ever threaten you or make you

feel that way?" Merk asked.

She shook her head. "No. I figured I got away with it." The corner of her lips quirked downward. "Of course I should've known better. People who dabble in corruption and fraud obviously have some safeguards in place. But the longer everything went along smoothly, the more comfortable I felt."

"Until ..." Merk prodded her.

"Until I got a strange email one day, and the subject line just asked *Where is it?* The body of the email was blank, sent from some generic social-networking site. I didn't know who it came from. No name was attached, just a series of numbers." She spread her hands, palms up. "I have no idea what the email meant. I didn't take anything. No"—she switched her wording—"I copied information, but I didn't remove any."

"So maybe they wanted the USB key you downloaded the data to."

Katina studied the man who'd spoken for the first time. He wasn't as big as the others, with dark hair and brows, but pure-white skin. He looked to be just as knowing and knowledgeable as the rest of them. She thought his name was Harrison.

"Maybe. But how would they know I put the info on one?"

"Hidden cameras for one but a keystroke capture—keylogging—would be my guess for all of it," Ice said. She shrugged. "Honestly, if they have a decent IT department, they should be able to find out what you did, when, and on what computer within minutes. If they can't, they aren't worth their paychecks.

Katina was sure her expression told everyone in this

room how little she knew about what Ice just said. Thankfully, Ice continued so the focus was off Katina's bewildered look.

"I understand professional accounting has checks and balances inherent in its system to catch basic human errors."

"That's very true," Katina said.

"However," Ice went on, "if you add in a tech-savvy CEO, maybe a boss who has dealt with embezzling employees before, then a third safeguarding layer could be in play."

Katina shook her head. "Not my boss. Not Robert. He's more of a salesman. He loves to interact with his employees, with people in general."

Ice raised one finger, her mouth a grim line. "Maybe so, but if the bad guys are one of those lower-level accountants, trying to sneak stuff by Robert, then things can get really intricate."

When everyone just stared at Ice, she shook her head and added, "I listen when Bullard speaks." She turned toward Katina to explain. "Bullard's expertise is in security hardware and software."

Katina nodded her thanks.

"Plus," Levi added, "it's common knowledge that you can't email information without leaving a trail. Even through the network to another location would've been traceable. And the easiest and most available method for data transfer would be a USB drive under normal circumstances."

She studied Levi's face and winced.

"I suppose that's possible. But why didn't they say something when it first happened or even when I gave notice?"

"Maybe it only came to light once that head accountant had returned, and it could've been a week or two after you left that she realized even the remote possibility that you had found this because she'd left that information accessible. Maybe she thought she'd get into trouble. Consider what it's like when you return to a job or begin a new one, which in this case, would mean she'd have a ton of catching up to do. And she might not have considered that you would find her private files."

Harrison spoke up again. "But it would've been easy enough for her to have seen the last time they were accessed, and she'd have realized what happened while you were there. For a while everyone might've even considered you didn't know what you had actually seen."

"In their mind, you're a junior accountant and possibly couldn't understand the material in front of you," Levi said. "But by then, it becomes a worry. Something they couldn't quite let go. And they followed you to see what you did with the information."

"From the time the accountant came back, how long before you felt like you were being watched?" Merk asked.

She flicked her gaze in his direction. "I can't be sure exactly, but maybe one or two weeks." She pursed her lips and thought about it a little harder. "The thing is, like Levi said, I was also really swamped because I had returned to my position which was no longer in the same shape I had left it and had a lot of work to fix, so I'm not sure I noticed right away. Maybe they were on to me fairly quickly."

"It doesn't really matter though," Levi said. "The fact is, we have to assume they know you have a copy of this information."

"And you said there were phone calls and more emails."

She nodded quickly. "Almost the same email came in repeatedly afterward. The numbers on the top were different as to whom it was from, but it was always addressed to me at work and had the same subject line, nothing else. And then they came to my personal email." She glanced over at Merk again. "That's when I really freaked out."

"Sure, but it wouldn't have been hard to find that, particularly if they've already accessed your business email and quite likely that computer because most people check their personal email at work anyway."

She considered that and winced once more. "Yeah, I did. Not often, but every once in a while. I'm very touchy about my stuff though. I've never been that trusting."

"The minute you opened that program and logged in, they had your email, and contacts," the dark-haired man said. "After that it was pretty simple to get anything else they wanted."

"But how did they know I was meeting Merk at the pub? Oh my God, my phone." She immediately stood and searched her pockets for it. "Merk, did you see my phone?"

"I took it before coming here in case they were tracking us with it. You were sleeping so I didn't wake you to ask. No signal can escape that box." He nodded toward a metal box at the end of the table.

She frowned and stared at it. "How did you know to do that?"

"Easy. Planting GPS trackers is what any of us would've done had our situations been reversed. Some phones come with their own built-in, but we would add one to be sure in most cases. We bug the phone so we can hear conversations and generally track the person."

"I'll give you a burner phone with a new number. No one can track you then." He smiled at her. "It's okay. This is what we do."

She stared at him in shock.

"You're safe here." Ice reached over and patted her hand. "Even if you were tracked to this compound, we have a disturbance setting that sends out a jamming signal. It stops anything within from being tracked."

There was a beat of silence.

Katina gazed back at the box, realizing the small red light on its side was now off.

Merk got up, walked around, opened it, and took out the phone. "Rhodes, got your tools with you to open this?"

The man called Rhodes stood up and walked around, pulling out a small tool kit from his pocket. The two men bent over the phone and proceeded to open it.

She'd never seen the inside of her phone, and couldn't really get a glimpse of it from where she was, but Merk reached over with a pair of tweezers and plucked out a small piece of metal. He held it up for the others to see. "Got it."

"Is that a tracker?"

"Well, it was. Now it's just a dead piece of technology."

He dropped it into the metal box and put her phone back together. He turned it on and held it in front of her so she could see it was working. She couldn't understand how someone had managed to get it in her phone. She'd wondered if she had been tracked to the parking lot by the men who kidnapped her, but still considered it impossible for somebody to have gotten to her phone and done this.

"It would have been an easy matter to wait for a moment when you had your back turned, even a short trip to the ladies' room, for them to have installed that," Ice said quietly in answer to her unspoken question.

"I guess you just never really know who you are dealing with and what's happening around you, do you?" Katina asked. "So does that mean my car has bugs as well?"

Rhodes laughed. "We have some detectors that will let us know if any are close by. If it was me, I'd have put one in there." He smacked Merk on the shoulder and walked out.

She turned her gaze to Merk and said, "Is he going to check?"

Merk nodded. "He'll have an answer for you soon enough."

"But I didn't want to bring the danger here to you," she wailed. "I didn't want anyone else getting involved. Do you see how dangerous this is? Why don't you just let me get my car and go?"

He turned and stared at her. Instead of the warm, friendly smile she'd seen earlier, the stark, flat gaze bore deep into her own as if seeing through the darkness of the last weeks, into the heart of her. "You really think I would let you take off after what happened to you? I knew there was a damn good possibility you were being tracked. I went through a lot today to save your ass," he snapped. "Like hell I'll let something happen to you now."

"That means they can follow us here. And that means people know where I am."

"Good. Let them come." As if too pissed to trust himself, he turned and stormed from the room.

She glared after him, understanding the feeling. She had no place to go. An uncomfortable silence took over the room. As they studied her, she turned to face them and said quietly, "I'm very sorry for any trouble I brought to your doorstep. It was never my intention." She turned her glare back to the doorway again and added, "I did tell Merk I wanted to be alone so I could just run, but he wouldn't listen."

"Good," Ice said. "That's not how we operate."

But Katina didn't know how they did things here.

MERK HEADED TO Katina's car where he watched Rhodes go over it. "See anything?"

"I've found one, but the meter's saying two."

"I'll check under the hood," Merk said.

But before he got there, Rhodes said, "Removed that one." He bent down and snagged the small item from underneath the running board behind the back wheel. He held it up, then turned the small meter in his hand toward the front of the car.

Together they poured over the engine, following the signal from hot to cold and found it just underneath the radiator. "This one was hidden better. It could easily have been missed."

They ran the meter around the vehicle again to confirm nothing else was here and then shut it down. Taking the trackers back to the shop, they added them to the box.

Merk turned to look back at her car. The hood and trunk were still open. He walked over and realized her bags were inside. A lot of them, as if she'd packed for a long trip. In fact, he was pretty damn sure she'd been planning to run. So why the hell did she call him in the first place? Maybe that was the best question he needed to ask her. The rest could wait. But if she was already running, why even bother letting him know?

He stormed back into the kitchen and stood in the doorway. Everyone was talking, but more about general topics, like the weather and type of cookies they had in their hands. He frowned when he saw them. Trust Alfred to bring out treats for company. Merk had been craving cookies for days, and Alfred had just smiled in that benign way of his.

Merk snagged one and said, "First question, and it's maybe the most important of all. If you were ready to run, and I can see from all the bags in the back of your car that you weren't planning on returning, why even bother calling me?"

She stared at him, and then he felt like a heel as her bottom lip trembled.

"I was afraid." She stopped to catch her breath. He could hear the tremor in her voice. "I was afraid they'd kill me, and nobody would know."

"Shit." What a hell of a statement, and it said a lot about the lonely state of her life if she called him just for that.

"I don't have many friends, just one or two, and not much family. My parents divorced, remarried, and redivorced." She made a face. "I don't have any relationship with them. And, as tenuous a connection as it might be, you are my ex-husband. I didn't know who else to call and was … still am, afraid to bring trouble to anyone's doorstep."

"So we would have had lunch, and you'd tell me bad guys were after you and then say, *If they kill me, hey, you'll know why I'm dead?*" he asked incredulously. "Does that make any sense?"

She shrugged. "I don't admit to having any common sense lately," she cried. "I've been reacting, not thinking, trying to stay alive and ahead of these guys. I needed help. I didn't know who to go to. I realized I had no reason to believe you really could help, but I just thought, maybe if I touched base one more time, then at least you'd know, if you never saw me again, then chances were I was gone."

"And how would I know if I never saw you again, when I haven't seen you in eleven years?" he snapped. He ran his hands through his hair, wondering why she'd do that, and then he stopped. He walked closer, his gaze on her. "You have it on you, don't you? You intended to give it to me."

He stood towering over her, hating when she cowered from him. He knew he was right. Now, instead of wanting to know why she'd called him, he desperately needed to know why she hadn't given him whatever it was she had.

Merk shoved his face closer to hers and said, his voice as soft as he could make it, "So why didn't you?"

Her lips trembled, and her eyes were bright with tears, but she stayed strong. "Because whoever has it is in danger, and I won't do that to you."

He threw up his hands in frustration and glared at her. "You are just as frustrating today as you were years ago."

"And you're just as domineering and arrogant and force-ful today as you were then," she shouted at him.

He stared at her and grinned. "We were good together, weren't we?"

"Oh, yeah, so good, that it lasted one night." She reached up with both hands, grabbing her hair, and snapped, "I don't know what I was thinking. I should never have contacted you. We don't even like each other."

"Oh, I like you just fine." Merk smiled. "I especially like the new model, but that's got nothing to do with it. You came to me because you knew I would help. And now, for whatever dumb reason, you're afraid I'll get hurt if I do."

"And that's because I like you too," she admitted. "And I like the new model better as well." She stood so she could face him squarely, but as short as she was, she couldn't gain any height on him. So she stepped atop the bench with her good leg, easing the other slowly there, and stared at him. Planting her hands on her hips, she said, "I can't let anybody

I like die because of my stupidity."

Ignoring the very real presence of the others in the room, he reached over, snagged her into his arms, and kissed her.

Hard.

She pulled herself free and cried, "Oh, no, you don't. That's what got us into trouble in the first place!"

He laughed. "That's what took us to bed," he corrected. "But what got us into marital trouble, well, I'll blame the booze for that."

"You could be right there. I haven't had tequila since," she confessed. She grinned at him. "It was quite a shock waking up the next day married."

"Ditto," he admitted. "But we fixed it and put it behind us. Until I got the bloody phone call from you."

She winced. "Here I go apologizing again. I should never have called you."

He hooked his finger under her chin and lifted it so she faced him. "If you say that one more time …"

Immediately she fisted her hands on her hips once more and glared into his face. "And what will you do about it?"

With their noses inches apart, he said in a very low whisper, "I'll do the same damn thing I did back then."

She gasped and immediately backed up. "No, you won't." She shook her head fast. "No more shenanigans out of you." She turned her back on him, stepped off the bench, and sat back down again.

He chuckled and realized how much of a spectacle the others had just enjoyed. "Don't get used to this," he said to his team. "We're not entertaining you people forever."

Sienna chuckled. "That's okay. Seems an awful lot of stuff is between you two that you should deal with. Then you can move forward in your relationship, like you're supposed to."

Instantly Katina shook her head yet again. "No relationship. We don't have one," she said a little too emphatically. "We aren't going to."

Merk stared down at her and wondered. All the same things that attracted him to her a long time ago were still there. She was feisty, fiery, and cute. And of course, now that she was in trouble, it appealed to his protective instincts all that much more. Maybe, just maybe, they should reconsider whether they wanted to rekindle their relationship.

Not like there were any barriers to it. They had their whole lives ahead of them. He tucked that little tidbit in the back of his brain and then smiled at Sienna.

"Time you took a little closer look to home in terms of relationships," he suggested.

She glanced at him blankly and in confusion asked, "What are you talking about? I don't have a relationship right now."

His grin widened and he said, "Yet."

Just then Rhodes walked inside and said, "You coming out to grab these bags for her, Merk, or not?" He stood in the doorway in exasperation. "I waited for you to come back, not sit here and play with your lady friend."

Merk watched Sienna as her gaze darted to Rhodes in the doorway and Merk saw the subtle shift. The interest, the softening of her features, tilted lips, and then a smile. When her gaze drifted past his, Merk deepened his grin, and with a tiny almost imperceptible nod toward Rhodes, he said, "Exactly."

For a moment she didn't understand what he meant, and then she got it.

Fiery red flushed over her pale skin. "Oh, no you don't.

No way are you pinning that on me." She rose, picked up her cup of coffee, and said, "Enough of that crap or I'll dock your paycheck." She turned and walked from the room.

Rhodes stepped up and said, "Boy, what did you do to upset her?"

"Nothing. Just pointed out her future."

Everybody else in the room chuckled.

Rhodes stared at him, then everyone else, and asked suspiciously, "What is this, an inside joke?"

"Maybe. No need to worry though, with time you'll become part of the joke too." He hooked an arm around his buddy's shoulders and said, "Come on. Let's go grab those bags. And we'll tuck Katina into one of the spare rooms."

Behind him he could hear Katina cry out, "I'm not staying ..."

"Yes, you are." And he headed to her car where they retrieved five bags.

When they had everything, they checked the front, including the glove box, and then walked back into the kitchen.

"Ice, any idea where we should put her?"

"Nowhere," Katina snapped.

But Ice stood in that smooth elegant motion that was so her and said, "A room has been prepped for her already." She smiled at Katina. "Come this way."

Chapter 6

"**W**HAT THE HELL am I doing here?" Katina murmured to herself as she wandered around the small bedroom.

She wasn't a prisoner. She hadn't been locked in. So why then did she feel like she had no choice but to stay here? She doubted Merk would enforce a prisonlike existence, but they'd all made this decision whether she liked it or not. And she didn't like it.

She also knew Merk was pissed at her. With good reason. She plunked down on the bed and flopped backward, her arms over her head.

Should she give it to them? She reached up and scrubbed her face, willing her exhausted brain to work. But her leg ached again, and her thoughts were definitely fogging up. She hadn't gotten much sleep in the last several weeks. The last few nights had been really bad.

After all, she'd been planning her escape.

And now everything had come to a dead stop. As if she'd jumped, but, instead of leaping off a cliff, she'd only managed to jump halfway *to* the cliff. And now somehow the cliff had been removed. She was left suspended in midair.

She remembered in Vegas how she hadn't had a doubt with Merk around. He'd been a powerhouse, even back then, and she'd fallen willingly into any plan he'd come up with.

They'd gone from game table to bar to the pub to the streets, laughing and cheering and crying, and had had the time of their lives. Whatever he suggested she'd gone for. She hadn't been coerced, but it had been so different. He'd been a magnet, and she felt that pull even now. She'd been delighted to be with him. That kind of power, that kind of self-confidence was sexy.

She'd fallen into instant lust with the man. They'd had one hell of a night. But by the cold dawn of the next day ... make that noon when they'd both woken up to realize what they'd done, well, she'd backed off and had been scared to find herself with anybody quite so powerful and dominant. Apparently she didn't have any brains when it came to him. She just fell completely susceptible to his whims.

Look at what happened today. Merk had no problem getting her to do what he wanted. And she wasn't going through that again. She'd learned her lesson—she hoped she had. But after today, maybe not.

There was a knock on the door. "Katina, it's Merk. Let me in."

She gave a half snort as she lay there. That was so him. No request, not even a question, more that he was entitled to come in. But not a direct order, just that you-will-do-what-I-say type of command. The trouble was her. She was already on her feet and walking to the door, which she flung open. "What is it about you that I just do everything you tell me to do?" she snapped.

His eyebrows shot up in surprise at the greeting, but he answered amiably. "At least you understand when it's imperative that you do something. That's important, instead of protesting and causing trouble for the sake of being difficult."

He gave her a gentle nudge, and she stepped back into her room. Instantly he followed and closed the door behind them. He glanced around the small space and smiled.

"They've done a hell of a nice job in this place. We have guest rooms that aren't just small holes in the walls and bunk beds tacked onto the plywood."

She walked over to the only chair and sat down. She had no idea what he was talking about with plywood and guest rooms, but she assumed he was just making conversation. Only she was tired. "Why are you here?"

He sat down on the side of the bed and studied her. "Where did you hide it?"

Immediately she crossed her arms over her chest and slouched deeper into the soft chair. "It's not safe for you to have it."

Instead of arguing with her, he gave her a smile that was gentle in understanding. "I guess you still like me then," he teased.

She glared at him. "Don't you dare do that lethal stuff again! I fell for your charms once. I'm not going there again."

He chuckled. She found herself smiling anyway.

"The thing is, as long as you're hiding it, we can't do anything about the men after you," he said. "If you give it to us, we can make copies to send to the right people."

She chewed on her bottom lip and worried on the problem. He was right. If something happened to her, those people would get away with it—and her murder—and no one would be held accountable. As much as she hated that, she didn't want them to go after Merk or the others and to hurt more victims due to her foolishness.

Only Merk wasn't giving her much of a chance to think about it. He leaned across the space, picked up her hand, and held it between his. The heat of his palm burned into her slightly cold skin. Shit, she didn't realize just how tired she was, or how stressed, until she felt the absolute comfort of the warmth of his hand and just knowing that somebody was here to help out.

"I didn't say thank-you for saving me. I didn't expect you to show up," she said. "When I was in the parking lot for so long, I figured you'd stood me up," she confessed. "And then all I could think about was that maybe that was you in the parking lot, after they threw me in the back of the van, and maybe you'd seen what happened, and maybe, just maybe, you would know what to do to help me."

She shook her head. "It never occurred to me you'd be quite so capable as to not only contact those who needed to be contacted but to also keep up the wild car chase and track me down to eventually rescue me." She smiled at him. "I guess all that military training did you some good."

"You did thank me for saving your life," he reminded her. "But you can't distract me from the main conversation."

She glared at him. "I don't know what I want to do."

He nodded. "Understandable. You're scared. You don't know who to trust, and you don't want to make the wrong decision."

"Exactly. If I make the wrong decision, the consequences are huge."

"And if you make the right decision, the consequences are also huge."

They stared at each other across the short distance, her hands, both of them now, cradled gently in his much bigger ones. She stared down at them and said, "As long as you promise to hand it all over to the right authorities and let them deal with it."

"I promise. You do realize that won't necessarily save you though, right?"

She nodded. "Unless they know you have already handed it all over … Then the game is up. The men will just get the hell out of the country themselves."

He laughed. "In our experience, the bad guys generally think it all works out in their favor, so they continue on. And they end up doing things in a very stupid way."

She sighed heavily. "I was hoping they'd be the kind to just run."

"And they might depend on the ties they have in another countries, if it's money laundering and tax fraud. Who knows? But they crossed the line when they kidnapped you, so what else is going on? Because, if anything more serious is involved, they won't hesitate to come after you again."

"Then we have to leave," she cried. "And now."

"We're leaving in the morning. You need to rest and to heal, to calm down and to breathe."

She looked up at him and hated that her eyes stung with tears yet unshed. "It just seems like I've been running for so long," she whispered. "Once that first email came through, I was living in a never-ending nightmare." She gave a broken laugh. "No, actually it was when I found those accounting discrepancies. … I felt trapped, like I just had no good options."

He tugged her forward into his arms and held her close against his chest—finally making her aware of the shivers wracking her body. His big arms were wrapped securely around her, as if he could instill the warmth and calm of his own physical body on hers.

Like that would happen. The only thing that ever evolved when they got this close together was the burning up of the sheets. Although considering she was cold, maybe that wasn't such a bad idea. She almost smiled, then remembered the circumstances that had brought them together again. She pulled back. "I'll talk to you in the morning. I should be able to pick it up then without any trouble."

He nodded.

She could hear the unasked questions in the air, but she refused to give into them. She wouldn't tell him where it was right now.

"We must determine where to copy and disperse the duplicates." She leaned back so she could look at his face. "Before we head out and collect it, we need a list of who it's going to. Plus a laptop and a post office printer because I don't want just electronic copies. We need physical copies." She frowned, thinking as hard as her sore brain would allow. "And a secure place to do that, with no one looking over our shoulders."

She fell silent. Not understanding fully her hesitation to tell him where it was. Maybe ... because she was so damn tired and couldn't think straight. But it was like that damn key was poison. As soon as she touched that, shit went wrong.

HE DIDN'T KNOW how to get her to trust him. They really needed to get their hands on that information. Not that he gave a damn about it, but he knew, as long as she was the only one who held it, she was in danger. The sooner they spread the truth to those who could help, the sooner she'd be safer. Although he was pretty damn sure that the prosecution would want her as a witness in the event of a trial, and, once anything like kidnapping became involved, it would be a big deal all around. But he also didn't want those copies in the wrong hands. Therefore, they had to be careful who they picked.

"It's almost time for dinner," he said, checking his watch. "Let's go downstairs and discuss the list over our meal, figure out who we should send all the information to."

"It's not that I don't trust everybody here, but it seems like we're taking a big risk involving so many."

He smiled down at her and dropped a kiss on her forehead. "If it was any other group, I'd say you were perfectly right to be concerned. But, as it's this group, my team, my unit from the military, and the few women that we have involved," he said, "your information is perfectly safe here. Not one of them would betray us."

She smiled. "Okay. So is it safe to say I'm starving then?"

He laughed. Once she set her feet gently on the ground, he stood up and held out a hand. "Trust me enough to do this," he said with a smile. "I was honorable the last time we saw each other."

She gave a delicate half snort. "Yeah, at least you married me then."

At that, he burst into laughter. He led her down the hallway. "You know, I have wondered over the years where you were, what you'd done, and if we would ever meet again," he said. "But I never thought I would look back and remember how much fun we had during that time in our lives."

She turned and tossed him a teasing grin. "Now that it's eleven years behind us, it's easy to laugh. Back then … not so much."

"Did you ever tell anybody?"

"No." She gasped in horror. "Well, I told Anna, my best

friend, a little bit but not all of it. You know what they all would've said if they'd known." She shook her head. "Silence was the only option." But her voice carried a teasing note as she said it.

"There's nothing to be ashamed of, you know."

She laughed. "Also nothing to be proud of. Figuring out how many drinks it took to get to the bottom of a bottle is really not the goal I wanted to set in my life."

The others were already in the dining room. This time, instead of them just sitting around hugging cups of coffee, Alfred had filled the center of the table with roast chicken and vegetables. And a great big Caesar salad alongside it all.

Merk grinned. "My kind of meal."

"If it's food, it's edible, and it won't walk away on me, it's my kind of meal," Katina said.

He stopped in his tracks and looked at her. "That's why you went to Vegas. … You could eat cheap down there."

She shook her finger at him. "You forgot, drink cheap too."

With everyone at the table, and the lighthearted atmosphere, they all dug into solid food. It was one magic Alfred knew very well. Whenever they were active on a job or needed to be ready to go in an instant, he got their bodies filled with really good healthy food.

As soon as they all dished up their selections and settled down to eat, Merk said, "Katina has agreed to take me to the data. However, first she wants to see a list of who gets the information. Before we leave the house, she wants to know where we will copy this material, print it out, then send both email and snail-mail copies of it all at the same time."

Ice looked at Katina and nodded her head. "Good decision," she said. "But you're safest place is here."

"That's what Merk said too," Katina said. "But we already know my vehicle has been tracked to this place. Therefore, they could come looking for me here. And I don't want them to find it."

Levi and Ice exchanged glances. Merk watched them, wondering what they were up to.

Then Levi turned to look at them directly. "Merk, what about Gunner, Logan's dad? He lives in Houston. He's ex-military, upper brass. His place is like a small Fort Knox. Logan went into the military because of his father. I'd ask Logan to take you, but he's in California doing the guard-duty detail."

Merk snorted at that. "Right. Maybe ask him if that would be possible."

Levi shook his head. "I'll call direct."

"You sure it's safe to bring another person into this?" Katina asked quietly. "I don't want anyone else to get involved."

"True," Levi said cheerfully. "But, if Gunner thought we were protecting him, he wouldn't be happy. And he was always a man looking to help a damsel in distress ..."

"Isn't that the truth?" Merk said with a smile. "He misses the military, in a big way. He was secret ops. But now retired he's bored as hell."

Merk looked at Levi and said, "Good call." He pulled out a notepad and pen, putting it on the table beside him, then said to the room in general, "Names. Who are we sending this information to? Talking fraud, offshore accounts, possible money-laundering. Kidnapping. But who is it that we trust to look into this safely?"

"The new DA in Houston is good." Ice reached across the table for the jug of water and filled her glass. "Formerly from California. I remember hearing good words about him. He closed a lot of high-profile corruption cases."

"I don't know him at all, but I'll take your word for it." Merk wrote down his name on the list. Then he wrote down Gunner. "Gunner probably has other people to suggest we contact as well."

"If there was a military angle to this, then I'd suggest Commander Jackson. Or just Jackson, as he is known now," Rhodes said quietly from the far side of the table.

Stone added his agreement. "He's always been straight with us."

"He might be worth contacting anyway. Remember he's still in the military, just not the same department, so he has a long reach."

The conversation carried on for another forty-five minutes until Merk had six names.

Then Ice said, "What about Bullard?"

Merk stopped and stared at her. "You think Bullard would know somebody, or are you saying we should include him in this?"

"That man surprises everyone. He knows a lot of people. In a case like this, he might very well have a good idea of who we can trust." Ice took a sip of her water and said, "I'll call him after dinner."

At that point, Alfred cleared off the plates with everyone's help, and then came back with a cheesecake. It was Katina's comment that made everyone grin.

"Oh, my God, I've died and gone to heaven."

"No, my dear, the whole point of this is to not have you die and go to heaven," Alfred said with a cheeky grin before he turned to grab a bunch of smaller plates and dessert forks off the sideboard.

Chapter 7

AFTER DINNER, KATINA didn't know what to do with herself. She offered to help clean up the kitchen and wash dishes, but Alfred scooted her out of his area. She'd wandered into the huge living room with several different sitting areas but found it empty. Merk caught up with her a few minutes later, after she'd sat down in front of a large gas fireplace that wasn't turned on.

"There you are," Merk said, startling her with his sudden arrival. "I wasn't exactly sure where you went to. Levi's contacting Gunner. Ice will call Bullard, and Stone and Lissa are moving into one of our newly completed apartments. They've been unpacking just these last few days, so they're in turmoil." He shrugged. "Everyone has normal lives to live."

She laughed. "Maybe that's the problem. I've forgotten what it's like to live a normal life."

"This too shall pass," he said reassuringly. "Don't worry about it. We'll deal with this and get you back to a normal work routine."

"Work?" She shook her head. "I have to find a damn job first."

"Not right now." He studied her face for a long moment as she watched him. Then he reached out a hand and gently stroked her cheek. "Did you hand in your resignation? Or did they fire you? You never did finish that part of the story."

"I couldn't stand it," she said quietly. "Always that sense of being watched, feeling I never had the freedom to do anything. After a particularly bad day, I gave my two weeks' notice. The last day I worked was Thursday."

"So you didn't work those two weeks?"

She shook her head. "I had six days of holidays coming, but I didn't actually tell them that. I was getting really scared, so I just took the second week off. And I quickly packed and moved out any personal stuff and was done," she said. "When I first found the information, I realized I would have to do something about it eventually. So I gave up the lease on my apartment and moved into a tiny studio for the last couple months. I gave away all my furniture as the studio came furnished." She shook her head. "Who knew I would have thought so far ahead? The thing is, I did it without thinking."

"It's called instinct," he said. "The company would've had your old address." He narrowed his gaze at her and added, "And may have accessed any forwarding info you shared with the post office. Unless you told somebody. Did you?"

She shook her head. "No, I didn't. I put an ad in the newspaper to sell the furniture but in the end just gave it all away. It was years old anyway. I never had much to begin with," she confessed. "So when I moved out of the studio, I could pack everything in my car. When I left, I still had another week's lease on the studio. Another reason for the timing of giving notice at work, but it's not like I'll go back and sleep there anymore."

"It's better not to go back, just in case somebody had been following you and knew where you had moved."

She felt a little ill at that thought. "In that case, maybe

my landlord's in trouble. He's a senior and lives above the small apartment," she said. "I don't want anything to happen to him."

"Give me his name and address. I'll see if any police reports or anything have been filed. There's probably been nothing, but I don't want him—or you—to worry unnecessarily."

She thought about that and then nodded. "Honestly I didn't feel like I was being followed to and from there, but ... his name is Ryan Brown." She rattled off the address.

"Give me a second to phone the police station and confirm nothing has been reported." He stood up and walked to the other side of the room.

She called after him, "Can you just call and say, hey, I'm worried about somebody, and ask if there has been any incident?"

He turned to gaze at her and smiled. "I know several people in the local police department. A couple friends I went to school with. We can trust them to tell me of any problems in the area."

She wondered about that. Wouldn't it still trigger an interest? She couldn't quite decide if it was safe to make inquiries that led to other people's questions.

She sat there, trying to relax until he returned, marveling at the size of the place she was in. Windows were everywhere, but they were tinted, and she was sure some security system had been installed because barely visible wires were on the top of each window and door. She didn't know what Merk's group was all about, but the living room itself was the size of five normal living rooms with little gatherings of couch seating areas. She really liked it. She'd never been in a place quite so large.

This wasn't a traditional house. She could imagine twenty to thirty, even forty people staying here it was so big. Especially with the huge commercial kitchen area—definitely Alfred's domain.

The dining room itself could easily hold that many people. At the moment they had a huge long table, but then on the far side they had a bunch of smaller tables too. So space was not an issue. She'd really like to go for a walk out on the grounds but wasn't sure if that was okay or not. As soon as Merk got back, she might ask. Just something to help her relax before bed.

He returned a few minutes later. Instead of a smile on his face, the corners of his mouth were pinched, and his eyes were hard.

Instantly her heart froze, and her stomach heaved. "What happened?"

"The studio you lived in was broken into last night. The place was ripped to shreds."

"Oh, no. What about the landlord? Is Ryan okay?"

Merk nodded. "He called the police when he heard the ruckus going on, but, by the time they arrived, nobody was there. And, yes, he does have insurance to help cover the damage, but he's obviously upset."

"You think?" She shook her head. "So even though I was so careful, they still knew." She stared out into the evening sun and said quietly, "Dear God. What if I hadn't left?"

MERK HAD A little more to the report that Jonas had given him, but she didn't need to hear the details. The old man was safe and sound, and the police had been there and were working on the assumption that somebody was just angry.

Katina had actually absconded out from under their noses, and they were pissed. He patted her shoulder and said, "I'm heading over to talk to Levi and Ice about this development. You stay here. I'll be back in a few minutes. If you want to, maybe we could take a walk around the complex, or I can show you around the house."

When she nodded and sank back into the couch, he gave her a smile and headed to the office. He didn't know if Levi and Ice were in the control room or the office; he hoped they were off the phone so they could all match up their data at the moment.

In the office he found Levi writing notes, setting up a large whiteboard with what he knew. Merk stood in the doorway, glancing behind to ensure he was alone, then stepped in and closed the door. "Levi, there's been a development."

Levi turned, studied him, then asked, "What's up?"

He proceeded to tell him that Katina's place had been trashed, ending with, "Threats were written all over the walls too. Things like, *Bitch, we'll find you*, and *Where is it?*"

"What were the threats written in?"

Merk shrugged. "Didn't ask."

"Doesn't matter." Levi picked up his pen. "Either way they got the message across."

"Did you get a hold of Gunner?" Merk asked. "Is he okay if we see him tomorrow?"

"Hell, that man is excited already. He's delighted to be asked and overjoyed to help. He's really looking forward to being part of the action." Levi laughed. "I told him it was just documentation to be copied and dispersed, and he was like, *Best kind. Clandestine. I miss that.*"

At that, Merk had to laugh as well. "Too bad he had to

retire. That old man's got a lot of juice left in him."

Levi stopped, sat behind his desk, and studied Merk. "I'm actually wondering, since I got off the phone, if we could use him. He has a hell of a lot of information and skills. I just don't know to what extent those skills can be of help to us now."

"Depends on how many connections he maintains," Merk said. "If he's still in touch with those in the industry, then he's a huge resource. His intel would be massive for us."

Levi nodded. "Check him out while you're there. See just how interested he may be in doing some fact-checking," Levi said with a grin.

Merk knew perfectly well *fact-checking* meant *gathering intel.* "I think that's a good idea. We know and trust him, and he knows and trusts us, so ..."

Silence settled between the two of them for a long moment, then Levi said, "How attached are you to your ex-wife?"

"Not sure how to answer that. I was barely attached to her when she was my wife," he said with a grin. "We were literally together overnight. She flew out early the next afternoon, after we'd done necessary paperwork. We were married for all of a handshake when you look at it compared to the rest of our lives." He laughed. "Actually we've spent more time together this time around than we did when we got married."

"And how do you feel about it this time?" Levi's gaze narrowed as he studied Merk's face.

Merk sat down on the corner of the desk. "I'm not sure. Intrigued. Interested. Worried. It's all happened so fast I'm not exactly sure what to say."

"Like when you first met her."

"Absolutely. Only there's more to it now. She's tougher than she was then, and I like the woman she's become." He kept his face open and honest. He'd been friends with Levi for a long time. Merk knew the man was sorting something out, but he didn't know what. "What's really bothering you here?"

Levi heaved a sigh, stretched back in his chair with his hands behind his head, and kicked his feet up on the desk. "Just that we have a pattern setting in here. Look at Stone. He meets Lissa, moved her here to protect her, and she stays. Ice meets Sienna and decides to help her. Don't know about you, but I've certainly noticed the attraction between her and Rhodes no matter how much they try to ignore it."

"Oh, I've noticed," Merk said with a grin. "Now you're thinking how I get a call from Katina, needing my help. I moved her in to protect her." He tilted his head to the side. "And you're afraid she'll stay."

Levi's boots hit the floor as he leaned forward with a big laugh. "I'm not afraid of it. I just see it happening. I'm wondering if you do as well." He crossed his hands on the desk and said, "Has Terkel said anything to you about it?"

"No." Merk frowned. "In fact I haven't heard from him in a couple days. Of course Katina just contacted me." He turned to stare out the window. "Sometimes I worry about my brother."

"And so you should. The man who sees more than he should and tries to help everyone he can is destined for trouble," Levi said quietly. "I'd love to get his take on this. I wasn't planning on Legendary Security becoming a match-making service or to have our nickname, Heroes for Hire, which is bad enough, becoming Heroes of the Heart."

"They call, say they need help, so we move them in."

Merk laughed as he stood up. "The good thing about it is, it's a big place, boss. Sounds like we need more apartments finished." And he walked out, laughing.

But inside, the reminder of his brother not calling was worrisome. Not that they talked every day or every week; sometimes they went months without a word. Usually when something happened in Merk's life, Terkel knew. And he always called, sometimes with advice, sometimes with one of those little notes that came from having sensed something, and sometimes it was just that good old brotherly warning.

The fact that he hadn't contacted Merk was odd, what with Katina back in his life. He pulled out his phone, glancing down at it. He should call Terkel. Without questioning himself, he pulled up his brother's number and hit Dial as he wandered down the hall. He'd spent far too many years with Levi, was thinking like him.

With his phone to his ear, ringing and ringing endlessly, he found Katina curled up in the corner of the couch, sound asleep. When his brother's number finally went to his voice mail, Merk left a quick message and put away his phone.

He walked to the sideboard, opened the bottom drawer, pulled out a blanket, and returned to cover her up. He stood over her and wondered. She couldn't sleep very well in that crumpled position. Should he wake her or should he carry her to her bed?

As he stood, frowning down at her, she opened her eyes, saw him, and screamed.

Chapter 8

WITH HER SCREAM reverberating throughout the room, Katina struggled to get free of whatever was wrapped around her. Suddenly somebody snatched her up, and a familiar voice whispered in her ear, "Easy, Katina. Take it easy. It's just me, Merk."

Instantly she stopped struggling but lay shuddering in his arms, her gaze locked onto his face as the truth settled in. It really was him. She buried her face against his chest, but she couldn't stop the shivers that wracked down her spine.

He sat down on the couch with her, holding her close.

Footsteps raced into the room. Levi and Ice both stopped at the entranceway, and Levi asked, "What's wrong?"

"Is she okay?" Rhodes asked from the other end of the room with Alfred.

"It's okay. I covered her up with a blanket. She woke up, saw me, and screamed."

Katina, her face red with humiliation, said, "I'm so sorry, everyone. I didn't mean to panic like that."

Stone snorted from the side by the kitchen. "Who could blame you? If I woke up with that looming over me, I'd be screaming like a girl too." He gave her a wink and walked from the room.

Alfred said, "I'll bring a pot of tea to calm her down

some." And he rushed away.

Merk glanced at Levi, gave a tiny shrug and a smile.

But Katina noticed. She glanced at the two of them and apologized again. "I am sorry."

In a bright voice Ice said, "Don't apologize. There's no need. You've been to hell and back. That you haven't fallen apart before now is already admirable. When you sleep, the subconscious does all kinds of horrible things. Don't worry about it. It's all good." She nudged Levi in the shoulder and said, "Come on back to the office. Stuff you need to deal with."

Feeling better but still embarrassed, Katina sank back into Merk's arms, only to realize where she was. She struggled to sit up. "I can sit on the couch."

But his arms tightened around her, and he said, "You could sit on the couch, but I really don't want you to. You scared me," he complained. "I need to hold you to know you're okay."

She snorted. "Does that line really work for you?"

He glanced down at her with a wicked grin and said, "It must. You're in my arms still."

She leaned back to gasp in his face. And then laughed. "You're incorrigible."

He tucked her up close again and kissed her lightly on the temple. "As long as you're okay, then I'm fine."

She let herself relax into the warmth of his chest. After a few minutes of just resting, she said in a small voice, "Did you think about me ever?"

Lying against him as she was, in no way could she could miss the surprised start of his body. But he didn't stiffen in outrage, and she knew whatever answer came would likely be the truth.

"A few times," he admitted. "We didn't have much time together, but the time we did have was … incredible."

Once again she tilted her head back so she could see his face. "It was, wasn't it?" She beamed up at him. "Nice to know we got something right back then."

He chuckled. "We were both very young. Both of us had plans for our lives. And it didn't include getting married to a stranger. We had a good time. We did what we did. Afterward we fixed it, and we moved on."

"Yep," she said with a comical tone. "And then I called you for help." She shook her head. "Who does that?"

"And why me?"

"I don't know," she said. "Honestly I didn't think the number would work."

"I kept your number all these years," he admitted. He pulled out his phone and checked his contacts. Sure enough there, way down at the bottom under Marshal, was Katina's name and number. He turned to look at her and said, "I honestly don't remember getting your phone number back then."

"Oh, I do. At brunch the next day—when we were exchanging information so we could get a divorce," she said in a dry tone. "I called you several times this week." She reached out and slugged him lightly on the chest. "But you never answered."

"I was off on a job when you first called," he admitted. "Depending on the type of mission, I leave my personal cell phone at home. We have a special one for the unit as we go out on jobs."

That made sense. She sank back and said, "Thanks for answering my call."

"Even then we didn't meet up as intended. I was inside

the damn restaurant waiting for you."

At that, she sat up straight and said, "What I said was, meet me at noon. So you mean, you were inside having lunch and a beer while I was standing outside waiting for you?"

"You said noon, but you didn't say outside in the parking lot. I automatically assumed it would be inside, where it was nice and comfortable. We'd have lunch, and you'd explain whatever problem you had." He shifted her slightly so she was in a better position on his lap, then added, "I wasn't expecting to see you picked up and tossed into a vehicle in front of me and carted away."

"Yeah, isn't that the truth." She yawned, quickly covering her mouth as she did so. "Sorry. I guess I'm still tired."

Just then Alfred walked in with a tray. She glanced at his face and said in a heartfelt voice, "Thank you, Alfred. You are such a gem to treat me so nicely."

He patted her gently and said, "You need a little bit of loving care right now, so a cup of tea is a perfect way to just let the world fade away."

She glanced at the tray, realizing that the loving cup of tea came with a plateful of treats. As soon as she saw the food, she realized she was hungry. She scrambled off Merk's lap to sit beside him, picked up a slice of something that looked like banana bread. She broke off a piece and popped it in her mouth. "Oh, my God! This is so good."

"Alfred, this is a hell of a deal." Merk reached across and grabbed a slice of the second type of bread on the plate. "I think he's on a secret mission to fatten us all up," Merk said in a conspiratorial voice. "We're all very willing victims of his conspiracy."

She grinned. "While that's a good thing, if you can't eat

your share of this, I'll eat it for you."

"Not happening." As if to make sure, he broke off a piece of the treat she was eating.

As he sat back in comfortable silence, each enjoying their snack, she remembered where he had headed off to before she'd zonked out. "You went to talk to Levi. What was the end result of that?"

He shrugged. "A lot. We'll go to Gunner's house early tomorrow morning." He slid a glance her way and said, "After we pick up the key."

She didn't answer for a moment, then said, "Okay. That works. As long as you trust Gunner."

"With the type work we do, trusting the wrong people can get us killed. We trust very few, but, of those we do, we trust them implicitly."

AFTER FINISHING THEIR snack, he could see her eyes drooping. He stood up, held out a hand. "Come on. Let's get you to your room. You're almost asleep now. You'd sleep better after a shower."

"I would love a shower," she admitted. "Being tossed around on the floor in the van wasn't exactly a nice experience." She stood up. "Not to mention my bloodied leg. Nothing a good night's sleep won't fix," she said in a determined voice.

He led the way to the stairs, then changed his mind and went across to the elevator on the far side. "Shouldn't put any more stress on that leg."

He sent the elevator up to the second floor and led her down the hallway to the bedroom Ice had set up for her. When he unlocked the door and helped her back in, he pointed to her bags stacked on the side and said, "There's your stuff. If you want a shower, go for it. The bathroom is through that small door there." He paused and then said, "Call me if you need me. I'll come. I'm on the same floor but down the other side."

She nodded. "Thanks. I'm sure I'll be fine." She turned to close the door behind him, whispering, "Good night."

He stood outside, waiting to hear the *click* of the lock. But she didn't lock it. He frowned. She needed to get used to locking doors. A good habit to get into. Although she was safe here tonight.

He walked back to the office to see Ice and Levi discussing the budget and manpower allocation, picked up a chair, brought it nearer to them, and said, "Has this to do with tomorrow, or is it just me taking her to Gunner's?"

When Levi shook his head, Merk nodded. "Who's running backup then?"

Levi said, "I think both Ice and I will go in. We'll stay back to observe if anybody else catches sight of you. Plus we want to talk to Gunner."

Ice turned toward Merk and asked, "Has she given any indication where the key is?"

Merk shook his head. "No, but every time I mention it, she gets really quiet. I'm still not sure what the deal is, but she said she'll take us there tomorrow." He reached up and ran his fingers through his hair. "Whatever that means. Honestly I'm not sure, but something odd is going on."

"Do you trust her?" Levi asked. "It's not a good time for something odd to be going on."

"I know," Merk said. He glanced around the room and said, "It's quite possible she might actually have it on her and doesn't want to let us know. Not until we're ready to go."

"But then we would be better off dealing with it here," Ice said. "We can have the copies taken care of with our equipment and send it out through our secure system."

"I told her that, but she's not buying it."

The three exchanged glances.

"We didn't ask to search her luggage, and, of course, we didn't take that opportunity when we had it."

"No, wouldn't want to either," Merk said firmly. "She asked us for help. That she hasn't handed the key over already means she doesn't trust us. So it's up to us to encourage her."

But inside he worried too. He had no idea if she was telling the truth about even having the information. And his friends had gone out on a limb to help her. He wanted her to be on the up-and-up, but was she? What did he really know about her? Like he'd said, trust was hard.

"I really hope she doesn't turned around and trip us up with this." And then, because he just couldn't keep that thought to himself, he said, "I can't see any reason for her to do so, but …"

"Unless she tries to run in the morning."

Merk stared at Ice and frowned. He considered the fact that the gates were locked and that Katina knew she couldn't get out.

"What she could do, when the gates are open, is make a mad dash for her car and run," Ice suggested.

"Even then we can't take it in a negative way," Merk said calmly. "Because, for all we know, she's hidden it in the car." He stood up. "Nothing more we can really do until morning. I'll call it a night then." He turned and walked out.

He didn't know what tomorrow would bring, but, as he'd originally planned to walk past her bedroom and make sure she was all right, he deliberately forced himself to go in the opposite direction. There was just too much uncertainty right now.

He'd been betrayed once on the job. Hell, they all had. The physical fallout had been brutal. Just look at Stone's missing leg. But that wasn't the same thing as betrayal by a lover, ... yet learning to trust was hard. Still, someone must take a leap of faith here. He only had the little insight he knew of the girl from over a decade ago. But she'd been real, authentic back then. So what had the intervening years done for—to—her?

Chapter 9

W HEN SHE OPENED her eyes the next morning, it was to a heavy heart and a weird groggy sensation. She understood what was happening today but still worried it wasn't the right thing to do. A part of her felt she should just run, get the hell out of Dodge. Forget about the USB stick. But she wasn't sure she could outrun her past. And did she really want to look over her shoulder forever?

Neither did she want to let go of that tenuous relationship she'd found again with Merk. She could've given them the key already. They could've taken care of everything in their office here.

But what if someone had followed her, was here already? For the same damn reason she was concerned about going to this Gunner's place. Particularly if the bad guys followed them to his house.

She just didn't know enough, and that scared her. She'd been so exhausted last night that she had collapsed into bed without a shower, but now she was feeling dirty and desperately in need of something to wake her up. And to loosen the tight hold on her chest. Her leg was sore but not painful. More of a dull ache that just bloomed inside her.

She headed to the bathroom, turned on the shower, and stripped out of her underwear and T-shirt. She stepped into the warm water and let the spray take away some of her pain.

She was so lost and at a crossroads right now. She had no job, no home. She had her vehicle but was living off the generosity of Merk.

Which reminded her a lot of her childhood. She'd been permanently caught between families and yet belonged to none. Now it seemed as if nothing had changed, and she was still repeating childish patterns of existence.

What the hell did that say about her? This was not where she had expected to be. She'd had such high hopes when she went to Vegas. Eleven years later, it seemed she'd gotten nowhere. During all that time she'd kept quiet about her marriage. She'd told Anna but no one else. Then Anna had been in Vegas with Katina. She'd graduated, done all the normal things, but she had never found another relationship quite like the short one she had had with Merk. Maybe she didn't trust herself anymore.

She'd had relationships; she'd had lovers, but nothing went the distance. And yet, as soon as she saw Merk again, the same damn attraction lit up her insides like a firecracker. They'd been combustible back then, and she already knew it would be very difficult to stop that same fuse from blowing up this time too. He was lethal. He was also a hell of a lover, and she knew that, with the passage of those eleven years and a lot more experience under his belt, he'd be just as lethal, if not more so.

She turned off the shower and reached for two towels, one for her hair, then carefully dried herself off and took a good look at her leg. Clean, it didn't look so bad. The bandage had come off in the shower, and she didn't have another one to put on. No way could she wear pants over her wound without the stitches catching every few minutes.

Katina frowned. What were her options? Shorts? She

glanced outside and realized it was hardly shorts weather.

With her bags open, she studied her clothing. She really didn't want to wear a skirt either. She had a couple, but they weren't practical if things went down the shitter.

So shorts it was. At least until she could ask for another bandage. She unwrapped the towel from her head, quickly dressed, brushed her hair, and braided her long rich locks. She tossed the braid down the center of her back and efficiently packed up the last of her clothing. She left out a pair of jeans to change into.

Quickly glancing around the bathroom to ensure it was clean and she'd left nothing behind, she made her way to the door. It was still early, but she suspected it wasn't early for this household. She opened the door and found the hallway empty. She knew her way at least to the stairs.

She slowly worked her way down the risers, happy her leg was a lot more flexible and her joints moved easily. Her body was pretty bruised and achy after the van ride, but, all in all, today was a whole new day. Maybe, with any luck, she could get rid of this burden she'd been carrying. As long as nobody else got hurt, she was fine with that.

The main floor was empty, but she could smell coffee. She followed the aroma and found Stone sitting at the main table with Lissa. She smiled at the two of them and said, "Good morning, I smell coffee."

Stone nodded his massive head and said, "Yep, that's the one standard around here." He pointed to the sidebar where the coffeepot sat.

She grabbed one of the cups sitting on a tray and poured herself a cup, then turned to the couple and asked, "Is it okay if I sit here?"

Lissa jumped to her feet and said, "Oh, my goodness, of

course, sit down. It's all really very casual around this place."

"I figured as much. Just hadn't quite sorted out how everything worked yet."

"The team lives here, and those of us who are partners live here with them," Lissa said cheerfully. "Stone and I just moved into one of the apartments on the far side, but we haven't got our place organized yet, so we're still effectively living in the main building." She patted Stone's big hand and said, "Hopefully this weekend we can get that all done." She laced her fingers with his and continued, "Not sure it will change much though. We're still over here for every meal."

Katina looked at her and asked, "Why is that?"

Lissa laughed. "I can't cook. Other than just the very basics. And Alfred here will be heartbroken if he has two less people to cook for."

"Actually that I can believe. I think Alfred is someone who likes to feed the world and be surrounded by lots of family."

Hearing voices, she looked up to see the rest of the crew in various states of wakefulness grabbing coffee. The men appeared to be relatively alert. She expected, with their jobs, that they had really little choice. They were all expected to get up and go at any given moment.

She sat quietly watching everybody in their natural setting. It was a unique way to see these people. Merk said they were a private security company, all ex-military, and she had a pretty good idea that the term "private security" was just a euphemism for doing whatever the hell the world needed them to do.

Finally Merk walked in, his gaze checking out the table before landing on her. Instantly his shoulders eased, and she realized he'd probably gone to her room looking for her. She gave him a crooked smile and said, "See? I didn't run away in the night."

He shrugged. "There's no place you could run to." He poured coffee and sat down beside her. Glancing at her bare legs, he raised one eyebrow and said, "Not sure it's a shorts kind of day."

She laughed. "It's Texas. Isn't it always shorts weather here? However, my bandage came off in the shower. Anybody have a medical kit handy? I need another bandage to cover the wound," she said, glancing down at her leg admitting, "I wasn't looking forward to putting on jeans and having the stitches rub."

Ice spoke up from the far end of the table. "You want to do it now or wait until after breakfast?"

Just then Alfred walked in with a great big platter of sausages, bacon, fresh bread, and a big bowl of scrambled eggs.

Katina raised her head to sniff in appreciation. "Oh, after breakfast for sure."

Everybody laughed and settled into eating.

When she was done, Ice led her down another floor into what appeared to be a full medical clinic.

Katina walked into the room in amazement. "This is something else." She noted several hospital beds. "Are you equipped to do surgery here?"

Ice laughed. "We've certainly done several, but, if it's major, we go to the hospital." She motioned to Katina's leg. "That, however, is something I can handle." She patted one of the beds and said, "Hop up so I can take a look at what size bandage we need."

Carefully Katina stretched her leg out so Ice could get at it. She brought over a couple bandages and found one that was about the right size.

"This should last you for the day. Let me know tonight, and we can change it out after a bath or shower again, if you want."

Katina didn't say anything. She wasn't expecting to be here tonight. These people had done more than enough to keep her safe, but she didn't want to trespass on their generosity. When Ice was done, Katina murmured, "Thank you. Much appreciated."

After that she went up to her room and quickly changed into jeans. She packed up her shorts and carried her bags out to the hallway. She had so many that it would take several trips to get them all in her car again.

As she picked up several, Merk joined her. "Just leave them here for now," he said in a firm voice. "You can decide what you want to do after we deal with the issues today."

She stared at him and chewed on her bottom lip. "I don't want to stay here another night," she explained. "You've done enough already."

He snorted. "Don't even start with me." He picked up her bags, took them inside her room, then shut the door behind her. "Let's go. We're taking my truck."

She was afraid of that. It meant she couldn't run away while in town. The fact of the matter was, he was right. She had no place to run to. So no point in arguing.

He led the way to the truck. She climbed into the passenger side, her purse at her side, and waved at the others on the driveway. Merk pulled out of the compound and headed through the gates. At the road, he stopped and said, "Which way, left or right?"

She turned to look at him. Of course, the USB key. He had no idea where it was.

She said quietly, "Right."

He put on a signal and turned right. For better or for worse she was committed now. No way would he let her get away without handing over the information.

Maybe it was for the best. Something had to be done. And she couldn't do it alone.

IT FASCINATED HIM to watch her facial expressions as her thought processes worked. Still uncertain of him, yet worried for him.

He clenched the steering wheel a little tighter as he let go of some of his anger. She had no good reason to trust him. She didn't really know him. They had had a fling a long time ago, and that was it. This was a life-and-death situation for her, already evident by her kidnapping. But surely she had to understand she needed help to handle this.

He followed her directions and came to one of the main banks. Then he realized she'd probably hid it in a safety deposit box. It made him feel a whole lot better. Not in her purse after all. He hopped out, walked around to open the truck door, and helped her down. Inside she asked the teller to get in her safety deposit box.

The woman nodded, and, within minutes, they were inside the small room with the box in front of them. The bank employee left.

With a glance at Merk, Katina opened the box and pulled out what looked like a child's souvenir. Then he realized it was a cheap souvenir key chain from Las Vegas.

He watched her carefully, wondering why she would've hung on to something like that all these years, or had she gone back recently? Oddly enough the thought hurt that she may have returned to Las Vegas without him. And that was just ridiculous.

She pulled apart the souvenir, and he could see it was a USB drive as well as a key chain. He nodded. "Good. Let's go."

She closed the box and left the room with a smile at the employee.

Back outside he wondered at her slow footsteps. As he got back into the truck, he said, "Are you still bothered about handing the information over?"

She gave him a shuttered look and then said, "I guess. Will you be upset that this is only part of it?"

He froze. Instead of turning on the engine, he slowly dropped his hand on the seat beside him and turned to look at her. "What do you mean?"

She stared down at the cheap plastic item in her hand and said, "I only had time to copy part of it."

"So you don't have all the evidence you were talking about?"

Again that same look came his way. "I do, just not in this form."

He slowly let out his breath, realizing he was clenching his jaw. He understood fear held her back, and he had to be patient. But, at the same time, he was frustrated as hell, needing reassurance of something else. "You're not playing games with me, are you?"

She shook her head. "No."

"Do we have to pick up anything else up in order to have all the information?"

"No." She opened her mouth as if to say something else, then closed it again.

He shook his head. She was damn infuriating.

He pulled from the parking lot with a quick glance to double-check they weren't being followed. Traffic was light. They arrived at Gunner's house in just under fifteen minutes. A trip made almost in complete silence.

What had she meant? Not only was she silent but she was curled up in the corner of the truck, like she wanted to be anywhere else. Too damn bad. This had gone way too far to stop the train now. Having the USB key was only part of it. The damaging information had to be intact as well.

At Gunner's they got out and walked up to the front door. It opened automatically in front of them. She looked at Merk in surprise.

He shrugged. "Gunner's into security. The door wouldn't have opened if he didn't know who was here."

They stepped inside the entranceway to stand on the huge hardwood floor, and there was Gunner, a big smile on his face.

"Well, look who is here."

Merk shot out a hand to shake his. The two exchanged greetings. Gunner had always been one of the white-hat guys. That was a good thing. Little enough of that in this world.

Gunner gently reached out to greet Katina. "Hello, my dear. I hear you got yourself in a spot of trouble."

That startled a hiccup of a laugh out of Katina. "You could say that," she whispered. "It's really not where I expected to see myself."

He motioned them inside and said, "Life is like that. Levi and Ice will be here any minute. I'm so happy to see you all."

They waited until Levi and Ice walked into the entranceway, both looking cool and composed. They were a power couple in their world. Interestingly enough, Merk could sense more nerves coming over Katina as their numbers doubled. He caught Ice's questioning look. He shrugged. He had no clue what was going on.

Gunner said, "I understand we have a bit of work to do. I'll arrange for coffee." He walked into a large office where his assistant sat. "You can give the key to him. He'll bring up the data, and we can take a look at what you've got."

Katina froze. In fact, she took a step back. Merk instantly wrapped an arm around her shoulder and whispered in her ear, "What's up?"

"I don't know him," she whispered. She winced. "It's stupid, but I'm struggling to hand it over."

Merk studied the assistant. He knew the man, and he was looking quite uncomfortable at the obvious attention.

Merk turned to Gunner and asked, "Do you mind if I handle this?"

Gunner waved his hand. "Go for it. I trust you won't access anything else in my computers that you don't need to."

"Your man can stand and watch. I don't mind that."

Merk sat down and held out his hand for the key. Without questioning, Katina handed over the trinket. He opened it up and popped the USB into the drive. There were three files. He opened the first one, and, as she said, it was spreadsheets of accounts.

Everybody moved to study the monitors. The assistant leaned down and switched a couple things, and then the spreadsheets opened onto the monitors higher up. That way they could take a closer look at the information. Merk moved the first file to one monitor, and then, with the assistant's help, he opened up the other two files so they could see the three files at the same time.

Behind him Ice commented, "Interesting."

Merk turned to look at Katina. "And where's the rest of the information?" He felt both Ice and Levi stare at him.

She flushed. "I have it," she said. She looked over at Gunner and then at his assistant, and said, "Do you happen to have a laptop with a mike attached?"

Gunner picked up a nearby laptop and brought it to her while the assistant grabbed one of several headsets sitting on the shelf. Quietly she hooked everything up.

She pulled up a chair to the desk and spoke into the machine. She relaxed in the chair, and the words just rolled off the tip of her tongue. She closed her eyes and settled in.

Merk stared at her in shock. He stood behind her to see the words as they rippled onto the notepad. And then he realized what she had meant. She couldn't download a lot of files without triggering the wrong kind of attention, so she'd memorized the contents. He shook his head, watching as the information floated almost magically onto the page. Beside him, Ice and Levi just stared. Merk knew how they felt.

Gunner stood beside him. "You know, this looks like it might take a while. Time for that coffee." And he left the room.

No way would Merk interrupt Katina at this point. But now he realized why she'd been so secretive. This wasn't something she wanted anybody to know she could do. Hell, it was quite a skill, but it wasn't one he'd want the bad guys to know about either. What methods they would use to force her to get info—or, even worse, to forcefully get data from her—would be horrific.

He pulled up a chair and sat down, reading the information as it went. After forty-five minutes of steady dictation, she stopped suddenly, sat taller, opened a spread-sheet, and verbally filled in the tables from memory. Merk looked at Ice and Levi. Both frowned at the shift.

Ice said, "You must have been dynamite in school."

"Hell, she'd be dynamite in any team." Merk wondered how the hell she could do this.

Finally she fell silent. He checked his watch and realized she'd been speaking steadily for over ninety minutes. He shook his head. He reached for a glass of water on the tray being wheeled in and handed it to her. With a grateful smile she drank the whole glass at once.

"Do you want more?" he asked.

She shook her head. "I should be fine now."

"Besides that magical display of whatever it was you just did," Merk said quietly, "is there any other information you haven't given us?"

She shook her head. "No. That's all I have."

Chapter 10

WITH A CUP of coffee in her hand, and her work done, she relaxed. Now that she finally got it all out, a sense of relief came as she had finally committed to a pathway—good or bad. Whenever she had to do something like this, it always terrified her that she'd miss some information. Forget it before she had a chance to write it down. But she knew this time she'd gotten it all.

She could see the look on their faces as they read the information she'd poured out. Somebody should transcribe it to correct the errors inherent in any dictation program. She made a couple corrections, but, as far as she was concerned, the information was complete. Between what she got on the key and what she remembered, it should be enough. At least enough for the police to go on.

And now she was tired. Which was stupid because it was not even lunchtime. She felt like she'd been through the ringer and back.

She sat quietly while the others discussed the information. Gunner's assistant was already going through it, cleaning it up and making it more legible. She watched, making sure he didn't change anything important. It wouldn't take too long, she knew from experience. When he finally finished, he sent it to the printer and gave them each a hard copy to read over. She didn't accept the one he handed her way. She knew what it said. The last thing she wanted to do was go over it again.

"So why is there a file with all these names of places and money? I understand what you say now about a code and the word *cop* beside three of them. It's not much of a name to go on, but surely we can get somewhere with this."

"That was the accountant's private file," Katina said quietly. "All kinds of restrictions were on that copy. I couldn't print it. It wouldn't let me do anything. The accountant was the only one who could edit it in any way. The only thing I could do was memorize it."

"You can use programs to take copies of stuff like that on screens."

She nodded. "But they also keep copies of what you've taken copies of," she murmured. "And I couldn't afford to let anybody know what I was doing."

Gunner stepped in and said, "But obviously somebody does if you were kidnapped, dear."

She grimaced. "Yes, but at the time I didn't think anyone knew."

He nodded in understanding and said, "Write down all who should get copies of this."

And that settled into a heavy discussion of names, options, emails, and contacts. They all elected to go with duplicate mailings, both print and digital, just in case. Ten names were finally settled upon.

To her that was a lot. Hesitantly, when they were finally done, she said, "Are you sure all these people are trustworthy?"

"No being sure about any of it," Gunner said in his best military voice. "All we can do is assume that people we have known and worked with and have witnessed how they acted in various situations are on the side of right."

"In other words it's a crapshoot …"

Merk laughed. "Back to Vegas again, are we?"

At that moment, the assistant removed the key, popped the cover on, and handed her the trashy Vegas trinket.

Merk looked at her and smiled. "It seems like things come full circle."

She dropped it into her purse and zipped it up. She glanced at the assistant and smiled, saying, "Thank you."

He nodded but was already back at work. The spreadsheets were printing off right now. Ten copies. She looked back at the list of names and said, "Are any of these people media?"

"One is a journalist of high repute," Gunnar said. "He's well-known as a whistleblower."

She nodded. "If it's as good as we can do, then I leave the names in your hands."

"And that," Ice said with a smile, "is why you called Merk in the first place, so relax. This is what we do."

Before Katina had a chance to answer, Merk reached across and picked up her hand, holding it gently in his. "It will be fine."

"Really? I'm pretty damn sure that's what you said before you led me into the Elvis Presley Wedding Chapel."

The entire group burst out laughing. That was good because she'd rather laugh than cry and that was her only other option at the moment.

"Photographic memory?" Merk asked quietly at her side.

She turned to look at him and nodded. Then shrugged. "Or maybe not. It's something like that but not quite. I never asked anyone."

His intense gaze locked on hers as if he was seeing if she

had more secrets hidden away. She let him look all he wanted. She knew she'd been emptied right out, and the process had exhausted her.

She closed her eyes and just rested.

"How come I didn't know about this before?" he complained in a lighthearted manner.

Without opening her eyes, she said, "You weren't too interested in *what* was inside me. More interested in getting inside me," she said in a very low voice. But, at the sudden silence in the room, she knew everybody had heard. Feeling the heat wash up her face, she whispered, "Damn. No one else was supposed to hear that."

Beside her, Levi snickered. "At least you understand Merk very clearly."

"Hey, that's not fair," Merk said with a grin. "I was very much interested in a lot more than that." But the humor ramped up in his voice as he added, "Although I was definitely concerned about that part."

She laughed. "I have to admit that's one thing we did a lot of. Laugh." She'd already brought up more sexual innuendos than she had expected to. Apparently this was who she was with him. They had laughed and joked and had a grand time. But the experience had also soured and scared her. She still considered tequila one of the devil's best tricks.

The topic returned to the information and all the names. "Can I leave now?" she asked, fatigue getting the best of her.

All heads turned, and everyone zeroed in on her. But Merk voiced the unasked question, "Go where?"

"Anywhere. How about California?" she asked mockingly. "I have an uncle in Canada. Maybe I should go visit him."

"Do you want to run for the rest of your life?" Ice asked.

"That's no way to live. You'll always be looking over your shoulder. Is Canada far enough away? Maybe. Until somebody, somewhere, somehow finds out who you are, and it gets back to these people."

Katina frowned. "No, that's no kind of life, is it?" She looked around at the rest of them and added, "But all this is likely to do is make things bigger and uglier."

"In the short term, yes," Merk said. "I don't know what your financial situation is, but maybe a holiday isn't a bad idea. At least until this all blows over."

"Meaning Canada is possible?" She sat up, liking the idea. Her uncle was great. She'd love to spend a few weeks with him. "How different is that from running away to Canada then?" she joked.

"It's all about intention," Merk said. "One is staying low and getting out of the limelight until the kidnappers can be caught and brought to trial, and the other is not planning on heading anywhere in particular, running, hoping that you'll be free and always looking over your shoulder. One is planned. The other is not."

"I have handed over everything I know of," Katina said firmly. "Probably more information is in my brain if you can dredge it out of me. I really don't want to run away. But an extended holiday would be a nice idea. Only not to my uncle if that'll put him in danger."

"You don't trust your uncle?" Levi asked.

She turned to look at him. "As much as I trust anybody," she admitted, hating that trust appeared to be such an issue for her. She'd been alone most of her life. Independent by necessity and depending on others wasn't something she had experience in. "I don't think he has anything to do with this. But I don't want to bring any trouble to his doorstop either."

Levi nodded. "That's good to know."

Merk spoke from the other side of her, making her twist back to look at him. "Does anyone involved know about your uncle?" He nodded at all the spreadsheets in front of them.

She let out her breath, slowly thinking about what could be in her personnel file. "I don't think so, but I suppose, if they wanted to search deep enough, they would find that information somehow."

Gunner spoke up and said, "Absolutely they would." He waited a moment and then said, "But they'd have to think that's a place you would go. They won't go all around the world on a goose chase if they think you're close. Or if you have other addresses, other friends who might yield them better results."

Friends? *Anna.* Sitting up straighter, Katina turned cold, knowing the color had been leached from her skin. "Would they really go after my friends?"

Silence.

"You were already worried about the landlord living above you. How is it you haven't connected they might give any of your friends and family a shakedown to find out where you are?" Ice asked.

Shaking, Katina pulled her purse toward her from the side of the chair and dug for her phone. She brought up her contact list and hit the first one at the top. Her best friend worked in an animal shelter. When she answered the call, Katina sat back, relieved. "Anna, any chance you could disappear for a couple weeks?"

First came silence. And then Anna cried out, "What's wrong? Are you hurt? I heard about the kidnapping. You could have called to let me know you're okay. I've been so worried."

Katina lifted a hand to her forehead. "I'm so sorry. I was trying to keep you out of this. I didn't want anyone to track you down. Honestly my life's just been hell these last twenty-four hours. I haven't had time to think clearly."

"I've been so worried," Anna wailed. "Oh, my God, what's going on with you?"

Katina didn't know what to tell her friend.

"Katina," Anna continued in a sharp tone, "what's this about me leaving?"

"I got into a bit of trouble. I'm on the wrong side of a lot of people who are on the other side of the law, and they're after me," she said. "The people helping me are concerned that my friends—you—might be targets."

More silence then she said, "Oh, my God."

Katina winced. "I know. I know. I'm so sorry. And I understand this is sudden, but things are about to hit the fan here in the next twenty-four hours, and I want to make sure you're safe."

She could just imagine her friend standing in the middle of the shelter, looking at all the animals in need, knowing instinctively what she would say.

"I can't," Anna said. "You know I have almost no staff anymore. The shelter's struggling to stay afloat as it is. Somebody has to be here to look after these animals."

Her gaze zinged over toward Merk. "I know that, Anna, but I'd die if anything happened to you because of me."

"Are these the same guys who kidnapped you?"

"Likely, yes. Or the people who hired them."

"I have a security system here and at home," Anna said. "I can hardly just pack up and walk away. It's not that simple."

"I know." Katina sank back against the chair and wiped the tears forming in the corner of her eyes. "I know exactly how hard it is. Everything I own is in the back of my car. I've lost everything."

"It's that stupid accounting job when you got a promotion, right?"

Katina frowned into the phone. "How did you know that?" She sensed the interest coming from everybody around her. But she shook her head, holding them off.

"You changed after that. You got really nervous, kept looking over your shoulder. I asked if everything was okay, and you said it was fine. But I knew you were lying."

"It's not so much that I was lying. I kept looking over my shoulder, but nothing was ever there," she explained. "And then suddenly somebody was. And that's when I was kidnapped."

"Who are the people helping you?"

Katina hesitated.

"Don't lie. I have enough issues to deal with here. Exactly what the hell's going on? So who is helping you, and are they to be trusted?"

Knowing what was coming, she braced for the worst when she said, "I called Merk."

Anna snorted and said, "You're kidding me. You called your Las Vegas husband?" She had said it in such a loud voice, Katina was damn sure half the room heard her.

"Ex-husband," she said firmly. "Besides, he was going into the military, remember? I didn't know who else to call. I figured maybe he would know who could help me. I wasn't expecting him to insist on being the one to step up."

"Oh, that's too funny. Your Elvis Presley Wedding

Chapel experience turned into a white knight." And then she giggled.

Katina was pretty damn sure it was more of a release over the stress than anything, but Anna was enjoying herself a little too much.

Merk leaned across and tapped her on the knee. "Tell her you will call her back in a few minutes."

She nodded and quickly rang off the phone call. She put the phone in her lap and stared at him. "What?"

He looked over at Levi and said, "Do we have anyone who could go help out at the shelter and keep an eye on Anna?"

Levi frowned but turned to Ice, thinking. "All our full-time men are out on jobs."

"That's another thing," Ice said. "It could be several weeks to several months."

Merk nodded. "Gunner, what about you? It doesn't have to be a full-time cop or a security guard, but somebody with military training, somebody retired who is no longer in service for one reason or another."

Katina had no idea what that *one reason or other* would be.

"As long as they had good solid experience in looking after somebody and were okay to help out with the animals, it would be a win-win on both sides. She's completely short-staffed and is overwhelmed with animals."

"Speaking of someone good with animals"—Merk turned to look at Levi—"how is Aaron?"

Levi shook his head. "Not ready for that yet. Still has surgeries ahead of him for the leg and back."

Merk nodded. "Too bad. He'd be an ideal fit. He loves animals."

"Yeah, when he was a young man, before the military," Levi said. "From all accounts he's become very bitter and not dealing well with his changed circumstances." He frowned and dropped his gaze to the floor.

"There are many like him," Gunner said quietly. "Now the question is, who do I know who would be the right pick for the job?" He sat there and dropped his pencil up and down on the paper. "Let me think about that for a few minutes and see if I can come up with somebody."

With that, Katina was happy and hoped that some solution came up and soon. She'd be devastated if anything happened to Anna.

MERK WATCHED KATINA slip the phone around and around in her fingers as she fretted over the safety of her friend. "How many friends could be affected by this?"

She looked up at him in surprise. "Anna would be the closest and the most in danger. We did a lot of sleepovers. We were quite visibly friends since forever. Same schools and college. She's the reason I stayed in Houston. With no family to care about, Anna was closer to being my real sister than the two half-sisters I do have. It was an obvious choice to stay here. As good a location as any." She flushed. "Actually Anna was in Vegas too. And the only one who knows what I was doing there."

Merk frowned. "I didn't see her."

She gave him a pointed look and said, "No, you were looking at something else."

He grinned. "I have good taste."

She shook her head and rolled her eyes at him. Although this was the last thing she'd expected to be joking about, it really did help ease the tension in the room.

"I do have other friends, but they don't live in town, and I don't know how much danger they would be in. I guess somebody could go to them and ask about me, but I haven't discussed this with anyone. Honestly I wasn't terribly social at work either." And then her voice fell away. She pinched her brows together deep in thought.

Merk gave her a minute and then asked, "What are you thinking about?"

She chewed the inside her lip and said, "It can't be."

"What can't be?" Ice asked. "Better let us decide."

Katina stared down at her hands and how she continuously flipped her phone around in her lap. "Another woman worked for us. She replaced a different accountant but just temporarily because he was attending a conference." She shrugged. "But I don't know why they would replace anybody for that week. The job normally would have been off-loaded to another one of the senior accountants or just left until they got back."

"And?" Merk asked. "There has to be more to this if it's bothering you."

"It wasn't bothering me until just now, when I realized that she disappeared."

Instantly everyone in the room sat up and stared at her. "Okay, I don't mean 'disappeared.' She left the building one day, and the next day I noticed her coat was still there, as if she'd rushed out and never wanted to come back to collect it."

"Or is it that she couldn't come back?" Merk said quietly.

She stared at him open-mouthed, her eyes round as saucers, and she cried, "Oh, no, there's no reason for them to do something like that, is there, Merk?"

"Hard to say. What was her name?" Gunner asked.

"Eloise Hartman."

"When did she disappear?"

Katina frowned, thinking. "Middle of March, I think," she said. "I was already in the new position, but I had only been there a couple days. She made some comment about me having fun, but her tone wasn't normal. Not snide and it wasn't offered as a warning, but something was just off about it."

Merk watched Gunner tap on his laptop, searching for Eloise Hartman. He studied Gunner's face as it changed. And then he knew. "What? A drive-by shooting or was a body found in the woods?"

Gunner looked straight at him and nodded, then turned to Katina and said, "She was found in the park, a single bullet to her head." He glanced back at the laptop and said, "Her body was found March 19."

At her shocked cry of horror, Merk shifted in his chair so he could wrap an arm around Katina and hold her close. "Okay, take it easy. We don't know if it's connected. We obviously have to assume there *could* be a connection, but that doesn't mean that'll happen to you."

"Or to Anna," she said in a shaky voice. "Oh, my God, what have I done?"

In a firm voice, Merk said, "You haven't done anything. It's these assholes who did this."

She turned her glassy gaze to him and said, "But they killed her. Are they planning to do that to me?"

Merk wondered about the best way to answer and then decided there was no gain in making light of it. She needed to be aware. He nodded. "Chances are very good that's exactly what they plan for you. Eventually. They would get that information from you one way or the other."

"But they would only have gotten the key," she whispered. "The rest would have gone to the grave with me." At his surprised look she explained, "If I'm under stress or any duress, my memory doesn't work. I can't recall anything. I have to be calm and feel safe, otherwise ..." She shrugged.

"So not an easy skill to have then," he said.

"And very unreliable. I was getting much better at using it for ... something unrelated," she added cryptically. "But then I got derailed and went home instead."

He turned to look at her, studied her face for a long moment, and then a grin broke out. "You were card-reading in Vegas, weren't you?" he accused. "That's what you meant about Anna being the only one who knew what you were doing there."

Her face fell. She cried out softly, "It occurred to me, when I could memorize all the cards and win a little money, how that might be a way to pay off my student loans, but I wasn't there long enough to even make good on the practice." She sniffled and glared at him, then wiped her eyes in a childish motion that made him smile.

"Card-counting is illegal anyway, so consider me your savior back then too."

She snorted, then turned to Gunner. "If you have anybody you know who could help keep Anna safe, I'd really appreciate it."

He nodded. "I might. Flynn would fit the bill."

Ice gasped in surprise, and then she giggled. "He would at that."

Levi asked, "Is he doing jobs for you? I was hoping to convince him to come work for me. This job could be a good test."

Gunner shook his head. "I'm not taking on jobs. But I know him through Logan. And I know he needs something constructive to do."

"The only thing is, he's a bit of a wild card. That's why he's no longer in the navy," Ice said. "He went rogue on one of his missions, and they decided they couldn't deal with that anymore."

Gunner nodded. "He did, indeed, but for all the right reasons. Some children were stuck in another camp, and his unit had orders to leave them there. Flynn wouldn't listen. He went back and saved them. In the process he lost his career."

"And he's always been a sucker for animals too, hasn't he?" Levi asked. He turned to Ice and said, "He actually was helping out at Dani's Center for a while in the vet clinic."

"Well, then he's got the animal part covered," Ice said. "But he's a bit of a jokester and a ham." Ice turned to study Katina. "What's Anna like? Can she handle somebody with an over-the-top personality?"

"Anna's a bit like that herself. She's quite a firecracker." Katina grinned.

"Seems they'd be perfect together." Ice snorted.

"Hey, we're not in Mason's unit here. No matchmaking allowed," Levi growled at Ice. She smirked in response. His growl deepened as he added, "Like we need that shit."

Merk caught Katina's glance of confusion and told her, "I'll explain later."

To Ice, Merk said, "Nice that you two found each other and got all your shit dealt with. Even nicer that Stone found somebody and had surrendered to all that pain to move on. But don't go matchmaking all the men you know."

Ice just gave him a flat stare, but, in one of those tiny perceptible nods, she managed to include Katina with it. And his glare deepened. But, on the inside, something sparked. And for the first time he realized what their relationship must look like to the others—the way they got along, the way they joked about their past history, and the way he constantly comforted her, and the way she had turned to him. A case could be made for the whole white-knight-in-shining-armor thing but wasn't a basis for a lasting relationship.

Unless he looked at Stone's love life, which began just as suddenly and in a similar fashion.

He shook his head at Ice. "Don't even think it."

She gave him an innocent smile and said, "Don't know what you're talking about."

Levi turned to glance at Merk and said, "No point thinking about it. It's already a fact. Up to you to figure it out." He stood up, outstretched his hand to Ice.

As she stood, she said to Gunner, "If you could contact Flynn, that would be great."

"We're looking to hire another four men, and he was under consideration," Levi said.

"Well, I can't be an active member of your team, which makes me sad," Gunner said. "But, if you need anything, just let me know."

Levi studied him.

Merk knew this was the conversation opener Levi and Ice had been looking for. Merk stood, helped Katina to her feet, and said, "We're going for a walk in the garden. The fresh air will be good for Katina."

He knew they'd take the reasoning the other way around, and they were right. He wanted a few minutes alone with Katina, but, by rights, Katina could use a little bit of space. He led her through the double French doors out to the beautiful garden in the back.

As they stepped through the doors, she said, "Are you taking me away or giving them space?"

He'd always known she was perceptive. Just hadn't realized how perceptive.

Chapter 11

"**H**OW DO I pay for that security detail?" Katina said as soon as they were out in the bright sunshine.

She turned her face to let the sun's rays bounce off her skin. It was so hard to reconcile the bright sunshine of the outside world and those heavy scary topics going on inside that room. She knew they were one and the same, two sides of the exact same existence, but she'd much rather live in the sunshine.

"Anna doesn't have much money, and neither do I."

"You let us worry about that," Merk said quietly. "Especially if this is the trial run for Flynn. Something we would do anyway. The job's small enough that we can see how he handles it."

She nodded. "So would you take it on as pro bono?"

Merk shrugged. "Sometimes it's what we have to do. Some of our clients can pay, and some can't. It's a matter of balance."

She turned to stare at him. She'd been instantly attracted to him, both times. She looped her arm through his and said, "Let's walk for a bit. It'd be nice to forget all this is happening."

"You've been living with the stress for days, weeks," he said. "That makes it tough on anybody."

"I have but hadn't really realized the repercussions." She

stared off at the roses—a good dozen bushes, all in full bloom. They were beautiful. She reached out to stroke the soft petals. "I feel terrible about Eloise."

"What was she like?"

She turned to look at him. "Nosy. She was one of those people who forever asked questions, like, where you lived. How come you're not married? Did you ever get close to being married?"

She turned her gaze to the daisies and continued, "Initially it was really irritating. But then I realized she was just a gregarious person. She liked to know what everybody else was doing and thinking at any given time. Sometimes I rebuffed her. Sometimes I told her." She shrugged. "I never did tell her about the marriage." She walked over to a bed of beautiful blue flowers and said, "I don't see columbines very much."

She squatted beside the garden and pointed at the different types in front of her. "That's this bed here." She studied them for a long moment, struck by a thought. "They are one of the most delicate-looking flowers. Yet it's amazing how well they survive in harsh conditions. They also reproduce rather easily, considering their fragility."

She straightened and wandered a little bit more. He always stayed a couple steps behind her. Finally, when she got up the courage, she turned and asked, "Do you really think I'm in danger?"

He didn't hold back; he couldn't. "Yes. I do."

She gazed down at her fingers clasped together. "Can I stay with you at the compound, or should I be making arrangements to go somewhere else? Not necessarily my uncle's but someone a long way away?"

"The compound isn't the best idea, but it's better than

leaving the country." His face twisted into a wry smile.

At that, her face scrunched up. "Why?"

"Because it's quite likely to trigger an alert that you're traveling on your passport into Canada." He added cheerfully, "Relax. Levi will be working on a solution. It won't be Canada though."

Sure enough, when they went back inside, the men were all sitting together, making plans. Merk stood in the doorway. "When do we leave?"

Without looking up, Levi said, "This afternoon."

Stepping beside him, Katina asked, "Where are we going?" She slipped her hand into Merk's, loving it when his fingers closed securely around hers.

Levi turned suddenly and looked at her. "If you really want to know, I'll tell you. But it's better if you don't know right now."

"Am I leaving the country?"

He shook his head. "No, we have lots of places around the country we can send people to."

She turned her questioning look at Merk.

He grinned. "Safe houses. We own or have access to a good half dozen of them."

Her mouth was slightly open as she considered this. "Wow. It never occurred to me that was possible." Who knew such a thing existed outside law enforcement?

Just then a manservant walked into the room and said, "Lunch will be in ten minutes."

Gunner waved a hand in his direction, "Thanks, Bruno."

Katina watched the massive male walk back out. "Are you guys all on steroids or something? How the hell does everybody get to be that size?"

"When you're used to working with only military personnel," Merk said, "it's natural to have friends and people you trust and to keep them around afterward. In Gunner's case, he's employed many of his ex-military associates."

"Already trained, understand loyalty, and know how to keep quiet, right?"

Merk looked down at her and grinned. "Exactly."

Five minutes later they walked into a large dining room.

Merk led her to the table, set and ready for them. Very quickly the rest of the room filled up—with a lot more people than she had seen so far. A cold luncheon of sandwiches, salads, sausage rolls, and pies was spread before them. In fact it all looked delicious. And she was starving.

She watched as Merk carefully served himself a couple sandwiches and rolls, then nudged him with her elbow and said, "Please."

With a smile he added a couple things to her plate. She looked at him with a sorrowful gaze. He laughed and added another one.

At the far end of the table Gunner spoke up. "There's lots of food, Katina. You won't starve here."

"Good thing," she said with a big grin, "because I'm hungry. I'd probably outeat Merk in a heartbeat."

"She probably could," Merk said with a laugh.

That set the tone for the lunch. Lighthearted conversation, good food. All followed by a tray of desserts with some wonderful roasted coffee. She didn't know what kind it was, but it was rich and thick. She sat back and smiled. "You do know how to live, Gunner."

"My dear," he said in a very serious voice, "after a lot of years thinking I was likely to die ..." Then to another he said, "I learned a very hard lesson. And it's all about living every day as if it's your last. And it makes for a very good living." He lifted his glass of wine and held it up and said, "Cheers."

She lifted her coffee cup. "I haven't learned that lesson yet. It seems like all I've done for weeks is run."

"There will be an end to this," he promised.

Less than an hour later they were in the truck, heading back toward the compound. Levi and Ice stayed behind to work on a few things. Katina figured it would also give them a chance to get ahead slightly so they could see if anybody was following them. It just felt odd to know she was part of a convoy at all times. But it also felt good. She felt secure.

And now, for the first time in a long time, she had people who she could trust to help her. What a heady feeling.

When they pulled into the compound, she no longer had the same sense of shock. Until she realized her car was gone. She gasped. "Where's my car?"

"Alfred moved it into one of the garages while we were gone, so it's out of sight."

"Oh." She slumped back down again. "I wouldn't have thought of that."

"Yes, you would've. Just not right off the bat. And you don't have to think about it now. This is what we do. Trust us to do it."

She nodded. As he parked and turned off the engine, he turned to her and said, "Now go and pack. You can have two bags maximum—one big and one small. Pack for cold evenings but hot days."

She frowned. "Cold evenings or just sweater-cool evenings?" She shook her head. "I don't think I have anything for cold evenings."

"Sweaters will be fine."

She opened the door and eased out. Together they walked into the compound. Sienna, Stone, Lissa, and Alfred waited for them. Lissa handed Merk a notepad and an envelope. "Contacts, keys, company card."

Stone said, "You're switching to a rental in Houston." He handed over the information.

Merk nodded, accepted both and said, "We'll pack and leave in thirty minutes."

Alfred stepped forward with a large basket in his hand. He handed it to Merk. "Traveling food. If you need more, you'll have to stop and pick up something along the way."

Merk stared at the size of the basket and chuckled. "I know she likes to eat, guys, but ..."

"This hopefully will last you for your first day," Alfred said. "After that, you'll have to shop."

Sienna smiled at Katina. "How do you feel about becoming a brunette?"

Katina's eyebrows shot up, but she understood immediately. "I'd rather be a redhead, but brunette is just fine."

The two women headed to her room. Sienna managed to dye and rinse Katina's hair, then blow-dried it enough that Katina could braid it and not have a sopping-wet braid dripping down her back. She quickly changed into traveling clothes with a sweater and sneakers. She kept her jeans on and had a T-shirt under the sweater. Then she packed.

With a bag in each hand, she cast a final glance around the room and turned to stare at Sienna. "I guess I'm ready."

Sienna led her out into the hallway, saying, "You'll be just fine. Merk will look after you."

"I know. He always did before."

"I think it's great that you two were married. Obviously something is still there."

Katina shook her head. "I don't know. That one night was great, but we divorced the next morning. ... That was brutal."

The two burst into laughter as they met the group in the hallway. Merk stood there with his bags ready to go.

He looked at her, nodding. "Nice hair." He grinned and asked, "Shall we?"

"Thanks." She took a deep breath and said, "Yes, absolutely."

INTERESTING. HE'D WONDERED if she would renege at the very last moment, but apparently she'd decided to put her trust in them and was prepared to follow his lead. Good. It would make things a whole lot easier if he didn't have to fight her. Because he had every intention of protecting her, whether she wanted him to or not.

With everything loaded and both of them buckled up, he honked the horn lightly. He knew Levi and the unit were tracking the vehicle. They'd follow Merk straight through.

He and Katina were heading to New Mexico, not too long a drive but long enough. By the time they hit the main highway, he told her they had several hours of driving, so she settled in the front seat.

"Did Gunner ever connect Flynn to Anna?"

"I understand Gunner was talking to him. I don't know what the end result was. As soon as they have something settled, they'll let us know."

"Sure. And in the meantime, what happens to Anna?" She turned to study Merk and added, "Maybe we should stay with her until they get somebody."

He shook his head. "No. We're taking you out of here.

Flynn will help Anna."

He didn't bother to look her way. The car doors were locked, and they escaped the city, traveling full speed ahead. No way in hell were they going back to babysit. Somebody else could do that job. He trusted Levi to make that happen.

"Did you ever contact your uncle?" he asked. He hated to bring up the subject, but it was possible somebody would go after him.

"He travels a lot normally, so I don't know if he'd be home right now. Plus I was still afraid to lead trouble to him." She sighed. "A whole lot of negative possibilities are crowding my mind, worrying how something is wrong."

"Don't borrow any trouble right now. We have enough to go around."

Her laugh was bitter. "You think? If anybody else I know dies ..."

"Don't think about it," he said firmly.

He drove steadily, stopping in Washington, Texas, for a gas break once. When they got back in the truck, she looked at the basket, then at him, and asked, "Shall I check out what Alfred packed for us?"

He waved his hand. "Absolutely. I'm feeling hungry myself."

She dove into the basket and pulled out large sandwiches beautifully wrapped up, a thermos with maybe two servings of something, and what looked like a selection of savory pies and handmade pastries. Her coos of delight made him smile.

"Alfred is one hell of a cook." She quickly unpacked a sandwich and handed him a half.

As he studied the creation in his hand—a great big thick black multigrain bread full of vegetables and meat and cheese—Merk nodded. "That he is."

They munched down their halves in no time. She was kept busy opening a second sandwich and then a third. He figured she had to be full, because she'd stopped opening sandwiches, only to find her examining the small pies. She handed him one and then took the second one for herself. Looked to be miniature quiches. He had his done in about three bites, but she curled up in the corner and moaned as she slowly ate hers.

He grinned. She was very sensuous in all she did. Just another example of what intrigued him. With the first wave of hunger taken care of, she could sit back, relax, and enjoy her quiche.

He really liked that about her. A time to be high-pressured and a time to be eased back. She seemed to follow her instincts in a natural rhythm that allowed for that type of on/off temperament.

That was a good thing. If she could relax right now, he hoped that also meant she could be ready to run at a moment's notice. Lord knew he might need her too.

As far as he could tell, they hadn't been followed.

But that didn't mean someone wasn't searching for them.

He had to get to the new location as fast as possible and hide out there. Maybe for weeks. Was she aware of that?

On the other hand, he was okay with it and was looking forward to spending time alone with her. All the guys would forgive him for thinking it was an opportunity too good to pass up. He knew they'd been dynamite in bed together. Now all he could think about was if she had changed and matured so much in bed and would he like that much better too? After all, he loved this older model of her already ...

He gave a quiet snort. He was a fool. Because even if she

wasn't exactly the same as she was before, she'd be damn hot now too. And one thing hadn't changed—he wanted her any way he could have her.

Chapter 12

THEY PULLED INTO one of the outlying subdivisions of Albuquerque. She loved the change of scenery. It was really stunning. Not to mention the reddish color of the hills. When he drove up to a small adobe house tucked into the hillside, she smiled. "Is this where we're staying? It's adorable."

He nodded. "Yes, this is one of ours."

"And you guys just come and holiday here? Perfect."

He shook his head. "We travel the world over," he said. "There are other places to holiday."

She sighed. "I'm a simple girl. This suits my heart just fine." She opened her door of the truck and slid out.

"Wait," he ordered sharply. "Let me check that it's all good."

At that, she froze. His words reminded her how she wasn't on holiday in any way, shape, or form. She stood at the truck and waited.

He walked toward the front entryway and quickly unlocked the door and stepped inside. She didn't know what to think. She understood why they were here, but, for just a moment, it had been nice to think it was an entirely different reason. When he stepped back out again and gave her a big smile, she knew they were good.

Reaching in the truck, she pulled out the basket Alfred

had sent with them. It was still heavily laden, but she knew it wouldn't last more than a day or so. She carried that up and stepped into the front of the house as he walked back to the truck to grab her bags. An Aztec theme decorated the inside, nice and simple with interesting floors, and what looked like plaster walls with stone and brick mixed in. A bit of old mixed with a bit of new.

She loved it.

All of it.

She set down the basket and explored the place. Three bedrooms were upstairs, one with a bath, and the other two shared a bath between them. As she looked out the windows at the small community nestled in the foothills, she just smiled to herself. She hadn't had a chance to go many places in her life, and she'd never been to New Mexico. It was perfect. No, it was better than perfect. It might not be a holiday, but she was damned if she wouldn't enjoy this.

Still laughing greedily like a fool, she ran downstairs and unpacked the basket. As she watched, smiling, Merk carried the bags upstairs. Good. He could take one of the bedrooms with the shared bath. She wanted the suite. But that was hardly fair.

When she had emptied the basket and had put away the food in the fridge and cupboards, she noticed the coffeepot and a bag of ground coffee. Even better. She immediately set up for coffee and realized she had no idea how much to put in. She made a good guess. She could always adjust the amount for the next pot.

When it was done, she still had no sign of Merk; she figured he'd gotten lost on his computer or talking to his unit back at the compound. She poured two cups and went in search of him. Sure enough, she found a room in the back on the main floor established as an office.

He had his laptop and gear ready to go. With his headset on, he talked to Levi. "Okay, that's good to know. I'll tell her Flynn is already at the shelter." He listened a bit, then a grin flashed on his face.

She placed his coffee on the desk.

"Let the sparks fly with those two," he said. "I'll give you an update once we settle in and head into town to do some shopping. I'll check in with Freddy when I'm there."

He hung up soon afterward and said, "Thanks for the coffee."

"What was that about Anna?" Katina asked.

"Flynn agreed to give her personal security." He paused for a second. "I guess the meeting wasn't too friendly. She didn't take very kindly to his presence."

Katina winced. "I should've warned her. If he walked in with any arrogance, she'd have chopped him to pieces."

Merk laughed. "He definitely walked in with that. He's a character and a half. But he's a good man. He's an even better soldier."

"Okay then, the rest doesn't really matter. As long as she stays safe. She might hate me when this is over, but that means she's alive, and I'm good with that."

"Levi wants you to make contact with your uncle," Merk said. "Just to be sure he's safe."

She took out her phone right then and found her uncle's number. Once again it rang and rang. "No answer," she said to Merk. "And no voice mail."

"Okay, what's his name? I'll send the details to Ice and Levi—see if they can track his passport."

She quickly gave him the name, address, and phone number. "Maybe somebody could physically check to see he's all right?" she asked quietly. "He lives out in the country, so it needs to be the RCMP that stops by."

He nodded. "No idea if Levi knows someone up there or not."

"I am pretty damn sure Levi knows somebody everywhere," she said with a snort. "That man has connections."

"He has. Gunner might help too."

"And didn't you say you had somebody in England?" she asked, having only a hazy idea of how that all worked.

"That would be Charles in England, and he might very well have some idea of how to track your uncle down too." Merk frowned and continued to type.

She didn't know if he was emailing or if he was in a secure chat room. All the stuff they did was way over her head.

"Ice has news. Several of the board members of Bristol and Partners, Ltd. were in a private plane crash. The authorities assume there were no survivors." He raised that piercing gaze to study her. "Did you ever meet any of them?"

She sank slowly into a chair and stared at him in shock. "I don't know. We had CEOs where I worked, but I don't know that any were the head of Bristol." She shook her head. "I didn't really have anything to do with any of the board members. I'm not sure I even know their names."

He nodded. "And this may have nothing to do with what information you've gathered."

"On the other hand, how could it not?" she asked. "Just think about it. I find all this information, and people connected to that same company are dropping dead now." She shook her head, staring out the window closest to him, studying the rock formations, not really seeing them. "I wonder what kind of shakedowns are happening in the company? Were those people, the directors, the ones responsible for the information I found?"

"Stop," he said sharply. "This is not your fault."

She turned her gaze back to him, but her lower lip trembled. "You sure? But, if I had just left it alone … It's just money. So what if they were stealing money, evading taxes? Do I really care?" She shook her head. "Not when compared to the loss of life."

"And you don't get to ask that question," he said quietly. "Because if they had done this already, you have no idea what else they've done—like Eloise. And, for all you know, some of this money is being laundered from drug deals or sex-trafficking rings. At this point, somebody has to take a stand and shut it down. You've done that. Don't second-guess yourself now. This is too damn important."

She stared at her hands. "I know that. Really I do. It's just hard to see the cause-and-effect of one's own actions."

"Standing on the side of right, you'll never have to question that again. Because, even if you don't know the outcome, you have to believe what you are doing is the right thing." He took off his headset and stood. "Let's go for a walk. It's a beautiful little town. Nobody knows who we are, and we can play tourist."

She finished her coffee in several gulps and said, "That would be lovely." She put the two cups back into the kitchen and turned off the pot.

At the front door, she stopped and looked around. Hard to imagine they could possibly not be safe here with the idyllic sleepiness to the area.

Merk stepped up beside her, locked the door, then held out his hand. Without hesitation she placed hers in his. And together they walked into town.

HE HAD WORRIED about telling her of the plane crash. Knew it would be hard to hear that other people were suffering or had been killed because of her actions. But she couldn't look at it that way. Because that was not how reality was. These people had set themselves on this path a long time ago. He didn't know if the plane crash was connected. But, like her, he had to assume it was. The coincidence was a little too damning. Like Eloise's execution.

Merk led Katina down a series of narrow pathways. He'd spent a week here a year ago and had really enjoyed it. This was a lovely place to hide out for a few days.

He had several other locations, and, if this one got compromised, they would pick up and move again. But, for right now, he planned to take her for dinner at a great little restaurant downtown.

It was late afternoon. If they were lucky he could get to the repair shop and find Freddy. Afterward they had a chance to explore a little, then they could sit down, eat, and rest. Everything could be done here on foot; no need to drive around. That would help, because he was driving a big-ass truck, and, though trucks were common here, it would be obvious they were strangers in town.

What a beautiful time of year with the gardens and the trees. Not that there was much in the way of trees, but the little bit there were, they were bright and cheerful. The afternoon brought a low-level heat. He'd told her to bring cold-weather clothes, but, at the time, he figured they were heading to the Colorado Mountains. At night it would still be cold here. He hoped she also brought T-shirts and shorts.

Once they'd walked through town, and she had a chance to admire the quaintness and the simplicity of the place, he led her to a TV repair shop at the far end. He was glad

Freddy didn't have to rely on this business for his income. Not many people repaired TVs anymore. They were a disposable commodity nowadays.

He did repair other electronics, but, as far as Merk was concerned, damn near all broken electronics—other than computers you could rebuild yourself—fell into the same category: garbage. He pushed open the door and let her enter ahead of him.

Once inside the dingy room, he turned to study the walls of dusty electronics. Not a great disguise for what really went on in the back of the store but seemed to work for Freddy. At the front counter Merk hit the bell. And waited. Finally he heard shuffling in the back. And that was actually reassuring as it meant Freddy was still here.

As he waited, the old man stepped through the long lines of beadwork, letting them jangle as they dropped back into place. Merk watched Katina's face as she studied the bead-work and smiled. Merk turned toward Freddy and said, "Long time no see, Fred."

Freddy's face lit up beautifully. They reached across the counter and shook hands. Merk placed an arm around Katina's shoulders and tucked her up against him. "And this is Katina, my girlfriend," he said with a big smile. He found it interesting that he saw no sign of surprise from Katina. But, then again, they had to play roles of some kind. This one just made sense. The only question was, how committed a relationship was he going to try to pull off? He figured "girlfriend" had to be the easiest on her.

"What the hell are you doing in town?" Freddy asked with a big grin that showed missing front teeth.

Freddy had been a bruiser in his day, a boxer in a ring where he lost teeth, busted some bones, and had taken more than a few blows to his head. But, unlike a lot of prizefighters, he was still going strong in his late 60s.

Merk knew one of these days he'd come into town and find that nobody would answer the ring of the bell. "We're just here for a week's holiday," Merk said. "Getting away from the stresses of life. Needed to relax a bit."

Freddy nodded sagely. "Stress will kill you," he warned. "Been telling you to move to the country and farm or something."

Merk gave a booming laugh. "I don't think farming and I would get along. I might handle the machinery just fine, but dealing with the animals and planting the acres? No way."

Freddy cackled. "No, no, you don't look much like a gardener to me." He studied Katina and gave her a toothless grin. "How did you ever get hung up with this guy? You sure somebody better wasn't around?"

She gave him a beautiful smile and said, "No, I never had any doubt. Merk is for me."

Merk clenched his fingers around her shoulder a little tighter than he expected. But her words pierced his protective shield. She was either a damn good actress or she meant what she had said. He desperately wanted to ask her which.

They exchanged a few more banalities, then Merk said, "Anything new happening around here?"

"What kind of time frame you talking?" Freddy asked, immediately getting down to business. "Last twenty-four hours?"

"We just arrived, so it'd be nice to know if anything came in ahead of us."

Freddy shook his head. "Nothing I've heard. No strangers, no new vehicles, but, you know, it's early days yet.

Be warned."

Merk nodded. "Give us a heads-up if you hear any-thing."

"Or see something?" Freddy asked. His piercing-blue gaze narrowed. "I've got some new equipment if you want to take a look."

Merk wanted to take a look badly. He nodded his head casually. "Sure, love to."

Freddy led them to the back of the store, and Merk smiled at Katina's gasp of surprise. As the front had been a dusty, dodgy old store where nobody seemed to give a damn; the back room was entirely the opposite—everything gleamed, shiny and bright—and full of top-of-the-line electronics.

Merk walked over to one of the huge monitors set up on a system off to the left and said, "Satellite? How did you get the connection?"

"*Connection* is the truth behind that statement. But I never give out my sources." He cackled and sat down in his chair. With a couple clicks they had an overview of the entire town. He shifted the cameras to the house they were staying in. "Now would you look at that?" Freddy asked.

"Looks damn fine. You've certainly had some upgrades since I was here last."

"Yep. I work for my friends, all over the world. Any excuse for new equipment is a reason to buy new toys."

Merk laughed. "That is the truth." He leaned in to study the town, realizing they could see people walking along the streets. He didn't recognize anybody.

Freddy said, "You're still using the same phone?"

"I'll give you a new number." He quickly rattled off the one for the phone he kept in his pocket. "If there's any emergency, use that number and call me immediately."

"Will do. Who am I charging?"

"Call Ice. I think it's still all the same accounts, but who knows? That's her stuff."

"You got it. By the way, this new little restaurant is in town down that way. French bistro," he said with a twist of his lips as he accented the last word. "I don't know the name. Most of the dishes have a fancy name no one can pronounce, but the food tastes damn good."

On that note, Merk turned Katina around and led her toward the front door. At the last moment he turned and said, "Anything interesting in the last year around here?"

Freddy shook his head. "Nope. The place is dead. And that's the way I like it. I'll be joining it soon." And he cackled with laughter.

"Anything in other parts of the world that might interest me?"

Freddy narrowed his gaze and studied him, then said, "Maybe. Let me think about that."

Merk nodded. Freddy was always a good source of information and normally the unusual stuff. "I have another address of interest. Wouldn't mind if you keep an eye out for it."

Freddy nodded. "Extra charges though."

Merk nodded. "That's not my problem. Ice won't have a problem either. Just call her." He rattled off the name of the shelter and the address. "The owner running the place is a potential connection to a murder case with long tentacles."

Freddy frowned. "I got no truck with that. Nobody should be touching women in this day and age. The fact that she's running an animal shelter, yeah, that's just low. I'll do this one for free." He snickered. "I presume you have somebody there on guard?"

That's when Merk remembered that Freddy knew Flynn and had to laugh. "You'll like this. Flynn's there."

Freddy's jaw dropped open. "Ha! Now that's perfect. What the hell did you do to get him to agree to that?"

Merk shook his head. "I didn't have anything to do with it. Levi did."

"Where the hell's Logan? I figured he'd be here with you."

Merk smirked. "Logan is in California, protecting some entertainer. A singer, I believe."

Freddy's jaw dropped for the second time. "Really? That's just too funny. Who'd have thought Logan would've fallen so bad that he'd be bodyguarding?"

Merk said, "There's no way I could do it, but somebody has to, and Logan was picked." Merk shook his head. "I think she might've known him before. So ..." He shrugged. "Logan got the short straw on that one."

Freddy chuckled. "I'm glad you stopped by. Haven't had this much fun for a long time. Just thinking about those two guys will keep me in laughter for years."

With a wave, Merk led Katina from the store. Walking down the sidewalk of the main street toward the restaurant, she said, "What the hell was that all about?"

He chuckled. "Just somebody else who the world doesn't have a clue about, but one who keeps an eye on the world. We've used Freddy for years. Levi has known him for decades. With any luck he'll still be around another couple decades because, when it comes to keeping an eye in the sky, he's dynamite."

"So can he really keep watch on our place and on Anna?"

"And on the compound," he said with a smile. "And, if

we can establish that your uncle is home, then Freddy'll keep an eye on him too."

"I had no idea such things were possible," she explained. "And, if I had known, I would've assumed it was done by a government agency, like a supersecret spy organization."

"In a way that's what we are. Don't forget, we were all top military in the past. We just transferred those skills to the private civilian arena. Getting the equipment and setting up the electronics, now that was a bit of a challenge. But we're slowly getting there." He tucked her arm into his and said, "People like Freddy give us the opportunity to do what we do. And that's to help people like you. Now a small place just around the corner is where I want to take you for dinner."

"Did you say dinner?" she said with a drawl of humor. "I was tempted to snack when I unpacked Alfred's basket but held off. I'm starved."

"I have no idea where you put it." Still, he liked to see a woman eat. He'd had enough of the kind who worried about eating a small salad. He understood the need to maintain whatever image the women were working on, but to be with somebody who didn't give a damn was a nice breath of fresh air—and still looked great.

He kept an eye out for anyone following them or appearing to watch them a little too closely. He didn't expect to find anything wrong this fast, but it was always possible. Particularly after meeting up with Freddy. If Merk was on anyone's radar, just going into Freddy's shop would trigger interest.

The restaurant was up ahead and around the corner. He pointed at the various stores. "This town is lost in time. They make fudge by hand, and a couple little coffee places still do the old-fashioned moka pot coffees, if you want an espresso the classic Italian way."

"Yes, to all of it," she said with a smile. "Hopefully we can try something different every day."

"That's exactly what I intend. No reason we can't enjoy our time here."

"Am I still to pretend I'm your girlfriend?" she teased. "Even when we're not with Freddy?"

"It's even more important to do so when we're not with Freddy. Freddy's the one who understands." He turned to look at her. "Will that be hard?"

"No," she said with a smile. "Honestly I have been clinging to your side for days now. Nothing's really different, except for unexpected memories I had never thought to revisit."

At the entranceway to the restaurant, he stopped and checked it out. "A little early for dinner. Do you want to go in and eat or keep walking?"

"Let's go in and eat. A walk afterward would be nice, and then we can head home. That should help me digest whatever it is I happen to be inhaling for dinner," she said with a smile.

He held the door open and ushered her in. After a final glance around he followed her. This was one of the cozy cafés, but the food had always been good. Assuming his memory served him well.

Soon they were settled at a small table by a big window. They could look down the street and see if anybody walked by. Few people were out as most folks had gone home for the day.

When the menu was placed in front of her, she leaned forward and said, "You do realize we didn't stop at the bank, and I don't have very much in the way of money."

He reached across and covered her hand with his. "And you do realize that you're not allowed to touch your cards at any point in time? Because anyone searching for you can trace when your cards are used. So this week you are to forget about money. We will cover the cost of everything. And, yes, that means you still get to eat."

Merk motioned toward the menu. "Order what you want."

Chapter 13

WALKING BACK AFTER dinner was a good idea, as her stomach needed to settle. The food was excellent but rich. She was afraid it would upset her system.

By the time they walked into the house, she felt fatigue pulling at her. Now that they were safe and a long way from the danger, the waves of tension and stress rolled off her back, taking all her energy with them. She yawned. "Sorry. That came out of nowhere."

She snuggled in close when Merk wrapped an arm around her shoulder. "You've been running on empty for a long time. A good night's sleep will help."

"Do we have anything set to do on any of the days we're here?" she asked. "Or can we just relax, go for walks, and sit and talk?"

"I have work to do on the laptop but, other than that, no. This is downtime."

"Oh, good." She tossed him a sideways glance and grinned. "Don't wake me up before ten tomorrow morning."

He looked at her, his eyebrows raised. "Are you serious? Ten o'clock? That's like noon." But he grinned wildly.

"So not noon. Inasmuch as I want to say ten o'clock, chances are I'll be awake at eight anyway."

"Well, I'll be up at six, so it doesn't matter. You can sleep as late as you need to."

She put a pot of water on the stove and searched the cupboards for tea. She found a few suspicious tea bags but wasn't sure she wanted to try them. However, Alfred had put some fresh lemons in the basket. She sliced one and made herself hot lemon water.

Merk watched her and said, "What were you looking for?"

"Tea, but it doesn't matter."

"We'll go shopping tomorrow." He searched the cupboards to see what was here, as if mentally doing a list in his head. He stopped at the fridge, saw the amount of food Alfred had packed which was still uneaten. "Actually, if we go out for one meal a day, we'll probably have food for the rest of the week," he exclaimed. "Alfred must think we eat a ton."

"Well, it seemed we ate almost one-third on the way up." She laughed. "He isn't far from wrong."

She took her lemon drink into the living room and sat down on the big couch. Merk sprawled out on the opposite couch. It wasn't very late, and, though she was tired, she wasn't quite tired enough to go to sleep. She pulled one of the pillows close to her and stretched out. "What did you do right after you left Vegas?" she asked curiously.

"Reported for duty." He turned to look at her. "I'd been serious. I was headed for my training immediately afterward."

She nodded. "I didn't think you'd lied."

"In Vegas, I think we have to expect there'd be lies."

That got a laugh out of her. "Since I was in college at the time, I just returned to campus with Anna and the other girls down there with us. Because we'd been in a group, my absence wasn't noticed like it would have been if it had been just Anna and me. They saw you and me, of course, so I was bugged decently on the way home, but I never said a word."

"But you did tell Anna about us?"

"I did but not right away." She raked her fingers through her hair, letting the strands of braid fall apart. "And it's a good thing I waited because she was pretty shocked and horrified as it was. If I had told her about it right away, she'd have screamed all the way home."

Katina smiled as she remembered. "When I called her a firecracker, I meant it. She spouted lots and blasted me for being a fool and a number of different names, but she's a really good person inside. When she calmed down, she wanted to know exactly how to get me clear of you."

"Does she know I'm in your life again?"

"Not in that way."

She realized that, although she'd told Anna that she was with Merk, but not in that way, it meant something different. She quickly added, "Just what you heard on the phone call."

"Ah." He settled back on the couch.

"Did you tell anybody back then?" she asked.

"Only my brother, Terkel. First off, I was headed for training. I didn't know anybody else around, so I had nobody to tell. By the time I met up with old friends, it wasn't something I wanted to bring up," he said drily. "Later I told my brother, but then he had a good idea already."

"Wow, really?"

He quickly explained about Terkel's "intuition" and their Creole grandma with the sight. That brought up several more questions. By the time they ran out of topics, they lay in companionable silence while she drank her hot lemon water. When she finished, she said, "I think I'll try to sleep now." She held up her phone and said, "Thanks for this phone."

"Not an issue. We also put a tracker in that for our purposes, in case you get separated from us so we can locate you," he said. "Just remember you can't do is tell anybody where you are."

"Right, secrecy." She stood up and carried her cup back to the kitchen and rinsed it out. Turning to him again, she said, "I'll shower and get into bed. I can always surf the web on my phone until I fall asleep." She walked to the stairs and called back, "Good night."

At the first landing she heard Merk say, "Good night. Have a good sleep." And caught sight of him heading back to his office.

She should have gone to her room earlier. He obviously had work to do and didn't feel he could do it while she was with him.

At the top of stairs she wondered where he'd put her bags, but, as she glanced into the master bedroom, she realized he'd given her the suite. She smiled in delight. This house wasn't fancy, but it was different. And she really appreciated those differences.

Wandering into the bathroom, she squealed in delight at the really big bathtub. "This is what I'll do first."

She closed the bedroom door and quickly unpacked the few things she'd brought. If she would be here five or six days, she might as well enjoy it.

She bent down to plug the tub and then turned on the water. A selection of bubble bath packets and bath oils were on the side. She chose one, dumped in a liberal amount. She found a guest bathrobe, brought it into the bathroom with her, and quickly stripped down. When she settled herself into the bubble bath, she gave a moan of delight.

How long had it been since she'd just sat back and relaxed and enjoyed the moment? It seemed like forever.

She could hear voices below, but she presumed Merk was on the phone using the Speaker option. They hadn't had any visitors, and she hadn't heard anybody else come in.

She lay in the water until it cooled and then dressed in her nightclothes, which consisted of panties and an oversized T-shirt, and crawled into bed. Within minutes, she turned out the lights and tried to sleep.

But she couldn't. Not that she wasn't tired, because she was, and not that she wasn't relaxed, because she was. She just couldn't shut off her mind. Knowing so much had happened, and, just because she had the chance to shut everything down and rest, it didn't mean it was so easy to do. She got up and grabbed her laptop, turning it on. She couldn't really reply to the emails, other than to tell people she was fine and off on a vacation.

With that done, she brought up a webpage and checked out this area of New Mexico. What were the attractions? They should have picked up a brochure in one of the stores, but she hadn't thought of it at the time. With the lamp on, the pillow bunched up behind her back, she was comfy and cozy in bed.

Light footsteps sounded outside her door. She smiled. She already recognized Merk's approach. At the knock on her door, she said, "Come in."

Merk pushed open the door and stuck his head around the wooden panel. "I thought you'd be asleep by now."

"I can't sleep. I did try, but my head just won't shut down. So I did some web surfing, finding out more about this place and seeing what there was to do."

He frowned at the laptop. "That's the first I've seen you with a laptop."

"Oh." She peered over the top of the screen at him. "Does it matter?"

"Not unless it's being tracked." He slowly approached, his gaze on the machine in her hands.

"I've never taken it to work, and I lived alone, so I don't know how someone would've put in a tracking device."

"How long have you had it?"

"Over a year. This laptop is where I saw the first email asking me, *Where is it?*"

Interest piqued in his gaze. "Do you have those emails?"

She nodded and brought up her email program. She'd actually filed all the emails in specific folders. She brought up the folder and opened it so he could see. She turned the laptop slightly so he could have a better view.

"Do you mind?" he asked with his hands out.

She handed him the laptop. Drawing her knees up to her chest, she waited while he searched through the emails.

"I'll forward these to Levi, if you're okay with that."

She nodded. "I would have done it earlier if I knew you needed them."

"I understand. This comes under the heading of *you don't know what you need to know if you don't ask the right questions.*"

"Exactly." At least he wasn't blaming her for not having shown him earlier. She would have, but it had slipped her mind and obviously had slipped theirs as well. She waited in silence for him to finish whatever he was doing.

"Is there anything else on this laptop that would be of interest?"

She glanced from the laptop to him and frowned. "I

can't imagine that there would be, but feel free to look around."

She only had the one laptop because she assumed she'd need it, but, in truth, she never really did. She played some games on it, wrote a few emails, but she had a work laptop and that's where she spent most of her time. In truth, she'd wondered about just getting a tablet next time.

THEY WENT TO the office where he plugged in a second machine and set up a program to run through her laptop. It did a couple searches, plus a diagnostic. He doubted there'd be any trackers, but he wasn't taking any chances. Somebody had obviously known her personal email address and had sent these anonymous emails to her. They were of interest only for the fact that somebody knew she had something she wasn't supposed to have.

He glanced at her and said, "Go on to bed. This will take a while."

She crossed her arms over her chest and tapped her foot lightly on the floor. "In no known universe are you allowed to give me orders and I am to follow them."

He glanced at her in surprise, then grinned. "I always liked that spunk in you."

She snorted and sat down. "You didn't have long to like anything about me. Let's get real. We had sex. We got married. We had more sex. We got divorced, and we parted. The end."

He laughed. "We certainly didn't need the paperwork to have sex," he said with a leer. "We could have done just fine without that."

"Sad but true. I haven't had a drop of tequila since."

He shook his head. "Neither have I."

The two smiled in understanding at each other. He really loved the fact that they could joke about it like they were. In a casual tone, his gaze on the laptops in front of them, he said, "Did you ever wonder if we should have adjusted, you know, to being married and given it a try?" Because he wasn't looking at her, he hadn't really registered her response until the odd silence came through. He lifted his gaze and studied her.

And then she cracked up.

Slightly affronted he asked, "What? What did I say?"

She giggled. "You thinking that maybe we should have given it a shot." She shook her head as mirth shook her shoulders. "What, another shot of tequila?"

"I wasn't that drunk."

"Yes, you were. And so was I." When she finally sputtered to a stop, her shoulders slightly shaking with the humor still in her, she added, "I never gave it a serious thought. I wondered what the hell I was thinking in the first place, but I never thought about prolonging that madness by staying married to you."

He wondered if he was supposed to be insulted over that. "Was I such a poor catch?"

"I have no idea," she said candidly. "It's not like we knew each other at all. We don't know the first thing about each other."

"But something lured us together," he said honestly. "Not just a physical attraction—but I really liked that too. You were funny. You were honest. Something about you was just"—he shrugged his shoulders—"attractive."

"A man of few words," she said with a smile. "But you're right. We had a good time, then it was over."

He nodded and gazed at the laptops. "Still, a part of me wonders *what if?*" he said.

"It's too late to wonder *what if?*" she said calmly. "You've moved on and probably had a dozen-plus relationships since, and I've moved on and had a couple." She looked at him pointedly. "And, if you're honest with yourself, you know there was no future for us."

"Back then," he admitted. "But I'm not that person anymore." He waved his arms wide open to encompass the house. "Although the work I did and now do are similar," he said, his smile widening, "back then I wasn't thinking permanency either. Through the years, when—or if—I was out on dangerous missions, I had short-term relationships because I never knew if, one time, I wasn't coming back."

Instantly her humor died. "Were your missions that dangerous?"

He eyed her slowly and then nodded. "Yes. They were generally. We did what nobody else could do. When the final mission blew up in our faces, in a way, I figured it was something I had expected all along to happen, which had finally happened, and we deserved it. We had luck with us for so long, but we knew, at one point, our luck would run out."

"Did you have good luck charms or something to keep you safe?" she asked, half-joking.

"I had something better actually. My brother."

At that, she leaned forward, interest in her eyes. "What do you mean? Was he on the mission with you?"

"No. Remember my brother has my grandmother's gift of sight? He often warned us ahead of time if things would go sideways."

"Did he warn you on this one?"

He stared at her for a long moment and then nodded. "He said he could see something was really bad about the whole deal. But we couldn't take the chance of those people getting away. Terkel told us not to go, but we all made the decision to go anyway."

"Even after he told you not to? I bet he didn't think much of that."

"No, he hasn't warned us too much since," Merk said. "He said something about us not wasting his time. If he gives us intel, we should make good use of it."

"I bet he tells you if it's important though." She sat back and nodded. "Families are like that."

"How do you know? You don't have much family."

"I used to. My parents divorced a long time ago. I was bounced from one home to the other. They both had new families, and I was this third wheel, hanging on from a previous life that neither wanted to acknowledge." She stared out the window and said, "I left as soon as I could. Not for me." She waved her hand. "Now they have completely different partners."

"So you didn't go to them when you had trouble."

Her gaze zinged in his direction again. She said with absolute finality, "No."

He nodded. "My brother and I are quite close. We're twins actually. But he got the gift of sight, and I didn't." It never really bothered him until that mission blew up in his face. If only he'd listened, he would have stopped the entire team from going. But it seemed like he was bullheaded, filled with drive and ambition. And stupidity.

"Anybody else besides your brother has that insight?"

Merk shook his head. "No, and my grandmother passed away a couple years back."

"Did she know? Did she see what was coming for herself?"

"I don't know if she did," he admitted. "She died when I was on a mission. But what I do know is Terkel knew. He warned me that she would go while I was out of the country, and the following week she passed away."

She smiled knowingly at him.

"What are you smiling at?"

"Because I know you went to see her before it happened, didn't you?"

He leaned back in his chair and glared at her. "You don't know that."

"Yes, I do. You're just that kind of guy."

Chapter 14

KATINA WOKE THE next morning with a smile on her face. She'd slept like a dream. She'd left the office last night soon after their conversation and went up to bed. Her mood was lighthearted and fun. She was afraid she was falling for him all over again. No, she knew she was. He was right. They had come together for a reason in the first place, and that attraction was hard to let go of. Even now that same feeling still remained over a decade later. It was just amazing.

Now that he brought it up, she had to wonder *what if?*

As she lay in bed, the morning sun shining on her face, she realized one *what if* was that she could have had a family and a loving life. Living the dream.

Alternatively that might have changed something in his world, and he would not be doing the work he was doing, or he could have been killed on a mission because something about her had distracted him.

In reality, she understood that things happened for a reason. But that gave her leeway to think that maybe they had come together for a second chance for another reason. That she was sleeping alone here was also unique because Merk had been a hotheaded sexual male; he oozed sexuality, unlike any other man she'd met. She figured, with just the two of them staying in this house together, they'd end up in bed sooner or later. She had to consider, was she ready for that?

And the answer was yes. Even if it was just for the experience. Maybe a reacquaintance, to see if it was as good as she remembered. She smiled. He'd love that. "Let's go to bed to see if we're still as good as we were."

She shook her head. So not happening.

She bounded off the bed, dressed in clean clothes, brushed her hair back, putting it into a single braid down her back, grabbed a sweater, and walked downstairs.

And of course he was already up, drinking coffee at the kitchen table.

"Did you go to bed?" she asked as she poured herself a cup. She turned to the table and sat down beside him.

"I did."

"Did you find anything in the computer last night?"

He shook his head. "Nothing's shown up yet. I wasn't really expecting it to, but I needed to make sure."

She understood and appreciated the thoroughness.

"Any update on Anna and what was his name? ... Flynn?"

He nodded with a smile. "Apparently the two are slamming sparks off each other."

She thought about it and shook her head. "I wish I was a fly on the wall. It would be great entertainment."

He studied her. "Looks like you had a good night's sleep."

"Like a baby," she announced with a smile. "What's on the agenda for today?"

He let her lead the conversation as they discussed their shopping to be done—what groceries they wanted to pick up and any other household items they might need.

Just the thought of all that food made her hungry. She

got up and opened the fridge, brought out some of the treats Alfred had packed for them. She didn't want any of it to go to waste.

Together they munched through their breakfast as they made plans. With the sun shining outside, it would be another glorious day. She found no lake with her search for local things to do, but she'd love to go for a swim.

"Is there a place to go swimming around here?"

"There could be a few rivers but not in the immediate area. Not within walking distance."

"Okay. Maybe another day."

"We'll be staying within walking distance for the week," he said. "At least until we see if there's any repercussions from all the mail outs."

She froze. "I forgot they went out yesterday." She stared out the window blindly. "It could take them two or three days to go across the country."

"Levi's already getting phone calls, because, don't forget, everything went out digitally first."

"Great. So, then what?"

"People have to sort through the information, verify its validity, and then start the rounds of interviews and tie up the evidence." He gave her a reassuring smile. "The journalist is ferreting out more information, and the DA has requested a meeting with Levi. It's all moving. Let time do its thing."

She nodded. "We're dreaming if we think we'll be here only one week, right?"

"Stay positive. Now that the right people have the information, we need them to act."

"That's one of the things I learned about life. Just because someone does something, it doesn't mean the rest of the world has the same idea."

He smiled at her. "And we have nothing better to do than spend the week here and enjoy it. So let's head back downtown and get some shopping done."

She stood and grabbed the dishes off the table. As she washed them, he grabbed a tea towel and quickly dried the dishes, putting them away. Another ten minutes and they were walking out the front door.

She stopped on the doorstep and looked at the neighborhood, a big hill rising behind their nice house nestled into the bush with the driveway heading straight toward the road. She wanted to go for a walk by herself a little later. When he stepped beside her, they headed down the driveway and back on the pathway to town.

"Can we stop by Freddy's?"

He nodded. "Every day if you want."

"Okay. Routines are good for me."

She linked her hand with his, and they chatted about seemingly useless stuff. But, to her, they gave her an insight into who he was. She talked about flowers, talked about animals—getting his view on animal shelters for Anna's sake—and talked about food. She learned he absolutely adored steak. He was male. He also had a sweet tooth for homemade apple pie, and he was a mean cook of Creole food, a skill handed down from his grandma. They discussed a few dishes they might buy the ingredients for and would cook later. By the time they walked into the grocery store, she was feeling very much like they were partners. Certainly good friends.

That set the pattern. Every morning they got up, had breakfast and coffee, figured out what to buy for their dinner and walked to the stores in town. They went out for lunch sometimes, and occasionally they stopped for coffee in the small café. Every day they stopped in to see Freddy. So far everything was good.

On the morning of the fourth day, she got up to find heavy clouds and rain. "Phooey." But she dressed just a little warmer and walked downstairs.

Instead of seeing Merk at the kitchen table in his usual spot, coffee in hand, she had to track him down in the office. "Problems?"

"Movement," he said. "The DA's office is busy picking up various members of the company."

"Oh, that's excellent," she said with joy in her voice. "Maybe this will be over sooner than later."

"Not necessarily." He looked at her and said, "Don't forget they have to have more than just what you gave for proof. But they have agents with search warrants at the company right now. So, with any luck, they can check some of these files."

"I have log-ins and passwords," she offered immediately. "I never thought to give them to you earlier as I'd already given you all the information I had accessed with them."

He froze and turned toward her. "Pardon?"

"Remember, I have a photographic memory," she said. "I can give them passwords, file names, and the log-ins." She shrugged. "I can't say it's for everything, but it's what I have, and maybe it'll help them get access."

She sat down, and he tossed a pad of paper at her. She carefully wrote down everything she could remember about all the log-ins she'd seen and used. When she handed her list back to him, he immediately typed it up.

She walked into the kitchen to grab another coffee. Her mood was good. It might be dark and gray outside, but this was progress, and she was happy with that. She filled her cup and went back to the office. Realizing his cup was empty, she went to get him a refill. By time she returned, he was cross-referencing what she'd written to what he'd typed.

"I'm sending this off to Levi and Ice. They can forward it to the DA's office." Then he leaned back and looked at her. "That's done now. Hopefully that'll help them get the information they need." He picked up the coffee cup and held it up to her. "Thanks for this."

"No problem," she said. "So now the routine day-to-day thing?"

"To a certain extent. We'll check in with Freddy. Then maybe, instead of grocery shopping, we could have lunch at that French place he talked about."

She nodded. "I slept late, so I'm not terribly hungry for breakfast."

She finally realized how late it was when she got up to refill her third cup of coffee and saw the time on the coffee-pot. No wonder he hadn't been in the kitchen waiting for her. She was an hour later than usual. But she also had good news to share. She turned and said, "I heard from my uncle. He sent me a text saying he was in California at a friend's, and he was fine." She beamed. "So one less person to worry about."

"Excellent. I'm sorry about the rest of your family not being close."

"Definitely not an easy way to grow up. There were no constants. Nothing to count on. It surprised me when I married you so fast. Then, when it instantly fell apart, it seemed like a repeat of my life. Something I thought would be there, wasn't." She gave him a quiet smile. "Live and learn."

"Learning to trust is huge," he said quietly. "I've been

dealing with that a lot this last year in my work. But it bleeds into other parts of our lives even though we do our best not to let it. Still, we have to begin somewhere."

"So are we starting here—with us?" she asked abruptly. "Are we really looking at a relationship together? One where we can count on each other?"

"I'd like that," he said with a smile. "Is that why you didn't tell anyone about your photographic memory?"

She nodded. "Growing up, my siblings hated me for it. Anytime I used it, they'd get me into trouble. So I struggled with that along with that whole 'who is going to be there for me' thing."

He finished his coffee and stood, saying, "How about we head downtown? By the time we're done, we should be ready for an early lunch."

"That works for me." She filled the coffee cups with soapy water to soak while they were gone, turned off the pot, and waited at the door for him. She already had her sweater on. It was just that kind of a day. When he joined her, he took one last look around, double-checked that everything was locked, then wrapped an arm around her shoulders. "Let's go."

HE DIDN'T KNOW how truly perceptive she was, like, if she had noticed he double-checked the locks in the office, the kitchen, and then the front door. She probably understood they had entered a very different phase now—where people understood what kind of information she'd brought to life.

The truth was, things had started the day before yesterday, but only now was the word getting out to the public. Levi had called to warn them, not that Merk needed the heads-up. He knew how dangerous this next step was. They were all looking out for her. His job was to ensure no one found her.

So far his brother hadn't called. He'd take that as a good sign.

"First stop is Freddy's."

"Okay," she said amiably.

He really liked that about her. She knew when to follow orders, and apparently she also knew when to tell him off for giving orders. He grinned at the reminder of their conversation a few nights before.

As they walked down the street, the clouds above looked like they would dump on them.

"We should have brought umbrellas."

"I don't have any," he admitted. "We may have to stop in for coffee before lunch."

But they made it to the store before the rain came down. As they walked into the gloomy storefront, she asked, "Does he ever clean out here?"

"That would bring customers in," he said drily. "I don't think he wants anything to do with that."

That got a laugh out of her.

He tapped on the bell on the front counter and waited for Freddy to come out. But, when Merk had no sign of Freddy, Merk hit the bell several more times. The old guy could be in the bathroom.

When still no answer came, he held a finger to his lips and whispered, "Stay here."

He walked to the beaded curtain and peered through it. He couldn't see anything because of the boxes in the doorway. He would have to move them, and that would give away his position. Damn.

Moving as fast as he could, he slipped behind and stayed low as he snuck past the boxes, to the point where the room opened up in front of him. Freddy had it arranged so nobody could see anything until they reached the center of his big electronic shop. The monitors were off. He checked out the back room further, in case Freddy had collapsed on the floor from a heart attack, but no sign of him was anywhere.

He frowned. Merk walked back to the front of the store and brought Katina into the back room with him. "It's unlike him to step out of the store."

"He has to go home sometime," she said calmly. "Maybe he's gone for an early lunch himself."

Merk nodded. "Anything's possible." But as he continued to prowl the room, Merk walked past the back door, slightly ajar. He pushed it open and stepped out to check the alleyway—and froze. He'd just found Freddy, dead beside the Dumpster.

Merk needed to check things out here, but he didn't want her inside alone. With this new development, he turned and called in a low voice, "Katina, come here." When she walked out to him, he grabbed her hand and tucked her up close. That's when she saw the body.

She slapped a hand over her mouth. "Oh, no," she cried softly. "Did he die of natural causes?" she whispered into her hand with hope.

He walked over to study the body. As he got closer, he could see the blood pooling underneath his face. Because of a slight incline to the alley, the blood ran underneath the Dumpster. Now that Merk was close enough, he could see the gunshot wound at the temple.

"Damn." He turned to look at Katina and said, "He's

been shot."

She immediately stepped back to hug the door, her hand still over her mouth, staring at him wordlessly. He'd seen way too much in his life to be surprised by anything, but he hated to see this happen to Freddy. He was one of the good guys.

Immediately a gun fired close by and hit the metal Dumpster beside them. Instantly the sound of racing footsteps receded.

Merk bolted back inside, dragging Katina with him. He shoved her behind the desks and raced to the side of the door and peered out, weapon ready.

The alley was empty. Then it had been empty before.

Shit. He turned back to her. "Stay here. I'll do a quick sweep of the area. Stay hidden. I won't be long." With a hard look to make sure she understood, he waited for her response. She quickly nodded and slipped farther out of sight. Good thing. He slipped outside and raced in the direction the footsteps had gone. As Freddy's was the last store on the block, Merk peered around the corner but found nothing. He could feel that the asshole was gone, but he couldn't prove it. He tucked the gun under his shirt and quickly walked to the front of the block, searching for a likely killer.

Nothing.

Back at the store he stepped into the entrance from the alley and called out, "Katina?"

"Here." She stepped from her hiding place and raced into his arms.

"You're safe. He's long gone." Holding her close, Merk pulled out his phone and called Levi. When he answered, Merk gave him the details. Much swearing followed on the other end.

"Okay, I'll phone his boss and let them know. You call the local police and get that in progress."

"I can do that." After Merk hung up, he turned to Katina. "I have to call the police. In the meantime, Levi'll contact Freddy's company."

A frown line formed between her brows. "Freddy's company?"

Merk nodded. "Freddy was part of a network. We'll see what ends up happening to the store after this."

"And does that mean whoever killed him saw all that he was keeping an eye on?" she asked nervously. "Is Anna safe? Are we safe?"

"In this situation, we have to assume the worst," he said quietly. "Let me call the police, then I have to take care of the shop."

She stared at him from the doorway, her gaze going from inside to outside, and said, "But, if the police come here, they'll know what he was doing too, won't they?"

"Yes. That's something the company will have to deal with."

She turned to look inside again. "We should shut everything down then?"

He hesitated for a moment, then said, "Let's do that first, in case the police get here in the next five minutes."

She frowned at him. "There won't actually be any police in a small town like this, will there? Wouldn't they have to come from the closest city?"

He nodded. "I suspect so."

"We can't leave him lying out there like that for the flies."

Just then his phone rang. It was Levi. "I called the cops myself. They are sending an officer down this afternoon, probably take an hour and a half. Can you cover up the body to hide it from passersby?"

Merk nodded. "We were just working on that." And then he spied a series of boxes. "I can cover him up with cardboard. But if anybody comes back here, it's going to look suspicious."

"Take pictures now. Then cover him up and wait until the police and the forensics team get there."

"Okay, got it."

Merk took a few pictures with his cell phone, then walked back inside to look for something better to cover Freddy with. On the back of the door was an old blanket. He took it out and carefully covered the old man. Then using the boxes, he built up a wall around him. At least for the short term, it might keep the general public from seeing him. When Merk turned around, he found Katina, standing in the open doorway, tears in her eyes.

"It doesn't seem fair. He was a good man. He didn't deserve this."

"The hard fact of life is nobody deserves this," Merk said as he calmly ushered her back inside. "We'll keep an eye on him until the police arrive. According to Levi, that should be about ninety minutes. In the meantime, we have things to do here."

He systematically went through the back room and shut down all the machines. Then he carefully moved all the tables against the one wall, so they were all stacked up, as if not in use. He brought two more tables over, setting them up with some of the dusty old equipment from the front shelves, placing them in a way that made it look like Freddy was doing some repairs. Merk also remembered to lock the front door and to switch the sign from Open to Closed.

He turned back to her and said, "Now to wait."

She glanced down at her watch. "It's already been forty-five minutes. They could be here anytime."

He nodded and took one last glance around the place, hating that now they would be blind everywhere, and led her to the alleyway. "I'd feel better if I stand guard out back," he said. "I don't want to leave him alone."

She smiled mistily up at him. "Nobody should be left alone like this."

Chapter 15

W HEN THE POLICE finally arrived, she found them both efficient and cold. Not only did they not know the victim, they didn't know the town. At least not very well. They asked a few questions, which she and Merk answered easily, then they were ushered out of the way.

Merk grabbed her hand and told the officer they were heading to the little French restaurant in town for lunch.

By the look on the guys' faces, Katina didn't think they had heard Merk.

Although she wasn't hungry, she knew she needed to eat because they didn't know what they were facing now. The curtain of safety had just been ripped away. They'd entered a whole new ball game.

As they walked away from the alley, she said, "Worst case scenario, we have to assume we've been found. One of those monitors showed the house we were staying in."

He nodded and, in a low voice, said, "But, unless they happen to be locals, they wouldn't know where it was."

"Yet it wouldn't take much to ask a local," she countered. "Everybody would know."

Again he nodded.

When they got to the restaurant, he pushed open the door, and the two of them entered. The place was half full, and they took a seat in the back. A waitress with a big smile handed them menus.

Katina studied it but didn't see anything that appealed. He didn't even open his. She placed hers on top of his and said, "Good. Order whatever you want for both of us. I'll be in the bathroom."

She got up and walked back to the ladies' room, a small single room. She locked the door, hung her purse on the wall hook, and just stood, staring at herself in the mirror.

What a hell of a morning. She was so damn sad about Freddy. She lifted her hands, saw her fingers tremble. What the hell would they do now? Turning on the hot water, she briskly washed her face and then turned the water to cold, wet a paper towel, and patted it on her cheeks. She had to get a grip. Events weren't going back to the way they had been. She'd had her vacation. She'd had a few days of an idyllic lifestyle—a few days to forget. But that was it.

The reality of the situation stared back at her. People were being killed over the information she'd found.

She used the facilities, washed her hands once again, then grabbed her purse, and walked out to the larger room. She couldn't stop looking around this time because anybody in this restaurant could have killed that nice old man. At least, she told herself, the way he'd been shot, she doubted he'd suffered much.

Sitting at the table once again, she leaned forward and said, "Do you think he walked outside willingly, or was he at gunpoint?"

"I don't think it was willingly."

She nodded. "Did he shut off the monitors? They weren't on when we went in."

He looked at her and smiled. "I wondered if you noticed that."

"Do you think he knew?"

"Fred was a canny old codger who was wise in the ways of the world. I think he had some idea he might be in trouble."

She wondered why she hadn't seen it before. "I'm not cut out for this," she said. "It's only just now I wondered."

"Don't worry about it. Stress will do strange things to you."

She realized the menus were gone and in their place were two steaming cups of coffee. She cradled her cup gratefully. "What did you order?"

He said, his gaze intent on sending texts, "It's a surprise. Wait and see."

She nodded and had to be satisfied with that.

Finally the waitress returned and set down two plates full of crepes.

Katina grinned. "Oh, this looks wonderful. Thank you."

The waitress beamed, left, and returned with a big bowl of whipping cream and another of fresh blueberries. As she turned to walk away again, she said, "Help yourself to both, dear."

Nobody needed to tell Katina twice. She split the blueberries between her and Merk's plates, then dumped liberal splotches of whipping cream on top both. And still he didn't lift his face from his phone. She kicked him lightly under the table. He lifted his head and frowned at her. She nodded toward the plate at his side and said, "Eat."

He glanced at it and put his phone down. "Well, this looks lovely." He pulled it toward him, and then there was silence.

As soon as they finished, she knew they'd be leaving. What she didn't know was if they were actually leaving the house too. Because she hadn't been terribly smart.

She hadn't left everything packed, ready to run. In fact she'd unpacked everything and made herself at home. That thinking had come to a sudden, irrefutable end. She needed at least a half hour to collect all her stuff again. Foolish. If they were going home to something very ugly, she wouldn't have that much time.

Mentally she sorted through the items she had sprawled out, figuring out what she would take if she only had a few seconds.

By the time they paid and were walking outside, she realized that, if they were going home, they were going a different route. "Are we hiding our tracks?"

"Not necessarily, but we're climbing up the ridge to look down at the house. We're not walking toward the house like we normally do because, if anybody's watching, they'd see us before we made them."

"Right. I'll pack up as soon as we get home."

He nodded. "Good, it's for the best."

Her shoulders sagged for a long moment, then she bolstered herself with the knowledge that, so far, she was alive. Fred hadn't had that option. "It is what it is."

"That's my girl." He reached out and caught her hand as they climbed up the hill behind the house.

Once there, he dropped her hand and took the lead. She was in good shape, but she wasn't in fantastic shape. Merk was definitely in fantastic shape. He slowed his pace so she could keep up. By the time they made it to the crest of the hill, she was huffing and puffing.

He led her across the top of the ridge and then crouched, telling her, "Stay as low as you can."

And again she wasn't anywhere near as graceful as he

was, but she crouched down and kept moving fairly low.

Finally they came to the spot where they could look down on the property. Instead of him standing there, staring, he actually sat down cross-legged and waited. She joined him. "What are we waiting for?"

But he didn't answer; instead he studied the layout. She realized they would not be leaving this ridge until he was sure it was safe. In truth, she agreed with that, but she didn't know how long it would take. So she settled back to wait.

They didn't have to wait long. Forty minutes later, during which she'd shifted her position a couple times while Merk sat still at her side, she saw somebody come out the back door and stand on the small deck. She froze. The man's gaze never lifted to where they sat. He did a quick search, then turned and walked back into the house.

In a furious whisper, she said, "Who the hell was that?"

His voice low and deadly, Merk answered, "I'd guess the man who killed Freddy."

MERK LAUGHED INWARDLY at her inability to sit still. She probably thought she was doing really well in that department, but then she'd fidgeted with her fingers and hands. She had straightened her legs, then tucked them underneath, even rocked back and forth.

Whereas he'd been quite capable of sitting and just resting in a moment of stillness. He had had enough practice at it. His training had been brutal. As he sat, he considered. The man he'd seen, was he alone? And why had he come out on the back porch? There was no need for that. Merk wished he had his binoculars with him, then he would have a better idea of who all was in the house. As it was, Merk and Katina would have to creep back down the way they'd come and wait until dark to sneak into the house.

Just as he made that decision, a vehicle drove up the driveway. He frowned as it disappeared around the front of the house. He didn't recognize the truck. A few minutes later the vehicle backed out and turned, disappearing down the street toward the village. One man had driven in; two men had left.

Did that mean the house was empty? Or had he left bugs and camera equipment in lieu of manpower?

Merk had choices to make. But the outcome of those choices could be deadly. He didn't want Katina anywhere close to the place. He needed to go in and check it out himself.

Had they taken anything? His laptop was there, but he'd put it away in the drawer. Depended on how well they had searched the place.

He turned to her. "Where's your laptop?"

"I was watching a movie on it last night," she said, "so it was on the bed." She shrugged. "I was just thinking today, after we found Freddy, how lax I got and left my stuff everywhere." She looked over at him. "Do we need to stay here on this hill?"

"I want *you* to stay here," he said. "I'll slip down and see if the house is empty."

"And if it isn't? Can you handle one intruder, ... two intruders?"

He nodded. "That's no problem. The problem is whether they left bugs behind and/or a security system or video camera feed. If they had an hour, that would've been long enough to set up something simple. And we've been in town enough to get noticed. That's an automatic reason to check."

"I guess the neighbors would know the house wasn't empty."

"It's not as much the neighbors, because, as you can see, nobody is close, but the villagers always know." He studied her face intently. "You're okay to stay here?"

She nodded. He leaned over and kissed her hard on the lips. "I'll be back."

At that, she said, "You promise?"

"I promise."

At a light run he went down the hill, staying away from the rocks in his path. He didn't stop to look behind where he'd left her. He kept his eye on the house and on the windows, in case anybody saw him. With the momentum he had going, he used it to swing himself up onto the porch where the man had stepped out. There were stairs on the side, but he didn't want to do the expected.

He landed lightly and pressed against the wall, waiting to see if the door would open. But no sound could be heard from the inside. He tested the door and found it unlocked. He pushed it open and slipped inside. He stopped just inside the entrance and listened. As far as he could tell, the house was empty, had a hollow echo to it.

He looked up in the hallway and searched for camera feeds. They could be hard to find, depending on how well hidden they were. He presumed they actually had that kind of equipment. The men had to confirm Katina was here, and then they could come back with more men.

He moved through the lower floor and found nothing missing, nothing disturbed. Which was interesting in itself. Had they searched the place? At the office door he stopped, and it looked relatively undisturbed. He found his laptop still inside the bottom drawer where he'd left it. Then again it had a mechanism underneath to open it, and it didn't look like a drawer.

None of this was by chance. They'd spent a lifetime dealing with this kind of stuff. Even the furniture had been picked out for such reasons. He moved swiftly to the base of the stairs and crept up to the top floor.

One swift pass let him know the place was empty. He checked Katina's room first. She was right. Discarded clothing, blankets, and tossed pillows were all around her room. Not a mess but it was in disarray. However, it didn't look like anything had been searched. But a woman obviously was staying here. She had her purse on her, so nothing was left behind to identify the woman was Katina.

Except her laptop. He'd deal with that later.

He hadn't seen any sign of cameras up to this point. But he didn't trust it. It felt like somebody had been completely through the place. And that wasn't good. He walked over to his room with that same sense of somebody having been here. Also not good. If there were cameras, he couldn't afford to be seen.

At the closet, he pulled a pillowcase off the shelf and, with his pocketknife, quickly cut two holes and pulled it over his head. Then he walked into her room casually. Calmly and efficiently he packed up all her stuff. She'd brought two bags, and, sure enough, both were well stuffed by the time he was done. He made the bed and cleaned up the bathroom of toiletries, then carried the bags to the top of stairs and picked up his already packed bag. On a mission he was never anything but ready.

Carrying everything downstairs, including her laptop, he walked over to the office and grabbed his laptop. With one last look around, he headed to the kitchen, then to the back door. They had often walked out from here. He laid the bags and the laptop on the back porch and turned to look up at her, and waved, letting her know all was okay.

In the kitchen he pulled out Alfred's basket from the closet and proceeded to quickly pack up everything they had that was edible. The rest he threw in the garbage and secured the trash bag. They'd have to drop it down the road. He had no time to dispose of it right now.

The keys to the truck were hidden in it, and the vehicle was in the garage. He headed back to the porch, grabbed the bags, carried them down the stairs and opened up the garage door, thankful the truck was still here. Using up valuable time, he dumped what he was carrying into the back, opened the glove box, pulled out a tester, and quickly scanned the vehicle. When it came up clean, he raced inside for the rest of their belongings. By the time he had cleaned up the rest of the garbage he'd left, she stood at the bottom of the hill. Furious he turned to her and snapped, "I told you to stay there."

"And yet you waved. I thought that meant everything was okay." She shrugged. "I was wondering if you needed to pack up anything." She stopped and looked at him. "Why are you wearing that?"

He frowned and then realized she was referring to the pillowcase. He pulled it off his head and said, "Damn it. Get into the truck. We're done."

"Should I take a last look and see if you forgot anything? Did you grab all my clothes, toiletries, and my laptop?"

He nodded. "Unless you hid anything?"

Instantly she shook her head. "No, I promise."

He motioned toward the truck. "Get in."

He pulled the pillowcase back over his head and walked

through the house one last time, then quickly locked all the doors. Back at the garage, he hopped into the truck, took off the pillowcase again, and cranked the engine. And realized she was no longer sitting inside.

He bolted from the truck and raced around to the passenger side.

To see a man holding a gun to her throat.

Merk swore like the sailor he was. Where the hell had that asshole come from?

"Stay where you are, and she won't get hurt."

"Like hell," Katina said bitterly. "You'll kill me, like you did Freddy."

"Not if you're good." He pulled her back toward the side door leading to the yard, likely the way he'd come in after seeing Katina come down the hill.

"Piss off," she snapped and slammed her elbow into his gut, spinning and jamming his gun up toward the ceiling. A shot went off.

Merk was on him in two seconds, and the asshole was on the floor, out cold. Merk snagged Katina into his arms and buried his face in her neck. "Dear God, I could have lost you."

She was crying uncontrollably against his chest. He'd have done anything to save her from this. He gave her a moment, then gently moved her to the truck's passenger door. It was even more important to get the hell out now.

And easier to lift her up than to get her to let go. Finally he untangled her arms from around his neck.

"We have to leave before he comes to or his buddies return, but first I need to find out who this man is."

She nodded and swiped at her teary eyes.

He dropped to the unconscious man and emptied his

pockets. Opening the wallet, Merk found the man's driver's license with a matching photo, cash, and several credit cards all pointing to the man being Samuel Cheevers.

"Let me see," she whispered, now beside him. "You called Levi?"

Good idea. He dumped the bits and pieces in her lap and stepped back to take a picture of the man. He quickly sent that to Levi and followed up with an even faster phone call.

When he was done, Katina handed back the man's belongings and said, "There's no point in keeping his wallet."

Levi tossed it on the ground beside the man, then walked to the driver's side of the truck. By now a sense of urgency was riding him—hard.

All of this had taken too long. If the asshole's buddies were coming back, they were likely on the way. So Merk and Katina would be caught leaving. He made it outside the garage, hit the button to close the door, hiding the prone man inside, then slowly drove down the driveway, and took the corner. He headed in the opposite direction of the truck he'd seen earlier and gunned it.

With any luck they'd made it free and clear. But he didn't live in a world of luck. He usually found he had to make his own because damn little of it was handed out for free.

Chapter 16

S HE WONDERED HOW long it would take for her to relax enough to realize they were safe. Merk had been driving like a crazy man for an hour already, and she kept looking behind to see if they were followed. It would be a long time before she forgot the sensation of someone holding a gun to her. Still she'd gotten free, and Merk had taken him down.

She could be proud of that.

Yet tension coiled in her stomach like a snake ready to take her out.

Finally she forced herself to relax by practicing a few deep-breathing techniques.

"Feeling better?" Merk asked, his voice calm and quiet as it floated through the truck. He was obviously used to dealing with this kind of nightmare.

"I am, a little bit, yes."

"Nice job back there."

"Thanks. We made a good team," she admitted. "You don't realize just how badly your muscles are knotted until you try to unknot them. Where are we going now?"

"Another house, different state."

And that was all he offered. It really didn't matter. As long as nobody was shooting at them, she was good. The thought of being separated from Merk right now was terrifying. He was big, solid, a dependable barrier between her and those nasty assholes.

"How long do you think before we're safe?"

"No idea. Levi's dealing with the DA. They have to round everybody up and see how far the poison goes. These kinds of crimes can involve dozens of people." He took his eyes off the road to glance her way. "And he had the local police check out the Samuel Cheevers we left behind, but he was gone."

"Of course he was." Maybe they should have killed him after all. "The police don't care about the little guys," she said. "What they really want is the big fish." She reached up to rub her temple where the gunman had hit her. Between the stitches on her leg and the bruise on her temple, she would be a mess before she got home again. Wherever home would end up being.

"Depends if the little guys did the killing. Even if the big fish ordered them, the little fish are the ones who did the deed."

Right. Eloise and Freddy. And, of course, her own kidnapping and today's incident. Knowing they would be driving for a few hours, she curled up into the corner of the truck and tried to sleep.

Her phone buzzed. She checked the ID. It was Anna. "Is there any chance of my phone causing the trouble?"

"Not likely. Was that a text or email that just came in?"

"A text from Anna." She read the message and chuckled. "She doesn't appreciate Flynn. Wants him to get lost and wants to know how long before she can boot this guy out of her life."

Merk laughed. "That sounds like Flynn."

"So is it safe to answer?"

He glanced at her. "Yes."

She set about answering the text, careful to not say anything important, and adding that Flynn was a really good guy. Anna just had to get used to him.

Her response came back within seconds.

No getting used to this jerk.

Katina really hated that she had put Anna in this situation, but it was for her own good, and, if Merk said Flynn was a good guy, then she trusted him. Anna wasn't the easiest person either. She tended to be way too passionate and emphatic about everything in her world. And her world revolved around saving animals.

Hours later Katina sat up with interest as Merk slowed the vehicle and turned off the main highway. She rubbed the sleep from her eyes and realized she'd just missed a sign. He drove for another ten or fifteen minutes, then took a dirt road. Frowning she watched, peering through the windshield into the near darkness. "This time we're really off the main road."

"Absolutely. Doesn't get much more rustic than this."

She hoped it wasn't too rustic. She still liked a few modern amenities, like running water. But if staying alive meant doing without, then that was fine too.

When he finally came to a stop, it was in front of a small log cabin. He hopped from the truck, grabbed a flashlight from behind the seat, and came around to help her down. Normally she got out on her own, but she could see she would need help here as there was no pathway. He led the way up to the front step. She could now see it wasn't so much a log cabin but a rustic cabin with some planking for sides. While she studied the outside, he opened the door. And she realized he must have a hidden key somewhere. She just hadn't seen him look for it. No way he could have known they would go to all these places before they left. Or had he?

If he actually had planned for that level of problems, she wondered what else was planned.

Inside was wooden furniture and a fireplace with the wood stacked on the side. She wondered again if it had modern amenities. She was relieved when he hit a light switch, and low ambient light shone from above.

"I haven't been here in a while. I always liked this place though."

Merk walked into another room, and she followed on his heels. A kitchen with a fridge. He opened the fridge door to find it recently fully stocked.

Instantly her mood lifted. "I see you have helpers all over the place."

"We do at that."

"But does that mean the more people who know about this place, the more dangerous it is for everyone?"

"Nobody knows we're here. Just because the fridge was stocked, it doesn't mean anybody has a clue who's coming."

She considered that and realized he was right. If this was a rental cabin option, services like shopping were often supplied for the new arrivals. And who knew who was arriving because the whole point was peace and quiet and privacy.

Katina waited inside, studying the big fireplace, wondering if she knew actually how to light a fire while he walked out to the truck and brought in their luggage. She decided that her camping days weren't so far behind her, and maybe she could handle this.

She crumpled up some paper that was off to the side,

then opened the flue. Using the kindling, she got a small blaze going. She was actually feeling pretty cheeky and proud of herself as she stood and watched the wood catch fire. By the time Merk was done, she had layered a few bigger logs on top.

He came over to stand beside her. "Nice job. I was getting to that next."

And then the coffeemaker beeped. She realized he'd put on coffee while she'd been making the fire.

With a big grin she said, "We make a great pair."

He held out his arms, and she ran into them, grateful for the hug. He held her close. "We absolutely do. I know you're worried about all this, but we will only be here for a few days, maybe a week, and then will move on again."

She nodded her head, gently rocking against his chest. "Thank you for looking after me so well," she whispered.

"Ha. If I was looking after you, you can bet you would never have seen Freddy's body, and you wouldn't have been scared out of your mind when the intruders went into the house or then pointed a gun at your throat."

"But it's okay. We got away, and who knows where the hell they are now." She tilted her head back and looked at him. "I hate to say it, but I'm hungry."

He dropped a kiss on the tip of her nose and said, "I was expecting that actually. I'm surprised you made it all the way through the trip without asking for Alfred's basket."

"Then I shall go to the fridge." She stepped from his arms and opened the refrigerator door to explore. Beside her, he studied the contents and asked, "What do you want?"

"Sandwiches are fast so I vote for those." She reached into the fridge and pulling out the fixings.

Two kinds of meat, cheese, lettuce, tomatoes, and onions. He found a loaf of fresh bread and brought it over. Between the two of them, they found the rest of the things they needed, like a knife for slicing the bread, onions, and tomatoes. Soon they were sitting in front of the fire, which was now blazed happily, munching on sandwiches.

"How late is it?" She looked at her phone that she'd left on the table.

"It's after 8:00 p.m."

She nodded. "I suppose the bedrooms are upstairs, but, if it's not any warmer there, I vote we sleep in front of the fire."

"There are small heaters if we need them. But I don't believe there's a central furnace."

She shook her head. "How is that possible in this day and age? It obviously gets very cold here."

"Remember that request that you bring something warm?"

And that answered her previous question. "You planned to come here anyway?"

"Sure, this is our second spot on the route."

"Route?" She studied his face in the flickering shadows. They sat together on the same couch, and she was close enough to see the reflection in his eyes as the flames flickered and danced in the fireplace.

He explained, "We have to have several spots close and available, so I made a circular route that would eventually take us back home to the compound when and if it is safe to go."

"When and if?" she said, her voice rising. "Please tell me this won't be a long-term issue."

"It's possible," he admitted. "But we can't focus on that. You set something into motion, and we're dealing the best we can with the fallout."

Right. That put it back in perspective again. She slumped in place. "Well, I don't have a job I'll miss out on, but I can't just spend the next few months staying undercover without doing something," she said.

"We'll make do," he said cheerfully. "Let's not worry about the time frame. It's not even been a week yet."

She nodded. "Is anybody else likely to know this is the second place on your route?"

"Not to worry," he said.

"Does anybody else know about this place?" She studied his face. "If the truck and our phones weren't tracked, then nobody knows where the hell we are?"

"The only people who know our location are Levi, Ice, and the rest of the team." He tucked himself up against the corner of the couch and, with a gentle nudge, pulled her against his chest. "Relax. We'll get to spend a week in the woods, just the two of us."

Was it her imagination, or was a little hint of an innuendo in there? Or maybe a question to see how she would react? Inside she smiled. Because, damn, if one thing sounded really good right now, it was a week away in complete isolation. Just the two of them. Small towns were great, but this was going be a completely different experience.

As far she was concerned, it was time to get back to their relationship, whatever that meant. And what a great time to find out what was developing between them. It would happen either upstairs in the bed or down here in front of the fireplace. She didn't plan on leaving his side. And, no, not because she was scared, but because this man had been driving her crazy for a long time. She knew how good they were together. She just wanted a chance to find out all over again.

She shifted her position so she could raise herself up. She leaned forward and kissed his cheek. "A week together sounds perfect."

He turned and studied her face in the shadows. She could see the question in his gaze. But she held back her smile. She wanted to see if he would make a move. Or if she had to. Of course he was on the job, whereas she wasn't. She actually had no compunction about leading him down the wrong path, if that's what was holding him back.

With his free hand he slowly stroked her cheek, letting his thumb move across her lips. She kissed it, nibbling ever-so-slightly. When he raised one eyebrow, she smiled. He cupped her chin and tilted it toward him, then leaned forward and gave her a gentle kiss.

HE HAD TO admit, this was in the back of his mind when he realized they were coming here. He'd wondered about taking her to bed in the last place, but she hadn't settled down enough. And there'd been enough to do to keep their minds busy. Besides it had been fun watching their relationship grow and deepen. The little teasing glances and tantalizing looks. They were both heading for this moment. And now, on a couch in front of the fireplace, it was damn hard not to think it was the perfect moment.

He deepened the kiss, loving when she threw her arms around his neck and kissed him back. He crushed her against his chest, remembering how her passionate responses got to him the last time. They'd spent hours in bed, tumbling across the sheets, enjoying being so perfectly matched. He didn't expect this to be any different.

"Upstairs or here?"

She eased back, a slightly muddled look in her eyes that he loved. He dropped a kiss on her nose and, not wanting to let go of the taste of her, did it again and then again. He ended up exploring her entire face, kissing her eyelids, her cheeks, before finding her lips again.

She still hadn't answered. And he realized, chances were, they wouldn't make it to the bedroom. As far as space went, he wasn't sure a short couch was the best answer either.

He shifted her to sit beside him. He got up quickly, moved the coffee table out of the way, pulled her to her feet, and took her over by the fireplace. He took the big cushions off the couch, laid them in front of the fireplace, and stepped back to wait. Her gaze went from the fireplace to the makeshift mattress, then back to him again.

"I do love resourcefulness." In a surprise move, she kicked off her shoes, took off her socks, and then her sweater.

And stripped right down to her skin. She stood completely comfortable in her nakedness, shadows dancing across her hills and valleys. He was stunned by her natural beauty. He never really had a chance to see her in Vegas. Not like this. She stepped onto the mattress and took another step toward him.

"Aren't you a little overdressed?"

That galvanized him into action. He sat to pull off his boots and socks, yanked his shirt over his head. By the time he reached for his belt buckle, he was already hard and ready. He managed to open his belt buckle before she slipped her hands inside his jeans, and further progress undressing came to a complete halt. He leaned his head back, barely holding inside his groans as she caressed the tip of him.

In a thick voice he said, "If you keep that up, it'll be over before we start."

Her fingers undid the snap on his jeans and lowered the zipper. She said, "As I seem to remember, it was never very long before you were ready for round two." Slipping her hands inside his underwear, she dropped them down past his hips and followed them on her knees.

Jesus. He could barely step out of his clothes with her hands so eagerly exploring him. As he drew his hands through her hair, watching her, he thought he'd never seen anything more beautiful. She had a complete lack of self-consciousness that was lovely. She was content in who she was as a person. When her lips closed around the tip of his erection, a groan ripped free. Taking her wandering hands, he stepped back and shifted her until she laid the full length of the mattress. He dropped down beside her before she could scramble back to her knees.

He tugged her hands over her head to hold them still and lowered his mouth, kissing her like he'd been wanting to do for days, weeks it seemed. No way this would be over so fast. He wouldn't let it. He'd been looking forward to it for a long time. And the memory of what they'd had together had haunted him for even longer.

Because, although she'd laughed at the idea, he *had* thought about *what if?* ... He had thought about what if they'd actually given it a try? And he'd worried and wondered.

He had said that getting married was a mistake. But he had often considered if leaving her the next day had been the bigger mistake. At the time it seemed like nothing so perfect, so wonderful, could've been a mistake. So when he had walked away, ... he'd questioned his sanity.

When he left the military, he'd thought again about this, but he didn't put any time and effort into renewing his contact with her. He figured she'd moved on.

But, of course, she'd been just as busy as he had. They hadn't found time to reconnect. But he always knew he wanted to, in the back of his mind. Here he had a chance to prove to her they belonged together.

Because, if he'd learned anything, this last week or so had shown him that they'd come together once before because it was right. How could coming together now be wrong? If anything, he wanted a chance to fix his mistake.

Something this good couldn't be bad.

Chapter 17

A T THE FIRST touch of his lips, the memories came flooding back. Lord, she wanted him. From that kiss, she hadn't been able to get enough. Eleven years hadn't changed that. But, now that the moment was upon them, she had no trouble stripping down to her skin and standing up as she always had. She went 100 percent into something; she didn't hold back. This was who she was.

When he'd followed suit, she couldn't resist. She'd gotten into his pants, and her hands had been all over him. It had always been like that. She could never stop touching him, stop kissing him.

They'd made love over and over again in that hotel room. So engrossed in each other, enjoying each other's passion so much that it had fueled their own, the night had been endless. When they had finally fallen asleep, it was as if somebody had hit them both with a reality checklist upon waking. It was shocking. They'd gone from hot to cold, and now all she could see was the heat burning through them again. And she wanted him. God, she wanted him even more.

And here she struggled to remain sane as those damn tantalizing fingers stroked and caressed her between her legs; his tongue tasted and dipped and curved and nibbled. She was already wet and open for him.

And yet he held back.

"No teasing," she ordered.

A slow sexy chuckle drifted up to her. She frowned. She knew that sound all too well. She sat up and grabbed him by the shoulders and tried to tug him toward her mouth. Instead, he dropped his head and kissed her right in the heart of the matter. She cried out, lifting her hips, instinctively seeking more.

He wrapped his hands around her hips and held her firm and resumed his torment. His tongue delved and tasted, and his hands wouldn't let her go.

By the time he finally moved to her hips, into her navel, and then to her breasts, she was mindless jelly. Once again she was so enthralled being with him that her mind no longer functioned as she went straight into fury—a conflagration that threatened to burn them both. She stroked and kissed and teased and bit him right back.

When he entered her, it was so right because her body was already his.

At his first plunge she screamed. At the second she screamed louder, and at the third she came apart.

Only he wasn't done. He held her locked in his arms and rode her through it and then reached down and found her tiny nub and teased her right into the second climax. And on it went.

When he finally collapsed beside her, she shook, her shivers literally wracking her body.

He could pull no blanket over them because he hadn't thought that far ahead.

Instead he covered her with his own body once again and whispered sweet nothings in her ear.

"Easy, baby. It's so damn beautiful to be with you again.

You're so passionate. So natural. So honest in your response. God, I love being here. How is it possible we walked away from this?"

He'd been like that. Not only did he wield his fingers and his hands and his mouth but his ... voice. He always said the loveliest things to her. She felt cosseted. She felt adored. But most of all she felt loved. And that was the greatest feeling of all.

"Are you okay?" he asked in a low tone, his hand gently soothing up and down her shoulder.

"I will be," she whispered with a small laugh. "I forgot what it was like to make love with you."

He lowered his head and kissed her gently. "Hopefully it brought back just good memories."

She snaked her arms up around his neck and held him close. "The best."

He eased himself to the side and rolled her over so she was tucked against his chest. He slung a heavy leg over the top of hers and held her close. That was another thing she'd loved. After making love, he was the kind of guy who just held you close. Waited for the heartbeats to calm down and cuddled.

Every man should learn how to cuddle. She smiled at her thoughts and snuggled closer. "You were serious? Are we really getting to spend a week here doing this every night?"

She felt him startle, then the low, deep chuckle. Her smile widened. She tilted her head back slightly so she could look at his face. She batted her eyes at him and said, "Unless you had something else you want to do, like work or play cards."

He rolled her to her back once again, somehow landing between her spread legs. She could already feel the erection prodding her. "Already?"

And he slipped inside. "Already," he affirmed. "Besides, if we only have a week, we'd better make the most of it."

And they did.

That same night, they explored the upstairs and found several blankets, which they dragged back to the fireplace. With a bottle of wine they found in the cupboard, the night was endless. Of course by the time morning broke, they were so tired and dopey, the decision was to cuddle and just nap for the day.

And she loved it. She couldn't remember ever spending this much time in bed—except with Merk. The only two times it had happened, it had been with Merk. Well, no reason to rush away this time.

They moved upstairs later that day. Besides, the huge bed needed a christening.

Two days later, they slipped into a loverlike pattern of making love in the evening, making love in the morning, and then sure, why not make love in the afternoon? Because it all felt so damn good.

They were lost in a haze of romance she had never expected. No talk of their future, just lots of talk about their past, and who they were at this point in their lives.

On the third afternoon, while she cuddled with him on the couch, she said, "I don't know where to move. I don't think it's a good idea to stay in Houston."

"Where would you like to go?" He gently stroked a hand up and down her arm. "The world's a big place. Is there anywhere you want to go?"

She stared at him a moment. "Is it wrong to say, I want to be where you are?"

He gazed down at her with a smile in his eyes, making

her heart ache. She never expected to feel like this with anyone.

He gently stroked his thumb across her bottom lip. "But that would mean staying in Houston, or at least within an hour of that city."

She nodded. "I don't know if it would ever be safe for me."

"The company you worked for wasn't headquartered there. The business offices are in California, so chances are, by the time it's all shut down and cleaned out, it won't be an issue."

She liked the sound of that. Besides, it was a hell of a big city; the chances of ever meeting anybody she'd worked with were slim. And the ones she had worked with who were higher up would be, hopefully, going to jail.

Merk's phone rang just then. He shifted Katina to grab his cell from the side table. She lay on the couch, her head in his lap, and listened while he talked to Levi.

"No, no sign of anything here."

In her head she said, *Thankfully.* Because it had been idyllic, but she understood how something could interrupt their little vacation retreat anytime.

She waited for him to speak again. When she looked up, she could see a frown on his face and realized something wasn't good news. He shifted the phone so she could hear the conversation.

He smiled. "So they've picked up everyone but the big fish."

She waited breathlessly.

"And he was the one who had ordered Katina to be picked up. And had ordered the hit on Eloise. In other words, the one asshole we needed to catch is the one who's free. Shit." Silence again as Merk listened to Levi.

"Right, he's either on the run, or he's out picking off the witnesses who could put him away for life."

She listened, her heart getting heavy. Merk's tone of voice was harsh, and she realized this was probably the worst news ever.

The conversation continued but not a whole lot was different. When he got off the phone, the entire atmosphere changed. The side of Merk where she'd been resting her head was now locked down to hardened muscles.

"Are we leaving?" she asked quietly. Hating the idea but ready to go if necessary.

Immediately his hand came to rest on her shoulder. He then stroked the length of her arm and laced his fingers through hers. "No, not right now."

"So the main guy is still running around out there somewhere?"

He nodded. "And it's somebody who can identify you. Because it's your old boss. Robert Carlisle."

She bolted into a sitting position and twisted to look at him. "Robert?" At his nod she shook her head. "But he was a nice man. Why would he arrange a hit on me?"

He gave her a look that said, *You know why.*

She rolled her eyes back and said, "Okay, okay. I get why he did it. But he's the most normal-looking person you've ever met. He was nice. He always stopped and talked. He had time for everybody in the company."

"Chances were good he was just checking you were all following the company line and being good little robots," Merk said with a smile. "Do you know very much about him?"

"He loved to fish, and he had several favorite spots. His

family had a cabin on some lake. He often went there."

"And you know this how?"

"He used to bring back pictures of himself, holding up his trophies. On one trip, he came back with a particularly large fish, and he was so excited, he was telling everybody about where he got it."

"Do you happen to remember where?"

She frowned. "Something like Satsuma Lake or sounds like that." She shrugged. "Honestly, if he hadn't been my boss, I'd have turned and walked away. But, because of who he was, I stopped and smiled and made all the appropriate noises. But I really didn't give a damn because I can't stand fishing."

He gave her a look of horror. "You don't like to fish? That is every man's dream occupation."

She laughed. "And here I thought it was making love."

His grin flashed. "Okay, so fishing is a close second."

He opened his phone and called Levi back. "According to Katina, the man was an avid fisherman. And his family owns a cabin somewhere on a lake. Satsuma or something that sounds like that."

Katina reached across and grabbed his arm.

He raised an eyebrow. "Hang on, Levi. Katina has something else."

"In Samuel Cheevers wallet was an address—428 Morgan Street, Houston."

"Any idea what it means?"

She shook her head. "No, but it did say 11:00 p.m. beside it, so a meeting of some kind. But no date was given."

"Levi, did you hear that?" Merk hung up the phone and said, "Levi's checking it out."

"I really don't want to think about anyone still being out

there looking for me."

"It's all too possible. Which is why we never really can let our guard down. Until he's picked up, this isn't over."

THE NEXT DAY Merk answered the phone to hear the good news. He turned and beamed at Katina. "That was Levi. Apparently Robert was picked up at the cabin. As we suspected, he'd gone to ground. He didn't resist arrest—just came willingly. He's being booked downtown now."

She threw herself across him, screaming for joy.

He picked her up and turned her around. "Looks like we got this one beat. Cheevers isn't a threat any longer with all the bosses picked up. No incentive anymore for the low-level guys to keep on the job."

When he pulled back, he said, "Levi also said time to go home."

"Right now or tomorrow morning?" she asked with a leer.

He chuckled. "Considering it's only one o'clock in the afternoon, I would be hard pressed to come up with an excuse to not leave until tomorrow morning."

He watched her face fall, but she nodded. "I guess our holiday is over."

"Holiday? I thought we were building a relationship?"

She turned to look back at him in surprise, a smile dawning, slowly.

Breathtaking.

"We were too busy enjoying the moment," he said with a smile. "And you were talking about leaving. I didn't want to be the one who kept you from traveling, if that's what your heart desired."

She stepped into his arms and said, "Right now you're my heart's desire."

And she kissed him with those deep, slow, drugging kisses that she was so damn good at. His temperature was already peaking when she stepped back.

"Now we pack." With a laugh she left the room.

Damn. He sure wouldn't mind sticking around for a little longer. But Levi was right; it was time to get back to the real world.

He quickly emptied the fridge and cupboards. He pulled out Alfred's basket and loaded the remaining food in it.

As he put away the clean cups, he opened a different cupboard, his gaze, for the first time, going up to the second shelf, and he froze. His mind tried to not compute what his eyes saw, but it wasn't working. They'd been here, what, four days, and he hadn't noticed? Then again maybe it wasn't a listening device? He studied it, hoping for a different answer, but inside he knew exactly what it was.

In which case, if anybody was listening in, they would know exactly where Katina was. If it was one of Levi's devices, then no problem.

He considered the ramifications of that. Was it something Levi had in the house just in case? In which case, Merk hoped that his friends, for their sake, better not have been listening to the last three days of lovemaking. They'd have likely checked in, realized all was well, and checked out again. But what if that bug wasn't theirs? Others would know Katina was here. Except they'd been here for days already, and nobody had come. He leaned back against the counter as he pulled out his phone and called Levi.

He could hear the puzzlement in Levi's voice as he said, "I don't think we have a bug there."

Merk stood and waited, the bug in his hand, as Levi turned from the phone and asked Ice.

Merk could hear the muffled response as Ice said, "No."

"Okay. Any idea why nobody has come then?"

"The good answer would be because we've picked up all the perps who were listening or monitoring the situation. The bad answer would be they've decided attacking you in the house was no good, so they're waiting for you to make a move."

Shit. He ended the call as a second one came through immediately. He answered it, his gaze locked on the listening device. But his mind was on Levi's information. "Hello."

"Get out. Now. Drop everything and go." His brother, Terkel's, voice was hard and sure. "Don't argue. This is good-as-dead bad. Move your ass now."

Ah, hell. "Time frame?"

"You've got five minutes. In ten it's too late."

And in typical Terkel fashion, he was gone. But Merk could hear his brother's whispered voice in the back of his head, ending with the phrase he always did, *Good luck, brother.*

They had to move ... and now. His brother was never wrong.

Yet someone was out there lying in wait. Someone already on the move.

Chapter 18

G OING HOME WAS supposed be the easy part. But she knew nothing would be easy about it when Merk disappeared outside, telling her to stay inside and pack fast, he'd be back in two minutes, and they needed to go immediately afterward.

She bit down on her bottom lip to stop herself from protesting. She had to trust he knew what he was doing. If it was just cautionary measures, it was all good. But based on his words and tone, it was something so much worse. With her bags packed and sitting beside the door, she quickly made a pot of coffee while she waited. Then proceeded to fill two thermoses.

After cleaning up, she still had no sign of Merk. She made another round to check they had packed everything and deliberately left the fridge open and turned off. She didn't know if somebody would be in to clean the cabin, but, as it was empty, it seemed wasteful to leave the fridge running. Who knew how long it would be until someone else stayed here. She hated this dithering. Making a decision, then changing her mind, not knowing what to do. Finally she sat down on top of her bag at the back door and waited.

Until she heard unfamiliar footsteps on the porch ...

She froze.

From where she sat, she couldn't see who it was. She

didn't want to move in case it alerted whoever was there that she was inside. She cast her mind back to the last few minutes, wondering if she'd been in front of the windows and if somebody could have seen her.

When she heard no sound of Merk entering the house or calling her name, her nerves set in. Followed immediately by panic. She glanced at the back door she sat beside and realized it wasn't even locked.

The footstep she'd heard were on the other side of the porch. She didn't know if they were coming toward her or not. If she locked the door now, they'd know she was here. But, if she left it unlocked, they'd get in easily. It probably made no difference because none of these walls or windows would keep them outside anyway. If he wanted in, he would get in. Her only hope was that Merk had seen him and was even now hunting down the asshole.

She whispered a prayer in her mind, *Please let this be Merk.*

She waited, her jaw clenched, her arms wrapped around her chest. And again she heard nothing. She was just about to convince herself she hadn't heard a footstep, maybe just a branch cracking outside instead. She was being foolish ... when the doorknob in front of her moved ever-so-slightly.

She bounded to her feet, snapped the bolt down, and raced for the front door. She was outside, into the woods in seconds. She didn't stop running until she was in the middle of a thick stand of evergreens. She hadn't seen or heard anyone running after her, but that didn't ease her panic.

Catching sight of one big evergreen, she bolted for the low branches and climbed up. She didn't stop until she was buried in the upper branches and completely hidden from view.

In her mind she knew that couldn't have been Merk. He would have said something. No way he'd have terrorized her like that. And that meant somebody else was here.

Still not feeling safe at the level she'd attained, she crept up higher. She clung to the tree trunk, buried deep in the branches. She realized her jacket was a light blue and could be spotted easily. Her black T-shirt was on underneath. Stripping off the jacket, she stuffed it between her and the tree trunk.

She didn't know how long it would be before she was found, but no way in hell was she moving until she knew Merk was below her. Katina couldn't hear anything because her heart slamming against her ribs drowned out everything else. She worked at getting a deep breath out and then another one. Anything to prevent that panic attack from taking over. She'd never had one, but this was a justifiable time.

When she didn't hear anything for what felt like ten minutes, her breathing slowed to a more normal rate. By the time probably twenty minutes had lapsed, she peered through the boughs to see if anybody was around. After what had to have been a full half hour gone by, she wondered whether she'd been an idiot and had run for nothing.

But Merk wasn't back here with her.

And no way could she have misinterpreted that doorknob turning.

When she crossed what surely had been the forty-five-minute mark, she reassessed the branch she was on, wondering if another would allow her to rest her back or to sit down better. She still had no intention of climbing down, but, for the first time, reality set in.

Horrible thoughts crossed her mind. What if the intruder had taken Merk out already? Then, it would be just her and the bad guy. Hell, if he'd seen her come in this direction, he could just sit on the front step and wait for her. She'd have to get down sometime. She hadn't planned on this being an all-night thing. She should've found a place inside the house to hide. At least then, when he left, she would have supplies.

But her brain immediately kicked in and said, *To last until when?* Until he came back? And why would he leave at all? She felt in her pockets and smiled. Instantly she kicked herself for being such a fool. She had her phone on her. She pulled it out, turned off the sound so nobody could hear calls incoming and outgoing, and texted Merk.

Where are you?

The answer came back instantly.

Stay where you are.

At least he'd answered. So he was alive. And obviously hunting the intruder. He'd told her to stay inside the house, but what was she supposed to do when the intruder was coming inside via the back door?

Unless he'd planned on taking the guy out at the house. But killing herself with all those self-doubts wasn't helping. At the same time she didn't know if Levi had any idea what was going on. She wondered if she should tell him. Just in case things got ugly.

The thing was, if it went bad, she needed somebody to know where she was, and, if things went good, well, that meant she was looking out for Merk and reporting in. Which made it an easy decision for her.

She opened the phone, thankful she'd been given everybody's number at the compound. She didn't know if that was a sign of trust or if they just still considered her part of the problem. She appreciated it either way. She immediately fired off texts to Levi and Ice. She wasn't sure who else would be around but figured Stone might be and sent him one too.

The responses came back instantly.

Don't move.

Stay where you are.

Trust Merk. Listen to him.

She stared down at the short answers and shook her head. *Really? That's it? I'm supposed to sit in this tree and just wait?*

Still, the advice wasn't bad. She studied the few branches around her and realized she could carefully lower herself to straddle the branch she stood on, allowing her to lean back against the trunk. But she had to do it so the tree didn't move; otherwise somebody might notice where she was. And, although the intruder might know Merk was here, the intruder's end result was going after her. She was the target. Besides, she figured these guys were arrogant enough to think they could handle Merk. Idiots.

Moving carefully she finally settled on the branch in a more relaxed position. Waiting had never been her thing, but, given her options, she figured she could stay here and do as she was told. As she sat and thought about all that she and Merk had, and the future that lay before them, she got angry.

Because this asshole could destroy her chances at that future. She understood the last few days with Merk had been a fantasy bubble of sexy romance, but they'd needed that time. No way would she let the asshole destroy what she and Merk had forged together.

She reconsidered her options. They all sucked. She had no weapon. If she did have one, she wouldn't know how to use it. Merk was well-trained and was out there, knowing exactly what was going on and how to handle this asshole.

Just then she heard something that made all the logic in the world disappear in a flash.

Gunfire filled the air. Silence, then more shots cracked.

Instantly she went into panic mode, pulling her knees up against her chest, making herself into as small a ball as she possibly could. She held her breath, waiting for the dust to settle. Who had gotten shot? And the bigger question still in her mind was, is Merk okay? She snatched up her phone and texted the others to say **Gunfire**. She texted Merk next.

Are you okay?

His answer was short.

Yes. Don't move.

And she realized the fight was still not over. She bowed her head and swore she would never get involved in something like this again.

HOPEFULLY SHE'D LISTEN this time. He peered around the trees. He understood why she'd bolted from the guy trying to get into the house. And he'd seen her mad dash into the woods and figured she got up a tree. If she'd just damn well stay there until he took down this asshole, they'd be good.

This guy needed to be taken out so they didn't have to look over their shoulders anymore. Likely a contract killer, one asshole determined to finish the job. Merk had missed him at the house. He'd run around the deck and gone after her, but she'd run like a rabbit. Something Merk had been happy to see. He knew exactly how fit and in shape she was. Because he'd spent a lot of hours stroking those toned muscles. But she still couldn't outrun a bullet.

His gaze swept the stands of trees yet again.

Crack.

He instantly dropped to the ground.

A bullet slammed into the tree trunk where he'd been standing. Damn it. The asshole had somehow circled around and come up behind him. The game of hide-and-seek was on.

Merk pulled himself up on several limbs of the tree to get better visibility. He caught sight of movement on the left. He turned and let his gaze float across the area, still just waiting to see … anything. A small shrub shivered with movement from within.

He lined up the shot. The brush was a good thirty-five yards away. Depending on how many branches were in the way, he had a good chance of hitting him.

He took the shot.

A man grunted. Even that much sound echoed loudly in the silent woods. He might have hit him, but he couldn't tell for sure.

Sighting his target, he slipped off to the right and kept moving to higher ground. He wanted to come down from behind. As he watched, the gunman straightened, turned, and stared right at him, but his gaze drifted off to the side.

He hadn't seen Merk.

Perfect. Merk straightened up ever-so-slightly and fired. The only sound was a soft thud. Keeping behind the tree trunks, he raced toward his victim. And, sure enough, he'd shot him in the neck. The man was dead.

Kicking away the man's weapon just in case, he bent down and pulled out his wallet to check his ID. But when he read John Lennon with an address in Washington, he figured it was fake. He straightened up, intent on picking up the guy and carrying him around to the front of the cabin when he heard something that made his heart run cold.

And realized he'd been a fool. The dead man hadn't been alone.

"Just drop him. He was an idiot anyway."

Merk raised his hands and slowly turned to face his newest adversary. Merk didn't know him, but he obviously was a better professional than the one on the ground.

The man grinned and said, "Young trainees make great decoys. It's amazing how often you guys, who think you're so damn good, find out how dead wrong you are."

"That's because he's the only one who did any of the shooting," Merk said calmly. His mind raced, looking for opportunities—they were looking pretty damn shitty. Plus he had to keep in mind this guy was after Katina. Even if Merk took a bullet, that wouldn't end this. He had to take down this asshole too. Otherwise he'd go after Katina.

And that wasn't going to happen.

"Well, it's nice to know you can tell the difference between the guns." He motioned with the barrel of his. "Turn around." When Merk complied, he added, "Now walk over to your girlfriend. See if she'll come down from that tree on her own."

His heart sank. He walked a few steps and said, "You

know you won't get away with this."

The man behind him laughed. "Of course I will. Do you have any idea how many other missions like this I've completed?"

"Missions?" Interesting phrase. So he was military too. "You didn't like the military and moved into the private sector? Private contracts?"

"Yep, much better pay. The benefits are nicer too."

Merk nodded in friendly acknowledgment as he continued to walk closer to Katina's hiding place. "Just out of curiosity, what happens to your contract now that your boss has been picked up?"

"I've already been paid. Completing the job is a matter of pride. A contract can't go unfinished, as my word is everything."

Merk understood. It also meant it didn't matter that the DA had rounded everyone up and was even now preparing for the court case. If the DA wanted Katina as a witness, then having her go missing would weaken the case. So the men in jail were counting on the assassin to complete the job. "Too bad. I was hoping maybe you'd drop the contract when you realized it was over already."

"Not happening. I don't care how many of these assholes the law picks up. I hope the jailers throw away the keys. They aren't men I want in this world if they think killing a woman because she saw something is the way to handle their problems. If they'd hung on to her after the kidnapping instead of letting her escape, they'd not need me. But they are all idiots."

Merk changed direction slightly, heading away from Katina, only to get slugged in the head.

"Don't bother. You and I both know where she is hiding."

Merk turned slightly and headed back in her direction. He needed a diversion. Something to allow him to tackle this asshole. He might be military, ex-military, but so was Merk, so he'd be using his dirtiest techniques.

"Stop here."

And that just confirmed what Merk had suspected. They were literally below the tree where Katina was hiding.

"Call her down."

He hesitated, wondering at the sense of doing that. But he called out, "Katina, run when you can."

And he dropped to the ground and kicked the man's legs out from under him. The gunman was on Merk in an instant. The gun went flying, and it was down to fists and as many underhanded tactics as they could use. The fight was vicious. Both knowing, in the end, one was going down.

Each needed to be the victor. Merk had more to lose. He had Katina.

He punched, kicked, flipped, and took several blows to the face—delivering twice as many as he got—but he could never quite get ahead.

The other man swore, then cried out, "You son of a bit—"

A puzzled look came into the killer's eyes before they rolled up into the back of his head. And he collapsed on top of Merk.

Merk shoved him off and bounced to his feet. Katina stood in front of him. He turned to look down at the killer to see a thick stick, one end thinner than the other sticking out of his back.

Instantly he opened his arms, and she ran into them. He crushed her against his chest, realizing how close he'd come to losing her.

When he finally eased his grip on her, she stepped aside, swung her hand back, and smacked him across the face. Pissed, he yelled, "What the hell was that for?"

"For suggesting I run away and leave you to deal with him on your own." She fisted her hands on her hips and glared at him. "Did you really expect me to save myself and forget about you? We're in this together—remember?"

Shocked, he stared at her, then glanced down at the dead man on the ground and started to laugh. He opened his arms again, and she fell into them, hugging him tight.

"Together? As in together forever?" She tilted her head and stared at him with the question in her eyes.

"Are you asking me this time?" he said with a laugh.

As she sputtered, he lowered his head and kissed her. When he stopped, this time she looked up at him with tear-laced eyes and whispered, "I thought I'd lost you again."

"I'm not so easy to lose," he said with a smile. He wrapped his arm around her shoulders and led her back to the cabin. "We'll stay here a little longer to deal with the bodies."

At the surprised look on her face, he realized she didn't know about the first man. He explained, watching the color leech from her face.

She swallowed hard and asked, "Then can we go home?"

"Absolutely."

As they reached the cabin, his phone rang. He glanced down to see Levi's number.

That's when she said apologetically, "I contacted them when I was in the tree."

He rolled his eyes and answered the call. "Yes, Levi. I'm fine, and so is she. It's over, but we have two bodies here to be picked up."

He listened as Levi, all business, made plans and filled him in on the latest. "Samuel Cheevers was picked up alive and well at the Morgan address, so good job on that," Levi said. "I have someone on the way for the latest two you've taken out."

Merk snorted at that. "Not my fault. But we're here until law enforcement gets here."

"And then where are you going?" Levi asked curiously. "Are you coming back here or … are you heading to Vegas?" he finished drily.

"I don't think so. At least not right away," Merk joked. He rang off and put away his phone.

At the silence at his side, he turned toward Katina to tell her of the plans in motion, only to frown at the look on her face. "What's the matter?"

"Was it a mistake?" she asked softly.

He didn't know exactly what she was referring too and knew it was a pathway riddled with mines if he didn't navigate this safely.

"Was what a mistake?" he asked cautiously, feeling his way.

"Marrying me?"

His gaze widened. "Hell, no. As a matter of fact, I was thinking we needed to repeat it as soon as possible."

She narrowed her gaze at him.

He tilted her chin up and kissed her, then, with his lips quirking into a lopsided smile, he said, "We could make a fast trip to Vegas."

She snickered. "I will *not* get married for a second time in the Elvis Presley Wedding Chapel," she stated firmly.

"That's okay. How about a Dracula's Tomb wedding?

I'm sure that would be a scream," he said jokingly.

But her response surprised him. She threw her arms around his neck and said, "I love you. Might always have loved you, but no way in hell am I going back to Vegas to get married again."

He wrapped his arms around her and held her close.

"But ..." she added, her breath warm against his lips, "any other place in the world—I'm all for it."

He didn't dare tell her there were some pretty godawful venues in Reno too. He figured he'd leave that for another time.

He was partial to a Dracula's Tomb wedding himself.

Maybe if he gave her some time to consider it ...

Then he caught sight of her face and realized it wouldn't matter where the ceremony took place—as long as she became his wife again—so all was good.

Epilogue

R HODES WALKED IN with another armload of groceries. The compound had been flying high these last few days. The DA was particularly impressed with the job Levi and the team had done in protecting Katina and helping to bring a lot of serious badasses to justice. Of course the court system was long and arduous with no guarantee of a conviction, but the DA had said, with the amount of information everyone had collected, it should be an easy run.

After Rhodes dropped the box of groceries on the kitchen counter for Alfred, he walked back out to grab yet another one. He smiled at Katina and Merk, standing in a clench off to the side. As he walked past, in a loud voice he said, "Unless you're making wedding chapel suggestions, I suggest you two come and help unload the truck."

Katina pulled back, laughing. "Sorry, Rhodes. Every time I get close to this guy, it's like a magnet pulling me in."

"And that's the way it should be," Sienna said loyally from behind Rhodes.

Rhodes wanted to say something, but Sienna was a best friend's sister, and, as such, he was still treating her with kid gloves as he had done when she'd been a gawky teenager with stunning promise. Unfortunately that was the last thing he wanted to do with her now.

It sucked when all your buddies were pairing up, and

you were the one left out. Especially when the one you wanted was out of bounds.

Her brother, Jarrod, had been to the compound twice already and was due for a third visit later today, all to ensure his sister was truly all right, especially now that the place had calmed down somewhat after the two recent attacks here at the compound, plus Jarrod had been called on a second overseas mission. Rhodes planned to talk to Jarrod as soon as he got here.

Sienna might not know what she had gotten herself into by asking for a permanent job at Legendary Security, but she'd better stick around now because he had no intention of letting this one go—ever.

Rhodes just hoped his SEAL-brother Jarrod thought that was a good idea too.

This concludes Heroes for Hire, Books 1–3.

Book 4 is available.

Rhodes's Reward:
Heroes for Hire, Book 4

Buy this book at your favorite vendor.

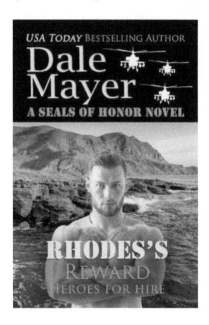

Welcome *to Rhodes's Reward*, book 4 in Heroes for Hire, reconnecting readers with the unforgettable men from SEALs of Honor in a new series of action packed, page turning romantic suspense that fans have come to expect from USA TODAY Bestselling author Dale Mayer.

Second chances do happen… Even amid evil…

Rhodes knew Sienna years ago. When she'd been young and gawky, more elbow and carrot hair than style, but she'd had something special even then. Now she's all grown. But she's a trouble magnet, and even at the compound it finds her...

Sienna had a super-sized crush on her brother's best friend years ago. Now he's hunky and even hotter than she could have imagined. Only she's new and doesn't want to jeopardize her position. When asked to help out on a job, she agrees...and triggers a sequence of disastrous events no one could foresee.

But someone will stop at nothing to silence everyone involved, especially the two of them...

Heroes for Hire Series

Author's Note

Thanks for reading. By now many of you have read my explanation of how I love to see **Star Ratings.** The only catch is that we as authors have no idea what you think of a book if it's not reviewed. And yes, **every book in a series needs reviews**. All it takes is as little as two words: Fun Story. Yep, that's all. So, if you enjoyed reading, please take a second to let others know you enjoyed it.

For those of you who have not read a previous book and have no idea why we authors keep asking you as a reader to take a few minutes to leave even a two word review, here's more explanation of reviews in this crazy business.

Reviews (not just ratings) help authors qualify for advertising opportunities and help other readers make purchasing decisions. Without *triple digit* reviews, an author may miss out on valuable advertising opportunities. And with only "star ratings" the author has little chance of participating in certain promotions. Which means fewer sales offered to my favorite readers!

Another reason to take a minute and leave a review is that often a **few kind words left in a review can make a huge difference to an author and their muse.** Recently new to reviewing fans have left a few words after reading a similar letter and they were tonic to a tired muse! LOL Seriously. Star ratings simply do not have the same impact to thank or encourage an author when the writing gets tough.

So please consider taking a moment to write even a handful of words. Writing a review only takes a few minutes of your time. It doesn't have to be a lengthy book report, just a few words expressing what you enjoyed most about the story. Here are a few tips of how to leave a review.

Please continue to rate the books as you read, but take an extra moment and pop over to the review section and leave a few words too!

Most of all – **Thank you** for reading. I look forward to hearing from you.

I love to hear from readers, and you can contact me at my website: www.dalemayer.com or at my Facebook author page. To be informed of new releases and special offers, sign up for my newsletter or follow me on BookBub. And if you are interested in joining Dale Mayer's Fan Club, here is the Facebook sign up page. facebook.com/groups/402384989872660

Cheers,
Dale Mayer

COMPLIMENTARY DOWNLOAD

DOWNLOAD a *__complimentary__* copy of TUESDAY'S CHILD? Just tell me where to send it!
http://dalemayer.com/starterlibrarytc/

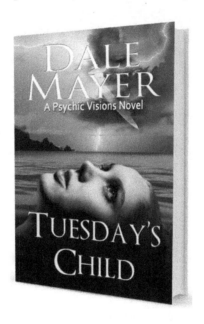

Touched by Death

Adult RS/thriller

Get this book at your favorite vendor.

Death had touched anthropologist Jade Hansen in Haiti once before, costing her an unborn child and perhaps her very sanity.

A year later, determined to face her own issues, she returns to Haiti with a mortuary team to recover the bodies of an American family from a mass grave. Visiting his brother after the quake, independent contractor Dane Carter puts his life on hold to help the sleepy town of Jacmel rebuild. But he finds it hard to like his brother's pregnant wife or her family. He wants to go home, until he meets Jade – and realizes what's missing in his own life. When the mortuary team begins work, it's as if malevolence has been released from the earth. Instead of laying her ghosts to rest, Jade finds herself confronting death and terror again.

And the man who unexpectedly awakens her heart – is right in the middle of it all.

By Death Series

Vampire in Denial

This is book 1 of the Family Blood Ties Saga

Get this book at your favorite vendor.

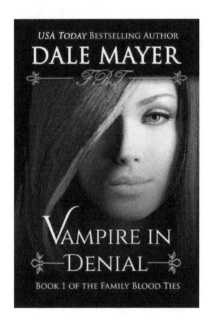

Blood doesn't just make her who she is...it also makes her what she is.

Like being a sixteen-year-old vampire isn't hard enough, Tessa's throwback human genes make her an outcast among her relatives. But try as she might, she can't get a handle on the vampire lifestyle and all the...blood.

Turning her back on the vamp world, she embraces the human teenage lifestyle—high school, peer pressure and finding a boyfriend. Jared manages to stir something in her blood. He's smart and fun and oh, so cute. But Tessa's dream of a having the perfect boyfriend turns into a nightmare when vampires attack the movie theatre and kidnap her date.

Once again, Tessa finds herself torn between the human world and the vampire one. Will blood own out? Can she make peace with who she is as well as what?

Warning: This book ends with a cliffhanger! Book 2 picks up where this book ends.

Family Blood Ties Series

Vampire in Denial

Vampire in Distress

Vampire in Design

Vampire in Deceit

Vampire in Defiance

Vampire in Conflict

Vampire in Chaos

Vampire in Crisis

Vampire in Control

Vampire in Charge

Family Blood Ties Set 1–3

Family Blood Ties Set 1–5

Family Blood Ties Set 4–6

Family Blood Ties Set 7–9

Sian's Solution – A Family Blood Ties Short Story

Broken Protocols

Get this book at your favorite vendor.

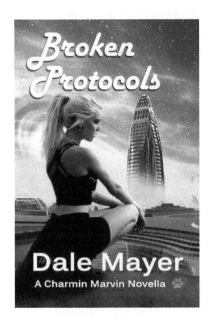

Dani's been through a year of hell...

Just as it's getting better, she's tossed forward through time with her orange Persian cat, Charmin Marvin, clutched in her arms. They're dropped into a few centuries into the future. There's nothing she can do to stop it, and it's impossible to go back.

And then it gets worse...

A year of government regulation is easing, and Levi Blackburn is feeling back in control. If he can keep his reckless brother in check, everything will be perfect. But while he's been protecting Milo from the government, Milo's been busy working on a present for him...

The present is Dani, only she comes with a snarky cat who suddenly starts talking...and doesn't know when to shut up.

In an age where breaking protocols have severe consequences, things go wrong, putting them all in danger...

Charmin Marvin Romantic Comedy Series

About the Author

Dale Mayer is a USA Today bestselling author best known for her Psychic Visions and Family Blood Ties series. Her contemporary romances are raw and full of passion and emotion (Second Chances, SKIN), her thrillers will keep you guessing (By Death series), and her romantic comedies will keep you giggling (It's a Dog's Life and Charmin Marvin Romantic Comedy series).

She honors the stories that come to her – and some of them are crazy and break all the rules and cross multiple genres!

To go with her fiction, she also writes nonfiction in many different fields with books available on resume writing, companion gardening and the US mortgage system. She has recently published her Career Essentials Series. All her books are available in print and ebook format.

Connect with Dale Mayer Online

Dale's Website – www.dalemayer.com

Twitter – @DaleMayer

Facebook – facebook.com/DaleMayer.author

BookBub – bookbub.com/authors/dale-mayer

Also by Dale Mayer

Published Adult Books:

Psychic Vision Series

Tuesday's Child

Hide'n Go Seek

Maddy's Floor

Garden of Sorrow

Knock, Knock…

Rare Find

Eyes to the Soul

Now You See Her

Shattered

Into the Abyss

Seeds of Malice

Eye of the Falcon

Psychic Visions Books 1–3

Psychic Visions Books 4–6

Psychic Visions Books 7–9

By Death Series

Touched by Death – Part 1

Touched by Death – Part 2

Touched by Death – Parts 1&2

Haunted by Death

Chilled by Death

By Death Books 1–3

Second Chances...at Love Series

Second Chances – Part 1

Second Chances – Part 2

Second Chances – complete book (Parts 1 & 2)

Charmin Marvin Romantic Comedy Series

Broken Protocols

Broken Protocols 2

Broken Protocols 3

Broken Protocols 3.5

Broken Protocols 1-3

Broken and... Mending

Skin

Scars

Scales (of Justice)

Broken but... Mending 1-3

Glory

Genesis

Tori

Celeste

Glory Trilogy

Biker Blues

Biker Blues: Morgan, Part 1

Biker Blues: Morgan, Part 2

Biker Blues: Morgan, Part 3

Biker Baby Blues: Morgan, Part 4

Biker Blues: Morgan, Full Set

Biker Blues: Salvation, Part 1

Biker Blues: Salvation, Part 2

Biker Blues: Salvation, Part 3

Biker Blues: Salvation, Full Set

SEALs of Honor

Mason: SEALs of Honor, Book 1

Hawk: SEALs of Honor, Book 2

Dane: SEALs of Honor, Book 3

Swede: SEALs of Honor, Book 4

Shadow: SEALs of Honor, Book 5

Cooper: SEALs of Honor, Book 6

Markus: SEALs of Honor, Book 7

Evan: SEALs of Honor, Book 8

Mason's Wish: SEALs of Honor, Book 9

Chase: SEALs of Honor, Book 10

Brett: SEALs of Honor, Book 11

Devlin: SEALs of Honor, Book 12

Easton: SEALs of Honor, Book 13

Ryder: SEALs of Honor, Book 14

SEALs of Honor, Books 1–3

SEALs of Honor, Books 4–6

SEALs of Honor, Books 7–10

Heroes for Hire

Collections

Standalone Novellas

Published Young Adult Books:

Family Blood Ties Series
Vampire in Denial

Vampire in Distress

Vampire in Design

Vampire in Deceit

Vampire in Defiance

Vampire in Conflict

Vampire in Chaos

Vampire in Crisis

Vampire in Control

Vampire in Charge

Family Blood Ties Set 1–3

Family Blood Ties Set 1–5

Family Blood Ties Set 4–6

Family Blood Ties Set 7–9

Sian's Solution – A Family Blood Ties Short Story

Design series
Dangerous Designs

Deadly Designs

Darkest Designs

Design Series Trilogy

Standalone
In Cassie's Corner

Gem Stone (a Gemma Stone Mystery)

Time Thieves

Published Non-Fiction Books:

Career Essentials

Career Essentials: The Résumé

Career Essentials: The Cover Letter

Career Essentials: The Interview

Career Essentials: 3 in 1

CPSIA information can be obtained
at www.ICGtesting.com
Printed in the USA
BVHW040951100119
537496BV00015BC/117/P